"STOP!" LACEY

Hawke sighed heavily but froze before raising her skirt any higher. "What's the problem, now, Lacey?"

"I'm wonderin' . . . what are you doing?"

He smiled. "Making you more comfortable. May I go on?"

"I'll take care of my clothing myself. I'd like to keep the boots on, if you don't mind."

"If that's what you want, Irish." Hawke turned his back. He'd heard of men who insisted on *dying* with their boots on, but this was a first.

Lacey quickly removed her underpinnings and lay back down. "I'm ready," she said softly.

Hawke moved alongside her until his lips were a warm breath away from hers. "Are you sure this time, Lacey?"

She gazed deep into his eyes. "Aye," she whispered throatily. "I'm ready for you, my husband. . . ."

CELEBRATE

101 Days of Romance with

HarperMonogram

FREE BOOK OFFER!

See back of book for details.

Books by Sharon Ihle

Wild Rose
Wildcat
The Law and Miss Penny
Marrying Miss Shylo
The Bride Wore Spurs

Available from HarperPaperbacks

"Tears will be running down your face at the touching conclusion. *The Bride Wore Spurs* is a book you'll reread and enjoy every time."   —*Rendezvous*

"A colossal western romance brimming with several superb characters."   —*Affaire de Coeur*

The Bride Wore Spurs

⚔ SHARON IHLE ⚔

HarperPaperbacks
A Division of HarperCollinsPublishers

This is a work of fiction. The characters, incidents, and dialogues are products of the author's imagination and are not to be construed as real. Any resemblance to actual events or persons, living or dead, is entirely coincidental.

HarperPaperbacks   *A Division of* HarperCollins*Publishers*
10 East 53rd Street, New York, N.Y. 10022

Cover illustration by Jean Monti

First printing: June 1995

Printed in the United States of America

HarperPaperbacks, HarperMonogram, and colophon are trademarks of HarperCollins*Publishers*

❖ 10 9 8 7 6 5 4 3 2 1

For Fred Dueber,
who keeps me on my historical toes—
have at it!
and
Larry, Larry, and ~~Darrell,~~ oops, I mean, Bertha;
for the wild, wacky, and wonderful memories
of our "pub crawl" through Ireland

With special thanks to Sharon and Wayne,
Barry and Sally, Don and Denise, all the warm
friendly folks from Laramie and Centennial,
Wyoming, and The Laramie Chamber of Commerce
and
To Jan Barone Poole and her magnificent
Arabian stallion, Marki, the stud on which my
fictional "Phantom" is based
and
To Lacey Christman for the use of her lovely name.

A man who wears spurs has high expectations.
A woman who wears spurs has a mind of her own.

1

I have spread my dreams under your feet;
Tread softly, because you tread on my dreams.
—William Butler Ycats

Ireland, 1878

Time for low tea, but instead of settling down like the others with a nice steaming cup and a bite of soda bread smeared with butter and jam, Kathleen Lacey O'Carroll was hiding in the broom closet doing what no proper young lady would even think of doing.

But then Lacey had never been particularly ladylike, and no one had ever accused her of being proper—and for a very good reason. Her place of residence was St. Josephine's Hospital for Women, sometimes referred to as County Tipperary's home for the insane. While Lacey wasn't exactly an inmate, she could hardly be considered as part of the staff, either. Although her status may have been in doubt, her situation was not; Lacey O'Carroll was every bit as cloistered at St. Josephine's as the nuns at Kylemoor Abbey. And had been since the age of seven.

Squinting hard at the paper she held in her hands, she

cursed the shadowy and vague ribbon of light cast off by the small candle she'd pilfered. "Damn the bit and this miserly flame! Surely you can do a better job than this."

Trying a different angle, she raised the candle above her head. After most of the shadows had drifted away from the wrinkled parchment, she narrowed her gaze to better focus on the neat handwriting, then read the last portion of the letter which was addressed to her favorite nurse.

". . . and do so look forward to meeting you this spring. Upon your arrival in New York, please wire ahead to let me know when to meet your train at the Laramie Depot. I will have the preacher standing by, and look forward to a long and happy life with you. Yours heart and soul, Caleb Weatherspoon."

Lacey's gaze fell below to the signature and hastily added postscript—both of which appeared to have been written in a scrawl which looked suspiciously unlike the rest of the cleanly scripted letter.

"And by the by. If you got a yung frend better than sisteen but les than twenny-five who mite be wantn a hoss ranchur, bring her wit you. I got a nabur coud use hisself a wife."

A wife! Her sense of excitement growing as a plan took shape in her mind, Lacey searched out the beginning of the letter and started to read it again to be sure she hadn't misconstrued anything. As she reached the romantic salutation—My Dearest Miss Quinlin—she realized that this time through, the lighting seemed better, making the message quite a bit easier to decipher. She glanced up at the candle she still held overhead to find that the tiny flame had set fire to a bundle of cleaning rags hanging off the shelf above her hair. The light was brighter because she'd set the broom closet ablaze!

With a terrified cry, Lacey flung the candle and letter

into the air, leapt to her feet, and burst out of the room, still screaming. In the next moment, everything went mercifully black, and she withdrew into herself, a place where her fears and the outside world couldn't reach her.

Later—hours or days, Lacey couldn't be sure—she struggled against the urge to remain buried within herself. Something on the outside was too important to indulge herself this way. Something that might have the power to change her life. What was it? she wondered.

When she remembered, Lacey surged through the darkness in her soul with a surprising burst of strength. Her eyes flew open to see four stark white walls. Then she caught sight of Nurse Katherine 'Kate' Quinlin who was pacing the white-tiled floor near the bed on which Lacey lay. A miracle of sorts, since by all rights, she should have been gazing upon stern Head Nurse Murphy. Blessed instead to find herself confined to a private room with her best and only true friend, Nurse Quinlin, Lacey breathed a sigh of relief. Somehow, dear Kate had managed to save her—once again—from what surely would have turned into a vicious birching, at the least.

Lacey lifted her thick coppery lashes and glanced up at her friend. "How long was I gone this time?" she asked guiltily.

Kate shook her blond head with frustration. "Just over an hour, but that were long enough! I was so sure ye could manage on yer own from here on out, but to find that ye've gone and set a fire is the work of the devil! What could ye have been thinking, lass, ye with the scars to warn ye away from all that burns?"

At the reference, Lacey automatically glanced down at her right hand. Staring at the web of scarring which made up the palm of that hand, she spoke in a soft, shaky voice. "It were an accident. I swear by the cross o' Christ that I ne'er meant to start a fire. I only thought to put light on a small paper so I might better make out the words written there."

Kate stopped pacing. "Did ye now? And what manner of paper would ye be reading instead of taking yer tea?"

Trying to sound as if she'd had every right to Kate's possessions, Lacey casually said, "'Twas a letter posted to you from one Caleb Weatherspoon."

"*What?*" Kate hovered over Lacey, whispering angrily, "How did ye happen to come by such a letter, lassie?—and do be sure to save the blarney for them that don't know ye like I do."

Still feigning innocence, Lacey gave a casual shrug. "What difference does it make how I got my hands on it? The thing is that I found your letter, read it, and now I know that you're planning to mail yourself off to Wyoming as a bride for this Caleb Weatherspoon. And soon, too."

With a heavy sigh, Kate sank down on the only other piece of furniture, a spindle-backed chair pushed up close to the head of the bed. She suddenly looked old and weary, aged beyond her thirty-five years. "Aye, and I canna argue the truth of what ye says, lass. I was about getting around to having this talk with ye anyway. Now's as good a time as any, I expect, to tell ye that I'll be leaving here Saturday, this week."

"So soon?" Lacey abruptly sat up. "For the love of God, Nurse Quinlin, you've got to take me with you!"

"What's all this?" Harsh lines suddenly appeared at the corners of Kate's pale blue eyes and her lips grew taut and thin. "'Tisn't possible to take ye along."

"But of course 'tis possible! I read the postscript of your letter myself—Caleb Weatherspoon said if there'd be a lass near my age, that you should bring her along as wife for a rancher friend of his."

"No! No!" Kate clapped her hands over her ears and rose to begin pacing again. "Ye canna ask this of me."

"But you've got to take me—don't you see? With you gone, there will be no one to care about what happens to poor Lacey O'Carroll. I'll surely die."

"*Raumach!* Ye've got your whole life ahead of ye—but yer right about the one thing. 'Tis time ye were free to go on yer own way. I was planning to speak to Nurse Murphy before I left about signing ye a clean bill of health, anyway."

"'Tisn't going to happen and you know it." Rarely did Lacey use sharp tones with any of the nurses, much less this one. But she used them now. "As long as there's a pound left of my money, I'll be stuck here as a woman of delicate constitution, and St. Josephine's will be all too happy to keep me."

"Bah! There canna be enough money left of your father's estate to matter now."

Since Lacey had no way of knowing her true financial condition, she had to accept Kate's word. "Even if I'm near to broke, do you think Nurse Murphy will believe the fire in the broom closet was an accident?" Kate couldn't look at her, and that was all the answer Lacey needed. "Why, quick as a hare they'd be locking me up in the mad-room and throwing away the key. You're my only chance, Nurse Quinlin, and we both know it."

"Bah!" But a few more sighs and moments of rapid pacing later, Kate offered an alternate solution. "What if I manage to get ye out of here, then set ye up in my old rooms, introduce ye around to a few—"

"I'm better off left here. Or dead."

Kate whirled around and stared at her with surprise. "But 'tis freedom yer wanting, isn't it? That's what I'm offering."

"There's no freedom for me in Ireland. Where would I go? What would I do? The townsfolk assume I'm a mad-woman since I've been at St. Josephine's near my entire life." And Lacey wasn't so sure they'd be wrong. "I have to leave the homeland if I'm ever to have the chance to try and be a regular woman—even to be a wife, God willing. I'm thinking maybe this Caleb Weatherspoon of yours might just know the perfect husband for me, a man who'd ne'er have to know of my past, or even guess at it."

"Oh, Lacey . . . I wonder. Even if I could take ye with me, and I'm not saying that I can, I dona see how ye can hide yer problems from a husband. What of yer spells, lass? How will ye explain them away?"

She hadn't thought of them, those occasional periods of silence brought on by stress, fear, or agitation when she simply withdrew from the world around her. Spells, they called them, which lasted anywhere from a few hours to a few days, when she couldn't speak, hear, or see. They'd started the night of the fire at the family castle, and occasionally got her locked up with the mad women—the way they had during the ten-year period between her seventh and seventeenth birthdays when she hadn't spoken so much as one word. But Lacey couldn't let those infrequent spells stop her now even though she didn't know how or if she could control them should she venture to America.

"I can handle the spells," she said with far more conviction than she felt. "The man need ne'er know of them."

Kate wrung her hands in genuine distress. "*Arrah*, like you handled them today? Is it so wise, or even kind to try and keep the life ye've lived from a man who'd pledge his troth to ye?"

"You tell me. Have you bothered to tell Mr. Weatherspoon what your previous calling was?" That Kate had *not* told him and didn't even plan to, was obvious by her pained expression. Being a "mad nurse" was sometimes looked on as one step away from the madwomen cared for.

Pleased by Kate's perplexed expression, Lacey felt a little smile tug the corners of her mouth. "I thought you might keep that bit of news to yourself, but do not

worry—you'll not be cheating your dear husband-to-be.
I've heard it said that a man should ne'er take a wife who
has no faults."

In spite of her obvious reservations over the proposed
plans, Kate burst out laughing. "True enough what ye
says, lass."

"So then, will you do it? Please?"

Kate raised her open palms to the heavens. "Lord
have mercy on me! Will ye ne'er set me free of this lass?
Ne'er?"

2

The more things a man is ashamed of, the more
respectable he is.

—George Bernard Shaw

Wyoming Territory
April, 1878

He was late. Hell, more than just late. A thick
coil of black smoke rolled across the clear blue skies to
the northwest, telling him that the train had already
pulled out of the station and was steaming toward
Medicine Bow at full speed. Caleb would have his hide if
he found out that no one had met his precious mail-order
bride, and if he ever discovered the reason why—that his
good friend and neighbor had been distracted by a small
band of wild horses—that hide wouldn't be worth a
plugged nickel. Not that most folks thought it was worth
even that, given the fact that it was cinnamon-colored
instead of pure white like the peaks of the Snowy Range
Mountains behind him.

But John Winterhawke, Jr. didn't really give a damn
what the townsfolk or his other neighbors thought about

⊸ 8 ⊱

the color of his half-breed skin. All he really cared about other than his long-time friend, was the ranch, Winterhawke, and the fact that if all went well, by summer, it might finally be his. All his. That is, of course, assuming his bastard of an uncle was ready to turn loose of the deed—and that Caleb's Irish mail-order bride was still waiting at the depot and Hawke could manage to deliver her to her crippled-up groom in one piece. If he couldn't handle that simple task, not even his *life* would be worth a plugged nickel after Caleb got hold of him. His sense of urgency renewed, Hawke slapped the reins across the backs of a pair of matched buckskin mares, and hurried the wagon along toward the Laramie Depot.

Fifteen minutes later he strolled through the station and out to the back where the train had deposited its passengers. There he spotted a lone pair of women sitting on a wooden bench, with a large trunk and small traveling bag at their feet. In a hurry to have this "bride" business over with so he could get back to his ranch, Hawke strode up to the women and gruffly said, "Is one of you Miss Katherine Quinlin?"

The lady to the left seemed to shrink into the oversized hood of her cape, and her eyes grew huge as she sputtered, "I—I'm Miss Katherine Q-Quinlin. S-surely yer not . . . ye wouldn't be my Mr. Weatherspoon, would ye?"

Although he was used to a certain disdain and even a fair amount of scorn from the fine citizens in these parts—especially now that Custer and his troops had been slaughtered some two years ago by his fellow "savages"—it rankled Hawke to think his best friend's bride-to-be looked on him with such obvious horror and revulsion. He even entertained the idea of responding, "Yes, ma'am, I'm Caleb Weatherspoon, the man you'll soon marry," just to enjoy the look on her face, but quickly dismissed the thought. As it was, he would be seeing less and less of Caleb once he wed. No sense adding to the distance that would naturally come between them.

"I'm John Winterhawke, Caleb's friend," he explained in a brusque tone. "He was cow-kicked last week during calving. Got his kneecap busted and can't ride in the wagon for at least a month. He sent me to fetch you." Hawke pointed to the baggage. "Which of these is yours?" He hadn't thought it possible, but the woman shrank further into her cape.

"M-might there be an inn nearby?" she asked nervously. "Rooms to let until Caleb can come for me himself?"

Hawke shrugged indifferently. "There's several hotels in town if you got the money to put yourself up for that long. Caleb's running a little short now with the accident and all. He was hoping you'd be willing to come out to the ranch and stay on until the circuit preacher makes it out that far. Shouldn't be more than a couple of weeks." He exhaled loudly, impatiently. "Are you coming or not?"

On her feet now, Caleb's intended glanced down at the other woman. "Mr. Weatherspoon wrote that he had a neighbor needin' a wife and to bring a friend along with me if I like. I ne'er thought to wire him about Miss O'Carroll here. Does he have room for her too until we get the weddin's over with proper-like?"

Since the other woman had been pointed out to him as part of the package, Hawke finally took a hard look at her. What he could see of her, that is. She also wore a velvet cape with an oversized hood, an indigo wrap that covered most all of her except for her intensely curious blue eyes, pert little nose, and small heart-shaped mouth—all features which told him she was at least ten years younger than Miss Quinlin.

"Is there a problem," Kate asked, "with me bringing her and all?"

Hawke shrugged. "Not for me, there isn't. I don't know

what neighbor asked Caleb to get him a wife, but if that's what he wrote in his letter, I guess that's what he wanted. He'll make room for her, I expect." Again he pointed at the baggage. "Both of these yours?"

"Mine and Miss O'Carroll's. Shall we wait for ye and the carriage out front of the depot?"

"No. You'll *follow* me." Hawke lifted the heavy trunk by one handle, then heaved it over his shoulder. His free hand dangling alongside his hip and the sheath containing his finely-honed bowie knife, he shot both women a smirk. "You two should be able to manage the bag just fine."

Hawke was a man who believed in keeping lists. In his business dealings, he always kept track of advantages and disadvantages along with possible profits or losses on paper. But when it came to his personal life, the list was usually stored in the back of his mind. That's where he kept the considerably lopsided ledger regarding his friend and mentor, Caleb Weatherspoon.

The man had taken him in as a young boy, taught him the tricks of the trapping trade, and even more important, how to survive on his own whether in the wild or among "civilized" citizens. When it became apparent that trapping could no longer earn a man a decent wage, Caleb took up cattle ranching, leaving Hawke to pursue his life's dream—the building of a horse ranch. He'd always figured that he owed his good friend a lot, so much in fact, he was sure he'd never be able to repay him.

Until today.

Hawke took a sideways glance at the women beside him on the bouncing buckboard, and felt the weight of that one-sided list shift toward a more equal balance. Not only did Miss Quinlin view him as somehow less than human, she hadn't stopped complaining about the hard wooden seat or failed to groan aloud each time the wagon bumped and thumped on its way out of town and onto the long stretch of rolling prairie which lead to the foothills of the Snowy Range Mountains. What had Caleb been thinking of to offer himself to a woman he'd never met? And which of his neighbors had been fool enough to do the same with the younger gal?

Except for an occasional inquiry as to the types of trees they passed along the way, Miss O'Carroll had been silent. Hawke liked that in anyone, female or male, even though something in this female's voice was compelling, almost musical in its effect upon him. It was probably that Irish lilt of hers, he decided, the delicate sprinkling of an accent which tickled his ears in a way the heavy Gaelic brogue spoken by Miss Quinlin could not. The sound was new and pleasant. A morning's diversion.

Judging Miss O'Carroll by those standards alone—quiet, but possessed of a pleasant speaking voice—Hawke decided that she automatically made the better choice between the two mail-order brides. Even so, the young Irishwoman left a lot to be desired as the wife of any rancher in the rugged, unforgiving mountains of Wyoming. Not only did she appear to be too delicate and meek to winter here, but she behaved as if she'd never been in the great outdoors before, much less the wilderness.

She'd been twisting this way and that throughout the entire journey, studying the clumps of sage and vast meadows with open awe. When a small group of antelope bounded across the path just ahead of the wagon a few miles back, she'd let out a squeal as if terrified to have been so close to such odd beasts. Didn't they have elk, deer, or something close to antelope in Ireland? If prey frightened her, what would she do when faced with a predator?—say a wolf, a bear, or a mountain lion? He almost laughed at the thought, something of a rarity for a man who didn't even feel the need to smile, then thought of Caleb and his impulsive decision to advertise for a bride.

Hawke knew why his friend thought he needed a wife—pure loneliness—and why he decided he had to have one of Irish extraction—to remind him of his dear, faithful mother—but it was crazy to bring women such as these up into these hills, sheer, unmitigated lunacy, no matter how long the winters might be or how lonely the nights. Pure idiocy.

After some eight uncomfortable hours riding beside the Irish ladies, Hawke guided the buckskins down a road that ran parallel to the Little Laramie River. Situated just below the tiny town of Centennial, the river's relatively straight banks were crowded with mountain mahogany and cottonwood trees, a colorful background for Caleb's Three Elk Ranch.

After tying the team to the hitching post out in front of the house, Hawke helped the ladies down off the wagon and hoisted the trunk on his shoulder. Then without so much as a "follow me," again he bid the women to handle the traveling bag themselves, and climbed the wooden stairs to his friend's modest frame home. Rapping twice against the white-washed door, he pushed it open.

"You up and about, and decent, Caleb?" he shouted into the room. After a moment of grunts and groans, his friend answered.

"I am now. Come on in!"

Hawke stepped into the wide-open room that served as kitchen, dining area, and living room, dropped the trunk on the freshly shellacked floor, then turned and gestured for the ladies to follow him inside.

Nurse Quinlin marched through the door with her head held high, but Lacey, who'd been left with the traveling bag, hung back. After what she'd overheard at the depot, she knew her arrival wasn't expected, and maybe, not even welcomed. She figured she was better off standing out on the porch at least until Nurse Quinlin—whom she was to address as "Kate" from here on out—had made the private introduction of her husband-to-be. Their escort, an unfriendly sort who wore a mountaineer-style hat with an inverted brim that hid most of his dark features, had other ideas.

He marched back through the door, took the grip from Lacey's hand, and snapped at her in a gravelly voice which made her feel like she'd done something wrong.

"Get on in here so I can close the door. Caleb doesn't happen to like flies in his soup."

The man's arrogance and gruff way of speaking were beginning to wear thin, but Lacey was much too new to both the country and her circumstances to do anything but obey him. Keeping her silence, she hurried across the threshold and took up a stance next to a huge pair of antlers that were nailed to the wall. Right behind her, this John Winterhawke pulled off his hat, hung it on one of the antlers, and stopped to stare at her. He held her trapped in his gaze for several moments, his deep-set eyes both green and gray at the same time and watchful, almost predator-like in the way he looked down at her from beneath the prominent ridge of his wide, strong brow. His open perusal of her was so intense and direct, Lacey honestly didn't know where or how she found the courage to keep looking up at him.

But she did.

He had *very* long hair for a man, long enough that he'd tied the coffee brown lengths into a kind of tail at the back of his neck, leaving it to hang down between his shoulder blades. Lacey had certainly never seen anything like *that* before, not even during the long journey across the American wilderness by rail! What manner of man was this? she wondered as he abruptly broke away from her and walked over to the stove.

Hawke lifted a pot from the burner and poured himself a cup of coffee. Turning back toward the stone fireplace, he blew across surface of the brew as he addressed his friend. "Is everything in order over there? Got the right woman, and all?"

Caleb, who was stretched out on a long couch positioned in front of the fire, gazed lovingly at his intended. "Couldn't be better, friend. I thank you agin for fetching my darling Miss Quinlin to me."

Kate blushed. Caleb was as rough and craggy on the outside as a weathered fence post, and he looked to be close to ten years her senior, but there was something about him that stirred her blood and made her feel cherished in a way she'd never known before—not even during the months of illicit trysts she'd had with her first and only true love.

"'Tis I who gives thanks for ye, Mr. Weatherspoon."

Caleb beamed. "See what I mean Hawke? I expect we'll be getting along like two pups in a basket."

Hawke cocked a thumb in the direction of the hat rack. "*Three* pups unless you've already sent for whoever ordered her."

Caleb glanced Lacey's way then, noticing her for the first time, and started with surprise. "And who might you be?"

Kate answered quickly. "'Tis the friend ye said I could bring along with me. The bride for yer neighbor?"

Caleb, a portly man whose girth was a perfect complement for Kate's apple dumpling figure, gulped audibly. "This here's a, a *bride* for . . . aw, dad-gummit. I forgot about that. My memory'd make a better sieve these days."

Hawke, who'd shed his thigh-length leather jacket and dropped it on a kitchen chair, strode over to the couch, coffee in hand. "I'm having a hell of a time figuring out just which neighbor asked you to get him a wife. Willard over at Box-T swore off women after that squaw of his went crazy and cut him up with his own knife, and if I remember correctly, Big Jim at Dirt Creek not only has a wife, but she's swollen up with their eighth child. That just leaves those moth-eaten miners around Centennial, and I can't imagine—"

"She's for you," said Caleb, plain and simple.

Hawke froze in mid-sip. Then in slow, molasses-like movements, the coffee cup slipped off the ends of his fingers and shattered against the shiny floor. The hot brew splattered his boots and leggings, soaking through to his skin, but Hawke didn't even flinch.

"*Me?*" he said, incredulous. "I never ordered me a bride! What in hell's wrong with you, Caleb? Have you lost your feeble mind?"

Caleb stretched himself up as tall as he could, although sitting there with his leg splinted from boot to butt, the gesture didn't add much to his squat stature. "Now don't go getting yourself all riled up," he said, working to calm his friend. "It seemed like a good idea at the time."

"It did?" Hawke's gruff voice was booming. "And what time might that have been, *friend*? I wrote all of your "courtship" letters for you, but I don't recall scribbling down anything to suggest that *I* might be on the lookout for a bride!"

Blushing a little, Caleb admitted, "Well, I kinda added the suggestion to the last letter we wrote cause I know what you're a needing even if you don't. I figured what you're a needing, is a wife."

"Like hell, I am!"

"Ah, if ye'll be excusing me, gentlemen?" Kate's tentative brogue cut into their conversation. "Me thinks I best go have a little chat with me companion so ye can have some privacy."

Pinning his half-breed friend with a purposeful gaze, Caleb said to his intended, "Thank you kindly, Miss Kate. That sounds like a fine idea. Me and Hawke got some straightening out to do."

With that, she maneuvered around the far end of the couch—the end which didn't feature the formidable obstacle in the shape of one Mr. John Winterhawke—and hurried over to where Lacey stood. "I canna *believe* what a dreadful affair I've got ye into, lass." With one eye on the men as they argued in hushed tones, she kept her voice to a whisper. "Yer only hope is that my dear Mr. Weatherspoon will sport ye the passage back to Ireland."

"Ireland?" Lacey dug in for a fight. "I'm not going back to the homeland, no matter what happens here."

"But girl!" Kate stared over at the men, her eyes huge. "Haven't ye noticed something . . . *different* about Mr. Winterhawke? Me thinks he's one of those wild Indians— ye know of 'em, heathens who'd just as soon peel the hair from yer head as pluck the bloom of a fuchsia to trim it."

"*You really . . . think so?*" Tremors of both awe and fear raced up her spine. "How can you be so sure?"

"Take a good look at him, lass, see for yerself!"

Needing no further encouragement as she'd been sneaking brief glimpses of the intensely mesmerizing man anyway since the moment they first stepped into the tidy little cottage, Lacey cast a furtive glance his way. Now that he'd removed the coat from his tall, lean body to reveal a rawhide shirt with fringe which swung down from his elbows, she could see how that, added to his rawhide trousers, colorfully-embroidered leggings, and hat which featured a pair of eagle feathers hanging over the brim, might give credence to Kate's theory.

Lacey had certainly never seen a man dressed in such a manner before, but something more supported the notion that this man might indeed be a wild Indian; his skin was reddish-brown, looking bronzed by the firelight, and he possessed a rather reckless, uncivilized countenance. John Winterhawke had a way of moving which all but said, "go to the devil." That, along with the feral gleam in his eyes insinuating that he might just *be* the devil, was enough to convince her that he could be the heathen Kate suggested he was.

Lacey shivered at the prospect of calling such a man, "husband," but she vowed not to turn back now. "I-I don't care about Mr. Winterhawke's heritage. I t-think he looks j-just . . . fine. If he'll be agreeing to marry the likes of me, then I'm staying."

Kate shot her a look of both anxiety and relief, as if she were worried about Lacey, but too eager to be rid of her to argue the point further. "If yer sure ye'll not consider returning to Ireland, lass, I'll do what I can to see that ye and . . . that the pair of ye are wed."

Across the room and in tones much louder than the womenfolk, the men were still slinging verbal mud at one another. Smarting from his protégé's latest accusation—that maybe he'd gone numb north of his ears—Caleb muttered under his breath, "Well just maybe *you've* gone *blind* as a post hole! Have you snuck a good peek at that gal?"

Grumbling to himself, Hawke said, "Isn't much to see of her all wrapped up in that cape the way she is, but I don't care if she's the best looking thing since the spring thaw. I *don't* want or need a wife!"

"Cape's off," Caleb said in a low whisper. "Take a look at her, have a gander at that nice skin. I'll bet that gal's face is softer than the inside of a school marm's thigh."

"You think so?" Hawke said sarcastically. "I wouldn't know that kind of soft, now would I."

Caleb ignored the reference to the fact that no self-respecting white woman would allow a half-breed to touch her, and went on with his argument. "Just take a look at the gal, god damn it! A good look—she's a beauty, Hawke, a real beauty. I swear, if'n I hadn't already made a pledge to Kate, I'd go after that young one myself."

Because Caleb was so adamant, Hawke grudgingly cast a disinterested eye in Miss O'Carroll's direction. What he saw surprised him with its impact, capturing him as surely as he'd captured Phantom, the renegade mustang stallion who now serviced the mares at Winterhawke Ranch. It wasn't just the delicate features he'd noticed earlier beneath the hood of her cape, but the way her hair and porcelain skin set them off. Hawke had never seen a woman with hair the color of a new penny, or skin so smooth and pale. She wasn't beautiful exactly, but stunning and alluring, the kind of woman who made a man stare at her with an almost morbid fascination. Hawke's mind told him to look away from her, that he was making a fool of himself, but for some reason, he couldn't react with his usual swiftness.

"Not so bad after all, eh?" said Caleb, delighted by his friend's response.

Finally able to look away from the young woman, Hawke furrowed his brow. "Yes, she really is very handsome, which makes me wonder—why would a good-looking white woman like that agree to marry a half-breed like me? What do you suppose is wrong with her?"

As Caleb mulled this over, Kate returned. "I hope I'm not interrupting ye, but I thought I'd let ye know that Miss O'Carroll has agreed to uphold her end of the bargain to marry Mr. Winterhawke. I assume that he's in agreement as well?"

Hawke turned on her. "You may as well assume that you never left Ireland, in that case, because—"

"Hold up a minute," said Caleb, cutting him off. "You know I've never called any markers in on you before, Hawke, and I didn't cause I never really figured that you owed me for all I done for you. I done what I done cause I like you and wanted what's best for you. Still do." He leaned back against the arm of the couch, resting his aching back, and leveled his friend with his gaze. "I'm calling in a marker now. I'm asking you to do this one thing for me; give the gal a chance. Give her time to prove herself to you, say till the preacher comes to marry me and Kate."

Hawke groaned. How could Caleb have put him on such a spot? There was no way in hell that he could deny the man his request—not if he wanted to enjoy his peace of mind and the solitude he'd grown to love, that is. He would have to at least look as if he were "giving the girl a chance," whatever that meant. Then, if he lived through it, he would simply declare this unwanted bride as unfit. There was really no other choice.

Speaking quietly and without enthusiasm, Hawke said, "I guess I could give her a try. Just what is it you want me to do?"

Caleb beamed. "Not much. Just test her a little, see if you don't find that having a wife around is a blessing, not a curse."

"Test her?" asked Kate, alarmed. "In what way? I'll not stand for any improper behavior!"

"Don't worry your head, Miss Kate." Caleb winked at her, then gave Hawke a meaningful look. "I *guarantee* you that my friend here won't be compromising your friend in any way. He can be trusted. Ain't that right?"

Hawke nodded, glanced at the young woman who still stood qu: tly against the far wall, and sighed heavily. "How do you want me to go about this 'test,' Caleb?"

"Why don't you come by tomorrow morning, pick Miss O'Carroll up—and in a wagon by the way—then take her back to your place for the day to see how she'll fit in?"

Again Hawke glanced at the woman, and again he wondered: *What's wrong with her?* Keeping a puzzled gaze on her, he asked, "Is that all right with you, ma'am?"

Lacey, who hadn't taken her eyes off the Indian since Kate had left her alone, had to glance away so intense was his scrutiny. "'Tis a good idea, I suppose, though I do not know what you'll be expecting of me."

"Not too much." Hawke strode over to the chair where he'd left his jacket, donned it, then proceeded on to the elk rack where he'd hung his hat. "Just the usual things," he said, speaking directly to her as he fit his hat to his head. "Cooking, cleaning, mending, a little help in the barn. Think you can manage those few chores?"

Rising to the challenge she heard in his tone and saw in his unnerving gaze, Lacey set her chin. "In my sleep, Mr. Winterhawke. In the dead of night."

Flashing a smirk—the expression really couldn't have been called a smile—Hawke touched the brim of his hat. "In that case, I'll be seeing you first thing in the morning."

It wasn't until after he'd gone, that what he'd demanded of her finally sank into Lacey's mind; *cooking, cleaning, mending?* Never mind the part about the barn—she'd never so much as *seen* the inside of a barn!

In fact, the only chores Lacey had ever been responsible for, or even expected to perform from the time she was seven years old, was to scrub floors and make certain that she returned the books she borrowed from the small library at St. Josephine's. She did this without question, for failure to return books resulted in the loss of library privileges, a thing Lacey would never have allowed to happen to her. Reading had been her only source of pleasure or avenue of escape from the hospital until the night Nurse Quinlin stole her away under cover of darkness.

But *cooking, cleaning, and mending?*

How did one go about the preparation of food or the fashioning of clothing? And how in the devil would she learn to do any of it—by morning, no less?

3

Never take a wife who has no faults.
—**Old Irish proverb**

Lacey had hardly slept since the night she escaped from St. Josephine's. She had been too excited about the upcoming adventure. Now as the darkness settled over her, she should have been resting, but her mind carried her back through her long journey, immersing her once again in the sights, smells, and sounds of all that was so new.

First there had been the huge ship and the rough, but thoroughly exciting crossing of the Atlantic Ocean. Then, after stepping foot on American soil for the first time, she'd felt a delicious, almost overpowering sense of freedom she'd never known, even as a child before "the accident." Topping all that, Lacey recalled the unparalleled excitement of making the train journey halfway across this great new country. She'd experienced a lifetime of memories in just a few short weeks. And now, God willing, she would finally know the thrill of having a man in her life. Someone to call her own.

Shivering with excitement over the idea, Lacey rolled to her side on the lumpy couch and faced the fireplace. Due to Caleb's splinted leg and the fact that he didn't fit anywhere else, he stayed in his big four-poster in the nice airy bedroom he would soon share with Kate, while she made herself at home in the small office at the back of the house, sleeping on the cot generally used by Hawke on those nights when he stayed over. This left the couch in the living room to Lacey, and though it was as comfortable as any bed she'd slept in since leaving Ireland, she'd tossed and turned for half the night. And it wasn't just the stimulation of the trip keeping her awake.

This Indian who was to become her husband had at least a little to do with her insomnia. Even if he was a bit on the gruff side, something about him fascinated her, something wicked and terribly exciting. What would it be like to become the wife of a man like that, she wondered, to walk side by side with such a proud and confident individual? Lacey thought back to the way he'd stared at her—in particular, to that intense, deliberate, and demanding gaze, a look with enough arrogance to suggest that it had the power to beckon her on its own. Even the color of his eyes was menacing, the same silver-green hue of the foam-capped Atlantic breaking against the Cliffs of Moher. Dark, powerful, and dangerous.

Lacey shivered again at the thought of being so helpless under this man's gaze, then tugged the blanket up tight beneath her chin. Still thinking of Hawke, and even daring to wonder if he might try to kiss her once they were wed, she finally felt herself drift off to sleep. In what seemed like moments later, there came a loud pounding on the door. Disoriented and confused, Lacey flung herself off the couch and tumbled down to the floor.

Again came the pounding.

"J-Just a moment," she cried, still dazed and confused.

Dragging herself to her feet, Lacey followed a thin beam of light cast off by the dying fire, and made her way to the door. After struggling with the thick plank which served as a latch, she finally removed it and pulled the door open. Hawke stood at the threshold between the porch and the house, his rugged features illuminated by the lantern hanging from the jamb. Beyond him, the sky was steel gray.

Hawke stared down at the sleepy woman, taking in the yards and yards of rumpled cotton nightgown, the wildly disheveled mop of coppery red curls, and the dull look in her normally bright blue eyes. His breath lodged in his throat. While he'd hoped to catch the Irish miss fast asleep, he hadn't figured on her looking so warm and cuddly, or so innocently provocative. Something warm trickled through his chest, then flared and spread below.

Shaking off the sudden, crazy effect her appearance had on him, Hawke cleared his throat and bellowed the obvious. "You're not dressed."

Lacey glanced down at herself, finally awake enough to realize she was standing before a man in a most immodest state. She quickly wrapped her arms across her bosom and crossed her legs at the ankle. "Of course not, sir! 'Tisn't even morning yet. What are you wanting at such an ungodly hour?"

"You," he said, pleased to see her eyes grow clear and alert, enough so he noticed they were not simply blue, but sparkling with minute specks of gold. Not so pleased by the effect this discovery had on him, Hawke brushed past her, stepped into the room, and headed for the fireplace. "I said I'd be here first thing in the morning," he muttered angrily. "This *is* the first thing in the morning in these parts. I'll give you till my hands are warm to get dressed, then I've got to be heading back to the ranch—with or without you."

Her mouth and eyes a trio of perfect circles, Lacey whirled around in a cloud of cotton, and hurried off to the office where her luggage was stored with Kate's. "I will not be long, Mr. Winterhawke," she called over her shoulder. "Do be sure to wait for me."

Muttering to himself now, Hawke reached inside his coat to where he'd sewn a wide, deep pocket in the thick lamb's wool lining, and pulled out his ledger. This was one list he did *not* intend to keep in the back of his mind. When the time came to turn down Caleb's generous offer of a bride, Hawke wanted concrete proof that she was completely unacceptable. After flipping the ledger open to the page already marked, "Miss Lacey O'Carroll," he slipped the pencil out of its sheath, moistened the tip with his tongue, then made his first entry under the heading, *Disadvantages:*

1. Slothful

Then, just because he was still irritated over the way his heart had lurched when he first saw her, and again when she'd looked at him with eyes like a gold-miner's dream, he glanced at the couch where she'd been sleeping. The cushions were askew and in need of straightening, and both the blanket and pillow she'd used had been tossed onto the floor in an untidy heap. Moistening the pencil again, he made another entry in the same column:

2. Messy

Hawke was toying with the idea of adding a third complaint to the column—something to do with tardiness— when Lacey came bounding into the room again.

"There, and I'm ready to go to work now," she said breathlessly.

Slowly turning toward her, Hawke saw that she'd changed into a navy blue skirt and plain white blouse, and that she'd twisted her mounds of springy red curls into a rather sloppy knot at the crown of her head. Wondering how long it would take for those unruly ringlets to explode from their precarious bun, he crossed the room and took her velvet cape from the antler.

"Is this cape all you've got by way of a coat?"

"'Tis a cloak, and yes, sir, 'tis my only wrap. Why?"

He shook his head. "I don't know what the weather's like where you come from, but even in summer, it can be colder than a witches . . . carcass in these mountains." He sighed heavily, making a point. "I've got some extra blankets in the wagon you can use for now, but we'll have to fix you up with some kind of coat if I'm going to be hauling you back and forth between ranches the next few days." Then he turned on his heel and went out the door without so much as a "follow me."

It took nearly an hour to cover the steep, twisting three miles of rocky road that led to Winterhawke Ranch. During that entire time, not one word passed between Lacey and her somewhat reluctant fiancé. He hadn't even offered to help her climb up on the wagon. She snuck a quick peek at Hawke, noticed his rigid, brooding profile, and supposed she was lucky that he'd even bothered to give her a couple of blankets to ward off the chill. It *was* cold outside, near to freezing she figured, and in mid-spring, no less! What must the winters be like in a place such as this? And how would she ever live through them should he decide to keep her?

Throughout the trip, Lacey contented herself by getting a lay of the land, the vague light of dawn giving her teasing glimpses of the forests and mountains ahead, their shadowy tree tops set off by shiny patches of snow still left upon the ground. After negotiating a sharp bend in the road, the final turn as it happened, the wagon strained up a tree-lined path, then finally came to a halt in front of a large log house. As before, Hawke simply climbed down from the wagon, leaving Lacey to fend for herself.

Wondering how the devil she would ever get this non-communicative man to accept her as his bride—and be kind to her in the bargain—Lacey stumbled along after Hawke across some kind of stone path, up five wooden stairs, and finally over a high threshold.

Once inside the house, Hawke struck a match and lit a wrought iron lamp mounted on the wall near the door. Staring into Lacey's eternally-curious blue eyes, he said gruffly, "I'll go find a coat that you can work in, then we've got to get busy. We're running late this morning."

"A moment, please?" He complied, but continued to stare at her from under a frown. "Forgive me if I've been at fault or if I've upset you somehow, Mr. Winterhawke, but—"

"Stop calling me that." No one, but no one had ever addressed him as "mister" anything. Hawke had been called many names over the years, to be sure, but never anything close to *Mr.* Winterhawke. It was an odd sensation to hear his name spoken this way—one he was pretty sure he didn't like. "Call me Hawke like everyone else does."

"If you wish it. As I was saying . . ." Lacey left the rest of the sentence unsaid, as her "doting" fiancé had walked away and disappeared into the bowels of his home. Now what? And exactly what made the man behave so rudely toward her? Blast the luck! What if he was *always* in such a bad humor, and his foul temper had nothing whatsoever to do with her? She wasn't at all sure that convincing him to marry her would be worth the trouble.

Deciding to have a better look at what might be her new home, Lacey glanced around the house. The place was magnificent. Made of thick, aromatic pine logs, the living room featured a high A-shaped ceiling braced by additional split logs and a center pole that featured eight spokes which reached up to support the ceiling in inverted tepee fashion. The immense stone fireplace at the narrow end of the room added a cozy touch, and with the fire burning as low as it was, turned the log walls to a rich dark maple color. But that was where this room's charm ended.

Caleb's modest little house had lovely lace curtains at the windows, shellacked floors, and thick rugs scattered throughout, whereas this place almost boasted of its lack of refinements. The huge bay window, including a pair of smaller ones to each side, was bare, inviting the night and its chill inside the room. As far as Lacey could tell, the floors were not shellacked—that was a guess since dirt and great clumps of mud seemed to be scattered everywhere—and there wasn't a rug to be seen. As for furnishings, the overstuffed chair and small lamp table positioned directly in front of the fireplace were apparently all he owned.

"Here you go, ma'am," Hawke said as he strolled back into the room and handed her a small jacket. "Take off that silly cape and put this on."

Lacey snatched the garment from his hand. "Forgive my insolence, Mr. . . . . Hawke, but if I've done something to offend you, I would like to know what 'tis. Seems to me that you're very unhappy in my presence, but for the life of me, I can not understand why. Would you mind telling me?"

She looked like a banti hen standing there, her feathers all ruffled, eyes flashing with a temper to match her hair, and for a moment, Hawke felt a little spot inside him go soft, the part of him that always melted for any kind of misfit be it human or animal. But then he reminded himself that fragile Miss Lacey was in no way, shape, or form, a misfit. Even though he still wondered what was wrong with her, he knew that all she need do was flash those blue eyes and toss those coppery ringlets, and she could have the man of her choice in any town. In any territory. She didn't need him. And he sure as hell didn't need her. Hawke toughened himself against those beautiful Irish eyes.

"The only thing that offends me, ma'am, is wasting time. This ranch runs on the same schedule as the sun, and I don't like that schedule messed with." He turned and headed for a wide arched doorway, but kept talking over his shoulder. "We've got to get breakfast out of the way now if we hope to get on schedule, so it's about time you went to work. I'll be right back to get you started on your chores."

Although still less than thrilled by the man's consistently bad attitude, after he disappeared into the other room, Lacey slipped out of her cloak to don the warm, sheepskin jacket as instructed. The sleeves were a wee bit long, but otherwise, it was a decent fit. She wondered briefly who it might belong to—it was much too small to have covered the Indian's broad shoulders—but then she heard what sounded like pots clanging together in the other room, and in the next instant, Hawke returned. In one hand he held a straw basket, in the other, a bucket.

Offering both items to her, he said, "I'll fire up the stove and put on a pot of coffee. Do you think you can manage to go out to the barn to get the milk and eggs?"

Again rising to the challenge in his tone, Lacey cocked her chin. "I'll be doing my best. Where is this barn?"

Hawke led her back across the threshold to the covered porch, lifted a lantern from its hook, and then lit it. "Go back down the path, veer to right and you'll walk right into the doors."

The sky, she noticed, had lightened considerably, making it easy for her to see the bell-shaped barn from the porch. Finding her place of work would be no problem.

Accomplishing tasks she didn't know the first thing about might not be so easy. Should she tell him she'd never gone after milk and eggs before? Or were these simple chores that even a child would be expected to manage?

"You'll need to light the inside of the barn," Hawke explained as he handed Lacey the lantern.

Shifting her load, she hooked the basket over her arm, gripped the pail with her left hand, then took the lantern with her right, careful to hide her scarred palm from him. The lamp swayed, nearly slipping off her wrist, but she managed to right it again.

"Be very careful with that!" Hawke warned. "I lost one house due to a careless fire. I don't plan on losing another." He thought of his other "guest" and the anxiety this woman's presence might cause. "There is one more thing; stay out of the loft."

"The loft?"

"Yes. Don't even climb the ladder to have a look at it. There's nothing but bedding straw up there, anyway. Any other questions?"

Tons, but she wasn't sure which, if any, should be asked. So Lacey repeated his instructions. "I go to the barn, get milk from—from what? A goat, a—"

"My cow, Hazel. She's the only one out there."

"Get milk from Hazel." Lacey nodded to herself. "And eggs from the chickens?"

"Yeah. I let my chickens have the run of the barn, so you'll find them everywhere. Just don't disturb the brooder in the stall against the north wall. She'll be hatching chicks in the next week or so. And stay away from the three closed stalls. I've got my best brood mares in them due to foal any day now. I don't want them upset. Understand what you're to do?"

North? Which way was north? And stalls, brooders,

and brood mares? Lacey really didn't know what he meant by any of that, but Hawke's impatient tone pretty well told her that she'd better have understood, so she gave him a wan smile. "I'll be doing my best for you."

"Well? You can't do your best just standing there—get a move on. It'll be noon before you get done at the rate you're going."

Although inflamed by his consistently critical tones, Lacey didn't want to give Hawke another reason to bark at her. Careful not to trip over the split-stone walk, she hurried down the path and made her way to the barn. The big double doors were closed, but not latched or padlocked, so she didn't even have to set part of her load down to gain entrance. She caught one of the doors with the toe of her shoe and pulled until the crack was wide enough for her to fit through. Then she stepped inside.

Lacey was at once struck by the warm, somehow comforting aroma of the animals, the pungent, earthy scent of horse and cow sweat in contrast to the almost odorless air of the frigid morning outside. As the animals detected her presence, chickens began to cluck, horses nickered softly, and a cow, Hazel, she assumed, cut loose with a loud bellow.

Fascinated by this strange new world, Lacey stepped deeper into the cavernous building and carefully hung the lantern on a hook she found driven into a center post. As she remembered Hawke's words about fire, and the fact he'd lost a house to flames, a violent shudder passed through her. It wouldn't happen again—never again. It *couldn't*. To reassure herself, Lacey double-checked the strength of the hook, satisfied herself that the lantern was secure and in no danger of setting fire to anything, and then took a look around the barn wondering where to start first. Surging with sudden excitement, she decided to head straight for the lone cow. She had a feeling that gathering milk would be a bigger challenge than the eggs.

"Top o' the morning to you, Hazel," she said, stopping just short of the animal's stall. "I've come for your milk."

The black and white creature heaved its head over its shoulder and stared at her with huge brown eyes. Never had Lacey seen such a large animal up close, and a sudden bullet of fright shot up her spine. What if the thing tried to attack her? It could flatten a lass like herself just by sneezing! Frightened, but determined to see this job through, she pressed herself tight against the stall divider, and eased her way alongside the animal.

Keeping one eye on the cow's every movement, Lacey glanced down at the bulging sack between Hazel's hind legs. That's where the milk would come from all right; she was pretty sure about that much, but how to get it out without putting herself in danger? Settling on a plan, Lacey set the bucket down, then slowly inched it under the animal's udder with the toe of her shoe. When it was in place, she quickly backed out of the stall to watch from a safe distance.

Hazel stamped her hind foot, twitched her long skinny tail, and bellowed, but milk was not yet pouring into the bucket. Obviously the animal needed help of some kind to produce the milk, but Lacey was much too afraid of the beast to actually touch her anywhere. Perhaps, she thought, if she went gathering eggs now, by the time she came back to check on Hazel, the bucket would be full. Of course, Lacey wasn't so out of touch with the world beyond St. Josephine's that she didn't realize the odds were heavily against such a miracle. But that didn't stop her from praying for one. Or from going on to her next chore.

She discovered immediately that she was *not* afraid of the chickens. In fact, chasing them around the barn was grand sport! Trouble was, they were afraid of her. Every time she tried to catch one, the thing would squawk, flap its wings, and take off running. Lacey ran after each and every one of the birds, even tripping and falling twice, but otherwise didn't slow down long enough to catch her breath. After a while, a pretty brown hen sporting little white speckles throughout its feathers fell over in a dead faint.

Concerned she'd frightened it to death at first, Lacey gingerly cradled the bird in her arms until its little eyes blinked open. Relieved to find that she had not murdered one of Hawke's pets, she positioned the revived hen in the basket and began stroking the tender spot on its back between its wings.

"There now, my bonny sweet chicken," she crooned breathlessly. "Be a good lass and give me up an egg, would you please?"

Almost as if cued, the hen clucked, ruffled its feathers, then stood, leaving a nice little brown egg behind in the basket.

"How delightful!" Proud to bursting of the accomplishment, Lacey scrambled to her feet with a renewed burst of enthusiasm, stood with her feet spread and hands on hips, and surveyed the rest of the scattered chickens. All of the birds were keeping a wary distance from her, but that didn't daunt Lacey in the least.

Strolling down the center aisle in an exaggerated swagger, she sang out, "All right, you sweet wee chickens; who among you will be the next?"

Inside the kitchen of the ranch house, Hawke glanced out the window above his small sink and stove—not just the one with the best view of the barn, but the only window in the house favored with a pair of actual curtains.

Wondering the same thing he'd been wondering for the past fifteen minutes, he thought to himself; *where the hell is that woman?* She should have finished her chores and returned to the house long ago. The stove was hot, the coffee was ready, and the sausage patties were arranged neatly in the skillet. Hawke was sorely tempted to cook and eat every last one himself, but then it occurred to him that the delicate Irish female might be having some trouble with Hazel, who wasn't always so agreeable to being milked. He *had* fed her awfully early that morning, and if she didn't have enough alfalfa left in her feeder to keep her occupied during the milking, well . . .

Again Hawke glanced out the window. All seemed quiet and he could see a steady glow from the lantern streaming out from the crack in the doors, telling him that she wasn't having a problem with the light. So what could the holdup be? Had she wandered up to the loft in spite of his warnings? Or was she just dawdling? He thought of the way she'd sauntered off toward the barn, of the almost too-innocent look in her eyes, and decided it would be better for them all if he at least went out to check on her.

Hawke moved the skillet and coffeepot back to a cooler part of the stove, went into the living room to get his coat, and had just slipped into it, when the door suddenly burst open and Lacey blew into the house. Her hair had indeed exploded from its bun and now fell in a thousand russet spirals across her shoulders, back, and even her face. The part of that pretty face which wasn't hidden by coppery little curlicues was streaked with dirt, and her rumpled skirt was dotted with bits of bedding straw. What the *hell* had she been up to?

"Top o' the morning to you," she said, her tone lyrical, cheerful. "'Tis something to be said for rising early and putting oneself to work in the collecting of the meal. I thank you, kind sir, for allowing me the pleasure of gathering what there is of ours. Oh, and don't worry yourself none about the lantern—'tis hanging right outside the doorway here, the flame blown out."

With a frown that was more of a playful pout, Lacey held the empty pail up for Hawke to see. "I'm afraid your stubborn Hazel was not up to giving us so much as a drop of milk this morning, but look here." She shoved the basket under Hawke's nose, beaming over the one tiny brown egg. "Your chickens were none too willing either, but see what I managed to squeeze out of that wee speckled one!"

"*Squeezed*—?" The conversation was so strange and Lacey seemed so pleased with herself, Hawke couldn't make heads or tails of it. But he could see that the bucket was bone dry. "There's no way in hell that cow's empty— her teats have to be near to busting by now."

Lacey shrugged. "I wouldn't know about her teats. I just know that she wouldn't give me so much as a drop of milk."

"Well," he said, grumbling a little, "maybe you weren't rough enough with her. She is used to me, you know."

"I suppose that could have been the problem, me new to her and all. Should I try her again?"

"If you plan on getting fed while you're here today, you're going to have to." She started to set the egg basket on the floor, but Hawke stopped her cold. "And that's another thing; I usually get close to a dozen eggs out of those chickens each day. I don't know what in hell you were doing out in the barn for so long, but from the looks of it, I'd say you weren't taking your chores too seriously."

"Oh, but 'twasn't that way a'tall! Let me try again and you'll see!" When he offered no immediate argument, Lacey dashed back out the door before he could change his mind, the bucket swinging from one elbow, the basket from the other.

Hawke had every intention of following her to find out exactly what she'd been doing instead of her chores. Her method for extracting the day's supply of milk from Hazel must have been pretty feeble, and even more curious, he couldn't wait to find out what she meant by "squeezing" an egg from the speckled hen. Before he could satisfy his curiosity on either count, however, he had a little chore of his own to see to.

Reaching inside his jacket, Hawke lifted the ledger from his deep pocket, turned it to the Lacey O'Carroll page, and moistened the tip of his pencil.

Under the *Disadvantages* column, he noted:

3. *Incompetent Farm Hand.*

Then he slipped the ledger back in his jacket and headed for the barn.

4

Falling is easier than rising.

—An old Irish saying

Hawke was watching his incompetent farm hand through a crack between the boards directly across from the milking stall, but he could hardly believe what he was seeing and hearing. Had his eyes deceived him, or had the woman just snuck up behind Hazel, edged the bucket under her swollen udder with the toe of her flimsy shoe, then backed out of the stall again? And was she now *shouting* at the animal? Hawke pressed his ear against the pine slats to better hear what she was saying.

"Notice that I'm not asking you," Lacey said, parroting Hawke by speaking in her deepest, gruffest voice. "I'm here to *tell* you that you'll be giving me some milk, and giving it to me now you miserable creature, or I swear by the piper o' Moses, I'll be bringing a curse down on you, I will!"

Chewing her cud noisily, Hazel glanced over her shoulder, regarded the boisterous woman with contempt, then went back to nosing around in the scattered alfalfa still left in her feeder.

Thinking a curse couldn't hurt, Lacey shook her index finger at the bovine and made good her threat. "If you don't have some milk in that bucket by the time I come back to you, may you melt like butter before a summer sun!" Then she turned around and leveled a determined gaze on the chickens. "As for you flighty wee lasses . . . "

Outside the barn, Hawke backed away from the slats in stunned surprise. What in the name of all that's holy had he turned loose on his animals? Either the Irishwoman's brains were as scarce as bird droppings in a cuckoo clock, or she came from such aristocratic stock, she hadn't even *seen* farm animals before, much less worked with them. Suddenly concerned for his chickens, who were squawking and carrying on like a fox was loose in their midst, Hawke hurried around to the front of the barn and tore through the doors.

There he found Lacey stretched flat out on the floor, belly-side down. She'd trapped his rooster in the egg basket, and even though it was struggling mightily, she held the cock firmly in place. Then she began shouting at it in the same gruff voice she'd used on the unimpressed Hazel.

"I'll have an egg now, my pretty wee chicken, and don't be wasting my time—out with it!"

"Stop!" Hawke demanded, afraid she would squeeze the very life out of his only rooster. "What in the hell do you think you're doing?"

Looking over her shoulder, Lacey blew a few spirals of hair away from her eyes, smiled at him, and said, "Collecting eggs, like I was told, sir. This one does not seem to be too willing."

"That one," Hawke explained as he reached her and hunkered down next to the basket to check on the bird, "is my *rooster*—do you know what a rooster is, by any chance?"

"Aye," she murmured, understanding. "'Tis a lad of a bird, and one that can not be making us any eggs for our breakfast." Lacey pushed herself to her knees and brushed the dirt and straw from her skirt. "Would you mind showing me how I might tell him apart from the lasses so I do not make that same mistake again?"

"There's no need for that." Hawke stood, extended his hand, and helped Lacey to her feet. "I don't intend to let you near my chickens again. As badly as you shook them up, I'll be lucky if they lay any eggs the rest of the week."

"Oh . . . oh, no." Tears sprang into her eyes, but Lacey fought to keep them inside. "I tried so hard to do it right, honest I did. Will you tell me what I've done wrong? I did get the one egg you know."

Oh, Christ—she wasn't going to cry, was she? Hawke hadn't been faced with a woman's tears since . . . well, since his mother so very long ago. He hadn't been able to help the only woman he'd ever cared about to stop the flow then, and he didn't even want to try now. But he had to do something. Feeling that spot inside him going soft again, Hawke purposefully hardened his voice when he finally answered.

"I'm not blaming you, so don't get all blubbery on me. Where did you find that one egg you brought me?"

Lacey sniffled and blinked her eyes. "I told you, it popped out of that wee speckled hen of yours after I set her upon the basket."

"*Popped* out?" The corners of Hawke's mouth twitched. "Do you mean to tell me that you put one of my chickens in that basket, *squeezed* her, and she actually laid an egg for you?"

Lacey nodded. "A course, I did not have to squeeze her much, but 'twas the only way I could think of to get me a basket full of eggs. If there be an easier way to get them out, I'd like to know what 'tis."

Chuckling to himself for the first time in a long, long time, Hawk's normally taut lips spread into a wide grin. "There's an easier way, I expect," he said, still grinning, "but it's not nearly as entertaining as yours. Come, I'll show you how to fill that basket up with eggs, and you won't even have to run after the chickens to do it."

Speechless, not over what she'd learned here, but by what she'd seen when Hawke relaxed enough to turn loose of his frown, Lacey followed him into one of the empty stalls. When this man smiled, his eyes, his mouth, his entire face—in fact—the whole *room* seemed to take on a brilliant glow! Why hadn't Hawke flashed that dazzling smile her way before now? It was better than coming across a four-leaf shamrock! If only she could keep him grinning that way instead of glaring at her as if she were the devil's disciple, their life as husband and wife might just be a very pleasant thing.

Could it be the man was not near so gruff as he appeared to be? Lacey had been taught by the nurses that to love with power was proof of a large soul; to hate was a thing in itself to be loved; and that hate was every bit as powerful as love. It stood to reason by Lacey's way of thinking, that this man who seemed so filled with hate, also had within himself the talent to love with power. Perhaps Kathleen Lacey O'Carroll merely had to find a way to coax it out of him.

"Are you listening and watching?" Hawke demanded of Lacey, who was staring a hole through him instead of looking at the feeder and other favorite nesting areas where eggs could usually be found.

"Oh, aye." She blushed, embarrassed to have been caught gawking at him, and glanced down to where a single egg lay peeking up through the bedding straw.

"You're saying that we look for the eggs then, and not the chickens?"

"That's the easy way." Hawke handed her the basket. "Try it and see."

As Lacey searched the fresh clean straw for eggs, Hawke wondered why she'd been staring at him so hard, and why she looked so . . . so god damn *wide-eyed* over what she'd seen. It probably had something to do with his hair, he decided. He was long overdue for a trim, and while he usually kept his sable mane longer than "fashionable," it had grown so much over the winter, that he had to tie it back with a leather thong at the nape of his neck to keep it from blowing in his eyes and mouth. He supposed that tying his long hair back that way made him look even more like an Indian than usual, but that was just fine by him. In fact, if he let it stay just like that until the preacher showed up, it might be the final inducement for this Irish aristocrat take off for greener pastures. Maybe he'd even twist it into a couple of braids. That would probably scare her all the way back to Ireland.

After the eggs had been collected—all nine of them—Hawke lifted a three-legged stool off its peg up high on one of the center posts, and put it in position beside Hazel. He nearly straddled it as usual, then decided he might as well give the Irish miss another lesson—and one to remember, at that.

Cocking a finger her way, he said, "Come on over here and sit down. If you want milk for breakfast, you'll have to learn your way around a cow."

Lacey demurred. "I—to tell you the truth, I can not imagine that I'd be any good at it. I must admit that I'm a wee bit afraid of the beast."

Hawke should have let it go right there, should have milked Hazel and got on with the day, but for some reason, he was compelled to instruct the apprehensive woman, to find a way if he could, to help her lose that painfully innocent expression which crossed her features so frequently. Her expressive eyes showed both wonder and excitement, yet they seemed shadowed with a fear of the unknown, giving her a look which reminded him of a caged bird suddenly set free. It was none of Hawke's business how she'd gotten that way in the first place, and it sure as hell wasn't his place to educate her in the ways of the world, but that soft spot inside urged him forward, and he couldn't seem to stop himself. Besides; what could it hurt to educate her where domestic barnyard animals were concerned? It wouldn't cost him anything but a little time.

Speaking to her in a tone he reserved only for his horses, Hawke gently said, "You have nothing to fear from Hazel. She *wants* you to milk her because right now, she's very uncomfortable. Come, you'll see."

His voice washed over her like a warm bath, surprising her enough that Lacey took a few tentative steps toward the animal. "She does not know me. 'Twill upset her a wee bit, me being here, no?"

"Not with me standing right beside you." He held out his hand. "Come on. Spread your wings and fly, little bird. You might even enjoy yourself."

Lacey wasn't sure why he'd changed his attitude or way of speaking to her, but she vowed then and there to learn the secret. If she could keep him treating her this way in addition to smiling more often, she might just be *grandly* happy for the rest of her life! Buoyed by the confidence his tender tones had inspired, she squared her shoulders and joined him in the stall.

"Just do what I say," Hawke murmured softly, "and everything will be fine." He reached for her right hand, but she jerked it away and offered the left. Deferring to what he assumed was her left-handedness, he gripped the small fingers of that hand and carefully set them down on the cow's back. "Stroke Hazel's coat gently and speak to her in a kind voice. Say hello, call her by name, and let her know you're her friend."

Lacey gulped, but it was with as much excitement as nerves. She'd never touched a beast such as this before, unless the wee pony she had as a lass of five would be considered in the same class. Even if it were, Lacey could barely remember anything of her childhood, much less what it felt like to touch her black pony, Coco. But Hazel was here and now, warm and slightly damp to the touch. She moved her hand, noting the cow's hairs were coarse, but surprisingly soft at the same time. Losing some of her fears, she lengthened her strokes.

"There now, Hazel lass," Lacey heard herself say as she continued to pet the animal. "I'm Kathleen Lacey O'Carroll come to ease the milk from your big swollen bag. I'll not hurt you, and would be ever so pleased if you could find it in your good graces not to hurt me back."

Pleased and encouraged by her gentleness, Hawke took Lacey's shoulders between his big hands. "She'll be all right with you now. The milk stool is against the back of your legs. Ease down on it. I'll be right behind you." Once she'd settled onto the little chair and he'd dropped to his knees, Hawke leaned across Lacey's shoulders to guide her hands toward Hazel's teats. A forest of coppery curls blinded him.

"You'll have to move your hair out of the way if we're going to get this done. I can't see what I'm doing or even reach your hands through it."

"Oh, goodness." Embarrassed to have been caught unaware of her disheveled state, and by the man she was supposed to be impressing, Lacey burst into nervous giggles. She quickly gathered what she could of her hair and dragged it over her left shoulder, sputtering as she tried to explain what had happened.

"I—I lost my pins while chasing the chickens earlier, and do not have anything else to hold my hair in place. I'm afraid it does get a wee bit unruly if there be the slightest dampness in the air."

"It's out of the way now," he assured her, aware of the hint of panic in her tone. There were still a few maverick strands left to tickle his nose, his senses, and most disturbing of all, something deep inside of him, but Hawke tried to ignore those sensations, and again reached across her shoulders. "Go ahead, take a teat in each hand and get a firm grip on them."

His warm breath caressed Lacey's ear, and even though Hawke wasn't really holding her, he did have his arms around her. Close enough, she thought, to preserve the moment as her very first embrace from a gentleman. The idea sent a little shiver up her spine, and Lacey had to bite her lip to keep from giggling over the strange sensations this man's touch ignited in her.

Hawke felt the tremor pass through her body. "Are you still afraid of Hazel?" he asked, concerned.

"Oh, goodness—no." Forcing herself to concentrate on the task again, Lacey tentatively reached out to touch the cow's udder. When her fingers made contact, she lost the battle with her giggles. "May the saints forgive me for my silliness, Mr. Hawke, but 'tis a very odd and strange thing your asking of me."

"I'm just plain Hawke. Now watch what I do." Still trying to ignore her hair and its fresh, floral scent, an aroma which reminded him of the first cherry blossoms of spring, his long arms reached beyond her delicate shoulders to Hazel's udder. To make contact with the cow, Hawke had to press his chest against Lacey's back. Never had he been in such close proximity to a white woman, especially one who didn't object, and the effect was as disturbing as it was pleasurable.

Working quickly to avoid any misunderstandings, he filled each of his palms with a swollen teat, then demonstrated the correct motion by squirting several streams of milk into the bucket in rapid succession. Lacey squealed with delight, turned her head to the side as if to speak, and damn near brushed her mouth across his. Halfway expecting her to scream or at the least, accuse him of making improper advances, Hawke immediately turned loose of the cow and leaned back.

"Now you try it," he said gruffly, wondering why in the hell he'd agreed to play out the little charade of "testing" a wife in the first place.

Aware that Hawke was irritated, and assuming that she'd done something to upset him—*again*—Lacey fought her runaway nerves. Trying mightily to ignore the squishy, squeamish sensations which accompanied the feel of the cow's udder beneath her fingertips, she grasped the teats and pulled. Nothing came out. A pout in her tone, she said, "'Tisn't working for me the way it does for you. I'm no good at this."

Again leaning over her shoulder, this time careful not to touch any part of her body with his, Hawke studied the position of Lacey's hands. "You're tugging on her instead of squeezing. Push your fists against Hazel's udder, then start a gentle up and down movement. And make sure you alternate your hands while you squeeze." He watched as Lacey positioned herself again, then added, "You have to squeeze hard—pretend you're trying to get eggs out of my chickens."

More relaxed now since the humorous reference to her earlier misdeeds made her feel somehow pardoned for the last, Lacey made a determined effort to accomplish her task. This time she was rewarded with a thin stream of milk.

"I did it!" she cried, enormously pleased with herself.

"'Tis like rain from the heavens, and I brought it about by myself!"

"What you've started is more of a light shower." Hawke chuckled softly. "See if you can't squeeze hard enough to get a thunderstorm underway, or we'll be here till nightfall." And that wouldn't have been a very good idea, he decided, given his sudden and surprising state of excitement.

Every time Hazel swished her tail or stamped a foot, which was frequently, a startled Lacey leaned back against him, bringing her soft body into contact with his and her heavenly scented hair flush against his nose. It wouldn't be a very good idea to just get up and leave her there, not while she was still so tentative and uncertain of herself. And yet if he was forced to stay in this position with his hips so close to her bottom—a curvy little backside in constant rotation as she wriggled back-and-forth on the stool while she went about her task—he didn't know how much longer he could keep his hands off of her. And as a half-breed, Hawke knew his status well enough to understand that could never happen, even if the Irishwoman *had* let on that she'd consider marrying him. For reasons he hadn't figured out yet, something wasn't quite on the up and up with Miss Lacey O'Carroll. Before the week was out, he intended to find out exactly what it was.

Dark as those thoughts were, the spark she'd set off in him flared instead of dying out as she worked, and Hawke finally had no choice but to abruptly stand and turn his back to her. "You can finish here by yourself," he snapped. "When the pair of teats you're working on go dry, switch to the other set until they're empty, too. I've got to go check on my mares." Then he stalked off down the aisle.

Surprised by Hawke's curt departure, Lacey paused to wipe a few beads of perspiration from her brow with the edge of her sleeve. She didn't know what the devil she'd done wrong this time, but the man seemed gruffer now than he was when he found her squeezing his rooster. More surly even than he'd been when he found out she was the mail-order bride he *hadn't* ordered. Why had he turned on her now? She was getting the required bucket of milk from Hazel—what more could he possibly expect?

Muttering to herself over the man's unpredictable nature, Lacey went back to milking the cow. Her poor hands ached so much by the time the first set of teats were dry, she didn't know how she would find the strength to empty the other pair, but somehow, she carried on. Just as exhaustion overtook her and she could squeeze no more, Lacey thought she glimpsed something moving across the aisle. Happy to release Hazel, she glanced toward the section of the barn featuring a couple of large, closet-like rooms containing all manner of ranch equipment and fodder. As she peered into the murky interior of the one which held several bins filled with aromatic grains and hay, something small and dark bolted around the corner and disappeared. She blinked and looked again. Now all was still. Had her mind begun playing tricks on her again?

To calm her suddenly racing pulse, Lacey tried to convince herself that if indeed she'd really seen a creature, it was nothing but a large cat—or something of that nature. But as she went back to milking Hazel, she could almost feel a pair of eyes on her. Disturbingly human eyes. Vaguely distressed by the fact that the sensation wouldn't go away, when at last the cow was drained, Lacey dragged the full bucket out of the stall, and quickly went in search of Hawke. She found him checking the feet of a pale yellow mare in one of the three stalls he'd forbidden her to disturb.

"Excuse me, Mr. Hawke," she said in a small, worried voice, "but I'm finished with Hazel. The bucket's full up with milk, too."

"Like I said before, the name's just plain Hawke." In better spirits now, he lowered Taffy's clean hoof and let himself out of her large, airy foaling stall. As he latched the tightly fitted door, he turned to Lacey and asked, "Do you like horses?"

"I can not say that I remember."

"You don't remember? How can you forget whether you do or don't like horses?"

"W-what I meant to say—" She stumbled around in her mind searching for a plausible explanation for the automatic answer. Lacey had considered mentioning the "shadow" or whatever it was she'd seen near the feed room, but after this blunder, she was afraid if she did, Hawke might get the idea that she was at least a wee bit foy. And, of course, she was. "I 'spose what I meant was that I can not remember ever being around them."

Apparently satisfied by her answer, Hawke shrugged and collected both the bucket of milk and the basket of eggs. Then he started for the house, calling to her from over his shoulder. "Let's go eat. I'm starved."

Lacey followed behind him until they stepped out of the barn and into the sunlight where she got her first good look at the grounds. The wide Wyoming skies were a pale silvery blue with just enough tendrils of fog still hanging in the valleys to remind her of the mists in Ireland.

"Oh, 'tis a fine soft morning," she murmured, her voice steeped in awe. "And such big, beautiful mountains you have here, too!"

Turning back to her, Hawke followed Lacey's gaze to the highest range of snow-capped peaks. "The big one, Medicine Bow Mountain, is over twelve thousand feet high. We're at about eight thousand."

The measurements didn't mean much to Lacey, but she knew there was nothing in Ireland which could compare. The homeland, what she knew of it anyway, was a pastoral country of uneven surfaces and mountainous terrain, but she knew that even the highest point, Carrauntoohill, was less than half the altitude at which she was standing now!

Revolving in place, she took a further look around the front of the property. Due east, a high fence surrounded a small corral containing only one horse, but just to the south of it and across the road, a long stretch of lush meadow with a sparkling creek running through it played host to several mares and their young foals. To the north, a much larger fence enclosed acres of pasture land with horses scattered along the sage-dotted mountaintop. Behind the log home, which looked far more impressive on the outside than its stark interior had, Lacey noticed a smaller building, also made of logs, along with the barn and a few sheds. Back of all that and lining the south side of the ranch, was a thick forest of dark green lodgepole pines set off by random swirls of lime colored aspens.

"Winterhawke" would be a fine place in which to live, she thought with anticipation. It was big, beautiful, and best of all, isolated from the rest of the world and its intolerance for those a little "different." Aye, she dared to dream, she could be very, very happy here—assuming, of course, that she could convince its owner to marry her. And, Lacey suddenly realized, she couldn't do that standing here gawking at his property. He'd gone into the house.

Hurrying along after him, Lacey caught up with Hawke in the kitchen where he'd set the milk and eggs on the rubbed pine counter near the stove. He was sitting at the table near the window writing something down in a long, narrow book.

Without looking up from his work, Hawk said, "I started the sausage. I'd like you to make some biscuits and gravy to go with it. Maybe a couple of fried eggs, too."

Lacey didn't have the first idea how to go about cooking

the sausage much less whipping up gravy, but this morning, she figured she had enough of an excuse to duck the chore without revealing that wee truth. Demonstrating with only her left hand, she held it out and tried to make a fist. "I'd like to be helping you with your meal, but I'm afraid your Hazel has give me finger cramps. I do not think I can even lift the skillet, my fingers ache so."

Hawke glanced over at her and had to admit, albeit grudgingly, that tending the cow could be hard on the hands, especially during those frosty mornings when the fingers were stiff to begin with. He sighed. "I guess milking does take a little getting used to. I'll cook today, but you can make breakfast tomorrow—if you plan on coming back, that is."

She raised a determined chin. "I am."

"In that case, I'll put in my order now. I'd like some biscuits, and I mean good fluffy biscuits that don't take a saw to cut into. They're something I've never had much luck with. How about you?"

"*Me?*" And though she had no clue as to how to go about creating the fluffy biscuits he craved, she said, "Why, goodness sakes. I've the luck of the Irish in my corner. Of course, I can make them—as long as I do not have to milk Hazel first."

"I'll take care of the milk and eggs tomorrow." Then, before he fired up the stove and got to work, Hawke added another notation under the *Disadvantages* column in his ledger:

Too weak and frail to be a ranch wife.

The following morning when Lacey stepped into Hawke's kitchen to begin dazzling him with her culinary talents, she came prepared. After spending half the evening with Kate working on ways to convince a "reluctant groom" that she could cook, Lacey watched as Kate made up a nice batch of fluffy biscuits. When they were done and cooled, the women wrapped them in paper, then tucked them in a basket along with a few "personal items" such as toweling, an apron, and a couple of cleaning rags. With the biscuits hidden and disguised this way, all Lacey need do this morning was warm them up a bit in the oven, smear a little flour and milk around in a bowl to make it look as if she'd mixed them up herself, and then serve breakfast.

Proud of the plan and the ease with which she'd carried it out so far, she sliced a couple of slabs off the big ham Hawke had set out, warmed the meat in the oven along with the biscuits, then set the pan containing the entire meal on top of the stove near the burner. Recalling Kate's final instruction—to put a nice cloth over the baked goods to keep them warm and moist like fresh biscuits would be—she covered the pan, then dusted her hands and apron with flour. Pleased with that extra bit of authenticity, she started for the barn to tell Hawke that it was time to come in.

As she reached the wide doorway, Lacey called out to him. "Your breakfast is ready—Hawke."

The familiarity implied by addressing him so felt odd, yet good at the same time. Humming to herself in anticipation of his reaction when he tasted "her" biscuits, Lacey listened for Hawke's deep baritone. All she heard was something that sounded like chickens scrambling around in the straw—that and perhaps, muffled voices. Recalling the "eyes" she'd felt on her yesterday and the twinge of fear the memory brought with it, she stayed at the fringes of the door and repeated his name a little louder. "Hawke? Are you in there?"

"In Taffy's stall!"

Relieved to finally hear his voice, Lacey hurried inside the building. After her eyes adjusted to the dimmer lighting, she marched straight down the aisle to the correct stall and peered over the door. Both of Hawke's hands were pressed against the horse's swollen belly, and his brow was creased with worry.

"Our meal is cooked," she said quietly. "Are you ready to eat?"

He straightened up and ran his hand along the mare's spine. "Something isn't quite right with Taffy this morning."

Lacey stood on tiptoe and draped her arms over the stall door. The mare's coat looked damp and kind of rippled all over. Chuckling softly, she said, "I see her hairs go all frizzy like mine. Is it because of the dampness in the air?"

"No, I think she's getting ready to drop her foal."

Lacey cried out with delight. "Those curly hairs are cause for rejoicing, then, are they no?"

Again placing his hands against the mare's belly, Hawke slowly shook his head. "Not with her they aren't. She's the sneaky kind who always foals in the dead of night—at least, that's what she's done the last three times. I think she wants me around for this one, and I can only guess that it's because she's in trouble."

"Trouble? In what way?"

He shrugged. "Could be a lot of things. I can't even be sure there is a problem yet."

"Then shall we go eat our meal? 'Tis ready you know, and when we come back, perhaps your Taffy will be up to telling us what her problem is."

"I'm not going anywhere until I know what's wrong with this horse." Hawke moved to the mare's head and rubbed his palm down the length of the white blaze running from her forelock to her nose. "Taffy's not only my best brood mare, but the first to drop a foal by my new stallion. I'm not taking any chances with her. You go ahead and eat. I'll get mine later."

"Oh, but—"

"Before you leave," he said, cutting her off. "Would you mind stepping into the harness room and getting me a couple of blankets?"

"No, a course not." Not only did she not mind, Lacey had no intention of leaving until she'd figured out a way to stay in the barn to witness an event she'd only heard about; birth. "Where might I find this harness room?"

"It's the first door on the right about mid-way into the barn. The walls are full of reins and gear hanging from wooden pegs. You can't miss it."

Her mind completely absorbed by the exciting miracle about to occur, Lacey found the correct doorway, stepped inside the room, and spotted the pile of blankets immediately. After helping herself to one, she spun around, hurried out the door—and froze in her tracks.

The dark shadow she'd glimpsed yesterday was straight in front of her. Today, it had a distinct shape, revealing that it definitely was *not* a cat. In fact, the figure hesitated a moment before darting away, giving her an even better view of it. Her heart in her throat, it took Lacey a minute to convince her legs to move again, but when they did, they carried her pell-mell down the aisle toward Taffy's stall.

"Mr. Hawke!" she screamed, recognizing the shadow for what it must be. "Mr. Hawke, come quick! 'Tis one of the wee people, a fairy come to bring bad luck your way!"

5

**The banshee only follows families whose
names begin with an 'O' or a 'Mac.'**
—A common Irish saying

It took Hawke a full fifteen minutes to convince Lacey that due to the variety of windows inside the barn and the yawning gap created by the open double doors, what she'd seen was really nothing but a shadowy illusion. When she finally quit parrying his explanations with more questions, he assumed she'd accepted his rationalizations, even though she hadn't stopped looking over her shoulder with each step she took.

In truth, it wasn't until they walked back to Taffy's stall and found the mare thrashing about in the straw, that Lacey turned loose of her fairy theory and forgot about what she thought she'd seen. The birth must be imminent! From that moment on, all she could concentrate on was the horse.

"Christ," Hawke muttered when he saw his mare struggle to her feet, then throw herself down in the straw on her other side. "This isn't right. Go back to the house," he barked at Lacey. "Get out of here."

"Oh, but I wish to stay, if I might. I've ne'er—"

"I'm serious, damn it all." His features grim, Hawke stomped over to the door. Lacey shrank away from him as he reached around to the outside of the stall and took Taffy's halter from the hook driven into the post there. "I have to examine the horse now, and—well, things could get really messy after that. You'd better go on inside."

"Please do not send me away." If it would have done any good, Lacey would have thrown herself down on her knees. Relying instead on the fabricated story she and Kate had agreed on to explain both their former lives and any accidental references Lacey might make regarding St. Josephine's, she said, "With me fresh from the hospital and all, maybe I could be of some help when her time comes."

"You're a trained nurse?"

Careful not to tell a bold-faced lie, Lacey merely hinted at her previous calling. "I worked right alongside Nurse Quinlin for a good long time." And she had, helping out with the newly admitted children by reading stories to them. "May I stay with you, please?"

Just then, with a considerable amount of effort and a deep, miserable groan, again Taffy took to her feet. That was enough for Hawke to make up his mind. Glancing briefly toward the spy-hole he'd drilled directly above each foaling stall, he shrugged slightly, then turned his attention back to Lacey. "All right. You can stay, but you've got to do exactly what I tell you."

"Aye, sir!" She could hardly contain her excitement. "And I'll not be in your way 'tall."

"We'll see." Grumbling to himself, Hawke spun around and walked back over to his mare.

Watching as he fit the halter over the head of the distressed animal, Lacey quietly let herself inside the stall. Taffy, she noticed, seemed to be having difficulty breathing and her engorged sides were heaving in a most uncomfortable-looking manner. After a moment, and speaking in a more gentle, caring voice than she'd ever heard him use, Hawke gave her his first instruction.

"Come here, Lacey. I want you to hold Taffy just like this."

Quicker than a hare, she was at his side. Then, following his lead, she slipped her hand between the halter and the horse's huge round cheek, and clamped her fingers tightly around the leather straps.

"Hold her still if you can and talk to her in the most gentle way imaginable." Dragging his hand across her damp coat, Hawke slowly walked alongside Taffy's heaving body until he'd reached her hindquarters. Then he issued a few more instructions. "Make her feel like she can trust you and that everything is going to be all right. I'm going to examine her now, and I don't want her getting upset or excited. Understand?"

Watching Hawke with one eye and the mare with the other, Lacey said, "Aye, and she'll not be having a worry from this nurse. 'Tis Kathleen Lacey O'Carroll come to save you from the trouble of bringing your babe into the world, lass. 'Twill be over before you know it." Wincing as she saw Hawke's arm disappear inside the horse, Lacey went on with her babble, segueing into an old Irish lullaby.

His examination complete, Hawke cursed under his breath as he said to Lacey, "Christ almighty, no wonder she's having so much trouble. One of the foal's legs is caught behind her pelvic bone. How's she doing up there?"

Staying in tune with the lullaby, Lacey sang her answer. "The lass's eyes are closed and her bottom lip is hanging down. I do believe the poor dear has fallen asleep. Imagine dozing whilst I've been feedin' her up with false music."

Hawke knew better than that, but he kept the information to himself; Taffy was exhausted, not sleeping, and probably dying to boot. If he was going to save either of them he had to dislodge the foal immediately, even if it meant breaking its leg. Slipping his hand back inside the birth canal, he gave Lacey another order. "What I've got to do now will hurt her a little and she might bolt, so don't stand directly in front of her. Keep singing the way you are, and whatever you do, don't cry out or startle her."

"Do not give another thought to me or the lassie," she sang in a gay Irish lilt, even though the force of Hawke's manipulations caused the mare to wobble forward, nearly falling. Her eyes wide with both fright and fascination as she watched the struggle to bring the foal into the world, Lacey went on singing, this time tossing in a few sayings in the middle of the lullaby.

"Oh, the south wind is soft and mild, a good wind for the seeds, but the north wind is cold, bone-chilling in your Wyoming. 'Tis a good thing, this wind, for when it blows, the darlin' wee horse puppies are born."

With a dull "pop" followed by a loud sucking sound, the foal's leg finally cleared the pelvic bone, allowing the animal to move along the birth canal and break through the birth sack with its head. With a final contraction, the foal shot none too gracefully into its owner's waiting arms. Staggering under the newborn's weight for a moment, Hawke fell to his knees and eased the slippery animal down into the straw. After quickly cleaning the filly's mouth and nostrils, then making certain that it could breathe easily on its own, he jumped to his feet and checked his mare.

"How's she doing?" Hawke asked Lacey as he helped Taffy discharge the afterbirth. "Eyes open yet?"

It took her a moment to answer, and when she did, Lacey was no longer singing or making nonsensical rhymes. She was astounded by the sight of the foal and its fierce struggles to rise up from the bedding straw, amazed by all she'd witnessed in these few short moments. She'd just taken part in God's most glorious miracle.

Tears spilled down from her eyes as Lacey pressed her own cheek against Taffy's, hugged her, and said, "The lass is trying. She's a wee bit tired right now, but I can feel that she's trying her best to come 'round."

Hawke heard the warble in her voice, and at first, thought she might be too nervous or upset to remain in the stall. Then he glanced up and saw that she'd wrapped her arms around the mare's neck, and that Taffy had taken her up on the offer by resting her weary head on Lacey's delicate shoulder. Both of their eyes were closed in quiet tranquility.

No longer concerned about Taffy's reactions to a stranger's presence in her stall, Hawke moved up beside Lacey and lightly tapped her on the back. When those blue eyes flashed open, he saw such a warm serenity and keen sense of wonder in them, he almost took her into his arms to celebrate the success of the difficult birth. Hawke managed to restrain himself, but did let her know how grateful he was for her help.

"Thanks for keeping Taffy so calm. She trusts you now, you know." Lacey glanced up at him, meeting his gaze, then favored him with a smile that brought the golden sparkle to the surface of her clear blue eyes. Startled by their continued impact on him, Hawke looked away and had to clear his throat before he could speak again. "Will you be all right if I leave you alone with these two for a minute? I've got to mix up some gruel for Taffy, and get some doctoring supplies so I can finish up with her and the foal."

Glancing at the mare, Lacey impulsively kissed the top of the animal's nose. "We'll be just dandy. There's no need for the angels to be laying a soft bed for this lass. She'll be runnin' and snortin' 'fore you know it."

Although she was obviously new with horses, her confidence, as well as Taffy's, was enough to reassure him that he could go about his business. "I won't be long. Just call me if she tries to lay down or does anything that doesn't seem right to you."

After Hawke let himself out of the stall, he took another look over the door at his best brood mare and the curious woman beside her. She'd surprised him, this Irish miss, not just over her willingness to learn, but because of her natural abilities with the horse. That in itself was almost a good enough reason to consider keeping her on, but why would a woman like that consider life with a man like him? he wondered again. What the hell was *wrong* with her?

Once they finished drying the little black filly with one of the blankets, then made certain that Taffy had recuperated enough to take an interest in her foal and begin nursing her, Hawke and his new assistant returned to the house for their very late breakfast. There they discovered that Lacey had left the pan which contained the meal too close to the burner. Not only were the bottoms of the biscuits burned black, but the ham was dried out, and the towel Lacey had used to cover the pan was scorched at the edges. Left unattended much longer, and the material might very well have burst into flames, catching the curtains afire and putting the entire house in jeopardy.

Hawke said nothing to her about the near-disaster or the ruined breakfast. He couldn't, not on the heels of what she'd done in the barn. What he did do after fetching her a leather thong for her hair, was set her down on one of his mahogany chairs, pour two cups of coffee, and deposit the pan of dried-up food at the center of the table.

Taking the chair opposite her, he gave her a plate and utensils. "Believe it or not," he said, trying to make her feel at ease, "I've been forced to eat food I burned a lot worse than this. I think breakfast can be salvaged." To demonstrate, Hawke chipped the top portion of three biscuits away from their moorings, stabbed a slab of ham, and dropped it all on his plate. After smearing a biscuit with a thick pat of butter, he popped it in his mouth and groaned with satisfaction.

Giving him a shy smile as she finished tying her hair back the way he did—at the nape of her neck—Lacey sawed the tops off a couple of biscuits and began to munch on them. They tasted a little like charcoal and had the consistency of a dirt pie, but grateful that he was taking it so well, she pretended to enjoy the scorched meal.

Hawke quickly dispatched the rest of the food on his plate, then washed it all down with his coffee. Watching her as she delicately picked at her ham, he said, "I've been thinking about a name for the new filly. I thought I might even name her after you."

Taken completely by surprise, Lacey choked on a piece of biscuit. After a swallow of coffee and the shudder the foul drink always sent through her, she said, "'Twould be a grand honor your naming the babe after me. Were you thinking of Kathleen or Lacey?"

He shrugged. "I'd forgotten about your other name, but I think Lacey sounds nice and it's different, too. Does it mean something special in Ireland?"

"'Tis a surname, my mother's actually. Most folks do not use it the way I do, but at the hospital, there were a lot of Kathleens. I took the name Lacey to avoid confusion." Which reminded her of that same problem here. "I'm grandly flattered to know you're considerin' naming the babe after me, but might it be a wee bit confusing once we're wed—you know, with two Laceys and all?"

Hawke stared at her a moment, his heart beating like a stampede. Wed, as in his . . . *wife?* He'd been so intent on doing Caleb a favor by bringing the Irish woman to his ranch, that Hawke had practically forgotten the reason he was "testing" Lacey. Now that she'd brought the subject up, he decided it was about time he set her straight.

"You can't be serious about marrying me."

Surprised by the blunt statement, it took Lacey a moment to respond. "Of course, I am. Why else would I be here?"

"If you mean here in Wyoming, I suppose because you traveled to America with Miss Quinlin looking for a husband. I understand that, I guess, but what I don't understand is why you'd consider me." He stretched his forearms out on the table, exposing his skin up past his wrists. "Respectable young women don't go around trying to attract half-breeds like me, much less think of catching one as a husband. Are you blind, or haven't you bothered to take a good hard look at me?"

She gulped. Of course she'd taken many hard looks at the man, and each time she did, she felt herself slipping under a new kind of spell, bewitched. Even now as he stared at her from across the table, the intensity of those silvery green eyes contrasting against his smooth cinnamon skin and rich sable hair, she felt the pull of something new and wonderful. In fact, in many ways, and especially after what had occurred in the barn, Lacey almost felt as if she were already a part of Hawke and his ranch.

"Aye," she finally murmured. "I see you and think you're a very pleasant-looking man, but I do not know what you mean by half-breed. Is it something to do with your kin?"

"To put it mildly, yes." Not sure whether she was serious or teasing him a little, he uttered a short, harsh laugh. "My mother was the daughter of an army captain at Ft. Laramie, and my father was an Arapaho scout for the troops. That makes me what we call here in America, a half-breed. Now do you understand?"

"Only where you got your nice dark skin—from the Indian side of you, I would guess. I do not see what this has to do with our getting married, though."

Hawke leaned back in his chair and shook his head. He'd never met anyone without prejudice of some kind, and he had a hell of a time believing that he'd met such a person now. Miss O'Carroll wanted something from him—what he didn't know—but he didn't believe for a minute that something was a lifetime tied to a half-breed. Testing her further, he told her a little more about his background.

"I'm not only part Arapaho, but a bastard." Her eyes flashed with shock or surprise at this news. So there was a little prejudice in her soul, after all. "My parents were never married, not that my mother would have considered living with a savage like my father, and as you might imagine, my birth wasn't exactly cause for celebration. You still so sure I'm the kind of man you're looking for in a husband?"

Lacey did not care for his defensive attitude or his tone, even though what Hawke had shared about himself didn't matter to her one way or another. Was his rancor caused by embarrassment, or was he just trying to chase her off? Too new at dealing with folks in the world "outside" to be sure of her instincts, Lacey decided to ignore the subject of his heritage altogether and work instead on getting their earlier sense of togetherness back. To do that, she thought a return to the subject which had brought them together in the first place would work best; the horses.

"All this idle chatter isn't getting that wee filly named. How would you like to call her, *Colleen dhas?* 'Tis a fine Irish name which means pretty girl."

The change of subject told Hawke that any further discussion about a marriage between them was over. Maybe the Irish miss understood prejudice better than he thought. "I've got a better idea," he said, not as relieved as he thought he'd be. "Why don't I call the foal, Irish?"

"Faith, and I would consider that a grand honor!"

"You helped bring the filly safely into the world. It's the least I can do."

"Irish." Lacey repeated the name, then laughed. "I do not know if that be such a good idea after all—the lass is black as the devil's heart. It might be bad luck to name a black horse after my homeland, *Erin.*"

Her gentle laughter was as lyrical as the song she'd sung to Taffy, and the sound warmed him far more than Hawke would admit to himself. Hardening himself against that feeling, he said, "She won't be black for long. She'll start to dapple out like her father in less than a year."

"Dapple out? I do not know the meaning of this."

"She'll begin to turn gray with white spots—dapples, I guess—and her mane and tail will turn silver. The older she gets, the lighter gray she'll turn. I'll introduce you to her sire later and you'll see what I mean. I named him Phantom, because he's so hard to see on a foggy morning."

"Aye, and I think I'm already understandin' what your sayin.'" Lacey paused, picturing the little filly all grown up. "I like the name, I do. It means she'll soon be resembling a fine Irish mist."

Hawke raised his coffee cup to her. "That sounds even better. Irish Mist it is then, in your honor."

*   *   *

For the next couple of hours, Lacey stuck close to Hawke helping him in any way she could. As most of his business was conducted in the barn around the new mother and her babe, the work was neither difficult nor beyond her limited capabilities. Hawke drove her back to Three Elk Ranch after that, and an exhausted Lacey barely kept her eyes open long enough to help Kate prepare another batch of biscuits.

The following morning when Hawke came back to retrieve her, again Lacey carried her basket of rags and towels, and as before they concealed the previously baked batch of biscuits. This time, the plan worked beautifully. Hawke, who'd been sullen since their discussion about his heritage, was mightily impressed with her talents in the kitchen and breakfast was a complete success. She spent that day trying to make the living room and kitchen of Hawke's home a little more presentable, mainly by using most of her time cleaning the mud and dirt off the floor. If she hadn't learned another thing during her life at the hospital, she had learned how to scrub floors.

The next morning when she awakened, every muscle in Lacey's body ached, and it was all she could do just to crawl off of her lumpy excuse for a bed. But, armed again with her basket of goodies, she managed the trip back to Winterhawke Ranch, and even began to feel a little better by the time they arrived.

As they stepped into the kitchen, Lacey set her basket on the counter and asked, "Will you be wantin' ham with your biscuits again, then?" She was already headed for the back door and the porch where the icebox was kept, when Hawke's answer stopped her in her tracks.

"Not today." He rubbed his belly. "I ate so many of your biscuits yesterday—every last one of them by the time I turned in last night, in fact—that I can't face them again this morning."

She whirled around and stared at him in shock. "Oh, but they do not cause me a moment's trouble. I do not mind making them, really."

"Thanks for the offer, but I churned butter last night and have some nice fresh buttermilk out in the icebox. I'd love some flapjacks made out of it."

"Flapjacks?" she repeated, her heart in her throat. "I ne'er heard of such things."

Hawke took the coffeepot from its warming burner and poured himself a cup. "Maybe you know them as pancakes."

"Aye, pancakes, I do know," she said without thinking.

Donning his hat, Hawke started for the door. "Let me know when they're ready. I'll be doing chores in the barn."

She couldn't think fast enough to come up with a reason to stop him, or an excuse as to why she couldn't prepare the breakfast he wanted. Lacey just stood there in terrible shock as Hawke strode on out to the porch, then banged his way through the screen door.

Pancakes! How was she to work her way out of this one? What in all that's holy did a person mix together to come up with the skinny little cakes? Once the shock of what she must do left her system, Lacey took a large mixing bowl down off the shelf and made her first real attempt ever at the art of cooking.

An hour and several aborted recipes later, she settled on a blend of flour, milk, and salt, then, remembering how much she liked the sweet flavor of the pancakes at the hospital, added a cup of sugar and a good measure of molasses. Lacey whipped and whipped the batter, smoothing it until the muscles in her arms cried out with pain before she decided it was silky enough to be the right consistency.

After thoroughly coating her hands with flour to keep the dough from sticking to her fingers, she arranged six little globs of the thick, gooey batter in the skillet, then set to mashing them into nice little cake-like shapes. They weren't the perfect small rounds turned out by the staff at St. Josephine's, she decided when she'd finally finished shaping them, but she thought they would most certainly do. Hefting the heavy iron skillet and its even heavier burden, Lacey set the pan on the stove near the hottest burner. Then she began cleaning up the dreadful mess she'd made of the kitchen.

Sometime later, she noticed that smoke had began to rise from beneath the little cakes. Lacey raced to the stove, grabbed the handle of the skillet, then released it in the next second. The iron handle was as hot as the stove, and she'd burned the palm of her good hand! Smarting, she raced to the table, cut off a small block of butter, then spread it across the burn and wrapped her hand with the only clean cloth left in the kitchen. By now, the smoke curling up from the stove was black, and the smell of charred flour hung over the room like the cloak of the devil himself.

"Damn the bit and the luck, too!" she cursed as she flew back to the stove. This time putting a soiled cloth between herself and the iron handle, she dragged the skillet away from the heat. After pushing her hair out of her eyes—a good deal of her bun had come loose during her frantic exertions—Lacey used a fork to try and lift the pancakes so she could turn them over. The dough was fused to the bottom of the pan.

Her frustrations mounting, she looked around the kitchen for something else to use as a wedge, anything, and spotted a large curved knife like the one Hawke wore at his waist. It was hanging from a wooden rack above the sink along with several other instruments. Taking the knife and the small wooden mallet dangling next to it, she jabbed the tip of the blade beneath one of the pancakes, then used the mallet like a hammer against the grip of the knife.

Chiseling away at her creations in this manner, after a time, Lacey managed to get all six of the little flapjacks turned. Her weary muscles nearly spent, she dragged the skillet back to the heat, then collapsed in a chair at the table. A moment later, Hawke burst into the kitchen.

The acrid aroma hit him first. "Christ, what are you burning in here?" he said as he walked into the room. "And why the hell haven't you come after me for breakfast yet? I'm—" He'd been about to say, starving, until he glanced at the stove and saw the crusty black lumps sizzling in the skillet.

Stalking over to the burner, he stared down into the pan. Breakfast, if that's what this was supposed to be, looked an awful lot like the buffalo chips he'd once collected for the evening campfire—after they'd been burned. "What the *hell* is this supposed to be?"

He turned to Lacey, who was still sitting at the table. Her head was in her hands, but what he could see of her face was covered with flour. Her hair was disheveled and her clothes were splotchy with flour and sticky dough. She looked like hell, but then the kitchen hadn't fared any better what with dough, flour, and molasses smeared on every counter and not a clean rag to be found anywhere. Taking care of the most immediate problem, Hawke folded his glove around the handle of the skillet, then shook his head in wonder as he lifted the pan from the heat and moved it to the counter. He was all set to join Lacey at the table to commiserate with her over the meal gone wrong, when he noticed his favorite bowie knife lying in the sink. This too wore a coat of gluey dough—and worse, the tip of the blade had been snapped clean off.

"You broke my knife!" he blurted out. "You've gone and ruined my best skinning knife!"

Lacey didn't even lift her head as his accusations rang in her ears. She was sinking, falling deeper and deeper into one of her spells. Soon, if she couldn't find a way to get hold of herself and stop the slide, she wouldn't be aware of anything except a great dark emptiness inside. If that happened, she'd be exposing parts of herself to Hawke she'd thought gone and buried.

No, no, not now! Not after all I've been through to bring me this far! Although Lacey fought against the inviting sensations, the pull of the slippery, effortless path into the mindless abyss was great, the promise of oblivion so strong, that it was almost like a warm caress. How she longed to hide there in that comforting lap of nothingness where she could escape responsibility for the mess she'd made of things, but from somewhere deep inside, she found the strength to barely hang on.

"Why won't you answer me," Hawke demanded. "What the hell has been going on in here?"

Lacey forced herself to stand, but when she tried to answer the charges, she still couldn't quite make herself form words. Glancing down into her hand, she noticed that she'd rolled a ball of dough up from the table as she'd sat there in her near stupor. *Speak to the man, tell him what he wants to know*, she begged of herself, but before she could begin, again Hawke prodded her.

"Lacey? What's wrong with you?"

Had he guessed? "I—'tis . . . because of your breakfast," shot out of her mouth followed by an equally impulsive statement. "'Tis the fault of your bloody pancakes . . . *sir!*"

Then, because she couldn't think what else to do, Lacey threw the sticky glob of dough at Hawke and bolted out the back door. Tears spilled down her cheeks as she ran and the urge to slip under the protection of one of her spells grew strong again, so strong, she knew she had to find a place to hide herself away until she could calm down. If Hawke confronted her now, Lacey knew she'd never have the strength to face him again. She'd be lost within herself for hours or maybe even days. What she needed was a good cry and a short nap. Solitude, above all. Thinking of the barn and the harness room with its thick pile of blankets, she dashed through the big double doors.

Once her eyes adjusted to the dimmer lighting, Lacey hurried down the center aisle without even stopping for a quick peek at Taffy and the newly christened "Irish." When she reached the harness room, she flung the door open and jumped inside.

There, a full measure of sunlight streaming in through the window to highlight its features, stood a thing more horrifying than even the banshees of her nightmares.

Lacey and the creature opened their mouths at the precise same moment. Then each cut loose with a blood-curdling scream.

6

When your hand is in the dog's
mouth, draw it out carefully.
—A common Irish saying

Surely her poor confused mind was playing
some kind of new trick on her! Wishing with all her
might for that to be true, Lacey squeezed her eyes shut,
then quickly blinked them open. The banshee was still
there, still staring at her in the same mute horror. It
glanced behind her to the door, but Lacey had blocked
the only escape route from the room. And she was far too
frightened to move out of its way.

"W-would you—" She paused to clear her throat.
"Would you be a banshee or leprechaun?" she asked the
thing.

The creature had a wild look about it, its dusty black
hair matted and sticking out in every direction, its skin
dark, smeared with streaks of dirt. At the sound of her
voice, its huge onyx eyes flared, making it look even
wilder. Then it flattened itself against the back wall of
the room.

"I-I mean you no harm," she said, recognizing a certain

insanity in speaking to what had to have been a figment of her imagination. Imaginary or not, the thing *was* the approximate size described in Irish fairy tales, its wiry body a little shorter than her own five feet five inches. The oddest thing was the fact that it was dressed in a most peculiar way, certainly not in a manner reminiscent of a leprechaun or an elf.

From what Lacey knew of those creatures, they went around pestering folks in caps, coats, and buckled shoes. Even *far darrig*, the mischievous elf, cut a dapper little figure as he ran amuck in his red costume playing jokes on children who did not obey their parents. But this wee person wore buckskin trousers similar to Hawke's and a fringed shirt to match. And he didn't giggle or dance about the way she would have expected of a fairy, but stood there frozen and mute instead. Like a child from the madhouse might do. If not a fairy, then what could it be?

She smiled and the creature seemed to relax a little. Then, surprising her, it leaned forward, tentatively reached out to her, and touched her cheek with the pad of its finger. It was all Lacey could do not to step back or cry out. Sensing something special about what appeared to be a young boy, she forced herself to stand still, and allowed him to examine her. He wiped a drop of moisture from her skin—a teardrop she'd shed as she ran to the barn—and made a careful study of it. As he marveled over the dew from her eyes, Lacey slowly came to recognize a certain manner about him. He wore a haunted look, one she'd seen often on the faces of children newly admitted to the hospital—and sometimes, in her own mirror. Her heart told her this was no banshee or fairy come to bring her bad luck; this was but another lost soul.

"I'm sorry if I frightened you," she said, keeping her voice soft and lilting. "I did not know you were here."

The boy's uneasy gaze remained on his fingertip and her dried-up teardrop. Fairly sure she knew how to reach him, Lacey pointed to his other hand where he held a gleaming band of metal tied up with what looked like a couple of thin leather straps. "Are you working for Mr. Hawke, then? What do you have there?"

This produced the first hint of communication from the boy. Without meeting her gaze, he shrugged and nodded at the same time, leaving Lacey to make what she could of his answer.

"I can see that you do not care to talk much," she went on, "and that is quite all right with me seeing that I never spoke a word for years on end during my early life. But would you mind seeing your way to answer me the one thing? Are you capable of speech, lad?"

Lifting his wary gaze, he slowly nodded.

"Well, then, I expect we'll be the best of friends! If there be one thing Kathleen Lacey O'Carroll can understand, 'tis the urge to stay silent!" The boy cocked his head and took a step toward her. Smiling at him again, she let him know exactly why she was there. "I'm working for Mr. Hawke, too, but I'm having a time of it!" She held up her sticky hands. "I was trying to make pancakes for his breakfast earlier, but I could not do it right. His kitchen looks every bit the mess my hands do, and all he's got to eat for the trouble, is a few lumps of charcoal."

The boy laughed, then held up the item he'd been polishing. "My work—spurs."

"Spurs, you say?" Determined to keep him talking, Lacey thought back to a story she once read about the American West. "A while ago I heard the tale of a small man from Texas who did not have the respect of his fellow cowboys. He went 'round with his face dragging the clover until he bought himself a pair of grand silver spurs. After that, when he went about wearing them on his boots, 'twas like the finest of charms for the lad. The cowboy felt so tall, so brave, and so fearless, that whenever he wore those spurs, the other men cleared a path for him. Are these the items you'd be workin' on, then?"

The boy's dirty sienna face broke into a wide grin, and he slowly nodded. "Hawke's spurs."

"Aye, then perhaps those are the charms I need to keep our dear Mr. Hawke from making his fill of complaints about my work." Lacey reached out and touched the edge of the silver for luck. "I can not seem to keep him in a fine temper when I'm around. Perhaps if I were to tie a pair of these to my apron . . . "

As if speaking his name had conjured him up, Hawke came into the barn and called to her. "Lacey? Are you in here?"

She turned her head as if to answer him, but the boy whispered, "No, lady, no!" Then he put a finger against her mouth.

"Lacey?" Hawke called again. "If you're in here, say so. I'm done hollering at you, if that's what has you worried, and sorry that I hollered before to boot." After a few moments of silence, his retreating footsteps met their ears, and then all was quiet again.

She turned back to the boy. "Why could we no answer him?"

"Spurs." He pointed up at the variety of leather goods and halters hanging from the wall. "You wear."

Lacey glanced up to find another pair of spurs, noting that they were of a far fancier design than the pair the boy held in his hands. The ones he'd been polishing had a horseshoe-shaped band of silver which fit around the heel of a boot. The actual spur—in this case, a protruding tube of metal one-inch long and blunted at the end—was attached to the center of the band at the back. The set on the wall appeared to have a silver wheel fashioned of what looked like shamrocks in place of this single spur.

"May I take them down?" she asked. The boy nodded rapidly, so Lacey stood on tiptoes and lifted them over their peg. The spurs indeed were shaped like small, pointy clovers, and when tapped by her finger, spun 'round and 'round, leaving a metallic little jingle in their wake. "They're like a good luck sign by the nine orders of angels!" she said with awe. "You think 'twould be all right if I were to try them on?"

Grinning to himself, the boy dropped to his knees, reached beneath the hem of her skirt, and captured one of Lacey's feet. When he saw her thin leather slipper, he frowned. Cautioning her to remain still, he jumped up, opened a small cupboard behind him, and pulled out a pair of boots.

Turning back to Lacey, he said, "These Crowfoot's. You try."

"Crowfoot? What is that?"

He beat his own small chest. "I Crowfoot."

Pleased by her progress with the boy, she accepted the offered boots. "Thank you, Mr. Crowfoot."

Lacey sat on a nearby stool to make the switch, and as she pulled off her own shoes, noticed that one of the boots Crowfoot had given her was stiff and new, the other, crumpled, worn, and a little misshapen. Automatically glancing down at the boy's feet, she saw that on his right foot he wore a fairly new boot, but that the left was wrapped in a large ball of hemp.

Sensing that it would be wiser to go slow with her new little friend, she decided not to comment or ask about his injury just yet, but quietly went about switching her footgear instead. Surprisingly enough, the boy's boots did fit her rather well, and were far more suitable for working on the ranch than her delicate slippers. Lacey offered her newly outfitted feet to Crowfoot, and he made a grand display of attaching the lovely "shamrock" spurs to her new boots.

"Try now," the boy said, encouraging her to stand up.

Lacey took a few hesitant steps, then got bolder. The more aggressive her stride, the louder the spurs jingled, and after a moment, she *did* feel as if she were ten feet tall, invincible, and all powerful. She even danced a noisy little jig for Crowfoot's benefit, then finally dropped back down on the stool.

"Now I'm knowing how that cowboy felt," she said, out of breath. "If only I had it in my power to wear these spurs in the house around Mr. Hawke! They have me feeling like there's nothing I can not do! Even to make pancakes!"

Crowfoot waved her away. "Go now."

Giving him what she thought he wanted—his privacy—she leaned over to remove the spurs and boots, but a grime-streaked hand reached out and stopped her.

"Go now. Keep spurs."

"You can not mean it," she said with surprise. "'Twill anger Mr. Hawke something awful if he finds me wearing his spurs, 'twill it no?"

The boy nodded, but placed a finger across his lips and grinned. Then he put the same finger across her mouth and grinned even wider.

"Forgettin' to tell the man seems like a very good idea, but he's sure to notice they've been taken from their peg."

Crowfoot shook his head and pointed to the spurs he'd been polishing. "Not hurt horse." Then he pointed to Lacey's feet. "Hurt horse, only for show."

"He does not wear them?" The boy nodded enthusiastically. "Then you're sayin' that if I were to tiptoe carefully to keep the spurs from jingling when Hawke's around, he might not ever know that I've borrowed them . . . would that be right?"

His grin wider than ever, Crowfoot stuck out his hand, took hold of hers, and shook it. "Right," he repeated. "No talk about Crowfoot, too. Right?"

Seeing a kindred spirit in this boy who couldn't have been more than ten or twelve years old, Lacey grinned back at him. "Right—and may I melt off the earth like snow if I should slip and make any mention of you."

Moments later, it was with a confidence that she'd never known before that Lacey made her way back to the ranch house and boldly stepped into the kitchen. Hawke was nowhere to be seen, so she went to work cleaning up the mess she'd made earlier, then tidied up the one he'd made cooking a pile of sausage patties while she'd been outside in the barn.

He checked on her only once after that, and then surprised her by starting the journey back to Three Elk Ranch at least an hour earlier than he had before—in fact, he hadn't even given her enough time to duck back into the barn and remove the spurs. On top of that, Hawke seemed to be in a "mood" throughout the long drive, speaking to her, but not really saying much. Oh, he said he forgave her for breaking his knife, and seemed to understand that she was new to cooking pancakes, but that little "connection" she'd felt between them after the foal was born had vanished. Tomorrow, she thought with renewed confidence, she'd return to Winterhawke armed with some of Kate's recipes and the luck o' the spurs to help her put them together right. Hawke would warm up to her *and* the idea of keeping her on once she fed his belly right. Lacey just knew it.

When the wagon finally pulled up in front of Caleb's wood-frame home, Hawke planted his foot on the brake, but didn't set it. "By the way—I won't be back to pick you up for a couple of days. I have to ride the fences and check on the horses out in the far pastures. Often, I wind up spending a night or two away from the ranch." That was a lie of course, especially during foaling season, but one he told to give him the break he needed from this confusing, confounded woman. He took his foot off the brake. "Be sure to say hello to Caleb for me. I've got to get back now."

"Oh, of course," she said, hiding her disappointment. "Then I'll just be wishing you the luck of God and the prosperity of Patrick that all goes well with your fences." With that, Lacey helped herself off the rig, careful not to jingle her spurs, then collected her basket and headed for the house.

Females, Hawke grumbled to himself as he drove away, *delicate ladies like Miss Irish in particular, had no place on a working ranch like Winterhawke.* She was nothing but trouble.

Nothing but a distraction with hair that smelled of cherry blossoms, eyes that sparkled both blue and gold, and a sweet lilting voice that went on and on with talk of marriage. The more he thought about it, the more Hawke was convinced there could be only one reason a woman like that might be willing to wed a half-breed like him; she had to be on the run. From the law, or even from a husband.

It didn't matter to Hawke in the least which it might be, because he had no intention of keeping her around long enough to find out. *He* sure as hell didn't have a need for a wife. He could cook better than this female, tend to the cows and chickens in less than half the time it took her to even *find* the eggs, and although he hadn't tested the little Irish beauty with a needle and thread yet, it wouldn't have surprised him to learn that he could out-mend her as well—and John Winterhawke, Jr. was the worst seamstress in all of Wyoming Territory!

If he had one brain in his head, Hawke decided, he

wouldn't even go back to Three Elk Ranch after her again. Sure he'd promised his best friend that he'd give her a full two-week try, but if Caleb knew how badly she'd turned his life upside down in just the few days she'd been at the ranch, the old man would have to release him from that promise—wouldn't he?

Hawke had assumed it would be a simple thing when he made the agreement, even a nice little convenience to have someone around to do the cooking and the chores while he went about his business with the horses. He hadn't figured on the smell of Lacey's hair or the sound of her voice, and he sure never thought she'd worm her way into his horse business the way she had. If all that wasn't shock enough for any man, because of her, he frequently found himself questioning the life he'd built for himself, and even wondering if he shouldn't reevaluate his goals!

Hawke had *always* known what he was about before. He was meant to be alone, and never expected to have much by way of company except for himself. He was an outsider, an undesirable, a position in white society he'd understood practically since birth. Even during those long winters trapping with Caleb, he'd known he'd eventually wind up alone, and he was fully prepared for that eventuality. What Hawke *wasn't* prepared for, was life with a woman underfoot.

Now that he'd tested Lacey these few days, he didn't know what to think. For reasons he still hadn't figured out, this O'Carroll woman was busy working her way into his blood, making him feel things he didn't want to feel, and at the damnedest moments—like in the stall over the birth of Taffy's foal, or worse yet, while she was milking Hazel. The spark of desire she'd ignited in him then was startling and something he'd thought he'd never feel for any white woman; a lust best left unfelt. If he were to suffer another day of such yearnings, it could prove disastrous. Ten more could be . . . Hawke didn't dare think beyond another day.

He knew, of course, that he was rationalizing his next move, and running scared from this woman, he who never ran from anything, man nor beast. But this was different, and now at last, he knew what he had to do. He would drive back to Three Elk Ranch a couple of days from now and tell Caleb that this trial with the Irish miss simply was not working out. If his friend tried to argue him out of it, he would point out that keeping Lacey around wouldn't be fair to Crowfoot—not after all he and Caleb had been through just to get the boy as civilized as he was. Hell, they'd already scared the kid out of Three Elk Ranch and into Winterhawke because of one mail-order bride. Crowfoot wouldn't have any place to run and hide if Hawke moved a second mail-order bride onto his own ranch. Miss Kathleen Lacey O'Carroll would simply have to find herself a husband elsewhere. Period.

Hawke told himself all that and more, convinced himself that he really had no choice in the matter, but over the next few days, he found himself listening for the sound of Lacey's Irish lilt and the little songs she hummed while working; hoping for a glimpse of those coppery curls and the fact that they could never seem to stay confined in a tidy little bun; but most of all, missing those sparkling blue eyes and the way they gazed at him—looking, always looking, yet never seeing the blood of a savage within. But he still didn't quite believe it.

Three mornings later, Hawke arrived at Caleb's ranch prepared to go through with his plan. It was best this way. He would soon forget this fascinating female had ever darkened his door, and she . . . she would have no trouble finding a husband for herself elsewhere. Anywhere, but here.

Shrugging off the last thought, he knocked on the door and let himself inside the house in the same motion. "Caleb? Is everyone up and about?"

"We're up!" Caleb called from the couch in front of the fireplace. "But Lacey ain't quite dressed and ready to go yet. Come sit a spell, catch me up."

Grateful for the relative privacy he'd have with his friend, Hawke settled down on the hearth across from the couch and got right down to business. "Miss O'Carroll doesn't need to hurry on my account. I'm not planning to take her with me this morning."

"Oh?" Caleb perked up. "You got troubles with the foaling, son? I can probably spare one of the extra men I hired on after my leg got busted up, but only for about a week or so."

"Foaling's going fine." Hawke took off his hat and busied himself by adjusting the crease in the crown as he went on. "In fact, Phantom's first filly hit the ground a few days ago, and from the look of her, I'd say in three years or so, she's going to be the best little brood mare I've ever had."

Caleb chuckled. "I heard all about the arrival of your little 'Irish Mist.' Lacey practically busted her buttons telling us the story of how you saved the foal and her ma. A tough one, eh?"

Hawke shrugged, oddly embarrassed. "More trouble than I care for, but they're both fine. What's not going so fine, is having that Irish female at the ranch with me."

"It ain't?" Pushing his backside against the arm of the couch, Caleb straightened himself. "I cain't hardly believe that after hearing that girl go on about you for the past two days. Why all she talks about is you and that ranch. I ain't heard nothing but Hawke this and Hawke that till—hell, listening to her, I'd a thought that the two of you were getting on thicker than calf slobber. What's the problem?"

Now fiddling with the brim of his hat as he turned it around in an endless circle, Hawke went on with his prepared speech. "It's not me I'm worried about when she's there. It's Crowfoot. I'm afraid having her around is upsetting him something awful."

"Oh, I plum forgot about him. Did they have a run-in of some kind?"

"I don't think so, but I'm sure the kid was watching her help me deliver Taffy's foal. I doubt he liked it much." And that much was probably true. Crowfoot loved working with the horses, and most likely viewed Lacey as a threat to his job. Thinking of a few other "facts" he didn't have to fabricate, Hawke added, "If that's not enough, Crowfoot hasn't spoken a word to me for the past two days. When I leave his supper in the barn, he waits until I'm good and gone before he comes down from the loft to get it. He's avoiding me, and I'm pretty sure I know why." He cocked a thumb over his shoulder in the direction of the bedroom. "Her."

"So what?" Caleb shrugged. "This ain't the first time he's gone and hid hisself from us, and I doubt it'll be the last. He'll be all right once he gets used to the idea of having a female underfoot." Caleb lifted his cane off the floor and tapped Hawke's knee with it. "Sounds to me like you don't got a problem a'tall."

Feeling as if he were losing ground, Hawke roughed up his voice. "Having that woman around has undone a lot of the progress we made with Crowfoot over the past four years. Besides that, she can't even cook up a slice of smoked ham! Frankly, Caleb, I don't think keeping her around is worth the trouble."

Kate drew the curtain aside she'd fashioned to separate

the living room from the kitchen, and picked up the conversation where Hawke left off. "I hope ye weren't referring to Lacey just now, Mr. Winterhawke—look at what the dear sweet lass has made up special for ye." Never slowing her stride as she crossed between the couch and fireplace, she passed the berry pie she was carrying beneath Hawke's nostrils and continued on her way.

"Was that a pie?" Hawke said, following his nose. "A *pie?*"

Feigning innocence, Kate paused dramatically. She, Lacey, and Caleb had discussed Lacey's culinary deficiencies at length over the past couple of days, that and the disasters she'd caused at Winterhawke Ranch. During the course of the conversation, Caleb revealed the only weakness he'd ever spotted in his friend, Hawke—the man absolutely, positively could not resist a slice of pie, no matter what the flavor.

Exchanging a conspiratorial glance with Caleb, Kate finally answered Hawke. "Why, yessir. Lacey got the urge to bake a nice fat blackberry pie, but if yer not wantin' *it* or *her* around, I'll just be handing it off to Caleb's men in the bunkhouse." She turned then, and headed for the door.

"No, wait!" Hawke was on his feet in a flash. Hell, he couldn't just let her walk out the door with a fresh berry pie—not without at least a taste of it! He actually *dreamed* about pies from time to time, but since he rarely had the chance to go to town, hardly ever got the chance to indulge this one obsession.

His mouth watering, Hawke swallowed hard. "Nothing's been settled about Lacey just yet. Caleb and I were only talking about some of the problems I've been having with her out at the ranch."

Taking her cue, the woman in question strolled into the room, her stride bold and purposeful—an almost impossible gait considering that she was walking on tiptoes. It really wasn't difficult for her today, however, for between the lucky spurs and the recipes Kate had written down for her, Lacey truly did feel as if she were invincible. Between her newly formed confidence and the English adage—the way to a man's heart is through his stomach—she had no doubt that after Hawke tasted the pie she'd "helped" Kate bake, the man would be as good as hers.

Her head held high, Lacey met Kate halfway across the room. "Did I hear my name spoken in the same breath with trouble?"

"Mr. Winterhawke seems to be concerned about bringing ye back to his ranch."

Lacey turned her bright blue eyes on him. "Are you now? If this has something to do with the dreadful mess I made of your kitchen, I apologize again. I should have told you that I'd ne'er made pancakes before. 'Twas wrong of me to keep that from you, I know that now, but I only meant to please."

There was something different about her. Hawke noticed that immediately even though most of his attention was still on the pie. What had she done to herself? he wondered. Lacey was dressed in a plain navy blue skirt and white blouse as usual, and her coppery hair was bound in a bun at the top of her head the way it started out every day. But somehow between the last time he saw her and this morning, a good deal of that "little girl lost look" had faded from her expression. In place of the formerly edgy, uncertain female who'd begun to haunt his dreams, stood a woman to be reckoned with. One, it suddenly occurred to him, who fascinated him even more than before.

Hawke glanced from Lacey to the pie Kate still held in her hands. They were waiting for an answer. Clearly, the pie would be his only if he made what they considered to be the correct decision. As he pondered his situation,

Lacey broke an edge off the golden crust, brushing away a few flakes which drifted down to her skirt. Then she popped the tender piece of pastry into her mouth. Christ! The pie was baked to perfection, Hawke could tell that just by the way it fell apart when touched. And, if the highly mounded crust and glazed purple streaks along the vents were any indication, it would be overflowing with sweet, succulent berries. He swallowed hard.

"Well, Mr. Winterhawke?" said Kate impatiently. "Am I to make the trip to the bunkhouse, or no?"

"Ah . . . no." His mouth watering so he could hardly speak, Hawke smiled at Lacey and made his decision. Hell, he'd once been strong enough to live through the worst winter blizzard he'd ever encountered, alone and unsheltered for nearly three weeks. Surely he could put up with this confounded woman and the unwanted feelings she brought out in him for another measly week or so. All he had to do, he assured himself, was stay on his toes around her—and make sure she kept on baking those pies.

"Are you ready to go?" Hawke said to Lacey as he sauntered over to the women and snatched the pie out of Kate's hands. "The place just hasn't been the same without you."

7

A lifetime of happiness: No man alive could bear it:
It would be hell on earth.

—George Bernard Shaw

Hawke ate the entire pie for breakfast; didn't even bother to use a plate. If he'd been alone, he probably wouldn't have troubled himself with a fork, either.

Not that he was a complete pig about it. More than once he'd offered to cut a slice for Lacey and share his bounty, but she'd insisted that she wasn't terribly fond of pie. Imagine that, he'd thought in amazement—a living, breathing person who didn't like *pie!* As he scraped the last bits of crust and berry syrup off the bottom of the pan, he belatedly remembered Crowfoot. Christ! how could he have forgotten about the kid? He imagined the look on the boy's face if he knew he'd been slighted this way, then guiltily wondered if it would be asking too much of Lacey if he were to suggest that she bake another.

Hawke glanced her way as she tidied up the kitchen. She was humming, filling his ears with sunshine, and methodically going about each task with slow precision—looking a lot like a woman who'd never so much as washed out a coffee cup before. This wasn't the first time he'd noticed her novice-like approach to anything he asked her to do, and he had a feeling it wouldn't be the last. Hawke had been watching Lacey closely since he'd brought her back to the ranch this morning, scrutinizing her like the winter hawk both his father and he were named after, looking for faults, he supposed, but finding riddles instead.

Something in Lacey's manner had *definitely* changed since the last time she'd visited; she carried herself more confidently, as if she suddenly had all the answers, and the faint tinkle of bells or something like them, accompanied her every movement. Jewelry of some kind, he supposed, although he'd yet to glimpse an adornment anywhere on her person.

"More coffee?" Lacey asked, her voice harmonizing with that metallic melody.

"No, thanks." Hawke patted his belly. "I'm about to bust as it is. That was, without exception, the best pie I ever bit into."

Lacey blushed a little, then turned back to the stove. "Thank you kindly, sir. 'Twas nothing."

"I'm glad you feel that way about it. I was hoping you'd see your way to baking me another."

"Oh . . . of c-course. I'll see to it first thing tomorrow."

He noticed the hesitation in her voice, but didn't press her. Tomorrow would be soon enough for Crowfoot to taste perfection, he supposed. Today he had to get some work done, and it was about time both he and the boy tended to the horses. Before he left, Hawke took a moment to lift the ledger from his pocket, flipped it open to the Lacey O'Carroll page, and perused his notes. So far, the only notation on the *Advantage* side read:

1. Good with horses.

Feeling generous now that he was full of pastry, he jotted another entry below the first:

2. Makes great pies!

Lacey swept over to the table and whisked the empty pie tin away, catching Hawke's eye again in the process. Never before had he even allowed himself to dream of finding anything like her in his kitchen, but here she was fussing over him like she'd been doing it all her life. Next thing he knew, Hawke was imagining Lacey as his wife and wondering what would it be like to find her at the stove each and every morning when he awoke. It might be nice, he thought, to hear that softly lilting voice murmur, 'Top o' the morning to you,' and to watch her lithe body swish across the room as she served his meals each day. And he sure wouldn't mind inhaling the sweet scent of cherry blossoms every time she brushed a few errant curlicues from her unmanageable coif across his cheeks. No, sir, he wouldn't mind that a bit.

Something warm stirred in Hawke at those thoughts, and his mind just naturally drifted toward the more pleasant side of marriage—to the fact that should he wed Lacey, he would be entitled to bed her, half-breed or not. Just thinking about this woman in his bed every night to do with as he pleased, drove him to add:

3. *Bed partner*, to the advantage side of the list. But it wasn't a moment later, that Hawke begin to think of the disadvantages to such an arrangement as well.

As much as the idea of bedding the copper-haired beauty tempted him, Hawke had a few reservations on that count—not that he was anything close to an expert in such matters. He could narrow the sum total of his experience with females down to one encounter on a long, memorable night around a dozen years ago when he was on the cusp of manhood. Caleb and a few of the Crow Indians they traded with at the time had unceremoniously tossed him into the tepee of a widowed squaw for an instant lesson on sex. There by the light of a dim fire, he learned several startling things about women and their bodies, even a few things about himself, but absolutely nothing of love. Wouldn't a woman like Miss Lacey O'Carroll expect that of him—love or declarations of love—if she gave herself over as his wife?

He sure didn't feel that for her now, and Hawke had a pretty good idea that he never would. Still, just thinking of lying with Lacey spread hot fingers of desire throughout him, tickling his nerve endings with a deep, hot lust he hadn't felt in years. When those fingers clenched into a fiery, pulsing fist as they reached the base of his groin, he forced himself to think of another disadvantage should he marry, then lie with this woman; children. Surely the Irish miss would want them. Hawke thought back to another lesson the Crow squaw taught him on that memorable night so long ago; rigid control, for coupling led to children. Hawke wasn't at all certain he wanted to bring any more mixed-breed children into the world to be shunned by both white and red alike. And he had no idea how well he could control himself now, especially around the fiery-haired Lacey O'Carroll.

"May I ask what you might be doing there?"

Lacey's voice surprised him so, Hawke nearly pitched backwards out of his chair. "What?"

She moved closer to the table and pointed to the ledger. "I was wondering what you're writing there, and if I might be of help."

"Oh, ah, it's just my ledger, accounting I keep whenever I go horse-trading." He glanced up at Lacey, oddly embarrassed to have been caught daydreaming about her, and felt compelled to explain even further. "I always make a list of the animal's good points and its bad. Whichever side is the longest when I've finished my examination, makes the decision for me."

"Ah, that sounds like a very good idea. Will you be buying another horse soon, then?"

"Something like that." Suddenly wanting out of the

conversation, Hawke hunched over the ledger to discourage her interest, then moistened the tip of his pencil and jotted two more notations under disadvantages:

7. *Bed Partner*

8. *Too damn nosy.*

The rough edge to Hawke's tone and his obvious dismissal of her didn't put Lacey off. How could she be angry with anyone who looked so adorable? Since he'd eaten the pie, the corners of Hawke's mouth, his tongue, and even his teeth, were all stained a nice periwinkle blue, making him look like a naughty little boy, even when he frowned. The only thing which disturbed her, was the catch in his voice, a little warble which suggested he hadn't been entirely truthful with her.

Sure he was deliberately hiding something from her, Lacey made up her mind to have a look at this ledger of his. Making certain to stay on her tiptoes in order to keep her spurs quiet, she took up a feather duster and casually began to clean the shelving which held dishes and crockery just behind the dining table. Hawke paid her no heed. So she moved a little closer to him.

She worked this way for several moments, flitting behind him occasionally as she did her "chores." When she opened the back door which was located directly behind the chair in which Hawke sat, Lacey walked through to the porch and took a couple of steps in the direction of the icebox. Then quietly retracing her steps, she peered around the jamb, leaned forward as far as she dared, and glanced over his shoulder until she could catch a glimpse of this mysterious ledger.

The heading on the page clearly read: *Lacey O'Carroll.* Beneath that were two columns, one called *Advantages*, the other, *Disadvantages.* She swallowed a gasp of surprise, and ducked back around the corner. Apparently Hawke was rating her in the same way he judged his animals! If that wasn't bad enough, it appeared that the list of entries on the *Disadvantage* side of the ledger was much longer than the other. So the man judged her and found her lacking, did he?

Incensed, Lacey hiked up her skirts and, forgetting to tiptoe, marched out to the far end of the porch. "The curse of the crows upon you *and* your miserable book of lies, Mr. Winterhawke!" she muttered under her breath as she flung open the icebox. Staring at the contents of the cold storage, she put the finishing touches on her curse in a much louder voice. "May you and your book of judgements rot in the hills for the crows to feed upon!"

Back in the house, Hawke cocked his head, alerted not just by Lacey's voice, but by that distinctive metallic sound which accompanied it. A sound, it suddenly occurred to him, which was beginning to strike him as vaguely familiar. What the hell was she wearing—chains?

"Lacey?" he called over his shoulder. "Did you just ask me something about crows in these hills?"

After a moment to calm herself, she tiptoed back to the door and poked her head around the corner again. Hawke had turned around in his chair, leaving her with no choice but to meet his gaze with a broad smile. "I was just wondering if your fine mountains are home to any crows. I thought I heard the cawing of one the other day."

"That's probably what you heard all right. Those pesky birds are pretty much everywhere up here." Hawke closed the ledger and slid it inside his jacket pocket. Then he stood, stared at her for a long moment as if weighing his options, and finally said, "I'm on my way out to the corrals now to get busy with the horses. Seems to me I promised you an introduction to Phantom the day his filly was born. Would you like to come along and meet him?"

Lacey beamed with pleasure at the suggestion, but she had not forgotten her earlier anger. She had every intention of getting hold of that ledger one day soon and finding out exactly what it was that displeased Hawke so about her. For now, she just smiled and said, "Aye, and I would be most happy to make his acquaintance at long last. Thank you kindly for askin'."

Though early morning yet, the day outside was bright and clear, nothing short of gorgeous. As they walked to the stud's corral, Lacey dropped her gaze to Centennial Valley, a gently sloping saucer of pastureland, rocks, and sagebrush lying directly below the mountaintop where Hawke had built his home. In daylight, she could easily see the sparkling creek winding through the aspens which bordered the mare's enclosure, and also that the ribbon of water cut across a meadow carpeted with bluebells and buttercups, a sight unlike anything she'd seen in Ireland.

Suddenly filled with a heady sense of freedom, the panorama before her drove away the last of Lacey's anger as she followed along behind Hawke breathing deeply of the pine-scented coolness all around her. Then at once, she picked up the distinct aroma of horses. They'd arrived at the smallest corral, a fenced arena whose walls were much higher than the other enclosures on the ranch. In that pen stood a sleek gray stallion with a thick silvery mane and matching tail which swept the ground.

As they approached him, the high-strung animal began to strut around the perimeters of his pen, tossing his head and snorting. By the time Lacey and Hawke were within two feet of the fence, the stud was charging toward them, skidding to a stop, then rearing and pawing the air in defiance.

"Don't get any closer," Hawke said, warning Lacey away from the fence. "As you can see, it doesn't take much to get Phantom excited."

The stallion reared again, this time emitting a shrill whinny, then spun on his hind legs and roared off across the pen in a dead run. After skidding to an abrupt halt just before crashing into the fence, the animal wheeled around and raced to the center of the ring where he began to paw the ground.

Instead of being frightened by the beast, a fascinated Lacey moved a couple of steps closer to the enclosure. "There now," she said, calling to the stallion as she stuck her left hand between two slats and into the corral. "'Tis Lacey O'Carroll come to meet up with you. Come smell the palm of my hand and you'll see that I'll not be hurting you or giving you any—"

Phantom suddenly charged the fence faster than she would have believed such a large animal could move. If Hawke hadn't grabbed hold of her shoulders and dragged her away from the corral in that same instant, the stud might have smashed against Lacey's outstretched arm, breaking her wrist, or worse.

His hands still firmly clenched to her shoulders, Hawke shook her a little. "Didn't I tell you not to get too close to him?" he shouted. "That animal's not only dangerous, but crazy!"

Although Lacey knew he couldn't possibly guess how that word stung her, making her feel defensive, and more sympathetic than ever toward the agitated stallion, she ignored his outburst. Instead, and even though he still held her shoulders bracketed between his hands, she defiantly turned her head away from him and stared at the beast. Phantom's nostrils were flaring and snorting at regular intervals, and he kept one big brown eye pinned to her as he loped around the perimeters of his enclosure. Was he committing her face to memory should she be fool enough to approach him again? Or was he simply as curious about her as she was about him?

Hawke shook her again, demanding her attention. "Lacey? Are you listening to me?"

"Aye," she finally said, too accustomed to doing what she was told to hold out any longer. "I'm listening and hearing what you have to say, but I can not tell you that I'm liking the words much. 'Tis mean of you to be callin' anything, man or beast, *crazy*."

"Well, excuse the hell out of me, ma'am." His expression and his tone were anything *but* apologetic. "Crazy pretty much covers the way that horse behaves on occasion, so crazy is what I call him. He deserves it."

With a toss of her head, Lacey turned her gaze back to the stallion. "Maybe that horse would not deserve it or behave so badly if you did not act as if you expect him to be so . . . so overwrought. Did you ever consider that? Seems to me that your prized stallion might be a wee bit saner if you did not treat him as if he were different from the other horses." At least that's the way she'd felt under similar circumstances. Feeling indignant on her own behalf as well as the animal's, she tossed in, "He probably wishes to run with them, instead of being penned up alone the way he is."

"One afternoon in a foaling stall, and suddenly you're an expert on horses, is that it?" Hawke's voice was deceptively quiet, for in the next moment, he hauled Lacey up close to his hips, almost, but not quite making full contact with her. As he'd planned, she snapped her head back around to face him, her big blue eyes wide with surprise.

"*Running*," he went on to say, "is not exactly what he wishes to do with the other horses. Phantom is my *stud*, understand? The rooster among my mares. If I were to turn him loose with them and their yearlings, he'd—"

"Arrah, and I-I think I understand what you mean." Blushing violently, she lowered her lashes. "I suppose I am sounding a bit the expert, but 'tis only because I do feel a kinship with the horses—really I do, and thought I might understand this gentleman's frustrations a wee bit."

At that moment, Hawke found himself wondering if she had any inkling of the kind of frustrations she'd set to growing in him—or if she understood how much *this* gentleman would like them eased. She was right about the one thing, however—Lacey did seem to have a natural feel for horses, an innate gift he hadn't recognized in anyone so quickly since the day he first introduced Crowfoot to his herd. In fact, it suddenly occurred to him, in many ways, the Irish miss and the young Crow Indian were a lot alike.

Puzzling over that realization, Hawke gentled his voice. "You are getting along with the horses just fine, but with that ability, you've got to learn a healthy respect for the animals. Without that respect, working with them could cost you at least a few broken bones, if not your life."

"Aye, and I suppose I might have learned that lesson by now if I had not been in a bit of a rush to make myself welcome here. I promise to listen better from now on."

"Do that," he said in a deep whisper. "And give yourself more time to get used to their ways. They're big—so big even they have no idea how big they are—and in the case of Phantom, still pretty wild."

"And would that be why you're callin' him names? Not to poke fun, but to warn a body that he's a wee bit 'crazy-wild?'"

"Yeah . . . something like that, I guess." Why would she have thought he was poking fun at his own horse? "Just remember this; even if Phantom seems to like and trust you, there's no way of knowing when you approach him whether he's going to nip at you, slash out at you with his hooves, or nuzzle your palm. He's *very* unpredictable. Do you understand what that means?"

"I would say that I do." Lacey flashed Hawke a meaningful grin. "The only thing I do not understand, is why you call the beast Phantom. He is mist-colored, true, but given his nature, I should think he might better be named . . . Hawke."

"Hawke?" Chuckling to himself as her meaning sunk in, he suddenly became very aware that he hadn't turned loose of Lacey's shoulders yet. Feeling curiously regretful, Hawke released his grip, but then, instead of putting some distance between them the way he should have, he impulsively brushed his fingertips across her porcelain cheek. "You're full of surprises, Miss Lacey O'Carroll. I always feel like I'm missing something with you, like there's a little secret or two you're keeping from me. What are you hiding, Irish miss? Anything I should know about?"

Lacey gulped, torn by a storm of conflicting emotions. Fright was one, to be sure, a fear that he'd somehow guessed exactly what she was hiding about herself. But at the same time, other, stranger sensations assailed her, overriding the concern that he might have realized by now that she was considered by those who ought to know, to be a wee bit fey. All she knew for sure was that when Hawke touched her cheek, she felt as though she'd awakened to her very first dawn. In fact, her entire body was alive with sensation, tingling with need and an undeniable desire to be held in his strong and, she suspected, capable arms. With no thought to consequence, Lacey swayed toward him, intent on experiencing that unnamed something.

The moment her breasts made contact with Hawke's rough buckskin shirt and the broad chest beneath it, so startling were the sensations, Lacey's head fell back of its own volition. Electrified by these new, surprising feelings, she instinctively moistened her lips, then raised her suddenly languid gaze to meet Hawke's. His eyes were darker now than before and less menacing, she noticed, almost the same black-green of the Irish yews. Even his expression had changed, his smooth cinnamon features looking more rigid and purposeful now. Most surprising of all, was the way he'd lowered his head and seemed to be moving ever closer to her opened mouth. Surely he didn't mean to . . .

It was wrong. It was beyond stupidity. And in just about any town he could think of, it was a hanging offense for an Indian to put his hands on a white woman. But in spite of all that and his better judgement, Hawke knew precisely what he meant to do. He was going to kiss Lacey, by God, kiss her until her teeth rattled, and to hell with the consequences—even if it meant the hangman was already measuring his neck for a hemp tie. He was going to taste that heart-shaped mouth, or die trying.

Hawke's lips touched down on hers so lightly at first, he wasn't even sure he'd made contact. Increasing the pressure, he slid his hands from her shoulders to her back, holding her tight enough now to feel the camisole beneath her blouse and its pattern of lace edging. Lacey's only reaction at first was to go rigid in his arms, as if frightened or outraged by the liberties he was taking. Then, as he deepened the kiss, she slowly melted against him, and her sweet lips softened and parted, making it easy for him to slide his tongue between them. She tasted better than fresh berry pie, more tender than the flakiest of crusts. As Hawke probed deeper in order to sample the sweet juice of her mouth, the rumble of approaching horses jerked him away from the luscious feast, and back to his senses.

Wondering irrationally if what he heard was indeed the hangman come to get him, Hawke released Lacey and turned his back to her. His legs heavy and sluggish, he stumbled in the direction of the hoofbeats. As he fought for control of his overheated body, he saw three riders coming around the last bend of the road which led to

Winterhawke. Keeping one eye on them, he bent down to retrieve his hat which had somehow fallen or been knocked from his head. As the riders drew closer, he could see that two of them were wearing army uniforms, and that the third was dressed as a civilian in a dark blue suit and tan overcoat. A very uncivilized one, at that, thought Hawke as his uncle's features became clear enough for him to recognize the man. Christ, why did his mother's brother have to show up now, of all times?

Quickly turning back to Lacey, Hawke slammed his hat on his head and barked an order at her. "Go into the house. Do whatever looks like it needs doing until I come get you. Go on now, and hurry!"

She looked disoriented, confused, and something he couldn't quite put his finger on—embarrassed?—but she wasn't moving fast enough to suit him. Again, he said, "Go to the house—*now!*"

Tears sprang into her eyes as Lacey's gaze darted from Hawke to the riders, and for a moment, he thought she was going to stand there no matter what he said. But then in the next instant, her fingers pressed tight against the lips he'd so recently kissed, she whirled around in a cloud of petticoats and dust, and scurried off toward the house. The metallic accompaniment which seemed to follow her every move was louder than before, and even more familiar than ever, but before Hawke could pinpoint the source, the riders pulled up in front of him.

It was late morning, but as he touched the brim of his hat, Hawke said, "Afternoon. What can I do for you?"

William Braddock climbed down from his lathered mount and tied his reins to the corral beside the stud pen before acknowledging that Hawke had even spoken. As he made his way between corrals, he wiped the grit from his brow, then broke into a broad, toothy grin.

"Afternoon yourself, breed." He rubbed his eyes, then

twitched his thick tawny mustache. "I must be going blind. Thought I spotted a female out here with you."

Although he'd already begun to erupt inside, Hawke managed to keep his cool exterior as he said, "It's nothing you need to trouble yourself about."

"I saw her run into the house, Johnny boy." Braddock speared him with a beady amber eye before he went on, his ample jowls jiggling as he spoke. "She looked an awful lot like a white woman. Now I have to ask myself what any decent white woman would be doing out here with the likes of a breed like you, and you know what I came up with for an answer?"

"It should be that she's with Caleb's mail-order bride, and only came by today to do some work inside the house for me." God how he hated answering to this man—or any man who set himself above another solely on the basis of skin color. Gritting his teeth, Hawke set a new course for the conversation. "In fact I've got to get the lady back to Three Elk pretty quick. What's your business here?"

"Work, huh." Braddock wasn't going to let go of the former topic so quickly. "What part of the house she working in, breed?"

Still pinning Hawke with that one judgmental eye, Braddock began to laugh, his girth rippling in time with his jowls. Hawke clenched his teeth, fighting a tremendous urge to fit his hands around his uncle's throat and squeeze until he could squeeze no more. He could hardly stomach the fact that he shared blood with such a man, much less believe that his gentle mother had been raised in the same household, but if not for thoughts of her, Hawke might actually have throttled him just to make certain he'd never have to do business with him again.

Reasonably certain he had his temper in check, he tried once again to shut the man up. "You're lucky you brought an army escort with you, Braddock." Hawke's uncle took a backward step, alarm lighting his muddy yellow eyes. Pleased to see such a cowardly reaction to the vague threat, he went on. "I'm not in much of a mood to put up with any of your shit today, so why don't you tell me what brought you out here, and save the rest for someone who appreciates it."

Taking another backward step, Braddock scowled from beneath his bushy brows, then cocked a thumb over his shoulder. "You're the one ought to be grateful that I brought these fellahs with me. These two gentlemen have come up from Ft. Sanders to have a look at your stock. I told them you've got yourself a breed of horses out here that'll run circles around the Indian ponies they're having so much trouble catching. If they like what they see, they'll pay top dollar for your entire crop of three-year-olds."

Almost thirty head! Hawke thought to himself, containing his excitement. Glancing beyond his uncle to where the officers still sat atop their horses, he allowed a tight smile as he said, "Those horses are scattered around the north pasture. We'll have to ride out to take a look at them. Mount up. I'll be right with you." Then he climbed through the fence and whistled for his favorite sorrel.

During the hours Hawke and his visitors were riding the fences and selecting stock, Lacey fluttered about the house trying to get it in order for his return. She'd watched him through the window after she'd run away, and observed his stance during his discussion with the man in the tan coat. He looked angry, certainly upset enough to give her the idea that he might not be in the best of moods when he came through the door later.

She decided to fix up the house for him, mainly in hopes that it would brighten his mood, but also because working kept Lacey's mind off the terrible indiscretion she'd allowed out by the corral. Cloistered as she had been for most of her life, she knew little enough about animals and their habits, and nothing of courtship, marriage, or men. She'd expected that Hawke might want to kiss her after they were wed—although for the life of her, she couldn't remember where she'd gotten such a notion—and even found herself day-dreaming about what it would be like to experience such a kiss with her mercurial host. But *never* in all her wildest dreams had she imagined that he would do something so shocking as put his tongue in her mouth! Not that she hadn't liked it, or found it a wee bit . . . exciting. But what were the consequences of such a kiss?

As she worked, Lacey imagined all sorts of repercussions from the sinful kiss, up to and including the possibility that she might be with child. The thought filled her with a terrible dread, even though she was sure there must be more to the creation of life than that, and she could hardly function once the idea occurred to her. Somehow, she kept going, and by Hawke's return at mid-afternoon, his mood was as she'd suspected, even blacker than the rapidly darkening skies. Lacey's wasn't a whole lot brighter.

Still, the moment Hawke stepped into his house, she began to flutter all about him, pointing out all the little things she'd done in his absence to make the place look more comfortable without making it look too frilly or feminine. She'd washed all the windows, thereby letting more light into the drab interior, picked a basketful of wildflowers then arranged them in fruit jars to grace both the kitchen and reading tables, and even freshened the air with a few sprigs of mint she'd found in his garden. All to no avail.

"Thanks for cleaning the place up," Hawke muttered

when she finished showing him what she'd done. "If you'll excuse me . . . " He started for the small room below his second-story bedroom which served as an office. "I've got a lot of work to do now, and I'd appreciate it if you wouldn't disturb me."

"Would you like me to put the kettle on—" Interrupting herself as she remembered that America was a barbaric land where as far as she knew, tea could not be found, she amended her offer. "I could warm the pot of coffee, if you like."

Thoroughly consumed by his uncle's final words— *You've got enough decent horse flesh here to pay your rent for the next year, but you've got a long ways to go before you'll see the deed to this place in your hand*— Hawke absently muttered, "Suit yourself, but don't bother me." Then he disappeared into his office and slammed the door behind him.

After that, Hawke pored over his books, adding and subtracting figures until he was bleary-eyed, but each time, the totals came out the same. By his calculations, Winterhawke was free and clear, but by Braddock's, the sum fell mysteriously short. Not that crying foul would do him any good. He couldn't even dispute his uncle's figures since their contract was verbal, not written, which was the only way, Braddock had insisted, that any banker could make a loan to a half-breed. Hawke knew he'd been a fool to agree to those terms, but he'd trusted this uncle of his to be fair with him. Hah! Fair. Now he had no choice but to wait until next spring to lay legal claim to the land he'd come to think of as his. Even though he'd been put off again, Hawke vowed that this was the last time—the *last time*, by God—that William Braddock and his bank were going to keep him from owning what was rightfully his.

Disgusted and angry, he slammed the ledger shut and

marched out of his office. The first thing he saw when he walked into the living room, was Lacey sitting in his brown tweed chair. Christ! He'd forgotten all about her. "I'd better be getting you back to Caleb's now. You ready to go?"

As he waited for her get up and come to him, Hawke glanced out the window and noticed how dark it had gotten, even though his internal clock told him it couldn't be terribly late in the day. A bright spear of lightning shot across the sky then, and moments later, a tremendous clap of thunder rolled through the valley, shaking the timbers supporting the roof. Shortly after that, the first heavy splatters of rain began to pound the shingles.

"Oh, *Christ*," he muttered as Lacey crossed the room to where he stood. "Just what we need. A big storm."

She paused in front of him, listening to the drops pummeling the roof. "It sounds as if it be raining hard enough to knock the top off your head! Are the storms in these parts always so grand and noisy?"

"Always," he said, resigned to their fate. "Trouble is, they also make a muddy bog out of the road between here and Three Elk, making it much too dangerous to drive a wagon across. I should have paid more attention to what was happening with the weather, but I didn't, and now . . . " He sighed heavily. "I'm afraid you're going to have to stay the night."

"Oh! But I can not stay here with you, not alone and . . ." Lacey's cheeks bloomed with a full riot of color, and she couldn't go on.

Hawke assumed that she was thinking back to the kiss they'd shared, and was probably worried that he might try to jump her sometime during the night. Hell, he could hardly blame her. He had been idiot enough to forget he was a half-breed, and had indulged himself with a taste of forbidden fruit. Of course once his uncle came along to remind him in no uncertain terms exactly what he was and where he stood in polite society, he'd seen things a little clearer again—clear enough to know that he'd been a fool to even daydream about keeping Lacey around.

"Don't worry," he said, trying to sound apologetic. "I promise you won't be disturbed in any way tonight."

"Oh, but . . . " She thought of Kate wringing her hands with worry. "I do not think that I should stay here."

"If staying troubles you so much," he snapped, his foul mood suddenly intensified, "then walk. You know the way to Caleb's place by now. I've got horses to take care of before this storm gets any worse." Sure the argument had been settled, and that she'd be staying the night, Hawke grabbed his hat and coat, then slammed out the door.

Shivering in time with the reverberating door, Lacey rubbed her arms, even though her tremors were not caused by the cold. Hawke was in a mood again, probably upset because he felt he had to play host for the night, and see to her comfort. That would certainly cause him a great inconvenience and involve the preparation of an extra meal or two, and even . . .

God in heaven! Wouldn't the man naturally expect her, Kathleen Lacey O'Carroll to fix the meals—a complete start-to-finish supper followed by a little something later in the evening? Well, she couldn't do it! Nothing past pre-prepared breakfasts and noontime sandwiches! Worried sick at the thought, Lacey could almost feel herself slipping toward the quiet comfort of her innerself, but she fought against the sensation, forcing herself instead to make a fast, rational decision.

If she stayed, it would mean putting Hawke out and irritating him even more than he was already irritated. It would also cause Kate to spend the night pacing the floor with worry over her. And last but not least, Hawke would demand that she perform several chores she simply was not capable of performing yet—namely, cooking.

She could not stay the night, no matter what. The only correct—the sane—thing for her to do was move on. Proud of the first big decision she'd had to make in her "outside" life, Lacey quickly removed her spurs so she wouldn't stain them with mud, and hid them in an empty crockery container at the back of the pantry.

Then, after slipping into her cloak and pulling the hood up over her head, a less confident Lacey walked through the door and started down the road toward Three Elk Ranch.

8

A woman is more obstinate than a mule—a mule than the devil.

—A common Irish saying

"Lacey!" Hawke called, just over a quarter of a mile down the road leading away from Winterhawke. His voice hoarse from shouting above the pouring rain, after another peel of thunder rent the valley, he called again. "Lacey, if you're out there, answer me!"

He stood still for a long moment, straining to hear her sweet lilting tones, but only the relentless tattoo of heavy raindrops battering his hat and slicker met his ears. He could hardly believe she'd been foolish enough to try and navigate this muddy, rock-strewn road in a blinding thunderstorm, but where else could she have gone? He'd searched the ranch high and low, and even questioned Crowfoot about her, but the boy swore he hadn't seen Lacey since she'd visited Phantom's corral—which also meant that the kid had probably witnessed their embrace.

Adding fuel to that theory, the moment after he'd given his meager information, Crowfoot scowled, then bolted up to the loft to burrow himself into his hiding place amongst the straw. There he would stay, silent and uncommunicative, until he was damn good and ready to talk again. Either that, or he'd disappear into the forests for a few weeks—or even months.

But Hawke couldn't worry about the kid or his fragile link to humankind now. Not with Lacey stumbling around in the mud somewhere and nightfall fast approaching. He cursed himself for going after her on foot instead of taking Hammerhead, the mule. He should have ridden him or one of the more sure-footed range horses for the view advantage, but he'd never been one to risk an animal unless absolutely unavoidable.

A vicious bolt of lightning shot down from the sky then, splitting the thick trunk of a nearby pine with an ear-shattering crack. A large section of the tree fell across the road, but instead of making him more cautious, Hawke deemed this search as one of those "unavoidable" risks. He'd just decided to turn back and start over again on horseback, but took one more long look down the road for good measure. Still nothing.

At the last second as he began to turn around, Hawke thought he saw a flash of white up ahead. Trudging through the thick, gooey mud, he saw it again. Something white flapping near the base of a lodgepole pine. At first he thought it was an injured bird or animal, but as he neared the tree, he realized the white streak was one of Lacey's arms—and that it was wrapped around the trunk of the tree she was trying to climb!

"Lacey—thank God!"

Obviously startled by his approach, she screamed, then lost her grip on the bark and slid down to the base of the tree.

Reaching her, Hawke pulled Lacey into his arms and half-carried her a good distance away from the lodgepole, berating her all the way. "Under a tree is the last place you should be standing during a lighting storm! Are you trying to get yourself killed?"

She blinked the rain out of her eyes—or maybe it was teardrops. "Oh, Hawke, 'tis you, an angel o' the Lord come to save me!"

Holding her in his embrace, he could feel Lacey's body trembling with both fear and cold. Christ, but she felt fragile in his arms, like a quivering frightened little sparrow. She nestled herself against his chest, prompting him to hold her tighter, and as she burrowed her head beneath his chin, Hawke became gripped by the damnedest urge to kiss her—not the way he had by the corral, but to lavish her forehead, her cheeks, and even her eyes with a thousand kisses. Nothing wrong or suggestive in that, he tried to convince himself. He was, after all, responsible for Lacey's safety as long as she was a guest in his home—he had to comfort her somehow, didn't he? That rationalization almost worked until Hawke looked into her golden blue eyes and realized that should he offer such a gesture, it might carry more significance than simple comfort to her—to them both.

Struggling against his own conflicting emotions, Hawke set Lacey away from him. "There's nothing to be afraid of now," he muttered in a hoarse whisper. "You're safe."

"Oh, b-but I w-was so s-scared," she said through a sob. "A-afraid to go on, a-afraid to go b-back. I d-did not know the road would be so d-difficult, or that I could not see w-where I was g-going."

"I told you the road was too dangerous to use in stormy weather. That's why I made the decision for you to stay the night at Winterhawke." As he spoke, Hawke tried to keep his tone from sounding to harsh or judgmental, but he couldn't keep the gruffness out of his voice as he asked, "What in God's name made you take off like that?"

She blinked up at him, wiping both rain and teardrops

from her eyes. "Why, y-you, of course. You said I c-could w-walk to C-Caleb's, if I like."

"Christ, I didn't mean it literal when I told you to walk to Three Elk. I didn't think you'd actually give it a try." A violent shiver racked her body just then, reminding him that she was soaked clear through to the skin. "Come on," he said, tucking her inside his slicker with him. He glanced up just as another lighting strike flashed across the somber gray skies. "It doesn't matter why you're out here now. We've got to get you back to the house before you catch your death of cold."

Lacey balked. "B-but I have to g-get to C-Caleb's."

"Damn it all, woman—isn't getting lost in the storm fright enough for you?" How could she still be so afraid of him or so intent on following through on this fool mission after what she'd been through? "I'm telling you for the last time that you can't go to Three Elk tonight. Standing out in the open during a thunderstorm and the chill you've taken are much bigger threats to your safety than I am, now let's go."

Still she balked. "B-but I just can not do this to Kate! She will be t-terribly worried about me. I m-must g-get to her."

"Why in *hell* can't you—" Hawke chopped his own sentence in half as he finally realized what she was trying to tell him. "Is worrying *Kate* the reason you didn't want to stay over at Winterhawke?"

Her teeth chattering, she nodded briskly.

"Oh, Christ, Lacey. I—I'm—" Hell, he couldn't even say he was sorry without explaining why. If he did, she would see him for the complete idiot that he was. Maybe Caleb had been right about his needing someone else in his life. Even to himself, it was beginning to look like Hawke *had* been the center of his own universe for much too long.

"Caleb knows I wouldn't be fool enough to try to bring you down this road in the rain," he said, reassuring her. Noticing how badly she was shaking, he scooped an unprotesting Lacey into his arms and began walking toward Winterhawke. "If I didn't show up with you shortly before it started raining, then he knows I'm not coming at all. He'll convince Kate that you're fine."

"Y-you're so very sure of this?"

"Sure enough to bet next year's foals on it." The hood of Lacey's cloak had grown so heavy with water, she'd been forced to peel it back, exposing her hair to the elements. As usual, it'd come loose from its bun, and now hung in wet spirals across her shoulders and face. Christ, but this woman had a way of burrowing into that soft spot of his, of making him feel things for her he had no right to feel. The sooner he got her off of his ranch and out of his life, the better off he would be, that was for sure.

Trying to ignore the way those drenched russet curls framed her enchanting eyes, Hawke muttered in a suddenly tight throat, "Press your head up tight against my chest and try to dodge the rain as best you can. We'll be back at the house in no time."

All too happy to share his warmth, Lacey snuggled up close beneath Hawke's chin, tucked her head against his buckskin shirt, and allowed his very strong and, as it turned out, extremely capable arms to carry her back to his ranch. She thought she'd warmed up pretty good too until he walked through the door of his home and set her on her feet in front of the fireplace. Once she was standing again, and without his protective embrace, Lacey began to shiver even more violently than before. Hawke left her standing there with instructions to stay put, then disappeared up the flight of stairs leading to his bedroom. When he returned a few minutes later, he was carrying a thick woolen blanket and a small bundle of clothing.

"These aren't very fashionable, but they'll keep you warm," he said, dropping the items on the couch. "Strip yourself and dry off the best you can with this blanket. After you're dressed, you can hang your wet things in the kitchen near the stove."

Lacey glanced around the large room, wondering how she'd be gaining her privacy, but before she could voice her concerns, he put her mind at ease.

"I'll just stoke the fire, then you'll have the house to yourself for at least several minutes. I've got to go out to the barn to check on the horses. Is there anything else you need before I go?"

Shivering too hard to speak clearly, Lacey just shook her head. After he'd added a couple of logs to the fire, Hawke left the house by the back door, but just to ensure her modesty, Lacey made a crude tent of the blanket, shielding her from the big bay window and anyone who might just "happen" by. Then she quickly stripped and dried her freezing body, careful not to get too close to the roaring fire, and donned the clothes he'd left.

By the time Hawke returned to the house, Lacey was dressed in a huge pair of dull red woolen drawers with matching long-sleeved shirt, a pair of rawhide leggings so big, they covered her legs beyond mid-thigh, almost to her crotch, and over all that, a buckskin shirt which hung well below her knees. Glancing down at herself, she decided that by anyone's standards, she was modestly, if bizarrely, dressed to receive visitors.

She'd just gone into the kitchen and finished hanging her clothes on the pair of chairs, when Hawke came through the back door. He paused, looking her up and down, and finally entered the room. His silvery green eyes were guarded, but Lacey thought she saw at least a flash of amusement in them.

Giving him a shy smile, she said, "Do you suppose

dear Kate will be jealous of my new wardrobe should she see me in this?"

"Definitely." His voice was still gruff, but he almost smiled as he spoke. Almost. "I hope you're warm enough in them."

"Oh, aye. I do not feel the least bit of a chill now."

His gaze drifted to the chair where she'd placed the damp pair of boots Crowfoot had given her. His eyes narrowed for an instant, but instead of making mention of the footgear, he turned to the stove and began to rub his hands together, warming them. "Suddenly, I'm near to starving. Aren't you?"

She almost said yes, right along with the rumble in her empty stomach, but then Lacey realized that if she admitted her hunger, he'd probably ask her to cook their supper—one of the very reasons she'd braved the storm! Realizing that she was almost as tired as she was hungry, she used her exhaustion as a way to excuse herself for the rest of the night.

"I thank you for your concern, but I could not eat a bite. All I am is very, very weary. Would you mind showing me where I might lie down?"

Without a moment's hesitation, or even the suggestion that she ought to put supper on before taking her nap, Hawke showed Lacey upstairs to his room for the night. She tried to decline his generous offer, but he insisted this was the warmest and most private place in the house, and that he wouldn't be using it anyway since he wanted to stay in the barn to keep an eye on Queenie, who'd yet to foal. Suddenly too tired to argue beyond that, Lacey allowed him to make a small fire in the lovely brick and mortar fireplace built into a corner of the room. Once he left, however, she climbed beneath the huge quilt and pile of blankets which made up Hawke's bed, and fell asleep the instant her head touched his soft down pillow.

When she awoke some time later, Lacey realized that at least several hours had passed. She stretched, luxuriating in the soft warmth of Hawke's bed, then inhaled the strong, clean woodsy bouquet of the man himself along with the faint aroma of horses. His scent was all around her, saturating his pillow, the bedclothes, and most of all, her senses. Startled by her reaction to the smell, a kind of restless yearning which started deep in her belly, she tore back the covers and swung her legs over the edge of bed.

Disoriented and a little groggy, Lacey glanced around, noticing that the lamp had been lit and that a bowl of stew and glass of milk were sitting on the bedside table. When had Hawke come to check on her? And why hadn't she awakened? Taking a look around the room to ensure her sense of privacy, she saw that it, like the rest of the house, was sparsely equipped. The comfortable bed, night table, and a small dresser were the only furnishings other than a rocking chair sitting to the side of the fireplace. Suddenly eager for the warmth of flames which looked as if they'd been recently stoked, she got up and worked her way a little closer to the hearth.

Except for the accident in the broom closet back at St. Josephine's, Lacey hadn't been this close to fire of any kind since "the incident" so many years ago. Staring into the flames with a stupor-like gaze, she thought back to the past—what she could remember of it anyway, then glanced down at the scar on the palm of her right hand. Oh, how she wished she could remember even one moment of the night when she'd burned herself—the very same night the lives of both her mother and father were lost. But that part of her life was still as blank as the walls in Hawke's home. Nothing came to her. Not even the images of the man and woman who'd brought her into the world. Lacey only knew that she was somehow responsible for the fire, and therefore directly to blame for her parents' fate: And that somewhere in the dark recesses of her mind, she held the key to the mysteries surrounding that tragic night.

Unable to stare into those flames any longer, Lacey moved over to the large bay window, a match to the one in the living room downstairs. Like the glass panes below, there were no window dressings to shut out the night or the cold, or to give the room a much needed touch of warmth. Feeling a slight chill, Lacey stayed her post a moment longer, imagining the breathtaking view of the valley and the distant range of mountains this vantage point would offer by daylight. On this moonless night, all she could make out were a few dark treetops and the vague outline of the barn.

Was Hawke out there sleeping? she wondered. And what of Crowfoot, the young Indian boy? Were the two related somehow? Brothers perhaps, or even . . . father and son? The idea disturbed Lacey almost as much as the thought of that young child staying out in the barn by himself. She hoped that he was allowed in the house, and only hid out in the barn when visitors came to the ranch, but something inside told her that was not the case.

Shivering a little, Lacey hugged herself around the middle, swaying to and fro as she stared out at the night, and wondered exactly where and how the little boy fit in at Winterhawke.

While Lacey was trying to figure out the relationship between the two, Hawke and Crowfoot were just settling themselves in the straw piled high in the loft. Queenie, a three-year old bay and first-time mother, still showed no signs of foaling, even though by Hawke's calculations, she should have dropped her colt by now. Very concerned about the animal, he propped his back against the wall near the open doors of the loft, and glanced outside. The skies were remarkably clear now that the storm had let up. As his gaze moved across the yard, he thought he noticed a blur across the way, and upon closer inspection, spotted Lacey's shadow as she moved about in his bedroom.

He'd left her a nice hot bowl of stew not fifteen minutes ago, but from the look of her then, he'd been sure it would be cold by the time she awakened from her deep sleep. Apparently he hadn't been as quiet as he thought. Lacey was not only awake but pacing the room as if deep in thought. She walked in front of the window then, pausing to stare up at the profusion of stars. The gentle glow of the fire and dim lighting from the lamp framed her along with the A-shaped pitch of the roof, making her look ethereal, like an angel captured on canvas despite the ill-fitting clothes she wore. Lacey's bounty of coppery curls were everywhere as usual, falling down along her shoulders, caressing her face, and he assumed, spilling down her back—a goddess by any man's standards. How did the woman manage to look so fetching in a costume that made him look rougher than a corncob pipe?

"She . . . pretty lady."

Caught up in watching Lacey, Hawke had forgotten he wasn't alone. When he heard that young, hesitant voice, he nearly yelped with surprise. Taking a deep breath as he looked away from the window, Hawke glanced at the kid and realized the boy had been staring at Lacey right along with him. He smiled indulgently as he said, "Yes, she's a mighty pretty lady, indeed."

Never taking his onyx eyes from the window, Crowfoot slowly nodded his agreement.

The boy didn't seem to be as upset by Lacey's presence

as Hawke had assumed he'd be. He doubted Crowfoot would remain so calm if he knew Lacey had been bold enough to disturb his possessions. "Did you know that pretty lady helped herself to a pair of your old boots?"

He shrugged indifferently. "I give to lady. Her shoes no good for work. No good for nothing."

"You *gave?*" This was entirely out of character for the boy. Crowfoot had a possessive streak of almost maniacal proportions, one that made him protective of even a tiniest scrap of paper should he count it among his belongings. "What do you mean, gave? Have you even met or talked to her?"

"One time, yes." Flashing a grin which appeared even more rarely than Hawke's, Crowfoot twisted his index finger around the middle finger and held them up. "Horses like lady, and I do, too. We friends. You keep her."

"Keep . . . ?" So that was it. Somehow, Lacey had managed to enlist the kid as an ally. "Well just forget about it, Crowfoot. Tomorrow Miss O'Carroll goes back to Three Elk Ranch, and there is where she'll stay. Understand? I can't keep her here anymore."

The boy hissed in return, an angry sound accompanied by a look of ferocity; Hawke hadn't seen anything close to that kind of hostility from Crowfoot since the day he and Caleb first tried to befriend him. It was enough to give Hawke pause, but he held his ground. The kid obviously didn't know what they would be subjecting Lacey to should she stay at Winterhawke—the scorn of their neighbors and townsfolk for sure—or how much she'd disrupt their lives.

His tone more resolute, Hawke said, "That woman is leaving tomorrow, and nothing is going to change my mind about it."

*   *   *

The next morning when Lacey awakened, she found her clothes neatly folded and set right outside the bedroom door. After dressing herself, she finger-combed her hair, then made her way down to the kitchen where Hawke was busy brewing up a pot of coffee.

"Top o' the morning to you," she said cheerfully. "I'm hoping you slept well in a bed not your own?"

"Yes," he said, pleasantly. "I slept just fine. Thanks for asking."

"I passed a very peaceful night, too. Thank you again for the use of your nice soft bed. I do not think I can ever repay you for all you did on my behalf last night." Blushing as she recalled the way he'd lifted her into his arms and carried her all the way back to the ranch, Lacey abruptly changed the subject. "And what of your mare? Has her babe made its way into the world yet?"

"Not yet, but I was just on my way out to check on her again." He poured himself a cup of coffee, then turned to her, catching her in the midst of trying to smooth her wild curls. Sliding the thong out of his own hair, he offered it. "Take this. I'll get another in the barn."

As Lacey accepted the thong, Hawke's fingers skimmed the back of her hand. His touch against her skin was like kindling to the flame, and Lacey marveled to think that such a wee bit of contact could make the impression it did on her. Her tummy ached with a foreign kind of hunger, not the sharp demands of the body's need for food, but with a dull relentless throbbing, insisting that she fill this aching void with every bit the same urgency as the other, as if both needs were crucial to survival.

Shocked to recognize such sensations from inside her own body, but not chagrined enough to look away from Hawke, Lacey studied him from behind as he strolled over to the kitchen table and picked up a tin filled with apples. As he walked, his dark wavy hair swung freely around his shoulders, showing her how truly long he'd let it grow. She would have expected a man with such a mane to look at least a little feminine to her eyes, but on Hawke, the affect was startlingly the exact opposite. Between his free-flowing hair and the close-fitting jeans and work shirt he wore in place of his buckskins today, John Winterhawke, Jr. was truly a feast for the eyes. By the cross of Christ! Lacey thought to herself, grabbing the counter to support her suddenly wobbly knees. The man looked even more virile and dangerous this way than before, a wild Indian and a mountain man all rolled into one irresistible package of muscle and brawn.

Unaware of her perusal, Hawke turned toward Lacey, showing off the fruit. "I went down to the root cellar first thing this morning and brought up what's left of last year's apples. They still look pretty good, don't you think?"

Gulping hard, thinking that *he* looked a whale of a lot better to her than anything she'd ever seen, Lacey forced herself to glance down at the pan's contents. "Oh, aye, they are a sight to behold, all right!" How come her voice sounded so breathless, she wondered, and why did she suddenly feel so . . . warm?

Hawke carried the tin to the sink where Lacey stood. "I hope there's enough here for you."

"For me?" Her throat tight, she tried to laugh, but it came out sounding more like a cough. What the devil was wrong with her? "I-I can not eat so many apples. I would be sick a month of Junes, if I did."

"You don't have to eat them," he said, setting the tin in the sink. "I'd be happy if you'd just bake them into a pie. In fact," he added, reaching for his hat, "if you do that, you won't have to do another thing around here today. Not even clean up the mess."

"Oh! Oh, b-but—" Lacey tried to think of something,

anything to help get her through this one, but nothing she could think of—not even the lucky spurs—could help. She'd watched Kate closely enough to know that she could never fake her way through the making of a piecrust, much less the filling. Worse, she couldn't even think of a way to talk her way out of it.

"Lacey?" Hawke reached over and touched the back of his hand to her brow. "You've gone all white. You're not going to faint are you?"

Gulping, this time over her own inadequacies, she finally raised her chin and looked him directly in the eye. "No, but you might be so inclined once you find out I've been feeding you up with false music."

"Music?" He raised thick chestnut eyebrow. "What in hell are you talking about?"

"Come, sit with me for a moment." She didn't even look to see if he followed. Lacey took the chair nearest the back door should she feel the urge to leap up and run away. After a very puzzled Hawke took the other, she laid both hands on the table, made a fist of the pair of them, and said, "I suppose 'tis better for you to know this one wee thing about me now than after we wed. I can not cook a lick."

"You . . . but what about the biscuits, the berry *pie?*"

"'Twas Kate's doings, all of it." Now that she'd admitted the one thing, the rest seemed almost easy. "Kate baked the biscuits the night before I was to come to Winterhawke, and I hid them in my basket. Same with the pie, but we didn't have to trouble ourselves by hiding it. I've ne'er tried to cook a thing in my life—well, except of course, for when I baked your buttermilk flapjacks."

The admission should have surprised Hawke, but he discovered that Lacey's revelations didn't shock him in the least. Hadn't he known there was something wrong with her from the start? "So you tricked me, and thought you could just keep on sneaking food over here from Three Elk indefinitely, is that it?"

"Oh, no! Kate is willing and working to teach me the ways of the kitchen. I've had lessons on how to make up your flapjacks and those fluffy biscuits you like, plus I even wrote down the recipes. I'm certain I can learn about pies and such, too, but maybe a little later."

"Uh, huh." He said it slowly, sarcastically. "Not that it matters to me, but what about sewing? Can you do that?"

Lacey hedged for just a moment, but then came clean there, too. "Not if you mean the actual construction of clothes, knitting, or quilting, but I can mend a button." At least, she *thought* she could. Then again, maybe not. "Truth is," she admitted with a sigh, "I can not sew either, but only because I've ne'er had the chance to learn. I'm willin . . . well, no." She took a deep breath. "Truth there is that I can not sew and I do not have the slightest inclination to want to learn how. But if you insist, I promise to give it a try."

Incredulous, Hawke pushed out of his chair and slowly circled her. Speaking behind Lacey's back, he said, "Let's see—you can't cook, can't sew, and seem to know nothing about keeping a man's home. Yes, ma'am! I'd say you fit all the requirements of a mail-order bride. What could I have been thinking of when I didn't jump at the chance to accept your proposal?"

Lacey twisted this way and that in her chair, trying to make eye contact with him, but he was always one step to the back of her. She threw her words in his general direction. "I-I know my lack of skills may seem a wee bit odd to you, but I meant—"

"Odd?" Hawke's voice was still coming from somewhere over her shoulder. "I demand more talents than you have in the horses I buy. Where were you raised, anyway—under a bush?"

Blushing violently, this time Lacey didn't seek his gaze. "Well, 'tis true that I do not come with the usual talents a man expects to find in a wife, but as I said before, I'm more than willing to learn."

"Servants, right? Isn't that it? You were raised in a house where servants did all the work so you never had to learn to do a thing."

That was close enough to the truth. Too close, in fact. Lacey nodded, but still kept her gaze averted.

"Just as I thought." Hawke was standing directly beside her now. "Maybe you figured a spoiled aristocrat could learn to cook, but what did you plan on doing about clothes? Even if I'd decided to keep you on—which I definitely haven't—I couldn't afford to buy you dresses in town. At least, not for a good long while, anyway."

"Oh, but those I have will do me fine." She finally glanced up at Hawke, beseeching him with her gaze. "They'll do for a good long while. I have two new white blouses and navy skirts—uniforms from the hospital." And they were that. They just didn't happen to be nursing uniforms.

"A very impressive wardrobe, I'm sure." Which didn't make a hell of a lot of sense to Hawke since he figured she was some kind of royalty who'd run away from home. Not that it mattered to him who she was or what she was running from. What mattered was that she'd tried to trick him—that and the fact that he had a mare to check. "Will you excuse me, please? I've got to get out to the barn and see how Queenie's doing. I'll be back shortly, and expect you to have your things ready by then. I'm taking you back to Three Elk just as soon as I get the horses hitched."

"Oh, well . . . of course."

He stomped out of the kitchen and into the living room. As soon as she was sure he couldn't hear her,

Lacey snuck along behind Hawke and watched his progress from the kitchen door. After he crossed the room to the peg where his jacket hung, he reached inside the garment to the inner pocket and withdrew his horrid little ledger. After spending several moments jotting something inside it, he returned the thing to his jacket, then continued on out the front door.

Lacey, understandably distressed over having to admit her shortcomings to the man she was supposed to be impressing, wasn't about to admit defeat just yet. After retrieving her spurs from the canister along with the confidence they gave her, she donned them and marched fearlessly into the living room. Then, taking the ledger from Hawke's jacket, she settled into the chair near the fireplace and opened the book to the page marked *Lacey O'Carroll.* First she read the *Disadvantages* column:

1. Slothful—How dare he suggest such a thing after getting her up before dawn each day!

2. Messy—The grandest of lies! This man's home was never so clean as it'd been under her care!

3. Incompetent farm hand—"Apprentice" farm hand, maybe, but eager to learn.

4. Too weak and frail to be a ranch wife—Maybe, she wasn't sure but she figured she deserved credit for being strong at heart.

5. Believes in fairies—Doesn't everyone?

6. Lousy cook—He had her there—but only temporarily.

7. Bed partner—This notation stumped Lacey. She'd get to the bottom of what he meant by that later.

8. Too damn nosy—What had she done to elicit this—other than what she was doing now?

9. Can't sew—Another area in which she could make no argument.

10. Lies/can't be trusted.

Crestfallen over number ten, for she couldn't even fake a fit of anger over the truth in that disadvantage, Lacey sighed and glanced to the right-hand side of the ledger. There under the *Advantages* column she found only three notations:

1. Good with horses—Her mood brightened considerably.

2. Makes good pie—That would have brightened her mood had he not drawn a thick, black line through it, voiding the entry.

3. Bed partner—Now she was more confused than when it had been in the disadvantage column—and how could one attribute be listed in both places, anyway?

"Humm," Lacey murmured to herself as she thought about what she'd learned. Tapping a fingernail against the little book, she was sorely tempted to toss the thing into the fireplace, but she decided to consider other options first. The score as she read it, was ten to two, a lack of eight pluses on the advantage side of the ledger. How could she make up that number, or even exceed it in the little time she had left to win Hawke over?

It occurred to her that she might as well list a few of her qualities now, and worry about proving them to the man later. What could such a plan harm at this juncture? Hawke had already made note of the fact that she was nosy and not to be trusted. Pleased with her rationalization, Lacey lifted the pencil from its little slot, moistened the tip, and got busy balancing the scale in her favor. Adding a new entry in place of the one that had been scratched out, she started with the obvious.

2. Resourceful.

9

Marriage is popular because it combines the maximum
of temptation with the maximum of opportunity.
—George Bernard Shaw

The circuit preacher had shown up a little
earlier than expected, but Hawke thought it fitting in a
perverse sort of way, that the man would be waiting at
Caleb's when he and Lacey drove up to Three Elk that
afternoon. That's how he looked at it anyway when the
small black carriage and single horse tied to the hitching post did indeed turn out to belong to one Reverend
Bob. Except for his white collar, the man was dressed in
black from his flat-brimmed hat to his polished boots—
an eerie twin to the imaginary hangman Hawke had felt
chasing him ever since he'd first laid eyes on Miss Lacey
O'Carroll. At the sight of the clergyman, it was all he
could do not to bolt and run back out the door.

But Hawke didn't go meekly into the fray, mind you.
He barreled his way into Caleb's home with Lacey hot on
his heels, she intent on soliciting the council of her
friend, Kate, he determined to get himself out of this
predicament once and for all. The Irishwomen hugged

and greeted one another, laughing and talking in their strange Gaelic brogues, but once Hawke got over the shock of meeting "the angel of death" in the guise of Reverend Bob, he got right down to business with Caleb.

". . . and nothing you say is going to change my mind."

"Hold your horses a minute, friend!" Caleb was lounging as usual on the couch in the front room. Righting himself, he propped his splinted leg up high on a milk stool. "What's all this about ledgers and lists? I thought we was discussing matrimony, not horse-trading."

"They're one and the same, as far as I'm concerned." Hawke dropped his ledger into Caleb's lap, then lowered his voice to a low roar. "Go ahead, flip it open to the page with her name on it and you'll see what I mean. She's just not proper wife material, and all the good intentions in the world aren't going make her that way. I thank you for the trouble you went to on my behalf, but we're just going to have to send Miss O'Carroll back where she came from."

His bushy gray brows bunched in contemplation, Caleb finally found the page with Lacey's name at the top, and began reading the columns, his lips silently mouthing each as he came to it.

As he waited for his friend to digest the entire list, Hawke embellished his complaints against the comely Irishwoman. "The way I have it figured, Miss O'Carroll comes from blue-blooded stock or something like that. For all we know, she might even be a runaway princess or whatever it is they call their royalty in Ireland."

Listening to his friend with one ear as he continued to read the ledger, Caleb said, "That don't make no sense. What would a princess be doing in Wyoming Territory of all places, and as a mail-order bride of all things? That don't make no sense a'tall."

"Hell, I don't know. I also don't know why she's here or what she's really up to." Aware the women had finally disappeared into the back bedroom and that the preacher was resting on Caleb's hammock out back, Hawke raised his voice. "I only know that *something* is wrong with her, and not just that she can't cook or sew. Something we're both missing somewhere."

"Humph. Not according to this here ledger of yours, there ain't. Why you've even got that gal scored one point higher on her advantages!" Caleb raised a squinty-eyed gaze to his friend. "Just how high does a woman have to rate to be good enough in your book, son?"

"I don't know what you're talking about." Hawke stuck out his hand. "Let me see that book. You're probably on the wrong page." But even before Caleb dropped it into his palm, he could see Lacey's name clearly inscribed at the top of the page. Hardly able to believe what his eyes told him after he'd studied the ledger a minute, Hawke sank down to the hearth in complete, mind-numbing shock.

"I—I didn't write all of this." Hawke's tongue felt curiously heavy, as if whittled out of wood. The neatly printed block letters did look a lot like his own handwriting, but there was no way in hell that he'd written what he was seeing. "Someone's been messing with my ledger!"

"Now, Hawke, my boy," said Caleb in his most cajoling tone. "I don't know what you're up to, or why you're a writing one thing and saying another, but if you mean to—"

"It's the truth, Caleb. I swear it!" Desperate to prove that he hadn't lost his mind or his ethics, Hawke dragged his fingernail along the advantage column, then jabbed it against one of the entries. "Does this sound like something I'd write? *Knows all manner of charms, riddles, and prayers from memory.*" Searching further, he stopped at entry number seven. "Or this? *Even-tempered for a red-haired person of Irish extraction.*" Then up to the entry in place of 'makes good pies,' which Hawke himself had scratched out. "And I don't even know what *this* is supposed to mean—*resourceful.*"

Caleb was chuckling by now, his round little belly bouncing like the south end of a northbound ass. "I got to admit, them are some mighty strange reasons for wanting to keep the woman on. My guess is you're a wantin' to get hitched to her so bad, you just made that nonsensical stuff up."

Hawke let out an exasperated sigh. "You're not listening to me, Caleb—*I'm* not the one who put those remarks in the book. Apparently, Lacey did—who else would have written that last entry?" He was referring to number eleven, the advantage which tipped the scales in Lacey's favor and really got Hawke's goat. *"Probably the only female in all of Wyoming Territory willing to marry a hard-headed man like you."*

Caleb's chuckles evolved to out and out belly laughing, and until he calmed down, Hawke knew it was useless to continue the increasingly frustrating conversation.

In the back bedroom, Kate was all questions. "And he didna seem to mind that ye canna so much as boil cabbage?"

Lacey shrugged. "He did not say really, but I think I can learn cooking and such fast enough to suit him. I just do not think he means to give me the chance."

"Ye mean to say the man does not wish to marry ye?"

"It would seem so." Tears sprang into the corners of her eyes, and until that moment, she hadn't realized how much she wanted this marriage between herself and Hawke. "Oh, Nurse Kate—what am I to do?"

"Hush, lass, and dona be calling me nurse." She handed Lacey a handkerchief, waited a moment for her to dry her tears and wipe her nose, then went on to ask,

"If not for yer lack of cookin' and wifin' duties, then why do ye think he will not wed ye, lass?"

Sinking down on the mattress of what was soon to be Kate's marriage bed, Lacey bit her lip and fiddled with the pile on the chenille spread as she tried to think of a delicate way to address the subject. "I can not say for sure that this is the problem exactly, but . . . " Her cheeks grew hot, her throat closed, and her breathing began to get erratic. "I—it's just that I have some concerns about . . . Hawke, and what he might think he's allowed to do to . . . I mean as a husband, of course, but if I did not please him in that way and cannot do—"

"God save ye, lass! Ye were alone and defenseless with the man last night!" Kate fell to her knees before Lacey and took both of her hands in hers. "Are ye tryin' to tell me that divil of a man has already taken some liberties with yer person?"

She hadn't thought it possible, but Lacey's face grew even hotter. "He, well . . . I do not know what liberties you speak of, but Hawke did . . . " Try as she might, she simply couldn't find a way to tell the woman who'd practically raised her that Hawke had slipped his tongue inside her mouth. It all seemed so sordid now that she was actually trying to put words to the embarrassing thing she'd let him do—and God help her, to remember the uncivilized way it made her feel. "I—I can not say what we have done, for it shames me to think of it."

"Arrah." Kate's nostrils flared, and in her rage, her voice dropped to a deep guttural growl. "May that heathen's last dance be a hornpipe on the air, the scurvy cur! He'll be makin' things right with ye, or he'll be payin' the divil till doomsday if Katherine Quinlin has a say about it!"

With that, she leapt to her feet still holding Lacey's hands, and jerked her up off the mattress. "Come with me, lass. We'll be gettin' settled on this 'fore another minute runs round the clock."

And because if she listened and obeyed anyone, it was former Nurse Quinlin, Lacey allowed herself to be dragged into the front room of Caleb's home where he and Hawke were still deep in discussion.

"Mr. Weatherspoon!" said Kate as the women approached the back of the couch. She would go no further, certainly not around to the front of the couch where the devil in question sat resting his lecherous hide on the hearth. "Your good neighbor here has committed a terrible indiscretion against my dear sweet Miss O'Carroll, and I'm afraid I can not entertain the thought of pledging my troth to you until the matter is settled to our satisfaction. What does your dishonorable Mr. Winterhawke intend to do to make things right with Miss O'Carroll?"

Hawke slowly raised up off the bricks, his mouth a big round O. "What in blue blazes are you talking about?"

"Easy, Hawke," cautioned Caleb, who'd also gotten up from his couch. Leaning heavily against the single crutch he used to get around, he turned toward his lovely intended. "What's all this about dishonor, my dear?"

"'Tis about the scurvy cur standin' beside ye and the liberties he took with my innocent young lass here. I demand to know what ye intend to do about it!"

His gray head swiveled toward the fireplace. "Hawke? What in tarnation is she talking about?"

Both hands raised high above his shoulders, he shook his head. "I swear to Christ, I don't have the slightest idea."

Kate lunged forward, nearly toppling over the back of the couch. "A high hangin' to ye then, ye dirty liar!"

"*Liar?*" Hawke stepped forward, bringing his nose within a foot of the enraged Irishwoman. "If there's a liar in this room, it's that sweet innocent lass over there with the big blue eyes!"

Lacey drew up alongside Kate, her breast puffed with self-righteousness. "I *ne'er* lied to you."

"Excuse the living hell out of me," Hawke said, cocking his head in Lacey's direction. "But I call stealing a man's private ledger and filling it with . . . with *whoppers*, is the same thing as lying—worse!"

Kate pushed her arms between the two, then spread her hands, effectively separating the quarreling couple, even though the couch did a fair job of that anyway. "Ye see what I mean about yer friend, Mr. Weatherspoon? The man's a *bosthoon* and a *blatherskite,* among other things, a divil who deserves a good beatin' with an oak shillelagh, but if ye can extract his promise to make an honest woman of my innocent Miss O'Carroll, then we'll just naturally have to be forgivin' him, then."

"In a pig's eye!" said Hawke, furious over the names he'd been called even though he didn't know exactly what they meant. "I'll be damned if I'm going to be tricked, forced or *bullied* into doing anything I don't want to by a pair of lying, cheating—"

"How *dare* you!" Lacey stomped a spur against the floor to help her gain extra courage. "I will not stand here and watch you pointin' your finger and shoutin' names at my Miss Kate. She's only looking after my best interests—which is a lot more than I can say for the likes of you."

Kate tossed in her opinion, spearing Hawke with a purposefully beady eye. "And I'll just be addin' my amen to *that*, ye malarkey-spewin'—"

"Just a dad-burned minute, all of ya!" hollered Caleb. "If'n you don't all stop talking at oncet, we'll never git this figured out."

"A—*hem*!" came a deep baritone from the back door. "Is it always this difficult for your guests to get a little rest around here?"

All four of the principals turned toward the Reverend Bob, each of them coloring from pale pink to bright red.

"Ah, beggin' your pardon, Reverend," said Caleb, master of the house. "It seems we have a little disagreement 'twixt friends, is all. Sorry if'n we woke you."

"Aye," said Lacey. "'Tis my fault I think, for mentioning some things to—"

"Now, lass, dona be taking the blame for insults this miserable cur has set upon ye."

"That's it." Hawke hitched up his jeans. "I've had just about all the name calling I'm going to take from your big—"

"A—*hem!*" Reverend Bob's voice was even deeper, more authoritative than before. "It's clear to me that you folks have some grievances to work out, but I think the Lord, and the rest of us, will best be served if you split up to continue your discussion. What is at issue here?"

All four of them opened their mouths as if to speak, but Caleb shot each of the other three a vicious, warning glance. Then he proceeded to explain as best he could. "It seems these two youngens here are having a speck of trouble deciding if they want to get hitched or not."

"Then may I suggest that we let the youngens in question work it out between themselves—alone?"

Kate bristled. "I'll not be lettin' the lass out of my sight with that, that—"

"I assure you," said Hawke in the kindest voice he could manage, "your friend will be quite safe with me." He turned to the reverend. "You have my word on it."

The preacher clasped his hands together and nodded solemnly. "Then why don't the two of you go on outside now and have yourself a calming walk around the property. When you decide what you're gonna do, let us know." He pulled a pocket watch out of his vest pocket, checked the time, and added, "We've planned the nuptials around a wedding supper Miss Quinlin has been preparing for a better part of the day. I'd like to get the ceremony underway within the hour, if possible."

Feeling a lot like the hangman had just pronounced the hour of his death, Hawke stepped around Caleb and his crutch, gave Kate a wide berth, then extended his elbow and said to Lacey, "Shall we?"

Her nose still angled at a properly offended tilt, Lacey slipped her left hand into the crook of Hawke's arm and allowed him to escort her outside to the grounds of Three Elk Ranch. They walked in silence for several moments, passing by a corral filled with both cow ponies and cattle, then around to the back of Caleb's small barn. From there Hawke led her to a large fallen log near the bank of the Little Laramie River where he invited her to sit down.

"This," he said, settling in beside her, "is my favorite view from Caleb's ranch." He pointed west to the rising slopes leading to his ranch and the Snowy Range Mountains behind it. "Winterhawke ends just past that last stand of aspens."

Looking up at the majestic mountains surrounding Winterhawke, she sighed. "'Tis lovely and peaceful your ranch, a place even the angels might call home."

Done with ducking the issue, Hawke turned to Lacey and caught her chin with his index finger, forcing her to look into his eyes. "Exactly what are you looking for in a home, Irish miss? Now that you know a little more about what to expect, are you really so sure you want to marry someone like me?"

She hesitated only a moment. "Aye. If you're willing to have me, that is."

Those beautiful blue eyes didn't flicker with even the slightest hint of duplicity. Releasing her chin, Hawke slowly shook his head and returned his gaze to the mountains he loved so much. "I just can't understand why a good looking gal like you would even consider marrying someone like me. From where I'm sitting, it seems I'm the only one who stands to gain anything by the match."

"You truly think so?" She sounded surprised, even pleased. "And what gains might those be, sir?"

Looking back at her, Hawke couldn't keep the sarcastic smirk from his tone or off of his lips. "For starters, the kind your dear Miss Kate seems to think I already helped myself to. Where'd she get the idea that I've already, well . . . touched you in a way I shouldn't have?"

Her cheeks flushed to a deep crimson, Lacey quickly averted her gaze. "I—I swear by the cross o' Christ that I ne'er told Kate what you done to me at the corral."

"Maybe not that, but you must have told her something."

"I ne'er said a word! I tried, but could not bring myself to say what we, what you done when you . . . kissed me."

"That's *it?* This is all about that one little kiss?" Still blushing, Lacey gave him a little nod, then blinked her long coppery lashes at him and looked away. Groaning to himself, Hawke rolled his eyes. To think he and Caleb—all four of them—had practically come to blows over almost nothing! Lord, what if things had gone further? What if—

"Well, then?" Lacey asked. "What's it to be? Are ye thinking you might like to marry up with me?"

Hawke sighed. "I honestly don't know what to say. I still can't understand why you'd want to hitch yourself to the kind of man decent white women wouldn't even look at, much less marry. You could waltz into Laramie or anywhere tomorrow and have your pick of fine upstanding citizens. Why choose me?" *What's wrong with you?*

She gave a tiny shrug. "You're the neighbor needin' a mail-order bride according to Mr. Weatherspoon's letter, and you seem to be a nice enough sort—most often, that is."

"Most often, huh?" Hawke pulled off his hat and began to smooth the eagle feather which hung down from the brim. "Apparently you don't have Indians or prejudice against them in Ireland, but here I'm considered, well . . . folks in these parts look down on my sort. Understand what I mean?"

"I can not say that I do."

Sorry he'd ever brought the subject up, Hawke considered dropping it entirely. He knew in his heart what fine white citizens thought of him, and had known since he was a small child, but to try and explain that kind of rejection was not only difficult, but extremely personal. Yet he couldn't just ignore that very real issue should Lacey continue to insist that she wanted to marry him. Sooner or later she'd understand the whispers and feel the hatred most whites held for their Indian brothers and those low enough to befriend them. William Braddock's recent visit was enough to remind Hawke what would become of Miss Lacey O'Carroll should she be fool enough to toss her lot in with that of a half-breed.

So distasteful or not, Hawke laid it all out for her. "I've already told you what folks around here think of my kind. Any white woman who'd marry someone like me, a half-breed Arapaho Indian, is considered even lower. I can't ask you to live that way. You'd never be able to hold your head up in Laramie, or anywhere you might go."

"How terrible." Lacey was truly appalled, but undaunted. "'Tis true, we do not have Indians in Ireland, but the Irish are not without their prejudices." She paused briefly, thinking of how she'd have been regarded in her homeland had she stayed in County Tipperary after the hospital released her. Just by virtue of the fact that she'd lived there most of her life, she'd be considered a madwoman, even though she'd never actually been declared as such by the county. Seeing a small irony in their situations, she gave in to a fragile smile as she said, "The fact that you're an Indian means absolutely nothing to me, Mr. Winterhawke. As for the fine folks in town who have a problem with you, or with the wife of a half-breed, they mean even less to me."

Hawke studied her for a long moment, hardly daring to believe what his eyes and ears were telling him, but Christ, if she didn't mean it! There wasn't so much as a hint of hesitation or exaggeration in her voice, and the dogged outrage and determination he saw firing the coals of her pupils could not have been feigned. Was it really possible that this woman honestly had no prejudices or tolerance for those who did?

Feeling humbled, Hawke could do no less than be completely honest with her. "If the thought of being snubbed by the good ladies in Laramie doesn't bother you, then maybe this will; all I have to offer a wife is the ranch and the horses I breed. Frankly, the business takes up most all of my time and energy. I don't see how any woman could be happy stuck up on this mountain with no one for company but me and my horses. I'd think you'd be better off in town with someone your own kind. As I said before, a woman with your looks would have your pick of men."

Lacey didn't want that—not another man or life in a civilized American town. She'd grown to love the Medicine Bow Mountains, the animals that lived in them, Winterhawke Ranch, and in some ways, even the man. Most of all, she knew her lack of social polish and the little eccentricities that went along with that lack, would go unnoticed here in the wild. In town, she would be judged—and found inferior.

Squaring her shoulders, she turned and looked Hawke in the eye. "This is where I want to be, a place I know I can come to love as much as the homeland. As for being lonely, Kate won't be that far away if I feel the need for a visit." Losing a bit of that confidence, she put the final decision in Hawke's hands. "I know that you do not feel so convinced this marriage will work. If you've found something lacking in me, if you feel I will make you unhappy as a wife, tell me what I can do to make myself a better bargain. Perhaps I can change or learn how to—"

"No, Christ . . . no." Hawke flung his hat to the ground. "There's nothing wrong with you—nothing I know about anyway," he added, his voice heavy with meaning. "I'm just trying to warn you about life around here, and me, too, I suppose. I haven't been around many folks, especially white women, and . . . " Hell, how was he explain the fact that he didn't need or want anyone in his life, that he was an outcast and rather enjoyed the role? "I don't have a lot of social graces—and don't want to learn them, either."

Lacey muffled her laughter. "I—I don't exactly have many social graces myself. I was somewhat . . . *sheltered* as a child."

Which strengthened Hawke's suspicions that Lacey was from royalty or something like it, and yet oddly enough, here she was still offering herself to him in marriage as if they were on equal footing. Surely she was running a bluff of some kind.

Testing her, Hawke solemnly said, "If you're still set on going through with this wedding, then I guess we'd best go inside and get it over with."

"Oh, and I thank you kindly, I do." She fairly beamed with excitement. "I promise to be the best wife I know how, and that I'll learn to bake the pies you love so before our first year is done."

Had he just proposed marriage and had Lacey accepted? Hawke wondered, his hand—his entire body—feeling numb as he reached down and collected his hat. Surely by the time they stood before the preacher, common sense would catch up with her, and she'd have a change of mind. Surely that would come to pass.

Fumbling around for a few words that wouldn't get him into any more trouble, Hawke said, "I, ah, guess we'd better get back inside then."

She smiled, her radiant expression alive with a maidenly glow. "Aye, and I imagine they're more than ready to be starting the ceremony."

An unusually healthy blush turning his own cheeks redder than his paternal forbearers, Hawke got up from the log, pulled Lacey along with him, then started back for the house—and the man in black.

Once Lacey shared the good news, Three Elk Ranch became a flurry of activity. A stunned, unprotesting Hawke was swept into the fray, and even helped figure out the agenda for all involved. Due to the lateness of the hour and the wedding feast scheduled to begin after the ceremony, there was no choice but for Hawke, Lacey, and the Reverend Bob to plan on staying the night right where they were. The road between Winterhawke and Three Elk Ranches could be difficult enough to navigate during daylight hours, but at night, especially after the recent rain, it could have been downright dangerous. Not that staying over was a problem; Crowfoot was more than capable of taking care of the horses during Hawke's absence, at least for a couple of days, and since Queenie had foaled shortly before they left Winterhawke, nothing of any urgency was pressuring them to return that night.

As the women primped in the back bedroom, Hawke called Caleb aside and said, "By the way, old friend, do me a little favor before the ceremony starts."

"Want me to give you a haircut? You are getting a touch shaggy."

As much as he wished he was a little more presentable for such an auspicious occasion, Hawke wasn't about to go calling attention to himself by doing something so obvious as cutting his hair. The whole affair was embarrassing enough as it was—including the assumptions on Kate's part.

"My hair's just fine," he said gruffly. "I want you to go have a little talk with your dear bride-to-be. There seems to be a really big misunderstanding about what I did or didn't do to Miss O'Carroll yesterday. I believe Kate thinks that I—" Hawke glanced around the room, noticing that Reverend Bob was within earshot, then leaned in close and whispered the rest of the sentence into Caleb's ear.

"Get out of here!"

"That must be what she thinks—I didn't, of course. I just gave Lacey a little kiss out by the corral. Will you straighten your woman out so she doesn't dig a shotgun into my spine during the wedding?"

Caleb slapped his good leg and laughed. "Sure, son. She's as good as straight."

"Thanks—and while you're at it, see if you can't find out what's really wrong with Lacey." Then, figuring he might as well do what he could to protect the reputation of his bride-to-be for as long as he could, he approached the preacher, who was sitting on the couch thumbing through his bible. "Excuse me, Reverend. Might I borrow a moment of your time?"

"Of course." The man closed the well-worn book. "What is it?"

"Would you be traveling east or west when you leave tomorrow?"

"West is what I planned. Is there someone I should visit on my way out?"

"Not exactly." There was someone Hawke *didn't* want

the man to visit—the entire town of Laramie. "I was wondering—what I mean, is that I would appreciate it if you wouldn't spread the news about me getting married, and all."

The preacher eyed him for a moment, reconciling himself to his own prejudices, Hawke assumed, then finally said, "I'm not the town crier, Mister. Just a man spreading the word of the Lord."

And that was just fine with Hawke. From then on, everything happened in a blur. After what he thought was an awfully fast ceremony with very few words leading up to the "I-do's," John Winterhawke, Jr. found himself a married man. He would have to remain this way in name only for at least this one night, due to the fact that rooms and privacy were in short supply at Three Elk Ranch. That, too, was just fine with Hawke, given the circumstances of the entire day. He figured he could use the next twenty-four hours to get used to the idea that from now on, he was responsible for a copper-haired beauty with eyes the color of a golden dawn.

As for Lacey, after she and Kate had served a wedding supper of roast calf's liver, boiled brisket, and potato pudding, then settled the men down with both mixed-berry *and* cherry pie, she was all too happy to retire to the back bedroom with Kate where she could completely relax. After Lacey slipped into her voluminous cotton nightgown, Kate tapped her on the shoulder.

"Sit a moment, will ye, lass? 'Tis time I spoke to ye of a few . . . things."

Her curiosity piqued, Lacey eased down on the edge of the bed and smoothed her gown. "Is something wrong? You look sort of worried."

"Sorry, lass, I dona mean to give that impression." She paced in front of Lacey, her hands clasped tightly together. "Caleb spoke to me of yer new husband and some confusion I had over the liberties he did or didna take with ye already."

"Oh," her cheeks bloomed bright, "that."

"Aye, and I apologize for presumin' the worst of the man. He seems a decent enough sort."

"Then what could be the trouble?"

Kate stopped pacing. "There is no trooble, lass, but since ye didna have a . . . normal upbringing, and no doubt, ye've not learned a thing about what goes on between men and women after they've wed . . . " She paused to wipe her brow with the back of her hand, her bountiful freckles fading under increasingly reddened cheeks. "What I'm wonderin' is how much ye know of what's expected of ye once yer alone at Winterhawke with yer man."

Wondering why Kate was acting so strangely, Lacey shrugged. "'Tis for sure that I'll have to learn to cook better!"

Kate sighed heavily and wiped her brow again. "'Tis a difficult thing, what I've to explain. A very difficult thing, me thinks, for ye to understand, but there'd be a wee bit more to marriage then cookin'. A good lot more, in fact."

10

Not bloody likely.
—George Bernard Shaw

"You can not be serious!" Now it was Lacey who paced the floor, her eyes wide and round as the pie tins Hawke had licked clean earlier. "This can not be!"

"Aye, but 'tis true, lass."

She stopped pacing and stamped her foot, sorely missing the jingle of her spurs. "But husband or no, I can not possibly consider doing such a loathsome thing with Hawke. I will not."

"Oh, lass . . . ye *must.*" Kate, sitting on the edge of the bed, averted her gaze. "'Tis the way of nature."

"Nature? And why would nature demand such an 'unnatural' act of me?"

"Why, for the begetting of children. I thought I made that clear to ye."

She hadn't, but even though Lacey found the entire conversation distasteful, she had begun to suspect as much. So *this* vile act was the thing which brought about the creation of children! She'd picked up enough whispers and innuendos from the nurses and other patients over the years to know that the process involved something private, something she probably didn't want to talk or think about, but to find this mating business was to involve her own private self in such an unprivate way, was just too preposterous to be real. Too monstrous to even contemplate further. Surely not everyone indulged in such goings on!

Eyeing Kate curiously, Lacey ventured forward. "You're not suggesting that even sweet-natured Nurse Flaherty, mother of ten babes, has done this business with gentle Mr. Flaherty, and as many times as children were born, are you? Surely she's found another way."

If not for sudden memories of her own lost love and the painful, bittersweet memories of their forbidden nights together, Kate might have laughed at Lacey's suggestion. She didn't, but went ahead with her lesson on sex with a little more empathy. "There is no other way, lass, and aye, sweet Nurse Flaherty did indeed lie with her man in that manner. I would guess that she also allowed him to visit himself upon her a good many times more than the number of babes she can claim— and still does."

Lacey gasped. "More than ten, you say! But why—"

"I canna in all decency go into more detail. I'll just say that 'tis possible the woman found a modicum of pleasure in the arms of the man she loves. 'Tis another of nature's ways when the match is a good one." She paused, her cheeks blooming like springtime as she wondered if she would ever feel those pleasures in Caleb's arms. "God willin', ye'll be findin' that out for yerself, and soon, I hope."

Her cheeks burning, Lacey turned her back to her friend and closed her ears to the incredible words she was saying. A modicum of pleasure, indeed! A ridiculous thought, but even if it were true, she simply wouldn't do it. She couldn't, and not just because the idea appalled her so, but because Kathleen Lacey O'Carroll Winterhawke could not in all good conscience take the risk of bearing children—not now, and not ever.

Although the authorities never pronounced her as such, she'd heard the nurses whispering among themselves about her precarious grip on sanity, understood they were insinuating that she had something to do with the mysterious way her parents had died. She herself had no recall of that terrible night save for the brand she would carry forever to remind her that it had indeed happened. Raising her right hand to eye level, Lacey stared hard at the scar on her palm and thought back to what it represented.

She'd gone mad the night her family perished in those same flames—she must have—and had been mad days and years after when she slipped into the longest of her mute, mind-numbing spells. Surely those were all signs of madness, and if that be so, couldn't this madness be a blight in the O'Carroll family blood? Lacey couldn't even bear to think of bringing children in the world not knowing if they'd be dangerous, judged insane, or locked away from gentle society. Somehow, she'd survived the taunts and whispers of others along with the thinly veiled pity and disgust that went with them, but she could never bring a child of hers into this world if there was even a chance it might have to endure the same stigma.

Kate cleared her throat. "Are ye all right with it then, lass? Yer awfully quiet."

Her mind made up, Lacey turned back to her only true friend. Kate met her gaze for a fleeting moment, then blushed again and looked away, acting as if she had something more to say on the matter, but didn't know quite how to say it. Then as before, she twined her fingers around each other and smiled an uneasy smile. Obviously the former nurse found this bedtime business between husband and wife as distasteful as Lacey did, and was ready to put the subject behind them as easily as they'd discarded their past lives. Which was fine with Lacey.

"Aye," she said, returning Kate's smile. "I'm all right with it and knowing what I must do. Shall we turn in then?"

The following morning, Lacey assisted Kate in the preparation of a huge breakfast, then jotted down several notes on the preparation of the foods both women thought she could handle with enough competence to succeed. She even scribbled careful directions for the making of pie crusts and one filling—berry—in the event she felt confident enough to try to bake one for Hawke before the women had an opportunity to see each other again. Then, with what Lacey thought was a fair amount of relief on her friend's part, Kate bid her adieu.

The ride back to Winterhawke was interminable, filled with long, awkward moments of silence between Lacey and Hawke. Even the little bits of conversation they shared were strangely shy and polite, as if they'd never met at the Laramie Depot or glimpsed the other's soul during the tender moment when Taffy's foal finally gained entrance into the world. Most awkward of all, was acting as if they'd never shared that passionate kiss out by Phantom's corral, the scent of the lathered stud and sun-drenched wilderness all around them.

Lulled by yet another long stretch of silence, the sound of Hawke's voice startled Lacey as the wagon rounded the final bend and started along the aspen-lined road leading to Winterhawke, her favorite part of the drive.

"I understand you've met Crowfoot," he said.

There was no question in Hawke's tone, and he didn't turn to her as if to gauge the veracity of her answer. It was a statement of fact. The lad specifically asked Lacey *not* to mention the fact that she'd come across him, and yet how could she just out and out lie to her new husband?

Hedging, she said, "Are you, by any chance, referring to the fairy I thought I saw in the barn?"

"I suppose so if you're talking about the Crow Indian boy who lives on my ranch. He says he gave you a pair of his old boots."

"Uh, aye . . . him." Nothing left to do but tell the truth. "Aye, and we did speak briefly. Will he be staying with us at the ranch house from now on?"

"He divides his time between Winterhawke and Three Elk, but as far as I know, he'll be at my place for a while. That's why I asked you about him, so I could be sure he wouldn't startle you if you should run into him in the barn again."

"Oh, aye, but what about in the house? Surely he stays in your office or somewhere when I'm not around. I do not wish to turn him out."

"You're not." Home at last, Hawke reined in the horses and set the brake. "Crowfoot lives in the barn."

Lacey's head whipped around. "But why? I do not mind if the lad—"

"He belongs in the barn," Hawke said abruptly as he climbed down from the wagon. Closing the subject, he added, "I just wanted to make sure you knew he was there, not argue about him. I'm going to check on the horses now. Why don't you get yourself settled in the house? I'll be along to help you in a little while."

Then, without waiting for her answer, he disappeared in the direction of the barn. Lacey thought of following her new husband to let him know in no uncertain terms what she thought of his cruel treatment of the boy. Then she realized she was ill-prepared to broach the subject without explaining a little of her earlier life and how well she understood Crowfoot's need for silence in order to nurse his inner wounds. But as the new mistress of Winterhawke, she decided it would most certainly be in her power to see to the boy's comfort. She would see to it, Lacey vowed, and soon—no matter what the master of all that surrounded her thought. No matter a'tall.

Much later that night, well after Hawke and his bride had nibbled on the basket full of leftovers from their wedding supper and he'd taken a large portion of those same foods to the barn for Crowfoot, he found himself fresh out of excuses for remaining downstairs while his wife waited upstairs in their "bridal chamber." He'd gone to his former bedroom ahead of her to light a nice fire and make sure the starkly furnished room was tidy and neat, then invited her in and left her to prepare for bed in private. By Hawke's calculations, he'd paced the length and width of his living room long enough for Lacey to have prepared for a month of wedding nights!

Thunder rolled in the distance, reminding him of the newly approaching storm and how quickly the temperature was dropping. Even though he still wasn't quite sure how best to approach this woman who was now his bride, he knew he couldn't just leave her shivering alone in his—*their*—room any longer. So with a deep breath and no small amount of trepidation, Hawke banked the smoldering embers in the downstairs grate, then made his way upstairs in hopes of lighting a fire of another kind.

When he reached the top of the stairs, it occurred to him that Lacey might have fallen asleep, so long was her wait. Considerate to the extreme on this most special of nights, he quietly turned the knob, then slowly pushed the door to his room open. She'd blown out the lamp on the bedside table, pitching the room into near darkness, but Hawke had no trouble spotting his bride. The glow from the low flames still crackling in the fireplace bathed her exquisite skin, making it seem pearly and almost translucent in the otherwise drab room. She'd freed her glorious hair, too, leaving the bounty of those coppery curls to spread across his pillow and down along the sheet. Lacey's eyes were closed as he'd hoped, but the sight of her lying there like a luscious angel, his for all eternity to boot, fed the sparks of his rapidly growing ardor, and turned it into a sudden inferno.

No longer remotely concerned about approaching her with stealth, Hawke strode purposefully to the edge of the bed and sat down. Behind him, Lacey stirred, her sweet voice reaching his ears in a mew-like sigh. Hastily removing his clothing and not caring where or how the articles landed, at last he raised the bedding and climbed in between the sheets beside her. Again she stirred, this time murmuring something he couldn't understand.

"What did you say?" he asked, rolling to his side and reaching for her.

"Hummm?" Lacey's eyes fluttered open. "Wha—oh!"

Hawke leaned up on one elbow, hovering just above her, and smiled down into Lacey's startled eyes. He brushed one of several errant curls off of her forehead as he murmured, "I thought you said something to me, but I guess you were just talking in your sleep. Sorry if I . . . disturbed you."

Her gaze fixed to his naked chest, Lacey favored him with a shy smile. "Umm, 'tisn't a problem."

"Did you find everything you need up here?"

Again a shy smile, this one punctuated with a sharp nod. "Aye, and thank you kindly for seeing to everything." She tugged the covers up tight around her throat and inched toward the edge of the bed—away from him.

"Look at me, Lacey," Hawke whispered, his voice low, coming from the core of his being. She slowly lifted a troubled gaze, meeting his eyes, but looked cornered, trapped as surely as his snares had trapped countless rabbits. It was a look Hawke didn't care for in the slightest. Relaxing the intensity of his own gaze, he softly whispered, "Don't be afraid, Lacey. I won't hurt you. You know that I would never hurt you, don't you?"

Her expression less worried, but still guarded, she whispered back, "Aye, and I'm believing that of you, my husband."

"Good." He ran his fingers along the column of her neck, feeling the tense muscles beneath her silken skin. "Relax a little, Irish. There's nothing to fear."

Keeping his movements smooth and unhurried, Hawke slowly eased himself closer to his nervous bride, then carefully settled his lips against hers. Lacey did not encourage him, or even shift herself to better accommodate his mouth, but she did allow the kiss. Even as he gathered her into his arms, obliging her to bear more of his weight, and then deepened the kiss, Lacey complied. Finally, at long last, he could feel her body moving beneath him.

Taking her busy hands and gently twisting hips as encouragement, Hawke slid his fingers up to the tight collar of her nightgown and began to unfasten the row of buttons there, kissing her all the while. He breathed deeply of this wife of his as he manipulated the little pearl fasteners, smelling the usual hint of cherry blossoms, but something more, too—softness? If such a virtue could even have an aroma, softness was exactly what Lacey smelled like, the downy, velvety essence of her seeping through his tough hide to perfume even the most acrid corners of his hardened heart.

Buoyed by the new sensation and the warming it spread deep within him, Hawke slipped his hand inside Lacey's nightgown and began to caress the gentle rise of her breasts. With an abruptness that startled them both, she pushed away from him. Lacey's little show of uncertainty did nothing to discourage Hawke, in fact, it prompted an almost primal aggression, one that had been building up inside him on its own. His ardor renewed, he followed the still-warm path Lacey had taken to the edge of the bed, then reached out to take her into his arms again—and came up grasping nothing but air.

First a soft *thump* met his ears, then this was quickly followed by a sharp cry.

"Lacey!" he called, leaning over the edge of the mattress to peer at the darkness below. "Where are you? Are you hurt?"

"Oh, goodness, me . . . no, I do not think so." She sat up and stared at him in the semidarkness, her eyes wide with surprise. "Are you wanting me to sleep on the other side of the bed? Would that be what you're hinting at?"

"On the—Oh, Christ, no, Lacey." He extended his hand to her. "Come back up here. I'm sorry if I was a little rough with you. I didn't mean to push you out of bed."

She slipped one of her hands in his, and with a gentle tug, Hawke had his wife beside him again. Exactly where he wanted her. "Are you sure you didn't hurt yourself when you fell?" he asked, caressing her hip through the thick layers of her cotton nightgown.

"No, no. I'm in splendid health, really I am." She swatted his hand away even as she leaned over and bestowed a chaste kiss to his cheek. Then, with one casual remark, she rolled over onto her side and offered her back to him. "The need to sleep has covered me up as surely as mist over a bog, so I'll just be bidding you good-night now, my husband."

An incredulous Hawke watched as Lacey snuggled her head into the down pillow, carving out a niche the way a wildcat fashions a soft bed by clawing the ground. Then at once, she lay perfectly still. What the hell had he done wrong? Hawke wondered. He'd been gentle and affectionate, sensitive to her innocence and her needs, and with the exception of accidentally pushing her out of bed, very considerate. He thought back to the way she'd opened her mouth to him, encouraging, then mimicking his every movement. Damn it all, Lacey had responded to his touch, and wanted him at least a little bit—he was sure of it. Where had he gone wrong?

Hawke and Caleb had touched on the subject of his wedding night as they drank their morning coffee earlier in the day. Although frankly, his friend didn't know any more about polite society and innocent maidens than Hawke did, Caleb did make a point of telling him that Lacey was inexperienced, and that she'd never had a husband or lover before. In the course of that discussion, Hawke also learned that Kate and Lacey had discussed this part of the marriage, and that his bride had been prepared at least mentally, to submit to her husband. While he expected that she might be a little afraid of him, and even understood those fears, he never dreamed she'd be so flat-out skittish as to shut him out completely. How was he to proceed from here? Or was he to leave her be, allowing them both a little more time to get used to the nearness of the other?

Much too stimulated not to at *least* give it one more try, Hawke inched closer to his wife and fit his hips up tight against her bottom. Then, after pulling the bulk of her coppery hair aside, he began to nuzzle the nape of her neck.

"What's that you're doing back there?" asked Lacey, swinging her hand around to swat him away—again.

After a long dark moment, a dazed Hawke backed away from her muttering, "Nothing." Then he punched the hell out of his pillow, carving out a canyon, not a niche, and buried his head in it. As he slept, a long ledger appeared in his dreams, the heading above the usual twin columns reading; *Marriage—For and Against.*

The next morning, Lacey awoke to a peal of thunder so loud that as it rolled through the room, it rattled the log timbers of the roof above her. A lightning strike went off, flashing brilliant shards of jagged light across the bay window, and then came another, louder clap of thunder. She opened her eyes to find herself nose to nose with her husband, their arms and legs tangled around one another. Her first thought was to bolt when she realized those masculine limbs so entwined with hers were naked, but she convinced herself that she was safe in Hawke's arms, secure and protected from everything, even the world outside. Taking comfort in the thought, Lacey clung to her husband's neck, showering his smooth tanned face with kisses. He groaned in response, then lifted his sleepy lids.

His eyes were warm and languid-looking by the morning light, the same rich soft velvety green of Irish moss. Oh, if only the two of them could stay like this forever! she thought joyously. How wonderful it would be to lie about in each other's arms, kissing with lips fused as one, time and time again. Lacey loved the way her husband kissed her and the tingly way it made her feel inside, and even enjoyed sleeping in the same warm bed with him— an extra special luxury on a cold, dark morning like this, she thought with a little shiver.

As for the rest, for what she thought he'd tried to do last night—join his body with hers—well, he'd stopped trying to do that, hadn't he? And never once had he said a word to her about the begetting of children. Maybe, she dared to hope, Hawke was in silent agreement with her in that regard. Perhaps he was no more eager than she to produce offspring. With another, more exuberant kiss, this one landing directly on Hawke's lips, Lacey rolled to the edge of the mattress, then hopped out of bed.

"Oh!" she cried, her teeth chattering. "'T-tis c-cold enough in here to f-freeze the heart of a n-nun!"

Hawke, who by now was sitting at the edge of the bed dressing himself, muttered darkly, "I'll stoke the fire for you, then go on downstairs to light the stove and put on some coffee."

"I thank you kindly, husband. I'll be down soon as I'm warmed and dressed to make a nice hot breakfast for you."

Curiously silent, Hawke finished with the fireplace, then started for the door. Thinking of the recipes she brought with her from Three Elk Ranch, she stopped him just before he walked out of the room.

"Do think of what you want for breakfast. My wish is to please you."

She listened for his reply, but all Lacey heard was

some incoherent grumbling before her new husband closed the door and left her to her own devices.

Downstairs, Hawke fired up the stove and waited for the coffee to boil. He was in a surly mood and definitely not interested in instructing his bride on the proper way to use the stove during her quest to try out the few recipes Kate sent along. There was only one thing on this morning that he wanted to teach Lacey, but rather than face the rejection she'd surely heap on him during daylight hours, he decided it would be best to wait until nightfall to begin that lesson again.

As for breakfast, there was still a fair amount of food left over from their wedding, remnants which included half of a cherry pie. Figuring if he couldn't sate the more urgent appetite gnawing at his core, he could at least, by God, gratify the hunger in his belly, Hawke devoured every last bit of pastry without ever coming up for air. Then he donned his hat and slicker, and went to care for his animals.

That night and the next proved to increase his surliness, not decrease it. The last filly to throw a foal by Phantom finally went into a difficult, protracted labor, but even after she dropped her colt, the foal's life, if not her own, was still in danger. Weak and underweight when born, the bay colt was listless and not interested in standing, much less nursing. Once Hawke finally got the youngster to its feet and directed its tiny head toward his mother's teats the mare, Cherry, balked, and kicked out at her son whenever he came near.

Hawke spent most of that night milking the big chestnut mare, the rest of it feeding her foal with this most important early milk by the teaspoonful. The following evening, by the time he was satisfied that the newborn could nurse on his own without risking his mother's wrath, a weary Hawke dragged himself upstairs only to find that his wife had fallen into a sleep so deep, not even his voice or touch could disturb her. Giving into his own exhaustion since he was sure he couldn't find the patience to go easy with Lacey should he manage to awaken her, he called it a night, his marriage still unconsummated.

Hawke awakened on the fourth day as frustrated mentally as he was physically. There were many reasons that he'd yet to claim his bride, most of them valid, he supposed, yet by morning's light, all he could dwell on was his own failure. How could it be that he, a man able to tame any wild beast he chose to, be it wolf, renegade stallion, or even someone like Crowfoot, who in many ways was more wild beast than boy when they first met, had been unable to find the key to taming his own wife? Why, with all his talents for gentling the savage beast, could he not bring this blue-eyed, flame-haired woman to heel? No matter what they said behind his back, there wasn't a man in any town he'd ever been in, including Laramie and his own uncle, William Braddock, who didn't back away from Hawke, giving him a wide berth and a healthy respect—at least physically. But this woman; this frustrating, completely adorable and unpredictable woman was driving him to complete and utter distraction!

Frustrated all over again, Hawke flung himself out of bed, dressed, and stoked the fire as he'd done the last few mornings. Then, muttering to himself as he went downstairs, he fired up the stove and put on the coffee. Giving in to a craving for the sausage he'd ground himself using equal parts of pork and venison, he went out to the icebox to get a package. When he returned to the kitchen, Lacey was waiting for him, dressed in her usual navy skirt and white blouse.

"Top o' the morning to you," she said, all smiles. "I

did not hear you come in last night. More trouble with the wee one?"

"Just a little. He'll be all right now." Hawke set the package down. "The stove's good and hot. I'd like you to fry up some sausage patties, and then make me a little gravy to pour over some of those good biscuits. Do you think you can do all that and make gravy, too? If not, I'll stay a while to help you."

Her smile grew radiant. "Of course I can manage on my own. Kate explained about mixing a few spoons of flour in with the pan drippings, smoothing it all out with milk, then tossing in a wee bit of salt and pepper." The biscuits were already made, so she just had to warm them, cook the sausage patties, and whip up this simple-sounding batch of gravy. What could be easier? "Shall I come get you when breakfast is done, then?"

Hawke glanced out the window just above the stove and sink. "No, it's still raining. I'll stick my head out of the barn from time to time, and if I see you waving at me from this window, I'll know it's ready."

With that final instruction, he took his slicker off the chair, slipped it on, then reached for his hat. Surprising him before he could turn toward the door, Lacey rushed across the room, threw her arms around Hawke's neck, and planted a big kiss on his mouth.

"There," she said, releasing him and stepping back. "I could not let you start your day without a good morning kiss. 'Tis a lucky sign that all will go well in your work."

Hawke paused, puzzling over this capricious wife of his—affectionate and almost loving one minute, cold and remote the next—then slammed his hat on his head and stalked out the door.

Sensing that she'd done something to irritate her husband, but without any idea what it might be, Lacey vowed to make it up to him by fixing the most memorable breakfast of his life. This morning, and for the first time, she simply would *not* allow any mistakes in the kitchen. Recalling Kate's instructions and the one glaring error she'd committed the day she'd attempted to create those buttermilk pancakes—neglecting to grease the pan first—Lacey scooped out a nice big slab of lard, popped it into the skillet, and slid the heavy cast iron pan over to the hottest part of the stove. Then she sat down at the table and went about forming a pile of perfectly round patties from the sausage meat.

Outside, Hawke stomped through the rain and mud, thinking that if he'd left his slicker and hat behind, the frigid storm might have done what his wife was apparently unwilling to do—cool off his overheated body. As he worked off some of those frustrations, he began to take a closer look at Lacey's reluctance from her point of view. What if in Ireland, marriage and all it entails was conducted a little differently? Who knows? Maybe there, a period of adjustment was the norm for a couple who barely knew one another. It could be that she just needed a little more time with him before getting to the most intimate part of their marriage. If that were true, at least it would explain her attitude a little better.

As reasonable as this hypothesis sounded, Hawke found himself hoping to God that the amount of time she needed wasn't more than the three nights he'd already waited for her to come around—even controlled as he usually was, he knew he wasn't going to last much longer if he had to go on sleeping beside his irresistible bride without touching her. To be sure of her reasons, he thought with a start, he probably ought to ask Lacey if this period of waiting was customary in Ireland. Of course, before he could do that, he would have to find not only the right words, but the right moment to bring the subject up—a difficulty in its own right considering the fact that he was damn near as embarrassed as Lacey when it came to discussing such matters.

As he mulled over this newest dilemma, Hawke's stomach growled, reminding him of the signal he'd set up with his wife. Strolling over to the barn doors, he glanced across the yard to the kitchen window. At first he thought he saw her springy hair bobbing this way and that in the glass pane. Then with terrifying clarity, Hawke realized that what he was looking at was not Lacey waving back at him, but the wings of a fire. The kitchen curtains were ablaze!

11

Fear is more fatal than hate.

—Canon P.A. Sheehan

When he burst into the kitchen through the back door, Hawke expected to find Lacey frantically beating off the flames, splashing water at them, or . . . *something!* But he found her standing stock-still, her hands firmly clenched into fists and her back against the farthest wall, just staring as if mesmerized by the fire which had already devoured his curtains and were now gorging themselves on the pine log walls of his home. The lid blew off of Hawke's temper as he realized everything he owned, his entire house was in jeopardy of burning down, and his own wife just stood there doing nothing—*nothing!*

"Christ, woman!" he bellowed, racing toward the window. "Have you gone *mad*? Help me, damn it! Run outside and fill the pail with water!"

Lacey was already pretty well gone when Hawke barreled his way through the door, slipping deeper and deeper into one of her spells as the terror of what was happening here in the kitchen mingled with blotchy memories of so long ago. If indeed she hadn't tumbled into the chasm of total withdrawal by then, hearing her husband refer to her as a madwoman was the final blow that pushed her over the edge.

Lacey ran from the house through the still-opened back door, bolting past both the bucket and the well, and continued to run, racing out of control as if the devil himself was at her heels.

Assuming that she'd gone after the water, Hawke grabbed up a towel and began beating at the flames which by now were licking the ceiling of his home.

Later, after he'd managed to put out the fire in spite of the fact that his wife had not returned with the water he'd requested, he went in search of her. Although his anger was still simmering on high, concern for Lacey cooled it considerably once he'd searched the grounds high and low calling her name and not found her.

Retracing his steps, Hawke stormed back into the barn and looked into all the stalls and feed rooms again in hopes of stumbling across some hint that she'd been there. Still he found no sign of Lacey. He paused for several moments outside the foaling stall, wondering if she'd been fool enough to try walking down the road to Three Elk again. After what happened here today, it made sense, he supposed, to seek her friend Kate. Deciding it couldn't hurt to take a ride in that direction, Hawke had just stepped away from the stall when he heard scratching sounds coming from above. *The loft!* Since it was Crowfoot's domain, he hadn't even thought of looking for his wife up there, but given the circumstances—none of which he understood—he decided to have a quick look. Once he'd climbed up the ladder and maneuvered through his dwindling supply of alfalfa, Hawke approached the carefully arranged bales of straw which served as the boy's lair.

He hadn't really expected to find Lacey there, so it was with a good bit of surprise that he discovered her sitting in the straw, wrapped in the boy's thin arms. "What the devil . . . ?" Hawke took another step toward them.

"No!" Crowfoot raised a hand, warding him off. "You go."

"The hell if I will." He moved in closer, only to be held at bay by a pair of lethal onyx eyes.

"You *go!* She not . . . she—" Crowfoot beat a tattoo against his own chest. "She hurt. You go."

"God damn it, son, you think I can't see that for myself?" And he could, easily. Lacey was staring out through the opened doors of the loft as if looking at the house, but her eyes were glazed over, seeing absolutely nothing. He didn't know exactly what was wrong with her or what drove her to this, but he did recognize the look for what it was: Shock.

Crowfoot renewed his grip on Lacey, then glanced up at Hawke and glared. "You go. She cannot talk. Maybe later."

"If anyone's going to go, it'll be you," he said, reining in his temper as best he could. "I'm Lacey's husband and I'll take care of her."

Instead of relinquishing his hold, the boy shook his head defiantly and pulled Lacey even tighter into his small embrace. Hawke could hardly believe this of Crowfoot, a boy who was barely more civilized than a wild animal at eight years of age when he and Caleb first took him in. It had taken them months to get even one word out of the withdrawn child. How had Lacey reached him so quickly? And how was Hawke to reach her? Something ugly rolled through him at the thought, and along with it, the feeling that he was on the outside looking in. Hawke recognized the sensation as jealousy, which he thought was ridiculous since the object of this insane rage was a boy, not a man. But Hawke was jealous, in any case. And he knew it.

Dropping to his heels, he softened his voice, using the tone he reserved for gentling horses. "I can see your concern for Lacey, son, but surely I'm the better choice to help my own wife. Have I ever done anything but help you when you needed it?" The bright glare slowly began to leave Crowfoot's dark eyes. "Didn't I even have enough sense to leave you to yourself when you didn't want anyone around? I never pushed or pressured you, did I?"

The boy gave a surly shrug, but averted his gaze.

"Then what are you worried about? You must know that I would never do anything to hurt Lacey. I only want to help her."

Releasing his grip on Lacey at last, Crowfoot hung his head. "You not hurt lady. I know."

"Then leave me alone with her for a while. Fair enough?"

The boy regarded him for a long moment before he said, "Hawke fair. And good, too. I go." Then in an instant, his wiry body moving with its usual stealth and speed, he jumped up and took off.

"Lacey?" said Hawke after Crowfoot had gone. "Look at me, will you?"

But as she'd done during his exchange with the boy, she just sat quietly without so much as flinching, and continued to stare out at the house. Trying another tack, Hawke approached his uncommunicative wife and sat down in the straw beside her.

After slipping his arm across her shoulders, he spoke to her in a low whisper. "Hello, Irish. A little mad at me, are you?" Not that he thought he had anything to apologize for, but even this didn't draw so much as a flicker from those wide blue eyes. "Well, if you are mad, don't worry about it. It's a common affliction to anyone who's unlucky enough to meet up with me—and I do know how much you Irish folks value your luck." Still nothing, so he tried a little silliness. "Why, I once got Caleb so damn riled over something I did, he kicked *himself* in the butt!"

Chuckling lightly, Hawke glanced at Lacey's expression, hoping to find at least a little crack in her armor. She was as stiff as a new saddle. Even Crowfoot hadn't been this distant when he and Caleb first came across him. The boy at least looked at them when they spoke.

As he considered other ways of reaching her, Hawke took Lacey's hands in his. Absently caressing the soft skin at the back of the hand she was always hiding from him, the right, he considered grabbing her by the shoulders and shaking her to awareness. Or perhaps, he thought, there was a less violent way. What if he were to kiss her or take her into his arms? She might even—

His thoughts stalled on the last word as his fingers passed over an extremely rough patch of skin on Lacey's palm. Turning her hand over, Hawke was startled to see that almost the entire area was webbed with scarring. When he recognized those scars as the telltale reminders of a bad burn, all of her little eccentricities began to make sense to him; especially her reluctance to get close to the fireplace or stove. It even explained in a small way why she hadn't tried to douse the flames in the kitchen.

Remembering how he'd shouted at Lacey when he found her standing there watching his house burn down, Hawke brought her palm to his mouth and pressed a kiss to it as he muttered, "Christ, Lacey—why didn't you show me this before now, or explain what happened to you?"

She heard Hawke's voice in the distant part of her mind, and had heard it since he started calling her name in the yard. It was a sound she couldn't shut out as easily as the nurses at the hospital, a deep, insinuating voice which had the power to reach her heart even through the walls of the spell. Still, it wasn't until his lips touched her scar that Lacey became fully aware of her husband's presence—and of what he was doing. A new kind of turmoil started within her at that display of tenderness, lifting her above the spell, but leaving her completely confused. She didn't know what to do, how to do it, or even who she was. Then the tip of Hawke's tongue touched down on that pad of damaged flesh, searing her body and mind clear through to the core.

With a sharp intake of breath, Lacey snapped out of her spell and jerked her hand from Hawke's grasp. Then she met his gaze, her mind and vision, if not her heart, clear. "Don't do that! How can you? My palm must feel like   like a plank to your poor mouth."

He glanced at the fist she'd made of that hand and shrugged. "Not to me, it doesn't."

"But it must! I can put my finger to this," she stroked her damaged palm, "and feel that 'tis like rubbing up against the bark of a tree or touching something . . . dead."

"Think what you will. It's just a little scar to me, a part of you." Hawke reached for her hand.

"Don't touch it!" Lacey shrank away from him. "Please don't even look upon me there."

He shrugged. "If that's what you want, all right. Is it still painful, or something?"

"Only to my mind." She hung her head. "I cannot bear to see the look in your eyes when you, if it . . . " Embarrassed, Lacey let the sentence die out. Her eyes filling with tears, she remembered what drove her to the barn and quietly added, "I'm sorry, too, for what happened in your kitchen. 'Twere an accident, I swear it. Is the house badly burned?"

"The house is . . . fine. I never did like those stupid curtains with the daisies all over them, anyway." Tilting his head toward her hand, he asked, "Tell me what happened to you. How were you burned?"

"I—I wish I could tell you, but . . . truth is, I cannot remember. I was but a wee lass not quite seven when it happened." Seeking his gaze, wondering how much more she could tell him and still have at least a little of his respect, Lacey watched Hawke carefully as she explained a small segment of her past. "I only know that my dear mother and father died in the same fire that burned me." The heavy sense of guilt that always weighed her down grew heavier at the thought, swelling her throat with a pain that ached all the way down to her heart. Lacey tried, but she couldn't go on.

Hawke didn't press her for more details. If he'd learned one thing through his experiences with Crowfoot, it was that information such as this came slowly and painfully, and that forcing too much too soon could do more harm than good. Instead, he slipped his arm across her shoulders again and gave her a gentle hug.

"Thank you for telling me about it, Irish. I just wish you'd have told me when we first met, or at least, after we got married." Hawke gave her a wry smile. "I wouldn't have been quite so determined to make you learn how to cook, that's for sure."

"Aye, you're right. I suppose I should have told you a wee bit more about myself before now. Please know that I'm truly sorry for everything."

Uncomfortable with the conversation and trying to end it, Hawke took his share of the blame. "Yeah, well I'm sorry for the way I hollered at you in the kitchen."

"*You*—sorry? Oh . . . oh, Hawke." Tears spilled down to Lacey's cheeks in spite of her efforts to hold them back. "'Tisn't a thing in the world for you to be sorry about. I only want, I only hope that . . . " She couldn't go on, so fast was the flow of her tears by now. Lacey brought her hands to her face in hopes of hiding this newest embarrassment, but Hawke caught them before she could stop him, then gently eased her down on her back in the straw.

"I don't know about you," he muttered, settling in beside her, "but I'm getting tired of all this apologizing and forgiving. I can think of a lot better things to do with our lips than talk."

When he saw the glimmer in Lacey's eyes and the tug of a smile at the corner of her mouth, Hawke impulsively touched his lips to the spot. The kiss started out slowly at first, the sealing of a pact of forgiveness, but soon it became much more than a gentle sharing of the tender feelings growing between them. In fact, this was different than anything they'd ever experienced before; more passionate to be sure, but also more profound somehow. Hawke could feel Lacey relaxing beneath him; his, in a trusting sort of way, for the first time since they'd taken their vows.

That kiss led to another, then another, until Hawke finally realized that he wanted his wife so badly, he'd almost convinced himself it would be all right to take her right there in the straw in broad daylight. Not the best of ideas considering that Crowfoot could stumble upon them at any time. The image this prompted gave Hawke the strength to tear himself away from her, even though regret and frustration followed swiftly on the heels of the passion they'd shared.

At first he assumed his normal rigid control and sense of privacy were the things which drove him to back away from Lacey, but as he glanced down at her lying there in the straw, Hawke realized there was something more than simple control at work here, a new force he'd never felt before. Perhaps, he thought, it was Lacey's expression. She no longer looked frightened, scared, or withdrawn, but shone with a radiant sense of peace, a happiness which lit her lovely face from within. He wanted her, there was no doubt about that, and wanted her still, but the actual physical joining between himself and Lacey suddenly seemed almost a secondary concern. Was this the way it was supposed to be between a man and his wife, or had that soft spot inside gotten the best of him again?

Wondering at the changes coming over him, concerned too, how those changes might affect the strong independence he coveted so, Hawke climbed to his feet. "I need a little air," he explained gruffly. "You lay there and rest a minute."

Lacey watched him stride across the straw to the doors of the loft, her captivated gaze fastened on Hawke's tight jeans and the firm round buttocks beneath them. Even if he was her husband, it seemed wrong to stare at the man so blatantly, but she could no more stop ogling him than she could cool the heat radiating up through her cheeks. In fact, her entire body was on fire with wanting him, an almost desperate need to have Hawke back in her arms. What had come over her?

Lord! she thought, bolting upright. Could this be that modicum of pleasure Kate mentioned? Or maybe, she thought, trying to find a way to rationalize her uncivilized reactions to Hawke, this had something to do with her spell after he'd hollered at her in the kitchen! Whatever the reason, Lacey knew if he looked into her eyes just right or touched her the way he had again, she'd probably melt like butter under the summer sun, leaving him to do his ghastly bidding on her poor helpless body.

As if he realized what she'd been thinking, Hawke chose that moment to look over his shoulder, gazing at her with eyes glistening in almost the same black green of the Irish yews. Then he favored her with a lazy smile. Unable to control the response, Lacey shuddered from head to toe. Her cheeks, which had finally begun to cool, instantly caught fire again, the flames within burning hotter than before. Why did the man have to look so bloody good to her? And how was she to keep her wits about her now that she knew how deeply he could affect her?

There was only one thing to do: Keep Hawke at bay. And the first thing she had to do to accomplish that was learn to avoid his demanding, disconcerting, and worst of all, hypnotizing gaze. As long as she didn't allow those incredible eyes of his to collide with hers, trapping her as surely as the most deadly of bogs, she'd be just fine.

"What is it, Lacey?" Hawke asked. "You look troubled again. Is there something you want to ask me about?"

"Oh, well, there might be the one wee thing." Buying a little time as she searched for that 'thing,' Lacey picked the particles of straw off of her skirt. "Crowfoot," she blurted out, after glancing around at the boy's small quarters. "Why must the lad stay here? I should think the boy ought to be given a soft bed at the house."

Leaving his post, Hawke approached her. "Crowfoot doesn't do a damn thing he doesn't want to do." He almost added, "like me." "He knows he can come into the house any time he wants and on a permanent basis too, but so far, he says he's more comfortable out here. This loft is a big step up for him since he pretty well raised himself in the wild."

She gasped. "You mean without a mother or father?"

"Yes, but he wasn't completely alone. Crowfoot has a way with animals, wolves in particular." He hunkered down beside her and began to pick the straw out of her disheveled hair. "After his mother abandoned him at birth, a trapper and his squaw took him in. Once the woman died, the trapper kind of lost interest in him. Near as Caleb and I can figure, the kid ran wild for around three or four years before we convinced him to come and stay with us."

"The poor lad!"

Hawke shrugged. Then without even realizing what he was doing, he worked at pinning a few of Lacey's russet spirals back in place again. "Crowfoot doesn't think of himself as someone to be pitied," he continued, even though the feel of Lacey's hair had the better part of his attention. "He loves working with animals, my horses in particular, but has also learned a lot about running a cattle ranch from Caleb. Once he gets to speaking a little better, I think he'll fit just about anywhere the whites will let him go."

Lacey couldn't help but hear the bitter tone in Hawke's voice as he said whites, but she didn't dwell on it. There was something else which disturbed her about the boy, something she knew she couldn't ask of Crowfoot. "What of the lad's injured foot? How much longer must he wear that smelly sack about it?"

"Again that's something he does by choice, and it's not to cover an injury, but to hide the clubfoot he was born with. He thinks if he wears that burlap bag and a boot, he looks more normal, I guess."

Fully aware at last that he was fiddling with Lacey's hair, and that the perfume of it and feel of the silken strands sliding between his fingers were driving him to distraction, Hawke abruptly stood up.

"I haven't tried to convince Crowfoot to wear a shoe on that foot since I think teaching him to speak better English is more important right now. You two seem to be getting along pretty good—maybe you can talk him into getting rid of that bag."

"Aye, and I'd like to try. Do you have a boot to fit him?"

"No, but I've offered to stitch him up a pair of custom moccasins, and the offer is still good."

Hawke was looking at her again, thinking of something other than Crowfoot. Lacey was as sure of that as she was convinced that "something" had to do with her—and kissing. That in turn reminded her of the burgeoning feelings inside her, the strange way his look and touch made her feel.

Forcing herself to look away from her husband, a suddenly panicked Lacey scrambled to her feet and carved an escape route for herself. "'Tis best, I think, if I go look for the poor lad now."

Then, with no objection from her husband, Lacey fled the loft.

Later that evening over a supper of T-bone steaks and pan-fried potatoes and onions that Hawke had cooked at his own insistence, he felt comfortable enough with the lack of tension between himself and his wife to broach the subject which had been weighing so heavily on his mind—and elsewhere. And he was sure, after spending the day working on the problem, that he'd come up with the best solution to broaching it—directness.

Hawke cleared his throat, then laid his knife across his fork, cavalry-sword style, and centered them on his empty supper plate. Commanding her complete attention with the business-like tone of his voice, he asked, "Have you finished eating? There's something I want to discuss with you."

Lacey eyed the slab of steak left on her plate. "Aye, I cannot find the room for another bite, but I thank you kindly for putting such a grand meal together for me. I don't deserve it after . . ." Her gaze drifted over to the scorched wall above the stove.

"Forget it," he said, even though a tear-inducing reminder, the acrid aroma of smoke, hung over the room like a great dark cloud. "I think I've been patient with you, Lacey, more than patient in fact. I also think it's about time for you and I to, ah, get to know each other a little better. In bed."

Lacey's gaze shot back to him. "In bed, as in . . . ?"

Hawke nodded. "That's right. As in performing your wifely duty with me."

"Oh, b-but . . . I was thinking that you did not want children."

After pausing for a long moment, Hawke said, "I'll leave that decision up to you."

"Well, then my decision is no. I don't want us to have children. Not now or ever."

Hawke didn't know which surprised him the most; the fact that Lacey didn't want children, which was fine with him, or the fact that hearing those words from her sweet lips stung him so badly. This was not the answer he expected or wanted from his wife—the result, yes—but not the bluntness which carried with it the unspoken words; *I don't want to bear your half-breed babies.*

From across the table, Lacey noticed that her husband's jaw was twitching in anger. Her voice barely above a whisper, she said, "I can see that you're upset with me again. Is the begetting of your children so very important to you?"

He swallowed his anger. "No, it isn't. In fact, I've never figured on having kids."

"Well, 'tis a good decision I've made then! Why do you look as if a banshee has come to visit? Can we not just go on as before?"

"No," he said quickly, loudly. "We definitely will not go on as before, but you don't have to worry about turning up in a family way. I know how to prevent the begetting of babies, and I assure you that I will."

"'Tis good to hear that," she murmured thoughtfully. "And I would suppose prevention is best done by keeping your private self just there—to yourself. True?"

"Not true, Mrs. Winterhawke." Hawke leaned across the table, dragging his clean flannel shirt across his supper plate, but he took no notice of the mess he made of it. Then he hardened both his voice and his resolve to let her know in no uncertain terms what he expected. "A man has needs whether he's planning on making babies or not. When you married me, you vowed to fulfil those needs. It's time you did—understand?"

"I . . . no, I cannot say that I do."

Silently cursing Kate for the sloppy job she did preparing Lacey for this eventuality, and increasingly uncomfortable with the topic, Hawke tried to explain another way. "As I said before, I can prevent the begetting of children. What I can't prevent is my wanting you." He narrowed his gaze, watching for the light to dawn in her eyes, but there was no sign of comprehension. Reaching for her hand, he gentled his voice and tried yet another way to explain his need. "I want you badly, Lacey, in the way a man wants a woman, and . . . I want you now. Will you come upstairs to bed with me? I think I can explain the rest of this better if I show you what I want."

"Oh, b-but, from what Kate has told me of this . . . this joining of men and women, well, I cannot do it. I will not! 'Tis too vile and awful a thing." She snatched her hand out of Hawke's grasp and pushed her chair away from the table. "If you care for me a'tall, you will not be asking such a ghastly thing of me again!"

"*Ghastly?*" Hawke could hardly believe his ears. "I think I can make the moment a lot better for you than ghastly, Irish miss; in fact, I know that I can. First you've got to give me a chance." He held out his hand. "Come upstairs with me."

"Ne'er!" Lacey folded her arms across her breasts in dogged determination.

"But—but you have to!" Hawke was losing his temper, he knew it, but he couldn't seem to stop himself. "I'm entitled to at least that much out of this marriage! God knows you haven't provided me with anything else. You can't cook, you can't sew, and you—"

"You're forgetting the floors, sir! Have you seen how well-scrubbed they've been since I came here?"

"I don't give a damn about the floors!" By now, Hawke's face was puffed and red from his eyebrows to his throat. "And I don't give a damn about cooking and mending. But you will, by God, sleep with me."

"I sleep with you, Mr. Winterhawke, and I have been sleeping with you since we wed, in case you did not notice. Now I—I'll just be thanking you for not trying to do your awful bidding on me."

"Damn it, Lacey! My needs involve more than just *sleeping* with you, and you know it!" His voice dropped to a low growl. "And trust me when I say, the only thing awful about that need, is the fact that you've kept me at bay for so long!"

"All right. If you're pig-headed enough to feel that you must have something more out of this marriage, I'll just be giving it to you, then."

"Well it's about time." Hawke sighed heavily. "For a minute there I thought I was going to have to toss you over my shoulder and drag you off to bed."

"You'll not be putting a hand to me this night, Mr. Winterhawke," she warned, "or any other."

Hawke's mouth fell open at her openly belligerent attitude, but he couldn't think of what to say or do in response.

Her cheeks burning brightly, Lacey stood up, threw the scrap of toweling she'd used as a napkin against the tabletop, then slammed her hands to her hips. It was then Hawke heard that distinctive metallic jingle that occasionally accompanied her movements, a sound so very familiar to him, that he was sure he could identify it at last. Before he got the chance, Lacey issued a final statement, drawing all his attention back to the issue at hand.

"As I was saying, Mr. Winterhawke; I'll be happy to tend to your needs in any way I can. Now if you'll kindly be showing me where you keep the mending, I'll just be getting to it."

12

I can resist everything except temptation.

— Oscar Wilde

Not at all sure he could get a grip on his anger, lust, or his usual self control should he stay with Lacey after her diatribe, Hawke stormed out of the house and made his way to the back of the barn. Cursing Kate's ineptness again and Lacey for her mulish stand against fulfilling her wedding vows, he split several pine logs in an effort to work out some of his frustrations. Exhausted at last, he and Crowfoot settled on a snack of venison jerky that the boy kept stored in the barn, then Hawke made himself a bed in the straw not far from the young man's lair.

He did all that, but didn't like any of the circumstances one damn bit—especially the fact that he'd be spending the night in the barn. But like it or not, Hawke figured that at least this way he had the opportunity to think things through in a calm, clear manner—something he couldn't seem to do when face to face with his new bride. So he looked at their impasse from every angle imaginable, including her side, and finally settled on the only theory that made any kind of sense: Lacey was afraid.

At least he hoped to God that was the problem, fear of the unknown, and not something more terrible that he couldn't understand, much less talk to her about. Assuming that he'd guessed correctly, Hawke moved on to the next dilemma: How to ease Lacey's fears and convince her that bedding him would be the natural, pleasurable thing to do. And there he hit another brick wall, one that would put him right back in the kitchen arguing with her over whether she would or would not sleep with him the way any other wife would do without having to be begged!

His frustrations renewed, Hawke burrowed about in the straw seeking a more conformable position, then settled back down to work on the problem. Admittedly, he didn't know much about women or marriage, but he was pretty sure that seducing this wife of his was turning out to be a lot more difficult than it should have been. Why was he having such a hard time of it? he wondered. After all, gentling untamed animals was his specialty, was it not?

Looking at the problem in those terms—that a wild horse was not so unlike this reluctant bride of his—a glaring similarity between the two struck Hawke like a bolt of lightning. Wildness, he'd learned, came from fear and the instinctive need for self-preservation. Maybe Lacey's fears were born of the instinct to survive and not from something she found repulsive about him. Could it be that carving a path to this woman's bed wasn't so different from breaking a wild filly? Growing more and more convinced that he'd hit on Lacey's reason for denying him, Hawke pondered new ways of approaching her.

Obviously, he wasn't much good at explaining the way things ought to be between them, so he ruled out having any more discussions about the matter. Force was out of the question, of course, no matter how long she stalled. The only thing left was to do what he did with the horses; gain her trust and employ the art of gentle persuasion. That meant learning to see the problem from her point of view, anticipating her needs and fears, and, most of all, spotting her desires and acting upon them.

Until he could get all that figured out, Hawke knew he couldn't go back to the house. Not with the way his blood boiled every time he saw Lacey, touched her, or caught the irresistible aroma of her hair. He didn't dare.

Lacey tucked her lucky spurs under her pillow that night, afraid to let them out of her sight. If she ever needed the luck and courage the little silver shamrocks provided, she figured she needed it now more than ever. Hawke was beyond angry with her, she knew that much just by looking at him. What she didn't know was to what extremes his anger might take him. She hadn't fared any better with Crowfoot when she tried to talk him into removing the sack from his foot. He'd grown sullen and moody, then darted off into the thick pine forest behind the ranch. By day's end, she felt alone, unwanted, and out of place.

The following morning things didn't start out much better. Lacey whiled away the hours waiting for Hawke to come back to the house, but he still hadn't shown up by noon for a meal or even for a cup of coffee. Early in the day, she thought she heard him out on the back porch, but when she'd opened the door, he was gone. He'd left the day's supply of milk and eggs there on the porch, but never returned for breakfast. Lacey supposed she should have gone after her husband then and asked him when he wanted to eat, but after the row they'd had last night and the fact that he never came to bed, she was afraid of his rebuke. And she most certainly had one coming.

Above all else, Lacey knew she'd been awfully free with her tongue last night in her quest to remain unsullied—in fact, she'd never in all her years talked to anyone the way she'd snapped at Hawke. But then no one else had asked her to perform this wifely duty thing before either. And she was afraid of all that might entail; she was so very afraid.

Later that afternoon, Lacey sat in the chair near the fireplace and struggled mightily to sew up a long tear along the sleeve of one of her husband's flannel shirts. Lord, how she hated this mending business, but she knew she had to do at least this much and cook for him too if she expected to get out of performing that other chore. After jabbing the needle back through the thick cloth and pricking her already tender fingertip again, Lacey hunched over her lap, glaring fiercely at the tangle of knots in the long black thread, and renewed her assault on the tear. Then she heard the front door bang against the inside wall of the house.

Startled, Lacey glanced up to see Hawke standing in the doorway, his large frame silhouetted by the explosion of sunlight behind him. Her heart lurched at the unexpected sight of her husband, then nearly quit beating altogether. Hawke didn't say a word at first, but just stood there, his feet spread, his expression full of purpose.

He was wearing his buckskins, she noticed, the shirt gaped open to his navel. That made it easy for Lacey to spot the sharply defined ridges of Hawke's smooth, muscled chest as well as the faint sheen of perspiration clinging to his cinnamon skin. If that wasn't enough to give her pause, his long hair had come free of its thong, and now hung loose around his broad shoulders.

Between the way he was dressed and his entire manner, she suddenly had the feeling that something had entered the room with him, a palatable sense of urgency . . . or danger. Alarmed by the idea, but somehow excited by it as well, Lacey drew in a sharp breath, then shivered from head to toe.

Although he was pleased by his wife's open fascination with him, Hawke remained tight-lipped and serious, but not harsh as he finally said, "Afternoon. Sewing are you?"

"O-oh, ah, aye, that I am. One of your shirts I found with a big tear in it, in fact."

Hawke stepped into the room. "Can you put it aside for a while? Crowfoot's gone down to Three Elk to visit Caleb for a few days and meet the other Irish bride. I could use some help in the barn, if you don't mind."

"Oh, aye!" Even if he'd suggested she bake a pie, she'd have tried it just to get out of the mending! "I'll come with you right away."

After she snipped the thread and tied the ends together, Lacey stored the needle and scissors in the cigar box on the table, then rose and tossed the shirt toward the chair. The flannel material touched down on the pine seat but then sprang back at her in the next instant instead. Puzzled, Lacey gave the shirt a good yank and tossed it again, but this time her navy skirt went along with it, and she finally saw the reason why. Somehow, she'd managed to sew her husband's flannel shirt to her own clothes!

Hawke struggled to keep a serious expression as Lacey raised her gaze to meet his, exposing her crimson features. Between the odd mating she'd done with their clothing, and her horrified expression, he almost lost the battle with his composure, but he couldn't laugh at her now! Not after coming up with the perfect plan at last.

Trying to diffuse the situation as quickly as possible,

Hawke strode over to the cigar box, removed the scissors from it, then dropped to one knee and snipped the threads which held the two items of clothing together. "There," he said. "No harm done."

"I—I ne'er tried to sew before, y-you know," she muttered, her tongue tripping over her teeth. "I told you that once, and also that I'm willing to learn how—"

"It doesn't matter," he interrupted, in too much of a hurry to discuss mending or her plans to become a better seamstress. "I was just going to use that shirt for rags anyway. Will you come with me to the barn now? That's where I really do need your help."

"Oh, well, of course."

The minute Hawke turned his back and started for the door, an enormously relieved Lacey glanced down at her skirt to look for any damage she might have inflicted upon it. The puncture marks from the needle had faded by now, leaving nothing but Hawke's memory—and perhaps his damnable ledger book—to point out her ineptitude as a seamstress. Lacey took it as a lucky sign anyway and lightly tapped the heels of her boots together, jingling her spurs. Then she followed her husband out the door. It didn't matter the manner of chore Hawke had selected for her to do in the barn, she thought with anticipation. Compared to the curse of this silly mending business, anything else he asked of her would be like picking clover!

Once they were outside, instead of going straight to the barn, Hawke directed Lacey to follow him to the hitching post out front where a horse was tied.

"This is Dolly," he said, taking the animal by the halter as he introduced her. "She's part mustang and, I suspect, a little bit of everything else that roamed these hills over the years. I haven't had much time to work with her yet, but I think she might be a good little saddle horse one day. Maybe even for you, if you like her."

"For me?"

He nodded. "What do you think of her?"

Surprised by the offer, but pleased since Lacey took this gift as a definite sign that Hawke had forgiven her outburst in the kitchen, she examined the cute little bay mare. Dolly was dark brown all over with a black mane and tail, a white blaze which ran from her forelock to the tip of her nose, and four white socks, the pair in the rear decorated with black spots which resembled anklets.

Lacey offered her left palm to the animal's muzzle. "She's a beauty, Mr. Winterhawke, a sweet little lass and one I'd be proud to call my own. I thank you kindly."

"Hawke, Lacey," he corrected gently, "just Hawke. And you're welcome. I'm going to clean her up a little now, and I'm not too sure how she's going to feel about having water splashed over her. I'd like you to hold her and make her acquaintance, speaking quietly like you did with Taffy. Just keep her as relaxed as possible. Can you manage?"

"Oh, aye—the lass is already acting like a very good friend of mine." And it was true. Everywhere Lacey touched Dolly, the animal leaned into her, begging for more. "You can go on about your business now. We'll be just fine."

"I'm sure you will." Hawke gave Lacey a long look as he pulled the tails of his shirt out of his trousers, completely unlaced the garment, then slipped it off and hung it over the hitching post. Taking the bucket in one hand and a rag in the other, he began washing the animal, explaining a little more about her as he worked. "Dolly's too small to sell to the cavalry, and because of her size I'd pretty much decided against breeding her, too. Now that she's in season, though, I figured I'd give her one chance to see what she and Phantom can come up with. It might just turn out to be a good match after all."

"You mean the lass is to become a mother?"

"If she catches, she will be in just under a year."

As if agreeing to the plan, Dolly raised her head and uttered a shrill whinny, the effort vibrating her entire body, and then she began to stamp nervously in place. When a resounding whinny echoed from the barn in response to her call, Dolly's tail began to twitch and she sidestepped, swinging her rump up hard against Hawke's backside.

"Easy, girl," he murmured. "It won't be long now. Hold her a little tighter, would you, Lacey?"

"Oh, aye." She renewed her grip, doing a good job of calming the horse, and was listening hard to Hawke's instructions and explanations, but the majority of Lacey's attention—and her gaze—was focused on the fact that he was wearing nothing but his buckskin trousers; pants, now that they were wet, that clung to his muscular thighs and rode down low on his trim hips.

She'd never seen so much of *him* before, always going out of her way to keep her eyes shut each morning and night as he slipped in and out of bed. Now that she had looked upon her husband's nearly nude body, Lacey couldn't keep her eyes off his nakedness, especially the way the muscles of his back and shoulders rippled and bunched while he worked on bathing the little mare.

Dolly whinnied again, and once more received a return call from the barn. This time, she tossed her head and tried to twist out of Lacey's grasp. "Behave yourself . . . lass," she said, her voice faltering, a little breathless. "You must obey Hawke and let him finish with you."

She glanced at him then, aware he'd turned his gaze on her, and found herself trapped as usual. Yet, something in the way he was looking at her today was different, ominous even. It gave her a little flutter down low in her tummy, but then Hawke's curious expression vanished, and in its place, he flashed the dazzling smile that always turned her insides to jam. A sudden tremor racked Lacey's body, and her knees went weak.

She tried to draw a breath of air, but gasped instead. "Lord," she said, fanning herself, "isn't it a hot one outside today?"

The wind that always seemed to be blowing through Centennial Valley felt cool against Hawke's skin, almost chilly, but he smiled as he said, "Just a touch." Then he picked up the long white strip of cloth he'd rolled into a ball, and began to wrap Dolly's tail with it.

Still having trouble holding the mare in place, not to mention keeping her own body under control, Lacey asked, "Why are you putting a bandage on the lass's tail? Has she hurt herself?"

"No, she's fine." He spoke to his wife in his best gentling voice, the tone low and husky. "Horsehair is very strong, almost like wire. The bandage is just a precaution to make sure Phantom doesn't get cut."

"Phantom? What does he have to do with her tail?"

"As I said earlier, I've decided I'd like to see what they can produce together." Hawke glanced at Lacey and winked. "Are you ready to go to the barn? Dolly's getting really impatient."

The horse was dancing in place by now, but Lacey barely took notice of the animal as the implications of what Hawke was suggesting sank in. Surely he didn't mean he expected her to help in the actual *mating* of the horses.

She took a breath, which again was more of a gasp, and said, "You intend to . . . to breed Dolly with Phantom, then?"

"That's the way it's usually done." Hawke circled the

mare's hindquarters, then moved up to the hitching post
to untie her. "She's getting awfully skittish. It might be
best if I walk her to the barn. You can take over again in
there."

"B-But . . . " Hurrying along behind Hawke and Dolly,
Lacey couldn't help but notice that he hadn't bothered to
put his shirt back on. And somehow he'd managed to get
water all over the seat of his buckskins; now they clung to
his backside, making that area look as if he wore nothing
at all. Allowing herself a little more of the visual luxury,
Lacey's gaze traveled up and down the length of her
husband's body as she asked, "But can't you just turn
Phantom loose in his corral, or in with the mares to
accomplish the, ah, deed?"

He answered her from over his shoulder. "No, Irish. A
million things can go wrong when you let horses breed
in the pasture. I've seen everything from stallions who've
been kicked in very, er, sensitive places, damaging them
badly enough to ruin them as studs, to broken legs,
which ruins them period. Phantom is too valuable to me
to be taking any chances with him." He paused then,
turned, and gave Lacey a piercing look. "This is one day,
Irish miss, when I'm not about to let anything go wrong.
Come along now."

With that, Hawke and the mare passed through the
wide double doors, and in a second were swallowed up
inside the barn. Lacey, who stood just outside, gulped and
wrapped her arms around her waist. Her heart was
pounding crazily, her mind a flurry of wild thoughts. Part
of her, a very wicked part, she thought, was enormously
excited by the idea of observing this ritual; an act, like
birth, she'd never witnessed before in any creature. And
yet to watch such an intimacy in the company of a man,
never mind that he was her husband, seemed terribly—

"Lacey!" Hawke called from the bowels of the barn. "I

need your help in here, and I need it now!" As if to punctuate the statement further, both Dolly and Phantom cut loose with shrill whinnies, startling her to action.

"Coming," she cried, rushing inside the huge building. As her eyes adjusted to the darker lighting, she saw Hawke standing in front of the sturdily built hitching rail he'd erected in the center of the barn. There he did everything from trimming hooves to doctoring sick animals, and apparently . . . breeding them, too.

Out of breath for more reasons than one now, Lacey stopped just short of Dolly. The horses were continually calling to each other by now, their shrill cries filling the inside of the barn with a deafening clamor. She shouted over the din. "What do you want me to do?"

"Stand right where you are. I'm going to run Dolly by Phantom a time or two. She's never been bred before and might be a little afraid." Hawke turned away from the mare and focused on his wife. "It's all right, though. Phantom will know how to relax her and make her want him as much as he wants her. It's his job. Just be ready to take her if I call on you."

Lacey nodded, but she had the strangest feeling that Hawke was talking more about her than the horses. Mesmerized as the drama between the equines unfolded, she dismissed the thought and watched as Hawke brought Dolly lengthwise against the stallion's stall. The mare squealed and kicked out at the wooden door separating her from the stud. Phantom arched his neck and reached out to her from over the top of the door, and she quieted in an instant. Nickering low but continually, he nuzzled her withers, then moved slowly down her spine, nuzzling and lightly nipping at her as he went along. When he reached her croup just short of her wrapped tail, the nickering grew louder, the nips more passionate. Dolly, responding to the stud, flipped her tail to one side and sprayed the stall door. Phantom raised his head high, stretching his magnificent silvery neck to its full length, and curled his upper lip to better enjoy Dolly's scent. Then he cut loose with a savage scream.

"That's it for now, friend," said Hawke as he forcefully led the excited mare away from the stall. Moving quickly now, he tied Dolly firmly to the hitching rail, then turned to Lacey. Things were going just as he'd planned with both the animals *and* his wife, if the look in Lacey's eyes meant what he hoped it did. Not only did she appear to be fascinated by the horses, but he thought he glimpsed more than a passing interest in her husband there, too.

"Come here, Irish," he said in hushed tones. She immediately moved over to where he stood, away from the animals, but in clear view of them. "I'm going to get Phantom now, and if all goes well, just the sight of you nearby will keep Dolly calm enough for her to behave. If I need you, I'll tell you exactly what to do. Got it?"

"Aye," is what she said, but it came out as more of a sigh. Flashing that dazzling smile her way one more time, Hawke turned and started for the stallion, his back and the wide expanse of muscle there glistening in the semi-darkness. Lacey caught her breath, then took another as Hawke released the latch and led the sleek stallion out of the enclosure toward the mare. The horses were calling to one another again, but Lacey paid no mind to the racket they caused. She was listening to her husband as he spoke to the animals, concentrating on the calm, firm manner in which he guided the powerful stud. There was no doubt to her or the beasts as to who was in control of the situation here.

"Easy, Phantom," Hawke said in that low dark voice. "Remember your manners, and speak softly to the lady. She's not going anywhere."

The stallion tossed his head impatiently, but didn't make a move that wasn't orchestrated by his master. When Hawke guided Phantom around to Dolly's haunches, Lacey saw that the stud was erect and so huge, she could hardly believe it. She gasped involuntarily, then quickly averted her gaze.

"Don't worry, Irish," came Hawke's soothing voice. "Remember they're made for each other, a perfect fit. Watch, you'll see."

His voice as captivating as his gaze by now, Lacey slowly turned in time to see Hawke lead the stallion up close to the mare. Then he gave Phantom the signal to mount Dolly. The stud rose majestically above the little bay, but lowered himself onto her back with a surprising gentleness, a lightness which didn't seem possible of this thousand-pound beast.

In spite of Phantom's gentle manner and his strict adherence to the rules set down by Hawke, Lacey cringed as the steed joined with Dolly. She started to look away, but then realized that the mare did not seem to be in any pain. In fact, not only was she pain-free, but the little bay had turned her neck around as far as she could get it, and was rubbing her nose against the stallion's muzzle as if kissing him! After a few powerful lunges, the mating was over. Now it was Dolly who nickered, Dolly who appeared the more aggressive of the two animals.

After guiding Phantom through a mannerly dismount, Hawke moved the stallion a safe distance away from the mare. Then he glanced at Lacey from over the exhausted stud's back, locking her in his gaze.

She wondered if he could see that she was trembling, short of breath, and completely consumed by what she'd witnessed here—consumed by that and the sudden image of Hawke joining with her, their steaming bodies entwined as one. At the thought, Lacey grew hot all over, filled with strange and wonderful urges, most of them the needy kind. Very, very needy. But in spite of all that, she was sure she could get control of herself. At least, she had been sure until it occurred to her that Hawke might be thinking of the two of them together as well. She studied his dark expression, looking deeply into his eyes, and thought that maybe he was.

After that, Lacey was lost. As much under Hawke's control as the horses had been. She would do whatever he asked of her. Strangest and most surprising of all, the idea didn't trouble her in the least. She just stood there, basking in the heat of her husband's intense gaze, and waited for him to make the next move.

Encouraged by what he saw in his wife's eyes, Hawke quickly put Phantom back into the stall, then walked Dolly directly to an enclosure several doors away. He did this without taking the usual precaution of walking the mare around a while, something he usually did to ensure retention of the stallion's seed. But today, Hawke wasn't particularly interested in breeding horses. Today, he was interested only in his wife. And if he hadn't completely misread her expression, she was fiercely aroused. Ready, at last, to give herself to him.

Swiftly crossing over to where Lacey stood, Hawke swept her into his arms. Muttering low under his breath, the sound not so unlike one of Phantom's nickers, he said, "Did you see anything ghastly between those two, Irish?"

She shook her head, unable to find words.

Hawke grinned, then slipped his hand down Lacey's spine and tugged her up tight against his hips. "Do you understand now that lovemaking, and all that goes with it, is nature's way and nothing to be afraid of?"

Blushing violently, her breath coming more rapidly than before, again she nodded, still too overwhelmed to speak.

"Good. Then maybe now you'll understand the need I was talking about before. I want you, Lacey." His voice dropped even lower, became guttural. "I want you badly." Hawke reached down to take her hand, then carefully placed her palm against his groin. His eyes closed, and a husky growl escaped his lips.

Lacey tried to pull away from him at first, but Hawke held her hand fast, insisting that she touch him and learn the depth of his terrible need. She allowed herself this, feeling the hardness of him through damp buckskin and the moist heat radiating through his trousers. Then, a surge of reckless desire driving her on, she allowed more, giving her fingers the freedom to travel along the entire length of that hardness. When she finally reached the tip, Lacey gasped and stepped out of Hawke's embrace.

"Oh, goodness, and by all that's holy! I don't think that I can accommodate you, sir!" Lacey snuck a quick peek at what she'd felt, then rolled her eyes.

Chuckling softly, Hawke said, "We're made for each other, remember? A perfect fit."

"Aye, I remember what you said about the horses, but I think there must be something wrong with me, for I cannot imagine that I have the part you'd be needing to, to . . . " She waved her fingers in the general direction of his crotch. "To make this fit."

Laughing out loud now, Hawke took Lacey's hand in his. "Why don't we give it a try anyway, Mrs. Winterhawke? You might be pleasantly surprised."

13

'Tis on her own account the cat purrs.
—A common Irish saying

The question he'd asked Lacey was purely rhetorical.

Hawke didn't even pretend to wait for his wife's reply. In spite of her insistence that their pairing could never work, he just swept her off her feet and carried her to a stall he'd filled with fresh bedding straw not more than an hour ago. He hadn't really planned on staying in the barn, but since a few doubts had already crept into Lacey's mind, Hawke was afraid she'd cool off by the time they made it to the house. As for those doubts, he suspected her protests were not protests at all, but pleas for him to reassure her that all would be fine.

Dropping to his knees, Hawke gently laid his wife down in the straw. He flipped his head, sending the long dark strands of his hair over his left shoulder, then lowered himself to her side. Lacey stiffened as he reached for her. "Relax, Irish," he whispered. "It's all right to be afraid of the unknown; that's nature's way of protecting you from harm, but please don't be afraid of me."

"I—I am trying to be brave, husband, but I honestly cannot see how this will work." It struck her that impossible as it seemed, she really did want this to work. She wanted Hawke.

"Tell you what," he murmured, scattering kisses across her cheeks and lips. "If I do anything you don't like, you tell me and I'll stop." At least, he was reasonably sure he could. "Fair enough?"

"Aye, 'tis more than fair." As she realized that she'd given him more than her trust—permission to proceed— the fire smoldering in Lacey's body flared, turning her cheeks bright enough to rival her hair. When Hawke reached for the buttons at the throat of her blouse and began to release them, she made no move to stop him, but squeezed her eyes shut.

"What's wrong?" he asked, wondering at her pained expression.

Lifting just one eyelid a crack, Lacey peered at him. "Nothing, I hope, but I cannot watch."

Lacey could hear Hawke's laughter, a kind of warm, low chuckle as he came to her and stretched his big body across hers. Then he began to smother her with kisses, most of them deeply passionate, others playful pecks not so unlike the gentle nips Phantom had given Dolly. In between kisses, he muttered short, endearing little phrases about how cute and shy she was, even as his hands busied themselves with her blouse, tugged at her skirt, and most enjoyably, caressed her skin as if he were putting a shine to a most delicate piece of china. It wasn't until those hands reached forbidden territory— her breasts—that Lacey realized he'd stripped her from the waist up.

"Stop!" she cried, remembering his promise. She

threw her arms across her breasts, then her eyes popped open to meet those of her husband. His chiseled face was less than an inch away from hers, and his eyes had turned an impossibly dark color, almost black, not green. His breathing was shallow, but labored at the same time. And when he finally spoke, his voice sounded husky, as if coming from a very tight throat.

"What's wrong, Irish?"

She glanced down at her chest. "I don't seem to have . . . you have . . . I'm naked, sir!"

Hawke's lips were set in a grim line, but Lacey could see that he was having trouble keeping that expression. The corners of his mouth wobbled and twitched a few moments before he finally said, "From what I understand, what we're doing here is much easier to accomplish without clothing. Besides, you may not want to watch, but I can't wait to have a good look at you. Do you mind so very much?"

Lacey bit her bottom lip. He wanted to *look* at her—*naked*? "I think . . . yes. I think that I do mind. That is, of course, if you don't mind."

Hawke minded one hell of a lot, but he gave in to her modesty. For now. Reaching across her to where he'd tossed her camisole in the straw, he collected the garment, then draped it across her breasts.

"Better now?" he asked. When Lacey nodded and gave him a shy smile, he slipped his hand beneath the blouse and slowly inched his fingers back toward her nipples. She opened her mouth—perhaps to protest—but Hawke quickly covered her lips with his own, kissing her hard, deep, and long; long enough that he had time to caress the crowns of her soft little breasts and coax their peaks to hard, tight nubs.

Lacey was moaning by then, moving beneath him and encouraging Hawke to take the next step. Keeping her

modesty in mind, he didn't remove her skirt or petticoats, but tugged them up to her waist. Then, still kissing
her eager lips and caressing one breast, Hawke caught
the waistband of her drawers with his fingers and started
rolling them down over her hips. When he got them as
far as her knees, he left her mouth in order to pull the
undergarments over her boots. A mistake.

"Stop!" she cried and sat up, pushing her skirt down
to cover her private self.

Hawke sighed heavily, but froze in place. "What's the
problem now, Lacey?"

"'Tisn't a problem as much as I'm wonderin'. What
are you doing?"

He cocked his head and smiled at her. "Removing
your drawers and boots to make you more comfortable,
is all. May I go on?"

"Er, ah—no. I would like to take care of, of my
clothing myself. As for the boots . . . " She pushed her
heels deeper into the straw, making sure he couldn't
see the spurs. "I would like to keep them on, if you
don't mind."

Hawke stared at her incredulously. He'd heard of
cowboys and gunmen who insisted on *dying* with their
boots on, but this was a first. He shrugged. "If that's
what you want, Irish, that's what you'll have."

"Aye, and I thank you kindly." She sat there waiting a
moment, but when he didn't move, Lacey waved her fingers at him. "If you would be so kind as to look away, I'll
be getting to it."

She thought she saw the corners of Hawke's mouth
wobbling again as he turned his back, but she didn't care.
This was embarrassing enough as it was without him
looking at every little private detail of her life. And
besides, if he watched, she'd never get her drawers over
her boots without him spotting the spurs. Lacey quickly

removed her underpinnings, buried them in the straw at her feet, then lay back down.

"You can turn around now. I am ready."

"Are you?" he asked, moving alongside her until his lips were a warm breath away from hers. "Are you sure this time, Lacey?"

She gazed into his eyes, not quite as dark with passion as they'd been, but mesmerizing just the same, then glanced down to his mouth. His lips were parted, moist and ready to claim hers again. Suddenly, Lacey wasn't just ready, but eager.

"Aye," she whispered throatily. "I'm ready for you, my husband."

Hawke's lips met hers before she could even take a breath, soothing a little of the need building up inside her, but increasing it in other ways as well. His hands were on her again, caressing, touching, learning each curve and valley of her breasts, her back, and even her legs. When he grew bolder, reaching around to caress and massage the gentle curves of her bottom, instead of being shocked or offended, Lacey found herself wishing, *hoping* he'd reach around and touch her in other, more private places.

Scandalized by the thought, but stubbornly clinging to it anyway, Lacey almost fainted with sheer excitement when Hawke finally parted her thighs and began to caress the soft skin there. So great was her need for him after that, she'd just about decided to brazenly beg Hawke to move his hands a little higher, when he did just that. The moment his fingers slipped beneath the auburn curls of her most private self and touched her, a lance of intensely surprising pleasure shot through Lacey. For a minute, she thought perhaps she had fainted; and maybe she did. She couldn't be sure. She was only sure that she couldn't stand it if Hawke stopped touching her now.

The need for something built up inside of her, an agonizing conflict of both pleasure and torture for which she couldn't imagine a cure. Her hips were moving of their own volition, writhing one moment, twitching the next, and then her husband left her, interrupting the moment to slip out of his trousers. In the next second, he came back to her, this time squeezing the lower half of his body between her legs. Lacey closed her eyes tightly in preparation for the coming assault, so tightly she thought she could feel the hair of her eyebrows brushing her cheeks.

But Hawke didn't force his way inside her the way the stallion had approached the mare. Instead, he slowly worked at filling her, pausing here and there to whisper encouragement against her burning cheeks. And then his progress came to a sudden, painful halt. He pushed against her again, only to come to the same crashing halt. It didn't take Lacey but a minute to realize that something inside of her was stopping him. She'd been right all along! There was no way Hawke could fit what she'd seen into her tiny body.

"Stop!" she cried, yet again.

"Oh . . . Christ," he muttered thickly, stopping as she'd requested. "Does it hurt you so much?"

The pain didn't worry Lacey in the slightest. "No, 'tisn't that, but I was right! You cannot possibly fit in that wee small space. I am not made right for you."

"Oh, Lacey, sweetheart." Hawke ran his hands through her springy curls, removing the few pins which hadn't already fallen out during their lovemaking. "Believe me, you've got plenty of room for me. I just have to get past nature's little barrier first." She drew her eyebrows together, telling him that she had no idea what he meant. "Hold on to me, Irish, and kiss me. I promise to get it out of the way as quickly as possible."

Although she still didn't know what was going to happen, Lacey obeyed her husband. She wrapped her arms around his neck and brought his mouth down on hers. Then with a shocking suddenness and a blinding flash of pain, he drove into her. If Hawke's lips hadn't been firmly clamped to hers, Lacey thought she probably would have cried out, but even his kiss couldn't stop the muffled sob that erupted in her throat.

When he heard that sound, Hawke abruptly ended the kiss and leaned his head back. Now that he'd filled Lacey completely, he didn't move at all, but stared down at her instead, hoping he hadn't hurt her too badly. She looked surprised, or something like it, but he could detect no hint of fear or discomfort in her expression. In fact, he could feel her newly-expanded muscles relaxing little by little. Then their eyes met, locking for a long moment in silent communication, and Hawke knew that she was quite all right. And ready for her next lesson.

He favored her with a crooked grin and asked, "How are you doing now that we've made things fit? You don't feel ghastly or anything like that, do you?"

Lacey giggled softly. "No, and I'm feeling just fine, thank you kindly."

"Fine? That's it?" She smiled shyly and shrugged. "Well, we'll just have to do something about that now, won't we?"

Another rhetorical question for Hawke began to move then, thrusting slowly, carefully at first, aware that she would probably be very tender. It wasn't long before, tender or not, Lacey began to respond with gusto, meeting his thrusts and encouraging a faster, deeper rhythm. Hawke was more than happy to accommodate her. Pleased beyond measure that his previously timid bride now felt secure and bold enough to move freely beneath him, he dug through the tangle of petticoats beneath them and lifted her thighs, encouraging her to wrap her legs around him. Moaning softly against his chest, Lacey immediately took the hint. She brought her knees up, then hooked her feet, boots and all, around his lower thighs. Something sharp bit into his skin, once, twice, and then, too caught up in the moment to care anymore, the sensation stopped or he failed to notice it again. His entire mind, body, and focus was on Lacey and the rapture building in her expression, the acute pleasure he could hear each time she moaned or called his name.

When a climax claimed a surprised Lacey, stunning her with its intensity and the enormous sense of relief it brought her, she cried out, then threw herself into the finale with abandon. Releasing her hold on Hawke's legs, she dug her heels into the straw beneath her and ground her hips against his in order to savor every pounding spasm of sensation. It wasn't a moment later that he withdrew from her, collapsing into the straw with a final groan, and, she thought, a good bit of cursing. He lay still, not touching or looking at her for what seemed a very long time. Then finally, his breathing more normal, he lifted his head, pushed his damp hair away from his face and smiled at her.

"Pretty ghastly, huh?"

Lacey burst out laughing. "Aye, I cannot remember doing anything so ghastly in my entire life."

Hawke crawled up beside his radiant bride, slipped one arm beneath her, and pulled her into his embrace. As he kissed her, nuzzling her throat and the soft rise of her breasts, the only part not decently covered by the camisole, Lacey became aware of the distant clucking of chickens and the rustling of straw as Hazel and the horses moved around in their enclosures. Had the animals been so quiet before, she wondered, or had she just been unable to hear anything else above the pounding of her own heart? She breathed deeply, picking up the usual warm animal odors and the crisp smell of fresh bedding straw, but also something new, a certain muskiness in the scent of her man that hadn't been there before they'd joined together as one. It was an earthy scent, not unpleasant, and one that sent a renewed shiver of excitement throughout her.

"Are you cold?" Hawke asked, raising his head from her breasts.

"Oh, no, not a'tall. I—I'm fine."

"Just fine again?"

She blushed deeply. "Better than fine. I'm wonderful."

"That you are." Hawke tapped the tip of her nose with his finger. "All in all, I'd say this turned out to be one of those 'fine soft days,' 'tis it not, Mrs. Winterhawke?"

Laughing over the way he'd imitated her, she gently corrected him. "When I say 'tis a fine soft morning, that means the weather is just a little misty, but not raining. I don't think we've had much mist or rain on this day, sir. What we've had, I would say, is a grand time of it."

"I would say that too." Reaching beneath her skirt, Hawke gave her backside a little squeeze. "I suppose if I were to call this a, 'fine soft bottom, Mrs. Winterhawke,' it wouldn't be right either, then?"

"Not a'tall, Mr. Winterhawke!" Lacey gave his chest a playful slap, then indulged herself by leaving her hand there. Caressing his smooth dark skin, loving the way it felt beneath her palm, she said, "I didn't know men could have such nice skin. The only man I ever saw without a shirt was my dear father a long time ago. It seems to me he was a very hairy fellow, indeed."

"That distinct lack of body hair comes from the Indian side of me."

"Ummm. I like it."

Disturbed by the memory that she didn't like it well

enough to bear children who might have that same skin, Hawke rolled over onto his back. He already regretted the promise he'd made about preventing babies; oh, not because he suddenly felt a deep need for progeny, but because of Lacey's reasons for wanting to remain childless. He'd felt robbed as he'd spilled his life's fluids into the straw, inferior to his bride, somehow, and that thought disturbed him as much as withdrawing had.

Aware suddenly of the straw beneath his body, and the fact that it scratched at him, stinging his thighs and calves in an odd way, Hawke sat up to investigate. He slid his hands up and down the backs of his legs, feeling several small welts over the area, and even a large one on his left buttock.

"What the hell have I gotten into?" he asked Lacey as he rolled to his side, exposing the area to her.

Blushing furiously at the sight of her husband's naked backside, but loathe to look away, Lacey peered at the little red streaks on his legs. She touched one of the welts, wondering what could possibly have happened to him, then stated the obvious. "You've been scratched up by something."

"I remember now!" Hawke suddenly righted himself and sat up. "It's those damn boots you insisted on wearing."

Before she could even think of getting out of his way, Hawke grabbed one of her legs and lifted it, exposing not just the boot she wore, but the silver spur attached to it. He stared at it as if he couldn't quite believe his eyes.

"What the . . . hell?"

" 'Tis spurs, sir."

"I know they're spurs! Where did you get them, and why are you wearing them?"

"I—you see . . . " Lacey gulped, wondering how to explain this to Hawke without getting him angrier than he already was. "I thought they would bring me luck, being made like shamrocks and all. I only meant to borrow them. I know they belong to you, and that I didn't have the right to—"

"You're my wife now, Lacey. You have the right to just about anything you want around here. I'd appreciate it if you'd let me know first the next time you see something you like." He paused, remembering the curious metallic noises he heard now and then when she was around. "Just how long have you had those spurs, by the way?"

Again, she gulped. "Ah, since the morning I made pancakes for you, sir. Crowfoot gave them to me."

The boy again.

Crowfoot and Lacey, two of a kind for reasons he hadn't quite figured out yet. Another of those irrational talons of jealousy slashed through Hawke's gut, vividly pointing out that no matter what had transpired here in the straw between himself and his wife, he really didn't know the first thing about her. Oh, he knew plenty about her body now, but nothing of her soul. She'd allowed the wild boy who lived in the barn a glimpse of that soul, Hawke just knew she had. Why wouldn't she show a little more of it to her husband?

14

No man is rich enough to buy back his own past.
—Oscar Wilde

"*Relax, Lacey, let your hips* move naturally and bend your knees slightly. Don't try to force the rhythm, fall in time with it. You're too stiff. Lean back a little."

Exasperated by the barrage of instructions, most of which she didn't quite understand, Lacey impulsively raised her hands to the skies as if begging for help from up above. Both reins slipped from her fingers in the process. The moment the leather straps hit the dirt floor of the training ring, Dolly stepped on one of them, causing her to stumble and pitch forward. Lacey flew out of the saddle like she'd been shot from a cannon.

Hawke rushed to her side, and Dolly, who'd retreated to the other side of the ring, stood there eyeing her as if to say, "What are you doing down there?"

Lacey, still sitting in the exaggerated sprawl in which she'd landed, cursed as she wiped the gritty Wyoming dust from her eyes. "Damn the bit and these miserable riding lessons, too!"

"Hey, Irish!" Hawke said, dropping to his heels beside her. "Are you all right? Anything broken?"

She rubbed the ache out of her right wrist, then shook it. "I think I've a few bumps for my trouble, is all."

"Why'd you let go of the reins? You're were doing just fine until then."

"I wasn't, and you cannot say that I was!" Tears sprang into her eyes. "I cannot do anything right around here. Anything!"

"Oh, now that's not true and you know it."

But instead of calming her, Hawke's words increased her tears. Because he couldn't think what else to do, he gathered Lacey in his embrace and held her, giving her outburst time to run its course. He'd learned to do that and more in his quest to understand the woman beneath the unruly mop of coppery curls; most of all, he'd learned not to rush her, but to give the both of them a little more time in which to become better acquainted.

After their first intimate interlude in the barn and the doubts which had assailed him immediately following, Hawke quickly made a decision to ignore the things that could never be, and to go to work instead on concentrating on what was. After all, he'd never expected to have a wife in the first place, much less a perfect match. And who was he to brood or complain about Lacey's tendency toward secrecy, when he was at least as guilty in that department?

Because of this silent vow Hawke had made to himself, as far as he could tell, he and Lacey had come to know each other a lot better over the past few weeks; if in no other way, most definitely physically. He hadn't had a minute's trouble convincing Lacey to bed him after the first time, that was for sure. Since both of them had a fondness for the out of doors, more often than not, that bed was a secluded patch of meadow grass or a mat of pine needles deep in the forest behind the ranch. They'd even learned to laugh together over the fact that Hawke always took the added precaution of checking his wife's footgear before they made love, and removing any objects which might cause him bodily damage. Not that she'd quit wearing her lucky spurs altogether.

Another bonus during this period was the fact that Lacey had gradually begun to get over her extreme modesty, allowing Hawke more than just an occasional glimpse of her pert little breasts.

That loosening of her modesty extended to him as well. Now whenever he caught Lacey gazing at his naked body—an almost daily occurrence—her glances were less furtive, more curious and open. Hawke rather immodestly put this down to the method he used for getting to know her better; gentling, his specialty.

Gentling worked so well on his horses, Winterhawke-trained animals were bringing top dollar in the area and Hawke's reputation as the finest horse-trainer around was spreading into the state of Colorado and the Dakota Territories as well. Some of the neighboring ranchers laughed at his methods, preferring the more rough and tumble force-breaking of stock, but with Hawke's way, there was less chance of ruining a good mount. And fewer broken bones.

So far, he'd never come across a horse that didn't respond to gentling, and had been able to turn even the most ornery steed into an animal worth its weight in gold. Now, he thought, holding Lacey tighter, even though he hadn't been looking for a wife or even thinking that he needed one, he'd found a woman who responded to him in much the same way. And she was worth far more than mere gold. The Irish miss brightened Winterhawke Ranch in a way he never could, making the entire spread seem more welcoming, warmer somehow. A part of that was the way she'd taken to the livestock. With the exception of the chickens, who still didn't know quite what to make of her, all the animals were very fond of Lacey, a talent that couldn't be forced or faked. Why did she have so much trouble seeing the good in herself? he wondered.

Her tears dried-up at last, Lacey pushed away from her husband and took a handkerchief from her skirt pocket. After drying her eyes and blowing her nose, she faced Hawke and made an attempt to apologize for ruining a perfectly good riding lesson.

"Please forgive my silliness, husband. I know that wailing is best left to the banshees," she paused for a hiccup, "and that all this blubbering cannot be much help in learning to ride one of your fine beasts. Maybe 'tis a better idea for me to leave the horses to you. I could try the mending again, I suppose."

Hawke couldn't have kept the burst of laughter in if he'd tried. Between Lacey's tear-and-dirt-streaked face, hair that as usual was half in and half out of its bun, and the memory of his flannel shirt sewed to the front of her skirt, he might have done some damage to his throat if he'd tried to keep it inside.

When his laughter ebbed, Hawke climbed to his feet, pulling Lacey up with him. "Is that really where you'd rather be on a beautiful day like this, Irish? In the house sticking your pretty little fingers with needles?"

Her stained features fell into a pout. "I would rather be shoveling up cow flop, and you know it, but I fear I don't have the talent to sit atop a horse. I ne'er will have."

"Well, then maybe I ought to send you to the barn. Last I looked, there was plenty of cow flop just waiting for someone to get on the business end of the shovel."

Lacey made an effort to keep her pout, but a grudging smile broke through anyway. "I wasn't serious about that, but I do wish I could cook your meals, mend your clothes, and ride horses the way you do. If I could only–"

"I like you just the way you are, Irish. Haven't you figured that out yet?" He caught her chin in the web of his hand, looked deeply into her eyes and impulsively added, "I don't care if you never do a thing around this ranch as long as you keep looking at me the way you do and smiling."

Afraid if he allowed himself to go on, he'd make a complete jackass out of himself, Hawke brought his lips down on Lacey's and kissed her for all he was worth. She'd begun crying again, he knew that when the salty taste of her tears slipped into the corners of his mouth, but Hawke kept on kissing her, holding her as if she might disappear should he let her go. Then at once, some second sense told him they were no longer alone.

Hawke abruptly released his wife and turned to find Crowfoot, who hadn't stopped by the ranch in over a week now, standing at the edge of the ring.

"Soldiers come," said the boy, pointing down the road. Then he turned as if to head for his hideout in the barn, but Hawke stopped him.

"Wait there a minute, Crowfoot. I want to talk to you." He took Lacey by the hand and led her to the other side of the ring. "You ought to go into the house now and wash up a little. I've got business to conduct with the cavalry, and you'd just be bored out here with us anyway."

She bristled, remembering the way he'd rushed her off the last time soldiers came to do business. "Save your false music for the animals without brains to understand the words or tongues to feed it right back to you." Lacey turned on her heel, her head held high, and added, "Just let me know when 'tis acceptable for me to come outside again." And with that, she swished her skirts and stalked off toward the house.

Hawke wasn't quite sure where he'd gone wrong with her, but he didn't have time to do a damn thing about it. The quartermaster from Fort Sanders was coming up the road along with a detail to fetch the horses he'd agreed to purchase. And Crowfoot was still waiting by the corral, pacing in place, looking more than a little anxious to get back to Three Elk—where surely he felt more appreciated. How in God's name, Hawke paused to wonder, had his life ever gotten so damned complicated?

As the cavalry officer neared, Hawke shouted, "Just give me a minute, and I'll be right with you." Then he hurried over to where Crowfoot waited, and asked, "Are you figuring on staying a while?"

The boy shrugged, averting his gaze.

"I'd really like it if you'd stick around here at least a week, Crowfoot. I realize that I kinda of ran you off before, but it was just so I could get acquainted with my new wife. I need your help around here, you know, and besides that—" Again he paused, swallowing a pea-sized knot of leftover jealousy. "Lacey's missed you, too. In fact, she's kinda upset right now. Maybe you could go to the house and say hello to her while I help the cavalry round up their horses."

Crowfoot stared hard at him a good long time, and for a moment, Hawke wasn't sure the boy was going to agree to anything. Finally, his eyes still a little hostile, he said, "I go see Lady. She likes Crowfoot." Then he was gone.

Inside the house, Lacey stalked from room to room, alternately cursing her husband for sending her away each time visitors came to the ranch, and lamenting the fact that she couldn't figure out what it was that made him feel so ashamed of her that he couldn't bring himself to introduce her to the soldiers outside. Hawke had told her several times over how pretty he thought she was, so Lacey was reasonably certain he didn't think her too plain to show off. She was well-spoken and mannered enough to get by in the American West, more so than most, in fact. So what was it about Lacey Winterhawke that embarrassed her husband so badly? Surely a stranger couldn't guess that she was unable to perform the most basic wifely duties just by merely making her acquaintance!

Pausing to glance at her reflection in the only looking glass in the entire place, a small mirror nailed to the wall by the hat rack, Lacey gasped. She figured she'd be a wee bit disheveled after the tumble she'd taken from Dolly, but not only was her hair messier than usual, her tear-streaked face looked like a map of the Laramie River and all its tributaries! Was it possible Hawke had sent her inside to spare *her* the embarrassment, not himself?

A light knock sounded at the door then, and Crowfoot poked his head inside. "Hi, Lady. I come in?"

"Oh, aye, and please do," she said, happy for the company. "Why don't you wait for me in the kitchen? There's a bowl of fresh-picked berries on the table just waiting for a lad like you to eat 'em all up. I need a moment to run upstairs and clean the dirt from my face."

Crowfoot didn't move toward the kitchen. He just looked at her closely, then let out a muffled giggle.

Her own image still sharp in her mind, Lacey laughed along with him. And in that moment, she saw a way to make a point with the boy. "'Tis a frightful sight a little dirt can make of a person, is it no? And sad, too, when that person cannot see how one little speck of dirt might turn other folks away."

Crowfoot's expression was guarded, but reflective, so she went on. "I'm thinking you and I have been so quick to defend ourselves, we haven't taken the time to learn what Hawke can teach us. He is a very good teacher, too, I'm thinking. 'Tis possible, I think, that we haven't let him help us all he could. What do you say?"

Crowfoot stopped laughing immediately, frowned, then cocked his head to one side as if thinking the matter over. "Yes, lady. Possible."

"Good, then. Would you like to help me make a little surprise for Hawke, something so grand he'll be proud of the both of us no matter how it turns out?"

Crowfoot gave her a shy smile. "A surprise? Good idea, lady."

"All right then!" She grasped his hands, ignoring the grit and days-old grime built up on his palms and fingers, and danced the boy around in a circle. "Time's a wastin.' Let us be getting to it!"

After the cavalry left with their horses, Hawke was in such a good mood, he couldn't wait to get back to the house and share the account of the new deal with his bride. He'd hardly stepped one foot inside the door before she stopped him, insisting that the floors were wet and asking him to stay outside and finish his chores before joining her for the evening meal.

He grumbled to himself over the delay, but agreed to her request and went to the barn in search of Crowfoot. He was nowhere to be found. Hawke supposed the boy had taken off for Three Elk in spite of the need for him here. In light of the way the young man had been treated at Winterhawke of late, Hawke couldn't really blame him for leaving, and thought he probably would have done the same thing under the circumstances. The next time Crowfoot stopped by, Hawke promised himself, he'd take him aside and do a little fence-mending.

As he finished the final chore of the night and headed

for the house at last, it occurred to Hawke that a good start with the boy might be to let him have his pick of the remaining three-year-old mustangs. He was old enough for his own horse, and more than capable of taking care of one. Feeling good about the decision, Hawke removed his hat and vest as he climbed the steps to the back porch, hung the items on a large brass hook near the door, and walked into the kitchen. Surprising him, a melange of aromas assailed his senses; slowly roasted beef heavily scented with onions, spices, and other unidentified vegetables, along with the contrasting odor of something sweet. Had Lacey cooked the berries they'd picked the other day? he wondered. If so, what in hell could she have made out of them?

Cutting off his thoughts, she stepped into the room from the back porch, carrying a pickle jar filled with fragrant bluebells. "Oh, I didn't hear you come in, husband. Have you finished your chores for the day?"

He nodded slowly, suspicious of her brightly innocent expression and general crisp clean appearance. She wore the same white blouse and navy skirt as always, but they were freshly ironed, and she'd even pinned a small cluster of bluebells to her collar. More unusual than all that, not so much as one spiral of russet hair was out of place, a feat all on its own.

"What have you been up to?" he asked bluntly.

Lacey looked at him as if to say, "Who, me?" then inclined her pretty head toward the stove. A large kettle gently simmered on the back burner, the low heat pushing intermittent bubbles to the surface where they exploded with a tantalizing fragrance.

Hawke was instantly hungry—and confused. Since the day Lacey had nearly burned the house down, he'd done all the cooking, and she'd been extremely grateful for the concession. "What's that on the stove?" he asked, "and who cooked it?"

"'Tis a pot of Irish stew I made using Kate's recipe, but I had to use beef in place of lamb. I think it didn't matter, though—does it smell good to you?"

Although it was unnecessary, as his mouth had been watering since he stepped into the room, he sniffed the air. "It smells wonderful. Did you just say that *you* fired up the stove and cooked the stew?"

"Well, a leprechaun didn't come along to do the chore for me, if that is what you're suggesting, sir." She deposited the flowers at the center of the table—rather, at the center of a sheet she'd fashioned into a tablecloth—then turned back to him with a sweet smile. "I did cook the meal, but I must confess that I did not build the fire in the stove. I had a wee bit of help on that score." Hurrying back toward the living room, Lacey poked her head around the corner. "'Tis time we were taking our meal. Will you join us please?"

It wasn't until then that Hawke noticed she'd set three places at the small table and added the rocking chair from upstairs to the two in the kitchen. "Who in the—"

Crowfoot, or rather a new version of the young man, walked into the room then, and the sentence died in Hawke's throat. The boy was, in a word, *clean!* His hair had been freshly washed, trimmed, and plaited into neat braids which hung down his back. Even more surprising, his hands and face, maybe his entire body, had been scrubbed clean, and he wore the new set of buckskins Hawke had been trying to get him into ever since the first day of spring. As the boy limped over to the table, Hawke couldn't help but notice that he still wore a ball of burlap around his crippled foot, but it, too, looked as fresh and clean as the rest of him.

Crowfoot took a seat in one of the old kitchen chairs, leaving Hawke to choose between the other and the rocker. "We eat now." He grinned, an expression as rare as a bath. "Good surprise you think?"

"A hell of a good surprise." Hawke found himself grinning back, then he glanced at Lacey and gave her a nod of admiration. Not only had he and Caleb been unable to get the boy to wash, but the kid had always been adamantly opposed to joining them at mealtime unless they were huddled around a campfire. How had Lacey managed the impossible?

Stunned, Hawke took the seat opposite the boy, leaving the rocker for his wife, and then he took a cautious glance at her. She was busy dishing up the stew and looking so confident, if he hadn't known better, he'd have sworn she'd been doing it all her life.

"And how did your business with the cavalry go?" she asked, the jingle of spurs accompanying her as she approached the table with two steaming bowls. After depositing the food in front of her "men," Lacey returned to the stove.

"Ah, it went better than I expected, another surprise I guess, in this day of strange goings on."

"A surprise? I thought you were expecting the cavalry to come get their horses. What is so odd about that?"

Waiting until she'd returned to the table with a basket of biscuits and her own bowl of stew before he answered, Hawke's news fairly burst from him. "While the quartermaster was here, he took the time to look over my two-year-olds. He was as impressed with their quality as he was by the way I've broken the horses he already bought. He decided on the spot to draw up a contract with me personally for all fifty head. There's no question now that come spring, I'll finally own this place lock, stock, and barrel!"

Although seated at the table, Crowfoot did not yet possess the manners this arrangement demanded. He banged his spoon against the crockery bowl several times over and leapt up and down in his chair. "Good, good! This is very good!"

"You bet it is," Hawke agreed, resisting the urge to correct the boy. "And just to make the deal even sweeter, the cavalry is going to pay me directly instead of going through Braddock Savings and Loan."

Again the boy reacted joyously, but Lacey was less enthusiastic. "I do not understand the part about the loan company. Why not deal with them if they be the ones you'd be owing the money to?"

"Because figures have a way of getting . . . confused at the savings and loan companies in town." And Braddock owned them all, which reminded Hawke of the only area in which he hadn't been completely truthful with Lacey. He had not told her that William Braddock was his uncle, nor would he. It was one thing ignoring the taunts and sneers of strangers over his half-breed status, but quite another to endure them from blood kin. That kind of shame he would never share with Lacey. Not even if his life depended on it.

"Just trust me when I say that it's best for the deal to be done this way, and definitely cause for celebration. Come spring, we'll not only own Winterhawke free and clear, but we'll have a good sum leftover to spend on ourselves for a change!"

Wanting desperately to share in her husband's joy, Lacey glanced around the kitchen, then put in a bid for a piece of the good tidings. "What you're saying is, that come spring we might be able to buy a few more items of furniture so we don't have to drag the chairs from room to room?"

Furnishing the house had never really been a priority with Hawke. He laughed at the oversight, then conceded. "I'd be happy to buy you some new chairs, Mrs.

Winterhawke. Maybe even a couch to put in front of the fireplace. Would you like that?"

"Aye. Almost as much as knowing that you like the supper I cooked for you."

After that strong hint, the three of them fell to the meal which turned out to be very decent considering Lacey's previous lack of training in the kitchen. Hawke had baked the biscuits the night before, and while they weren't terribly fresh, if they were sopped in the stew it didn't really matter and they made a perfect complement to the meal. Surprisingly enough, most of the conversation as they ate came from Crowfoot. His main reason for visiting Winterhawke was to inform Hawke that Caleb's leg had healed well enough for him to plan Three Elk's much-delayed cattle branding, an event that was to take place in three days.

Lacey had never heard of such a thing. Once Hawke explained how each rancher burned his own unique brand into the hide of the animals to keep them from being stolen, she shivered from head to toe. "I don't think the cattle can like that very much. I think I shall stay here and practice my cooking whilst you men do your terrible deeds."

"Nope, sorry," said Hawke as he shoved his empty bowl away. "Branding is as much a party as anything. The neighbors all come to help out since it takes a lot of muscle to get the job done, and afterwards, it's Caleb's responsibility to feed everyone. You don't have to come outside to watch the branding if you don't want to, but I expect Kate's going to need all the help she can get in the kitchen."

The thought of seeing her friend again after the weeks they'd spent apart made the branding sound a lot more appealing. "Aye," she said brightly. "I expect she ̶ould use my help. In that case, I'll go, but I do not think you'll be seeing these blue eyes observing you that day, sir."

Hawke knew he'd be seeing them anyway, if not in person, the way he did in his dreams every night. A rush of warmth spread throughout him as pushed away from the table. "Thanks for the great meal, Irish. It really was good."

"Not so fast!" She bid him stay in his seat by holding up her hands. "I have one more surprise, the best one that I saved for last."

He patted his belly. "I hope it isn't more food. I couldn't eat another bite."

"Oh, I expect you'll be finding room for a wee bit of this," she said smugly as she rose from the table. Lacey crossed the room to the counter attached to the sink, then reached behind the flour canister where she'd hidden her final offering. After removing the scrap of toweling she'd used to help conceal it, she turned toward the table and made a grand presentation of her hard-won dessert.

"'Tis a berry pie I baked just for you!"

She started for Hawke, her movements dramatic and regal, and set the offering down on the table in front of his nose as if she'd presented him a king's ransom in gold. His gaze incredulous, he stared at the pie, not knowing what to do or say next. The top crust looked as if it had been man-handled—there was really no other word for it—the whole thing pieced together so crookedly, he had to wonder if she'd gone outside during a high wind to put it together. It also looked as if she'd probably cut the required vents, but they were unnecessary since the edges of her patchwork "quilt" had come undone during the baking process, creating many more vents than were needed. The finished product, bleeding purple from its many ragged wounds, could have passed as the loser in a knife fight.

"Damn that looks good," Hawke said with a straight face.

Lacey beamed, handing him the knife. "Go on, then. Cut yourself as big a piece as you can eat."

Hawke brought the edge of the knife down on the crust, thinking a saw would have made the job easier, but managed to extract a good portion of pie and drop it into his empty supper bowl. Thinking he could have made Crowfoot a sturdy pair of boots out of the crust, Hawke stabbed at the pie with his fork and ate the entire portion anyway. He did so with a smile on his face, no less.

When he'd finished every last pebble—crumb really didn't describe the leavings of Lacey's crust—and pushed away from the table, this time the grimace of discomfort Hawke made as he patted his belly was real. "Thanks again for all your efforts, Irish. That was the best damned pie to ever come out of that stove."

"Really?" she said, as surprised as she was pleased.

Since Hawke was the original owner of the stove, he knew a pie had never been baked it in before. So he wasn't lying when he confirmed his remarks. "Absolutely. The very best."

Overjoyed, Lacey clasped her hands together. "In that case, sir, you can expect another little surprise tomorrow night after supper!" She pushed the berry pie toward him. "Go on now, be sure to save a piece or two for Crowfoot, but eat the rest of it all up. I'll be needing the empty pan first thing in the morning."

15

What cannot be had is just what suits.
　　　　　—An old Irish saying

By the time Saturday rolled around, and
Hawke and Lacey were off down the road to Three Elk
Ranch, he was as sick as a calf with the scours. After
he'd managed to wade through the rest of the berry pie,
as promised, Laccy baked another of those leather-like
crusts and buried something resembling apple mush
beneath it. The result of her efforts didn't taste much
like apples, but more like the inside of a sugar sack,
burlap texture and all. Since he'd pretty much asked for
it, Hawke had done his duty and finally managed to
choke down the very last bite after supper last
evening— all without so much as a lick of help from
Crowfoot, the little bastard, who was under no such
obligation.

After the wagon rumbled over the narrow wooden
bridge spanning the Little Laramie River, Hawke wasn't
sure he could make the last few yards to his friend's
ranch without tossing his breakfast. Somehow, he

managed to hang on, and made the final turn onto Caleb's road a few moments later.

"'Tis a lovely day," Lacey said, suddenly bursting with excitement. "What a shame Crowfoot could not come with us."

Coughing to cover yet another belch, Hawke paused long enough to be reasonably sure he wouldn't inflict any more of his stomach's misery on Lacey's delicate ears before answering her. "I already told you that he's just not ready to face so many strangers at one time yet. He's happy by himself for now." And besides that, he and the boy had cooked up a little surprise for Lacey that ought to be finished by the time they returned to Winterhawke the following morning; freshly shellacked floors throughout the house. "I appreciate your concern for the kid and all the progress you've made with him, but he does work for me, you know, and has to stay behind to tend the livestock."

"Aye, I'm knowing all that, but knowing does not keep me from wishing he could have come along."

"You're soft, Lacey, a little too soft when it comes to Crowfoot, but I suppose that's better than the other extreme." He was considering pointing out a few other places where she was soft, and acceptably so, when Hawke realized they'd arrived at the hitching post out front of Three Elk Ranch; and that Kate was already running down the path to greet them.

"Lacey!" she called, waving robustly. "'Tis a balm to these poor old eyes to see ye again!"

"Kate!" Lacey jumped down from the wagon before it even came to a complete stop, and flung herself into her former nurse's arms. "Oh, 'tis good to see you again, too."

By the time the women finished hugging each other, Hawke was already making his way toward a corral where Caleb and a pair of hired hands were saddling horses for the roundup. Recognizing that she and her husband would be separated for much of the day, and for the first time since they wed, it was with a pang of bittersweet regret that Lacey followed Kate into the house.

They caught up on the basics when they first entered the kitchen, each of them wanting to know if the other was happy, overworked, or comfortable at last, living in this great land called America. When all appeared to be fine on those counts, and in each household, Kate motioned Lacey to move closer and asked one final question about her well-being.

"And another thing, lass, if ye don't mind my askin'; after the lamp is blown out at night, is this man Hawke as kind and considerate of ye as he should be?"

Knowing instantly what Kate was inquiring about, Lacey blushed to her roots and averted her gaze, a satisfied smile giving her answer better than any words she could think of.

"I see," Kate murmured knowingly. "So he's as kind and considerate as all that, is he?"

Lacey's face grew even redder, hotter. She turned toward the window hoping the ceaseless wind would be blowing as usual, but all was still as her suddenly lifeless pulse. "H-he's, well, Hawke is simply . . . wonderful."

Kate, who'd been measuring out flour for the pies and cakes they were preparing to bake, dusted her hands on her apron and slipped up behind her former charge. "Then ye truly are happy, lass, really and truly?"

Lacey turned, her pulse in full swing again, and flashed a broad grin. "Oh, Kate, what I am is happier than I've e'er been in my entire life. Do you suppose I might be in love with my husband?"

Kate laughed softly. "Only ye can know that, lass, for only in your heart will you find the answer."

"But I do not know what love is or how this magical thing is supposed to make a person feel inside."

"Tell me, then," Kate said, her voice as soft as her previous chuckles. "How do you feel when ye think of yer husband? Say the words out loud, and ye'll know yerself 'fore I do."

Lacey drew in a deep breath and furrowed her brow in thought. "I do not know that words come to mind when I think of Hawke. Sometimes at the sight of him working, the drops fall from my eyes, even though there is no sadness in my heart."

"Hum, that would seem a very good sign of love and better than words, too. Anything more, lass?"

She paused again, thinking of her other symptoms. "I know, too, that I wish to follow and stay with Hawke always. He is the light in my eye, and he fills me up with joy in my heart. 'Twould that be the love the poets speak so highly of?"

Her laughter cheerful now, Kate said, "Can you na hear yerself, lass? What else could it be?"

What else, indeed, thought Lacey, so full up with this thing called love, she feared her breastbone might split. "Aye, and I'm thinking maybe you're right! I do love my husband, and with all my heart, it would seem, for there is only a wee bit of room left for anything more!"

"I'm so happy for ye, lass." Tears sprang into Kate's eyes, and she quickly gave Lacey a hug. "Ye canna know how I've prayed for this these past weeks."

Surprised by the depth of emotion in Kate's voice, as well as the tears in her eyes, Lacey asked, "Why are you crying? I should think your own happiness would be the top o' your prayers."

"I—well, lass, 'tis just that I feel so responsible for you, I expect."

"Why would you be feeling that way about me? I'm the one stole your letter and cursed you into taking me to Wyoming with you."

"Aye, but . . . " Kate turned away from Lacey and slowly made her way back to the table where her baking supplies were laid out. Then, her voice hesitant, distant somehow, she went on. "I'm the one brung ye half way around the world, and by my way of thinking, that makes me responsible for ye. Now enough of such talk. Tell me; does that husband of yers love ye back?"

There was something in Kate's tone or manner that disturbed Lacey, some little intimation that the woman hadn't been quite honest with her. What could dear, sweet Kate be hiding? Or had what she thought she sensed been imaginary?

"Dona tell me the man is a indifferent as all that!"

"Hawke? Oh, goodness no, but 'tis a wee bit difficult to tell what he's thinking," she answered honestly, even if she couldn't be sure that Kate had. "I can not say that Hawke does love me, but then, I can not say that he does not. I do know that he loved the pie I made for him, though!"

"Pie?" Kate turned away from her work to stare at Lacey. "Ye've gone and baked up a *pie* . . . and by yerself?"

"Aye, not one, but two!" she said proudly. "One made of berries at the start of the week, and one made of apples just Wednesday."

"And where, might I ask, did ye get the recipe for apple pie, lass? I dona recall jotting this down."

Feeling smug now, Lacey cocked her head to the side and said, "'Twas simple. I just followed the same recipe you wrote down for berry pie, putting apples inside the crust instead."

"And no spices?"

Lacey shrugged. "I put sugar in, if that be what you

mean. Since the lid come off the canister as I was measuring it up, a good deal more sugar than the recipe asked for fell in, too, I think. Hawke seemed to like it anyway. Finished it up last night, he did."

"Humph." Kate laughed to herself. "That big a fool for pie, is the man?"

"My Hawke . . . a fool?"

"Maybe just for ye, lass." Kate winked. "One can hope, anyway."

"Aye, one can hope, and then maybe, it'll be true." She rolled up her sleeves and studied the supplies on the table. "Where do you want me to start?"

Since Lacey clearly had a lot to learn about cooking yet, as she got to work with the supper preparations, Kate took the time to explain to her former charge about the importance of flavoring in fruit pies, then scribbled several notes about when to use cinnamon, cloves, and other spices: And while she was at it, she spent an extraordinarily long time showing Lacey exactly how to roll out an acceptable pie crust in only one try.

Around mid-day after all the cows and calves had been rounded up and confined in one large corral, the men came to the house for refreshments and a short break. Hawke propped himself against the fireplace mantle, leaving the couch for Caleb and his ranching neighbors, Willard and Big Jim. Both of the men had come to the branding alone, a surprise since the companion-starved womenfolk in the Centennial area always jumped at the chance to visit one another during these rare gatherings.

Then Hawke remembered that Willard's squaw had lit out for greener pastures, and Big Jim's wife had just given birth to their eighth child. The majority of the hired hands were bachelors, but the few married wranglers kept their wives back in Laramie, which left Lacey and Kate to tend to the needs of the branding crew on their own. Most of the men sat cross-legged on the floor with the exception of two of the more enterprising cowboys who helped themselves to the chairs in the kitchen.

Shortly after the crew gathered in the living room, Lacey appeared bearing a large platter of sandwiches, and Kate, directly behind her, carried an assortment of drinks on a heavy wooden tray. Both women mingled with the guests, offering the refreshments several times over, but no matter where Lacey went or who she was talking to, her gaze never left Hawke's. Easily reading the message in her glittering blue eyes—a wish, he thought, to be back at Winterhawke, alone with him again—he winked and blew out a sigh, sending a duplicate message of his own. Several furtive smiles from Hawke later, and tender blushes in return from his bride, it was time for the actual branding to begin.

As the men filed outside then scattered, each heading toward his appointed chore, Hawke walked alongside Caleb, who was moving slower than the rest of the crew due to his still-sensitive knee.

Remarking on his progress, Hawke said, "I thought you'd be laid up a good long time the way that cow cracked your kneecap. I can hardly believe you're walking so good already."

"I got my lovely Kate to thank for that." Caleb cut loose with a guffaw. "That woman put me through hell these past few weeks, making me work that knee three times a day no matter how much it pained me. Why, she even forced me to put enough weight on it that it brought tears to my eyes, but by God if she wasn't right. That son of a bitch is already stronger than Big Jim's prize bull—and it wasn't that strong before it got broke!"

Hawke thought Caleb was exaggerating mightily

about everything. "Kate *forced* you did she, friend, twisted your arm to make you keep bending that knee?" He laughed at the very idea of his mountain man friend so tyrannized by the short little Irishwoman.

"I ain't lying!" said Caleb, shouting to be heard over the roar of bawling cattle. "That woman was relentless, a regular slave driver! 'Course, if I did a good enough job of what she told me to do, my sweet Katie rewarded me pretty good at night." Caleb laughed again, then winked. "Maybe what Kate done was bribe me more than force me."

"Now that makes a little more sense." In a rare meddling mood, Hawke queried his friend further about the marriage he'd made. "How are things are working out for you and Kate?"

"Oh, I'd say they're more than working out, Hawke. Here I am, homelier than a hog's butt with a nose big enough to store a newborn calf in, and that gal treats me like I'm the best thing that happened to her since she was whelped. I don't know what I did to deserve Kate, but I aim to keep her happy as I can and with me for as long as I can." He elbowed Hawke in the ribs. "Leastways till she wakes up some morning and gets a good look at what she tied herself to. Think that woman needs glasses?"

Hawke gave a grudging laugh. "I doubt it, friend. She probably sees right through you like everyone else who bothers to take a good look." And what she saw, he knew from experience, was a good, kind, decent human being, the sort of man who'd never hurt another living soul or animal unless it was absolutely necessary. He knew why Kate had married Caleb even if the man didn't. What Hawke still didn't know was why Lacey had married him—or what was wrong with her.

Despite his recent promise to himself not to dwell on his doubts, Hawke found himself asking Caleb,

"Remember that little talk we had the day we both wound up married? I asked you to get Kate aside and see if you couldn't find out what was wrong with Lacey. You never did tell me what you learned."

Caleb abruptly stopped walking, and for a minute, Hawke thought maybe that newly mended knee had given out on him. "What is it, Caleb? Is your leg acting up on you?"

"Oh, ah, no . . . well, maybe just a little." Caleb dramatically rubbed his knee.

Recognizing something of a ruse in the way his friend was acting, Hawke prodded him further. "About Lacey?"

"Oh, ah, danged if I kin remember exactly what Kate said, what with the way these womenfolk go on and on . . ."

Avoiding Hawke's gaze as well as the question, he stared off toward the corral and hollered, "Hey, Willard! I want them calves in the side pen, not the middle one! Dad blast it, do I have to do everything myself?" And with that, he limped off toward the other men, leaving Hawke and his question behind in the dust.

Hawke made no attempt to follow his friend. He stood frozen, wondering what in the hell Caleb was hiding from him, and why all of a sudden he was acting so mysteriously. *Christ almighty*, he muttered to himself. How could his best friend—his only true friend—have lied to him that way? Oh, he hadn't come right out and said the words, but for a man like Caleb, omission was as good as a lie. Worse, maybe.

Until that moment, Hawke would have bet Winterhawke Ranch and all that went with it that Caleb, of all people, would never have lied or evaded him the way he just had. But he had done it. Hawke knew that as sure as the day was long. Caleb had betrayed the trust the two men had built between themselves, and he had done so on behalf of Kate and some terrible secret they shared. Hurt, angry, filled with a lot of sudden, uncomfortable feelings he couldn't put a name to, he stomped off toward the corral and threw himself into his work.

When he finally returned to the house that night, Hawke was exhausted as hell. He stumbled in through the front door to find most of the crew already lounging around the living room partaking of the supper being served by Kate and Lacey. Staying as far away from them all as he could, he took a seat on the floor just past the foyer.

"Hawke!" called Caleb. "I was wondering if you was ever going to come in. You did the work of ten men out there today—ain't you afraid rigor mortis will set in if you stop moving for too long?"

The crew chuckled at Caleb's reference to Hawke's stiff, sore muscles, but even as they turned toward him in respectful homage, he didn't join in their laughter. For one thing, he was too damn tired, but for another, he felt a little like an outsider, most especially after his talk this morning with Caleb. Kate, Lacey, and his good friend, miserable conspirators that they were, could just keep their little secret if it was so damned important. Hawke had never given a good god damn what anyone thought or did before, and he sure as hell wasn't going to start now.

Carrying a bottle of Caleb's home-brewed beer in one hand and a thick ham sandwich in the other, Lacey hurried over to where Hawke sat and kneeled down beside him. "You're looking very tired, husband," she said as she offered the items. "Maybe this wee bit of food will perk you up."

"I sure hope so." Hawke took the beer without meeting her gaze, and drank half of it down in three consecutive gulps. Then he accepted the sandwich, but before he bit into it, he impulsively asked, "How long did you and Kate work together at that hospital in Ireland?"

Her eyes flew wide open, highlighting the golden sparkles floating in their sky blue depths—along with a good bit of anxiety. "Oh, a few years is all. Why do you ask?"

He shrugged, the direct reverse of the way he felt. "I don't know much about your past. I was just wondering. Any reason I shouldn't?"

She gulped, not just visibly, but audibly. "I can not imagine why." Laughing nervously, Lacey got to her feet. "I had a very boring and . . . troubled childhood, so I do not like to talk about it much. That, or the time . . . you know, the fire."

That had somehow slipped his mind. Feeling a stab of guilt for prodding her, and too damn tired to think about it any more, Hawke pushed himself to his feet and said, "If I sit here any longer, my muscles will freeze up. I think I'll go back outside and walk around while I eat."

"That's a good idea. I'll come get you when we're ready to serve dessert." She leaned in close, lightly kissing his cheek, and whispered, "Kate and I made five—do you hear me?—*five* pies!"

Even though he was groaning to himself, Hawke managed to smile and say, "That sounds great." Then he strode out the door.

Glad to have escaped the conversation relatively unscathed, Lacey hurried back to her serving chores. Once all the other men seemed settled and well-fed, she cornered Kate and insisted that she join her in the kitchen.

Pulling her over to the farthest wall, Lacey huddled with her friend near the window frame and asked, "What, by all that's holy, have you been saying to Caleb? You did not tell him about me, did you?"

"Hush, lass!" Kate looked over her shoulder at the flimsy curtain separating the rooms, then turned back to Lacey. "I may have mentioned a wee bit about my past, and that ye were at the hospital with me, but I didna, er . . . er, well mention, too much of the goings on. Why troble yerself with worrin' about it so?"

"Because something's gone wrong between me and Hawke, and I just know it has something to do with the hospital! God in heaven, I do not think I could stand it if he e'er finds out about me. I might even die!"

"Hush, lass, and ye'll do no such thing. Dona fret so; Hawke will ne'er find out about you." She closed her eyes as if in prayer. "Dona give it another worry."

"You're so very sure?"

"Aye, lass. Come now, let us serve some of our baked goods to these weary cowboys. A taste of the pie we made today will put a smile back on the face of yer Hawke, just ye wait and see."

Outside on the porch propped against the wall directly below that same window, Hawke sat with a bite of sandwich frozen in mid-swallow. The hospital, the past, and the goings on? Jesus, he thought in horror, had those two Irishwomen run some kind of brothel back in their homeland and gotten themselves thrown out of the country?

A ridiculous theory, Hawke decided. He didn't know one hell of a lot about women, but he did know for certain that Lacey had been a virgin the day he made her his. And that automatically ruled out his previous "running away from her husband" theory, too. If not fleeing a house of ill repute or an enraged husband, then what? Kate's words rang a terribly ominous tone in Hawke's ears, one that told him whatever had happened in the past, it wasn't good. *Damned* if he didn't hate being in the dark, secrets swirling all around him that he wasn't privy to. Worse than that, he hated the fact that Lacey was so adamantly opposed to letting him in on the secret; she, his very own wife, a woman who already owned more of him than any human being ever had.

Hawke supposed he wouldn't be sitting out here driving himself crazy with suppositions if he'd have demanded some answers back in the house instead of just asking. Then in the next instant, he realized exactly why he hadn't done just that. He wasn't sure he wanted to know the whole truth of a past that frightened her so badly she was compelled to hide it. That, or to hear any lies from those sweet lips should she take the easy way out. Call it false pride, call it pure stubbornness. It didn't matter in the slightest to Hawke what name could be put to the decision he made then. He was just happy to have it over with, knowing that he'd asked Lacey for the first and last time to come clean with him.

The following afternoon as Hawke turned the horse-drawn wagon around the final bend in the road leading to Winterhawke, Lacey thought she detected a very odd expression on her husband's handsome face. When the wagon stopped, he insisted that she stay seated until he came around to help her down, and in the next moment Crowfoot appeared at the front of the house, a long black strip of cloth in hand.

Before she could ask what was going on, the boy met them halfway up the stone steps leading to the porch.

"Surprise, for lady!" he declared, circling around behind her. "No look yet."

Understanding that she was to be blindfolded, Lacey allowed the young man to tie the cloth around her eyes, then let him lead her into the house and to the center of the living room. A strong odor hit Lacey immediately, a bitter aroma which reminded her of the sharp tang of pure alcohol used at the hospital.

"You look now!" said Crowfoot as he whisked the cloth away from her eyes.

The freshly-shellacked floor sparkled beneath her feet, the trail of shiny varnish leading into the kitchen and up the stairs to the bedroom as well. With a gasp of sheer delight, she said, "Oh, 'tis a beautiful job you've done, Crowfoot. This will make scrubbing the floors e'er so much easier, too!"

"Hawke's idea," the boy explained, "but I make him pay plenty."

He laughed then, a sound she was beginning to hear more and more from Crowfoot, then turned to her husband. While he wasn't exactly flashing that dazzling smile she loved so much, Hawke was at least grinning. Thrilled to feel so close to him again, Lacey threw her arms around his neck, planted a big kiss on his mouth, and then said, "I thank you kindly, dear husband. 'Tis a wonderful surprise. Might there be something I can do for you in return?"

Clearly uncomfortable, and maybe a little embarrassed with Crowfoot looking on, Hawke took Lacey's arms from his neck and stepped away from her. "You don't have to do another thing, Irish," he murmured, before he turned and headed for the door. "This was just a little something we did to thank you for making those pies. I'm going out to check on the livestock. Need anything from the barn?"

Impulse almost coaxed her into blurting what she did need from him at that moment, but at the last second, Lacey pressed her lips together firmly, and shook her head. Then she resolved to find a way to properly thank her man if it took her all day and night to figure it out.

*   *   *

Much later, Hawke came back to the house half-way expecting supper to be on the table. The kitchen smelled faintly of smoke, lingering effects from the fire, but of nothing else. He wandered into the living room, still no Lacey, and then crossed over to the foot of the staircase leading up to their bedroom.

"Lacey? Are you up there?"

After a long moment she shouted down, "Aye. Can you come here for a moment?"

"In a little while," he hollered back. "I'm hungry. I'm going to go fire up the stove."

"The bloody stove can wait!" she shouted in return.

Startled to hear such a demanding tone coming from Lacey's normally sweet mouth, he started up the stairs as instructed. Vaguely wondering what the hell kind of trouble his occasionally inept wife had gotten herself into this time, he pushed the door to their bedroom opened and walked inside.

Lacey was standing in the middle of their bed, facing him. Her glorious copper-colored hair hung free, tumbling over the porcelain white skin of her back and shoulders. Her eyes appeared to be closed, but Hawke could see that she was peeking through her thick russet lashes in order to gauge his reaction—and, weariness aside, he definitely had one.

Although they were strapped around her ankles instead of her boots, his painfully shy bride was wearing her lucky silver spurs. And not another damn thing.

16

Contention is better than loneliness.
            —An old Irish proverb

It wasn't long after the branding that Hawke
and Lacey settled into their married life, each under their
own terms. The sensuality she'd unleashed on the night
she'd displayed herself so boldly, worked extremely
well in bringing them closer again, at least physically. But
Lacey sensed that Hawke still wondered about her past
from time to time, and with more fervor than mere
curiosity. If something was missing from their marriage,
she thought it might be trust, and so kept her declarations of love for Hawke to herself.

As the weeks wore on, the Wyoming summer slammed
down on Lacey, striking her like one of Caleb's red-hot
branding irons. Her fair skin was no match for the harsh
noonday sun, her Irish constitution unable to cope with
temperatures much higher than those of the homeland,
dry heat or not. She suffered the months of that first
summer bottled up inside the home she loved so much,
daring to venture out-of-doors only during the early

morning hours, or very late at night after the sun had gone down.

When fall came at last, whistling through the Centennial Valley on the coattails of a cool northern breeze, she all but dropped to her knees in the dusty parched earth to give thanks. The cooler temperatures even soothed her eyes, turning the lime-green leaves of the aspens to a bright lemon-yellow which was an even more striking contrast to the forest green pines. Then in what seemed like the space of a heartbeat, the very winds she'd so recently praised turned bitter cold, and in less than a fortnight! Although Lacey had thought herself prepared for weather such as this after her years in the wind-swept terrain of Ireland, the velocity and bone-freezing chill of the gusts that blasted her in Wyoming were a hair-raising contrast, indeed.

By Thanksgiving, the first few snowflakes of the season began to fall as Hawke and Lacey traveled from their ranch to Three Elk for a holiday supper with the Weatherspoons. Crowfoot, although he'd come a long way in grooming, manners, and speech, and was as comfortable at Three Elk as he was at Winterhawke, stubbornly refused to join the foursome, choosing instead to stay behind and keep watch on the livestock.

As the wagon pulled onto the road leading to Caleb's place, Lacey tilted her head back and stuck out her tongue.

Hawke caught sight of this out of the corner of his eye. "What in hell are you doing?"

She didn't answer him at first, but kept her tongue out until a snowflake finally landed on it. "There," she finally said. "I had to have a taste of the first snow. 'Twill bring us a very lucky winter, you know."

He chuckled gruffly. "Everything is lucky according to you. Is that an Irish thing, or just you?"

Lacey thought on that for a moment. "Perhaps a wee bit of both."

"In that case, see if you can't use that luck to wish for that snowflake to be the last of the day." He glanced up at the sky and frowned. "If there's a blizzard, we could be stuck at Caleb's for weeks."

Lacey hoped he was kidding. While it snowed in Ireland, it didn't happen often, and never to the extremes Hawke was suggesting. She kept a wary eye on the heavens even after they'd arrived at Three Elk, and intended on going outside from time to time to check on the weather. But then Kate bounded down the steps to greet them, pulled her inside the house, and insisted that she immediately go with her to the back bedroom. After that, never again did a thought of the weather cross Lacey's mind.

"What can be such a secret that we must hide in here?" she asked as Kate bodily dragged her into the room and quickly closed the door.

"I've a couple of surprises for ye and I wanted to let ye know about them in private so's we wouldn't blubber in front of our husbands."

"Blubber? If you're thinking to make me cry, then I do not want any of your surprises."

"Yer so sure?" Kate's pale blue eyes twinkled with both mischief and delight. Then she drew back the curtain which concealed her wardrobe, plucked a brown dress from the few hanging there, and draped it across the bedspread. "What do you think?"

With a sigh of admiration, Lacey said, "Oh, Kate—'tis beautiful. You'll be the envy of every woman in the territory wearing this down the streets." She touched the soft wool fabric of the mahogany overskirt and jacket, then slid her fingertips over the center panel and trim, which was made of crisp linen checkered in shades of black and brown.

"'Tisn't mine, lass," said Kate softly. "'Tis yers."

Lacey's heart caught in her throat. "Mine? B-But, how? You can not mean that—"

"I can sure enough. My dear Caleb has informed me there'd be a verra good chance we'll be snowed in by Christmas. 'Tis my early present for ye in case we canna share the day."

On second thought, Lacey decided right then that Kate's idea of coming to the privacy of the bedroom had been the best plan after all. She was most definitely blubbering! "Oh, heavens above," she cried, "I can not thank you enough! I've ne'er had a dress of my own before, only these uniforms."

"I'm well aware of that, lass. I thought it high time ye had yer own gown, so when Caleb and his men drove the cattle to rail in Laramie, I asked him to pick me up some pretty warm material to match yer lovely red hair. Do ye like the color?"

Lacey lifted the dress from the spread and pressed it to her bosom. "I love it, Kate, truly I do. Would it be all right, you think, to wear it to supper today?"

"That's what I was hoping ye'd do."

So excited she could hardly contain herself, Lacey dropped the gown to the bed and reached for the top button of her blouse, but before she could release it, Kate stopped her.

"There'd be one more surprise, first, lass." Moving to the edge of the bed, Kate sat down and patted the spot beside her. "Come, join me a moment."

Lacey dropped down on the bedspread wondering how she could possibly be any more surprised or pleased than she was with the dress. But she was—and very quickly, too.

"I've been verra suspicious about something for weeks now, changes in me that could have been caused by a number of things, especially since this tummy of mine is so fat, anyway! I wanted to be verra sure before I told anyone what I suspected, and this morning came the new sign I was hoping for—movement." A smile nearly splitting her face in two, Kate looked Lacey straight in the eye and took a deep breath. "Oh, lass, I can hardly believe 'tis true myself, but 'twould seem that I'll be having a wee one before the winter is over!"

"A wee one? You mean a . . . a baby?"

"Aye! 'Tis truly a miracle!"

"B-but, do you mean to say that you and Caleb have been, well, that you—"

"Aye, and I do mean to say just that." She laughed and patted Lacey's shoulder. "Surely you didna think the bedroom waltz was only meant for the young."

Blushing, Lacey looked away. "I guess I didn't think of it at all."

"Well Caleb did, and I'm verra happy for it. I ne'er even dared to dream this would happen to me so late in life—why I'll be thirty-six when babe is born!"

Lacey looked at her in surprise. She hadn't realized a woman that old could even get with child.

But Kate didn't notice her expression. She rambled on, spinning her joy around Lacey like a web. "I think I must be five months gone now, and as I said, this morning I felt the babe moving inside me." She closed her eyes and placed her hand over her round belly. Then she reverently whispered, "I simply canna believe 'tis happened to me again—'tis like the second chance I've prayed for all these years."

"Again?" asked Lacey. "I did not know you had a child."

Kate's eyes popped open as if awakening from a dream, then instantly, they became shuttered. "'Twas a long time ago, lass. I lost the babe well before it could be born. But . . ." She sighed heavily. "I dona wish to speak of it again. Oh! And ne'er breathe a word of that one to my Caleb. Please?"

"I wouldn't."

"Thank you, lass, and say nothing of this babe either when we go out to our husbands. Next to me, of course, ye were the first to know. I thought ye might like that."

Out in the living room, Hawke toasted Caleb's successful cattle sale with a bottle of home brew. "It looks like we're both about to see our way clear, at last. Congratulations, friend!"

After a good long pull of beer, Hawke shifted his hips against his chair, the high stone hearth of the fireplace, then asked, "What do you think the women are up to so long in the bedroom?"

"Hold yur horses. I expect it's got something to do with the bolt of wool I picked up in town last month. Have a little patience, and you'll see soon enough."

"I hope by soon you mean in the next minute or so." He sniffed the air again, torturing himself. "I don't know what all Kate has cooking out there, but I'm just this side of going out to the kitchen and helping myself."

Caleb wagged a finger in his face. "Better not try that, if you know what's good for you. That woman's got herself a temper, eww-wee, does she got herself a temper. I don't know why she ain't red-haired like Lacey with all the steam she's got built up inside that head of hers."

"It used to be red, Caleb," said Kate as she rounded the corner into the living room. "But I blow my top so often, I burned all the color off and now I'm a blond. Does that make ye feel better?"

Still facing Hawke, he grimaced and mouthed, "I got trouble now, friend."

But surprising them both, Kate began to laugh. "Get

up the two of ye. There'd be a lady coming into the room."

Hawke didn't waste any more time than Caleb did getting to his feet. As they glanced toward the hallway, Lacey suddenly appeared in an elegant new dress. Hawke whistled appreciatively, then twirled his finger, bidding her to turned around.

"Do you like it?" she asked, noting his admiring gaze. "Kate made it for me as an early Christmas present."

Hawke was stunned at the least, for he'd never imagined Lacey dressed in the same way as the fashionable ladies of Laramie. It was a style that suited her well—even if it did make him feel less suited to her.

"You look beautiful, Lacey," he said at last. "All dressed up with nowhere to go. It will be a good long time before I can take you to town, you know."

"I know that," she said, exaggerating the sway of her hips as she swished past the men on her way to the kitchen. "I intend to wear my new dress only on special occasions like today, and of course, the first time we go to town next spring. Now if you men will excuse us, we've a Thanksgiving feast to dish up."

Which was more than all right with Hawke. When they finally sat down to the meal, the table was laden with platters of ham, baked chicken, and stuffed pork fillets. Side dishes included something called donegal pie—a mixture of bacon, hard-boiled eggs, and mashed potatoes baked up inside a pastry crust—and mutton broth. Everything looked and smelled so good, it was all Hawke could do to keep from sneaking a chunk of pork during the prayer time Kate insisted on before they ate.

". . . and so Lord," she went on, "may the blessing of the five loaves and two fishes be ours; and may the King who made division put luck in our food and a good heart to the babe who's to come our way in March."

Hawke, whose eyes weren't closed, but at half-mast to better keep watch over the food, saw Lacey and Kate take a peep at Caleb, who almost looked as if he'd fallen asleep.

Picking up where Kate left off, Lacey cleared her throat and finished the prayer. "We give thanks, Lord, for all your earthly blessings, and pray that Kate and Caleb's child will be born with better ears than his father. Amen."

Hawke and Lacey exchanged a meaningful glance, while Caleb, who'd opened his eyes, just sat there staring at his empty supper plate. Finally he raised his head, looked at his wife, and asked, "What's all this chatter about babes and children?"

Kate sighed heavily. "Oh, Caleb, darlin'. Are ye sure that cow didna kick yer head after she finished with yer knee? Ye have na been listenin' to a word I said!"

Hawke, who was in a kind of mute shock himself, glanced at Caleb, noting the thunderstruck, confused look on his face. Friends to the end, he decided to take it upon himself to sum up the message in language more easily understood. "What she said was that she'd be calving sometime in March, and you're the herd bull responsible for the new breed of Weatherspoon. Get it, Daddy?"

Caleb went kind of white, which was saying something since the summer sun had baked his skin until it was almost as dark as Hawke's. "Calving? You mean . . . Kate is . . . " He couldn't think of a delicate way to put it, so he put his arms out in front of his stomach in an enormous circle.

"Aye, you silly fool," said the mother-to-be. "I think I shall be, er, *calving*, sometime around the end of March."

And just like that, the big former mountain man passed out. Then he pitched forward across the table, his bulbous nose digging a mighty deep post hole in Kate's donegal pie.

For a woman with child, she was up and out of her chair in a flash, pulling her husband's face out of the mashed potatoes and making certain his air passages were clear.

Seeing that his friend was in good hands but no danger, Hawke couldn't find a reason to keep supper on hold any longer. He stabbed a pair of plump juicy pork chops and dropped them on his plate.

Lacey turned to her husband, her eyes a little misty, and said, "'Tis a wonderful miracle, 'tis it not, Kate and Caleb having a child?"

His mouth full of pork, Hawke nodded, intending to stuff yet another forkful of tender meat between his teeth. But then he caught Lacey's gaze and the unmistakable glimmer of envy shining through her unshed tears. The fork fell from his hand, landing with a clatter against his plate as he finally allowed the news of Kate's pregnancy to go full circle in his mind. There was joy in the having of this child for the Weatherspoons, a joy Hawke didn't begrudge them in the slightest, but for some reason, all he could feel was sad. Is that what he'd seen in Lacey's eyes instead of envy? Sadness because she couldn't allow herself to have the children of a half-breed?

If so, that explained her expression, but it didn't go far in helping him to understand the source of his own melancholy—or whatever it was that had come over him. He sure as hell didn't want kids, so it couldn't be that. But even as Hawke reaffirmed that belief to himself, a gentle tug at the soft spot inside him suggested declarations such as those were no longer true.

With a heavy sigh, and an even heavier heart, he dropped both his hands to the table. His appetite gone, Hawke had to wonder; why in the hell couldn't he and Lacey visit Three Elk Ranch without having something pointed out to them that they could never have?

*   *   *

Fulfilling the prognostications at Thanksgiving, the weather turned bad late that night after the Winterhawkes returned to their home. And it stayed that way right through Christmas and beyond. At first, Lacey was absolutely delighted by the heavy snowfall, and could spend hours just watching it swirl down from the heavens to land in flowing white mounds sculpted by the wind. By Christmas she'd had her fill of nature's attempts at ice art. And by mid-January, she thought she might even go mad if she had to spend one more day locked up in the house.

As if in answer to her prayers, toward the end of the month she and Hawke awoke one morning to a beautiful dawn with miles and miles of clear blue skies overhead. Hardly able to believe her eyes or contain her excitement, Lacey leapt out of bed into the frigid air of the room, ran to the window for a better look, and stood there shivering in her cotton nightgown.

"Oh, Hawke!" she cried, surveying the carpet of sparkling white snow covering the valley. "Come look! 'Tis a gorgeous day outside, almost like summer!"

He joined her, but had enough sense to don his buckskin shirt before striding up behind her and wrapping her in his warm embrace. "Christ, Lacey. You're shaking like the quakies in a high wind."

"Q-quakies? W-what are they?"

He pointed to the trees which by now looked more like tall brown weeds amongst the dark green pines. "Those aspens out there are sometimes called quaking aspens."

She shrugged. "I don't care if I shiver till my hair falls out, just look at that sun. I think I shall go stand under it and spend the entire day there just warming myself." She slumped against her husband's chest. "Thank the Lord this miserable wintertime is over. I do not think I could have lasted much longer."

"I hate to bust your bubble, sweetheart," he said, pushing her hair aside in order to nuzzle the back of her neck. "But spring is still a good three or four months off. This is just a small break."

She turned in his arms, facing him now. "Then why are we inside? We must go enjoy the sun while it lasts." Then another exciting thought occurred to her. "Oh! And can we please go down to see Kate and Caleb? She can not be but two months away from having her wee one."

"I wish we could, sweetheart," Hawke pulled Lacey back into his arms, far more interested in her than in a fleeting patch of sunshine. "I'm afraid the roads are impassable down the way, and even if we could get through, I can't take the chance of us getting caught down at Three Elk. The days are short now, remember? At best, you're looking at only five or six hours of that sunlight."

"Then let us go now!"

He shook his head, hating to disappoint her. "No, Irish. We can't. The weather is nice now, but within a half an hour, another blizzard could hit."

Discouraged, she leaned into him, resting her head against his chest, and for a minute, Hawke thought he wouldn't have any problem convincing her to go back to bed. Then at once, she broke out of his embrace.

"If that is the way things must be, then I'll not be wasting one more precious minute of sunlight. If you're wanting your breakfast cooked today, you'd better get to it yourself, sir. I'm taking myself and the new rocking chair you and Crowfoot made me for Christmas, and setting us both down in the sun. There is where we'll be staying till there's no more sun to be had."

Convinced now that Lacey wouldn't be coming back to bed with him, Hawke stretched as he glanced out the window and said, "In that case, I guess I'd better round up Crowfoot so we can take a ride out to the north pasture to check on the shelters to make sure they're still standing. While we're up there we might even scare up some fresh meat for supper. This looks like a fine day for rabbit hunting."

"Oh? Why do you say that?"

"The rabbits around here are a little like you, Irish. They just can't resist sitting outside and sunning themselves on a day like this." He pinched her freckled cheek. "We'll be back before dark."

Before he left, Hawke cleared the snow from a nice patch of ground in front of the house and deposited Lacey's rocking chair smack in the middle of it. She sat there a good long time, basking in the warmth of the sun and enjoying the incredible view of the valley and snow-capped mountains beyond. Then later in the day—actually, toward evening by winter's hours—the winds suddenly came up, bringing with them the return of the bone-chilling cold. Lacey shivered once, a tremor which shook her body from end to end, then pushed out of the chair. Glancing up, she noticed that the skies were not only getting darker, but that they were clouding up again, the heavy dark mass of clouds telling her they were in for another big snowstorm.

Grumbling to herself, she reached over to pick up the chair, when an idea struck her. Maybe she couldn't stay outside, but there was no reason she couldn't bring the out-of-doors into her home. Hurrying to beat the onset of the storm, Lacey ran to the barn, collected a small saw, then dashed into the thick stand of lodgepole pines at the back of the ranch. After cutting several aromatic boughs from the trees, she gathered them into her arms and started for the house.

Lacey was out of the tree line but still several yards from the back porch when the first snowflakes fell, one of them landing directly on the tip of her nose. She impulsively stuck her tongue out in an attempt to reach it, but of course she could not. Laughing at her own folly, she started down the path she'd made earlier for the return trip to the ranch.

That's when she heard it.

A low, beastly growl that raised the hairs on the back of her neck. Lacey froze, her gaze darting from side to side. She could see nothing which might have made the sound. She took another, more cautious step toward her home.

Again came the growl, this time in a higher pitch, more of a vicious snarl. Staring directly at the house, her eyes wide, she finally saw the vague outline of a dog standing in the shadows on the top step of the porch. Lacey's blood ran cold, then ceased to move at all. The animal skulked out of the shadows and down the stairs where it stopped. It wasn't a dog, but *a wolf!*

She took a step backward, realizing the beast had blocked her way to both the house and the barn. It began to growl even more ferociously then, as if it knew it had her trapped. Then, the long hairs on the nape of its neck standing erect and mane-like, the wolf slowly crept toward her.

Already terrorized by the animal's snarls and menacing yellow eyes, when the beast curled its upper lip, revealing razor-sharp canines, a wave of dizziness swept through her. Fighting off a swoon as the animal bunched its body preparing to launch an all-out attack, Lacey screamed and threw the pine boughs she'd gathered toward its head.

Then, still screaming, she turned and ran back toward the forest. She ran and ran, occasionally stumbling over a fallen branch or large rock, but ran until she was nearly winded. When she realized she was also running out of steam, Lacey glanced over her shoulder to check the distance between herself and the wolf. As she skittered blindly through the trees this way, arms outstretched as guides, the toe of her boot collided with something solid, pitching her into the air.

In the next moment, her world spinning topsy-turvy, Lacey crashed to the ground. Then everything went black

At what should have been just before dark, Hawke rode back to the barn alone under very black skies. Crowfoot, as eager for some new scenery as anyone, decided to give Hawke and Lacey a little privacy until the next break in the weather. He split from Hawke after they'd finished checking the shelters, and went on down to Three Elk taking the rabbits they'd shot with him. The boy, still half-animal in some respects, was in no danger from the elements, but another weather break couldn't come too soon as far as Hawke was concerned. It was already snowing so hard, he could barely see the barn even though he was just two feet from it. After rubbing down his horse and tending to the rest of the animals, Hawke started for the house, planning on warming himself along with his sweet little bride the minute he got in the door.

Head bowed against the storm as he walked toward the path leading to the house, Hawke noticed several scattered lumps buried beneath a rapidly thickening blanket of snow. Curious, he kicked at one of the lumps to reveal a small branch that looked as if it had recently been cut from a pine. More than just curious now, as he moved down the path he unearthed a few more branches along with a small saw. Instinct alerting him, he glanced up ahead to the porch.

Something was lying on the top step. And it seemed to be gnawing on something. Slipping his Bowie knife out of its sheath, Hawke brandished it as he cautiously approached the porch. As he drew closer, he was able to identify the beast as a large timber wolf.

The animal turned its big gray head toward the path then, and bared its teeth at him.

17

Never poor till one goes to Hell.
　—An old Irish maxim

"Oh, Christ—it's you, Hattie." Hawke sheathed his knife, then climbed up to the porch. "And here I thought we'd finally gotten rid of your homely old hide."

Hunkering down beside the she-wolf, he rubbed the animal's big gray head and made a quick perusal of her body. Even though she wore her thickest winter coat by now, Hattie's ribs were readily apparent. "It's been a little tougher winter than you figured on, huh, girl?"

As if in answer, the animal dropped the item she'd been chewing between her front legs, then rested her muzzle against the toe of Hawke's boot. He laughed at the gesture, remembering the less-than-friendly greeting the animal had given him the first time they met some fours years ago. Hawke had come upon the wolf as she lay dying, her right rear leg firmly clenched in the teeth of an enormous steel trap. While he and Caleb had never employed such vicious instruments during their years of trapping, this was not the first time they'd found live quarry snarling and writhing in one of the hideous traps.

Knowing after one quick glance at the animal's shattered hind leg how badly she'd already suffered, Hawke's first impulse had been to put the wolf out of her misery. That and take the hide, even though he and Caleb didn't normally trade in wolf pelts. But as those wary, yellow eyes glared at him from across the clearing, showing him an unusual vulnerability and something he couldn't quite name, that soft spot inside Hawke took over instead, and he found himself trying to save the animal.

After rapping the wolf between the eyes with a thick pine branch, stunning her, Hawke tied her still-dangerous jaws shut with the thong from his own hair. Working quickly, he freed the animal, then amputated her mangled leg and stitched up the stump. Unknown to Hawke at the time, Crowfoot had been hiding in the thick foliage not four yards away, watching and afraid. Once the wolf was out of danger and lay hobbled by Hawke's fire, the boy slowly crept into view.

Unaware at first that the young man had been running with the she-wolf, her cub in all but the most basic of ways, Hawke welcomed the boy into his safekeeping, assuming that his family would come along looking for him sooner or later. Hawke laughed again as he remembered how Caleb had come upon him sitting in the middle of a snow bank with a wild Indian boy on one side and a three-legged wolf on the other. The senior trapper had accused him of going soft in the head, yet before the week was out, the older man was falling all over himself trying to win both the boy and the animal.

Crowfoot by comparison had been easy for Caleb to conquer; old Hattie, named after a woman Caleb had almost married, apparently had room for only one man and one boy in her wild heart. To this day, she still had a little trouble being nice to the older trapper, and even tried to run him to ground on occasion. Which prompted thoughts of someone else—*Lacey*.

"Christ!" Hawke jumped to his feet, talking to the wolf. "If you're figuring on sticking around a while, I'd best go warn my wife about you. And you'll treat her right, or you go, no arguments. Got it?"

Hattie cocked her grizzled head, then whined.

"All right, you can have a little chow first, but then you'll have to behave, or it's back to the woods with you." Hawke opened the icebox and removed a good-sized chunk of beef. As he tossed it to the animal, he noticed the item she'd been chewing on; one of Lacey's shoes. Not overly concerned since boots were about all his wife wore now, Hawke stepped into the house.

"Lacey?" Not only silence, but ominous darkness. He hurried inside, growing more and more alarmed as he realized she hadn't lit even one lamp. Then Hawke noticed her new rocking chair was not back in front of the fireplace. "*Lacey!*" he called again, the volume louder, harsher. Still nothing. A quick check out front confirmed his fears. Lacey had left her new chair out in the storm, but there was no sign of her. She wouldn't have abandoned the rocker she professed to love so much unless she had no other choice.

Gripped with cold fear, Hawke raced through the house and out to the back porch again. He'd been thinking of going to check the barn, even though she hadn't been there ten minutes ago when he tended the animals. Then he remembered the pine boughs littering the pathway. Retracing his steps, which was more difficult now as the increasing snow had begun to fill them in, he cut up toward the still-visible path which led into the forest. They were faint, not much more than small dimples in the snow, but the prints he found there had been made by a small pair of boots. And not too long ago, either.

Had Lacey come across Hattie, and panicked? he wondered. Adding the fiercely protective nature of the wolf to his wife's fear of wildlife—even antelope—supplied an answer to the question in terribly vivid terms. Sick at heart, his chest swelling with dread, Hawke glanced up at the rapidly darkening skies and the even blacker clouds splotching them. Not only was nightfall near, but the storm was increasing in intensity.

"Oh, Christ, no," he muttered from deep in his chest. "No!" Then, in an anguished howl to rival the leader of Hattie's old pack, he screamed, *"Lacey!"* And plowed headlong into the forest.

'Twasn't so different from a spell, Lacey though to herself, disoriented, but strangely cozy in her bed of snow. And like a spell, she knew deep down inside her that something about this was wrong, and that she really ought to get herself together and do what must be done. Oh, but this way was so much easier. Nothing to harm her, no horrible shouting or ugly accusations between her mum and da, no words of condemnation from the nurses as they whispered Lacey's name amongst themselves and pointed to the little girl gone bad; just peace and the soft, cold quiet.

The wind kicked up, swirling around Lacey's icy little bed, and she began to shiver again. "Leave me alone," she murmured, her lips numb from cold. "Go away and leave me alone."

Above the howling wind, she suddenly heard another sound, something more comforting than even her cozy little bed in the freshly-fallen snow. What was it? She lifted her head, breaking through the icy blanket which had covered her, and strained her ears. Again she heard the sound, this time able to identity it as her husband's voice. *How very nice,* she thought, her head aching. *Hawke will know what to do.* Then, smiling contentedly, she lay back down and burrowed into the snow and let herself be lulled back into her previously sleepy state.

In spite of the cold, and no matter how illogical it sounded, she was warming up. Content. She sighed, giving herself over to the elements, but heard Hawke's voice calling her name. He sounded hoarse, panicked . . . maybe even angry. *Come sleep with me,* she invited in her mind, unable to find the strength to put voice to the words. *Come hold me and sleep, my husband.*

Hawke called her name again, the sound louder and even angrier. Prompted by him and a sudden burst of energy, Lacey opened her eyes and raised her head, surprised at the havoc all around her. Snow was swirling in every direction, making it impossible for her to see a thing except the color white. The bitter wind cut through her velvet cloak, stinging the parts of her body that weren't already half-frozen. She began to shiver again, violently and uncontrollably. What was happening to her? she wondered, terrified for her own survival at last. Would she freeze and die?

Digging deep within herself for both courage and strength, Lacey struggled to her knees, then finally managed to stand. Bracing herself against a nearby pine, she cupped her hands around her mouth, took as deep a breath as she could manage, and screamed with every ounce of power she had.

When he heard the sound, at first Hawke thought he'd scared up a wildcat, or even stumbled across a predator in mid-kill. When it came again, and he realized the voice was definitely human and female, he shouted back, "Lacey! I'm coming. Keep hollering so I can find you."

She did. Even though her voice got weaker, the calls more infrequent, she kept it up long enough for Hawke to spot her draped between the low-lying branches of a lodgepole pine.

Rushing to her side, he pulled her into his fierce embrace, unable to speak. He held her that way for several moments, loathe to ever let her go, but then forcefully separated his heart from his mind. Hawke's instincts for survival were strong; strong enough for him to realize he couldn't effect their rescue if he let the intense emotions tearing at his gut rule his head. So it was with steel-like precision that he forced those feelings to a back burner, and in utter silence ripped off his heavy buckskin jacket, wrapped Lacey in it, then hefted her into his arms.

With only these words of instruction, he said, "Hold on to my neck, understand? Don't let go of me for anything!"

Then, with only instinct and his years of trapping guiding him, Hawke fell into a dead run and made his way through the blinding snowstorm to the ranch.

Once he'd kicked open the door and stepped inside, he paused only long enough to decide where Lacey would be the warmest. Then he bolted up the stairs with her still in his arms, and heaved her onto the center of their bed. Moving swiftly, Hawke built the biggest, hottest fire he could without jeopardizing the house, then went back to the bed where she lay shivering out of control.

His features still rigid, unreadable, Hawke brushed the dry snow out of Lacey's hair and quickly undressed her. Searching for signs of frostbite, particularly white spots or gray areas, he examined her fingers, toes, ears, and nose, but other than a general blue cast to her delicate skin, all appeared well. Moving quickly as she was still suffering from exposure to the cold and not out of danger yet, Hawke tucked her into their bed between the flannel sheets, then piled every blanket and quilt in the house on top of her.

Only then did he allow himself a moment to breathe, to look on Lacey's quaking form beneath the mound of covers as anything other than his solemn duty. The one breath of relief he took caught sharply in his throat, lodging there. Hawke took another, and another, until he was reasonably certain he could keep control of himself. In spite of those efforts, he continued to choke on emotions too deep and too new to recognize for what they were, much less acknowledge them. Ignoring his inner turmoil, Hawke stripped off his own clothes, never taking his gaze from his wife, and climbed beneath the blankets.

Knowing the heat from his own body would be the best and safest way to warm her, Hawke gathered Lacey into his arms. After cuddling her stiff limbs and unresponsive body this way for several minutes, she finally rewarded him by slowly twisting in the circle of his embrace. Moaning softly as her blood began to flow warmer and faster, Lacey burrowed against Hawke's body as if trying to climb inside him for the extra warmth there.

The emotions he'd so carefully buried surfaced then, pointing out to Hawke one undeniable fact; he'd have split his belly open from stem to stern if he thought for one second the deed would help save Lacey. Anytime. Anywhere.

"T-t-was a-a-a . . . "

"Hush now, Irish," Hawke muttered, surprised at the husky, cracked sound of his own voice. He kept her wrapped in his arms and legs, and continued to caress her frosty skin with both his hands and feet. "Don't try to talk. Let's just get you warm for now."

"B-but a-a-w-w-wolf!"

"I know, Irish, I know. We'll talk about that later."

Unable to harness the rush of emotions burgeoning

inside him at the sound of her sweet lilt—a voice he'd thought he'd never hear again—Hawke fell on Lacey's mouth, kissing her so deeply, it was as if he were seeking life-sustaining warmth for himself. Something powerful and intense, a certain recklessness gripped him, and for the first time in his life, Hawke was afraid of what he might do or say. He squeezed his eyes shut, trying to ward the sensations off, to call a halt to whatever held him in its grasp. If he couldn't do that, he feared he might do the unthinkable: Dissolve into tears.

The effort to hold himself back finally exhausted Hawke. With a low cry, a groan that was at least half-sob, he buried his head in Lacey's hair, and drew her body beneath his. If he hadn't known before, Hawke knew then how terribly incomplete he'd be if he should ever truly lose the woman he held in his arms. Desperate to feel whole again, urged onward by a terrible need to become as close to Lacey as humanly possible, Hawke slipped his hand between her legs and nudged her thighs apart.

"Forgive me, Irish," he whispered, his voice hoarse against her hair. "God forgive me, Lacey, but I've got to have you. I've got to have you now."

"Aye, m-my h-husband." Her breath skipped out in soft little pants, but the tremors wracking her body now were shivers of another kind, and not from the cold. She ran her hands through Hawke's loose hair, pulling him to her. "There'd be nothing to forgive, for I, too, have a . . . a grand need for you."

With a decided lack of both finesse and patience, Hawke immediately slipped into his wife. She felt better at that moment than any time he could remember, including the first. She was hotter than the roaring fire filling the entire hearth of his great stone fireplace, his in a deeper, more fulfilling way than he'd ever imagined.

It suddenly occurred to Hawke that he loved Lacey. He

loved her, by God! Amazed and buoyed by the discovery of such an intangible thing in his own heart, he suddenly wanted nothing more than to share the realization with Lacey, to make it somehow more concrete between them.

But then John Winterhawke, Jr., former mountain man and one tough son of a bitch, stumbled across another revelation about himself—he was afraid to tell her. Afraid that little piece of herself Lacey kept hidden from him would prevent her from loving him back. Would make him seem a fool. He was disappointed by that thought, to be sure, but rather than letting it cool the frantic, emotional rhythm of their lovemaking, Hawke kept hold of the love he felt for her, making the moment even more intense than before.

Knowing he couldn't last much longer this way, he called out to Lacey, urging her onward with both his voice and his touch. When at last she reached her peak, triggering his own, the promise he'd once made demanded that Hawke withdraw, and withdraw at once. Something stronger than self-restraint, a more savage and possessive part of his primitive self urged him deeper within her instead. Then he was lost, shuddering in the throes of a mind-numbing orgasm which stripped him of all control.

Moments later when he'd regained his breath and a small measure of his sanity, Hawke raised up on his elbows to relieve Lacey of the burden of his weight. Guilt flickered through him as he gazed down on her sweet trusting face and contented smile. Although he figured he ought to at least apologize for what he'd done here, Hawke found he didn't quite know what to say or how to explain exactly what had happened to him. Maybe, he thought, hoping it were true, nothing would come of his lapse in judgement. Maybe there would be nothing to apologize for.

Exonerated by the thought, he asked, "Are you warm enough yet, sweetheart?"

Lacey glanced up at her husband through misty blue eyes. "Aye, that I am." Her hand fluttered to her left breast and remained there. "Especially in here."

His throat tight, aching unbearably, Hawke hoarsely muttered, "Me too, Irish. Me too." Then, feeling more guilty than ever, he rolled onto his back and lay staring up at the knotholes in the ceiling.

Snuggling herself into the crook of her husband's arm, Lacey tried to explain again about her near-attack. "I must tell you how I came to be in the forest. 'Twas a wolf on the porch when I came round to the back of the house today! A wolf!"

"I know," he murmured. "I figured that's what sent you into the forest."

"Do you know that it tried to eat me?"

"Lacey, I doubt that—"

"I swear 'tis true! I ran off before it could catch me, then I fell over a boulder or something, and hit my head. When I woke up, I was truly surprised to find the wolf wasn't making a grand supper of me!"

Feeling her scalp for lumps, Hawke chuckled softly as he said, "I doubt old Hattie wanted to put you on her supper menu, but I imagine she must have scared you half to death when the two of you met up." Lacey winced as his fingers slid across a small bump on the left side of her head. The skin wasn't broken, and since she hadn't drifted off or passed out since he found her, Hawke wasn't concerned that she'd suffered a concussion. "Are you hurt anywhere else?"

"I do not think so." She tested her legs. "Maybe a wee knot on the one knee, but nothing to doctor." Raising her head so she could look her husband in the eye, Lacey asked, "Did I hear you call the wolf by name?"

"Yes, Irish, you did." Reminded of yet another apology he owed her—one he had little difficulty in making—Hawke explained. "I should have told you about old Hattie at the first sign of winter, but then, well, I guess I just forgot all about her."

Lacey abruptly sat up, careful to keep the blankets around her shoulders. "You *know* this wolf well? You speak of her as if you raised the beast on your ranch!"

"I didn't exactly do that, but she has been a frequent visitor around here."

"A *visitor* you say?" Lacey slapped Hawke across the chest, stinging his skin. "Six eggs to you for your breakfast, sir, and half a dozen of them rotten!"

"Hey!" Hawke reached up as she drew back her hand in order to slap him again, and caught her by the wrist. "I told you I just kind of forgot about old Hattie! Don't take it so personal, Irish."

"Hell's cure to you, Mr. Winterhawke! 'Twas because of you I almost froze to death out there, and because of you that friendly wolf of yours almost made a meal of me. 'Tis very personal to me, indeed."

Even though he knew she was halfway kidding, a burst of those new, overwhelming emotions swept over Hawke, taking him by surprise. He pulled Lacey down on top of him, folding her in an embrace which almost prevented the two of them from breathing. Easing his grip just a little, he whispered against the bounty of curls at her ear, "Forgive me, Irish. I never—I didn't dream that wolf would come back here so late in winter, and it sure never occurred to me that she'd show up when you were here alone."

"Oh, I suppose what you say is so, but why in all that's holy do you allow such a creature the run of the place? 'Tis a dangerous beast, 'tis is not?"

He shrugged. "I expect she can be, certainly if she

doesn't know you, but with me, and especially Crowfoot, Hattie is just an ugly old pussycat."

"Crowfoot?"

"Uh-huh. They were together when I found her caught in a trap, living on the run near as Caleb and I could figure." She gasped, a thousand questions mirrored in her eyes. "It was an unusual arrangement all right, but not completely out of the question. Crowfoot, who'd been named Crow Boy With Crooked Foot at birth, was abandoned by humankind as you already know. We suspect that Hattie was also shunned by her own wolf pack for some reason. Anyway, they were together, and together they stayed that whole first year they lived here at Winterhawke."

Sighing with disbelief, Lacey shook her head. "'Tis difficult for me to understand, but if the boy and wolf are so close, why have I ne'er laid eyes on her before today?"

"Hattie's wild, and always will be. Don't forget that for a minute." Thinking of Lacey's close call with the animal, Hawke pulled her mouth down to his for a quick, but meaningful, kiss. "She's gradually been spending less and less time around here, weaning Crowfoot in a manner of speaking, I guess. The old gal generally takes off at the first hint of spring, then comes back in late fall or early winter. This year she left well before the last snow hit, and frankly, we figured that she either found a mate who considered an ugly, three-legged wolf adorable, or was finally strong enough to care for herself through an entire winter again."

Mulling over all she'd learned here, Lacey eased her head down on her husband's chest. "'Tis a beautiful story, I'm thinking," she murmured. "A tale to bring the splendor of fire into my heart. Do you know what I mean, husband?"

"Aye," popped out of his mouth automatically, but for

Hawke it was more an endearment than an answer. Lacey brought more than the splendor of fire to his heart; she burned brighter and hotter there than the core of a cinder. Hawke glanced above the wild tangle of her hair to the shadows flowing into one another as they danced across the ceiling. In those gracefully reflected flames of the fire still roaring in the hearth, he found the perfect portrait of the intangibles in his heart.

That brief respite from the weather was the last the inhabitants of the Centennial area saw of the sun for another six weeks. Snow piled up deeper than Hawke could ever remember it, trapping him and Lacey in their log home, the tunnel he'd dug between the barn and the house their only avenue of escape. When the sun finally broke through the clouds in the first part of March, bringing with it a promise of spring, Hawke and Lacey ran outside like a pair of little children, laughing and playing, and flinging snowballs at one another.

Crowfoot returned to Winterhawke during that same break, and enjoyed a happy if short reunion with Hattie. Once the boy was back where he belonged and she examined him to make sure he was all right, the wolf took off again. This time, Hawke had the definite feeling she wouldn't be coming back.

It wasn't until mid-April, however, that the Winterhawkes could chance a trip to Three Elk to check on the Weatherspoon family. The baby, a fragile girl, had been born a few weeks early, but with her mother's expert care, was getting on very well. Kate had named her Kathleen, in honor of Lacey, and when it was time for Lacey to go home, the women fell into a prolonged and teary farewell. Shortly after that fast visit, foaling began at Winterhawke, and before they knew it, it was mid-May and the cavalry had returned for the horses ordered last spring. Lacey, who hadn't been to Laramie since she'd arrived over a year ago, was so excited about the prospect of traveling to town with her husband, she'd hardly slept for two nights. Hawke, caught up in the idea of owning Winterhawke free and clear at last, shared in her restlessness. Neither of them thought Saturday would ever come.

Three days before the planned journey into Laramie, Hawke made his way back to the house early in the morning with the eggs and bucket of milk. He walked into the kitchen expecting to find Lacey busy at the stove. Instead, she was kneeling by the pantry, retching into a bucket.

"Christ," he muttered under his breath, going to her. Leaning down, he lightly patted her back, and asked, "What's the matter, Irish, did you choke on something?"

She shook her head, but continued to retch, bringing up nothing but air.

His suspicions roused, he thought back to Big Jim and the symptoms the rancher grumbled about each time he suspected that his wife had caught—again. Hawke hadn't paid much attention to the man when he started talking about woman-matters, and he had pretty much put the possibility that Lacey might be pregnant out of his mind. Now as he put everything together, he did remember Big Jim mentioning something about his wife's tendency to throw up a lot in the early months.

"Christ," he muttered again, louder.

After wiping her mouth, Lacey rolled away from the bucket and looked up at Hawke from her seat on the floor. Her normally bright complexion was pale and wan, showing her freckles off far more than usual.

"My stomach," she said, holding her belly. "'Tisn't quite right this morning."

Hawke didn't beat around the bush. "How many mornings has this been going on, Irish?"

She shrugged, a slight hesitancy in her voice as she admitted, "For the better part of a week, I suppose. Why?"

Hawke sighed heavily, uncertain how to proceed with the discussion from here.

Noting his concern, Lacey climbed to her feet. She swooned, nearly falling, and would have, had her husband not been there to catch her. Had Big Jim mentioned anything about dizziness? Hawke thought that maybe he had.

"Sit down, Irish," he said a little gruffly. "In fact, maybe you ought to go lie down a while."

"B-but the sickness is gone again. I was just a wee bit weak there for a moment, is all."

Despite her objections, Hawke firmly sat Lacey down in the nearest chair. Then, actually contemplating fatherhood for the first time since the night he'd lost all control, he traced the soft curves of Lacey's cheek with his fingertip. Surprisingly enough, the thought of her carrying his child really didn't disturb him at all anymore, if indeed it ever really had. In fact, he realized that he was actually looking forward to the prospect, teeming with a new kind of joy.

Hardly able to keep a serious face, he forced a stern expression to hide the smile lurking just beneath it as he said, "You're not sick, Lacey. I think you're going to have a baby."

He hadn't thought it possible for her delicate skin to go even whiter than it was before, but it did. "A babe— *me*?"

Hawke nodded, just the corners of his mouth upturned.

"B-but . . . but you *promised* that would not happen!"

At both her tone and the words, Hawke's joy deflated to an ominous kind of bewilderment. "I'm not a hundred percent sure that's what's wrong with you, Lacey. It's just a guess. When we get to town Saturday, have the doctor take a look at you after he examines Crowfoot."

Tears sprang into Lacey's eyes as she read the truth in her husband's expression. Lowering her head, for she couldn't bear to look at him any longer, she prayed to God that Hawke was wrong. But she knew, somehow, that he wasn't.

Ever since the night he'd found her near to freezing in the snow, then loved her with a passion she'd never felt in him before, Lacey had been afraid something like this might have happened. Things were different between them that night, physical differences to be sure, but the morning after, too. Hawke's silvery-green eyes by morning's light seemed to gleam with a hint of guilt, and she thought she could almost see an unspoken apology perched at the tip of his tongue. She'd known something was wrong, but had been so happy and content, it was far easier to go on as if nothing out of the ordinary had happened.

Well clearly, something had. Was she now supposed to present the man she loved above life itself with a mad baby? How would she ever accomplish such a thing? Lacey wondered with horror. She'd have to explain everything to him—her involvement in her own parents' deaths, the spells that came over her with less frequency as she grew older, and the periods she spent as a mad girl locked in with the others at St. Josephine's. She could never find the words to show Hawke this part of herself. Never!

Both terror and grief pouring out of her in a muffled sob, Lacey lifted her head and lashed out at the only thing she could think of—Hawke, who'd put her in this position in the first place.

"No, no, no!" she cried, pounding the table beside her. "This can not be true. You must tell me 'tisn't true!"

Not so much as a hint of his former joy remained as

Hawke snapped back at his wife. "I don't see why you're so damned upset." Or maybe, he did. "I've seen the way you look at Kate's daughter when we're over there. Maybe having a baby of your own won't be such a trial for you."

How could bearing a mad child be anything but a trial? "Well, I don't agree with you, sir! I also don't think you're a man of your word!"

"Lacey," he said, the warning in his voice low and clear. "You're not being fair about this."

"As fair as you! I told you I did not want a babe, and you, you p-promised it would not happen to me. How could you have done this dreadful thing anyway?"

"God damn it, Lacey," he snarled. "I'm only human. I didn't figure on getting you in a family way. If you'll recall, I didn't exactly want children either! I just made a little mistake."

"I think there'd be nothing small or wee about it! And a dreadful, dreadful mistake it 'tis." Overwrought and overwhelmed all at once, the tears began to fall harder as Lacey folded her arms on the table and dropped her head on them.

"As I said before," Hawke muttered, his heart breaking, "go see the doctor in town. Maybe he can do something to help you with this dreadful mistake. God knows, I can't do anything for you now except say I'm sorry."

18

A man cannot be too careful in the choice of his enemies.
—Oscar Wilde

The next three days were rough on Hawke and Lacey. He spent most of his hours in the barn with the hired hand he'd borrowed from Caleb, making sure the man knew exactly what was expected of him and what to do in case of an emergency. Lacey pretty much hid out in their bedroom, crying and miserable. And alone.

The long drive to town should have been a joyous one for everyone, what with money enough for Hawke to buy the ranch free and clear as well as to send Lacey on a shopping trip for herself, at long last. More importantly, there was hope for Crowfoot to lead a normal life. Lacey had worked hard with the boy over the winter, and finally convinced him to let both her and Kate have a look at his foot. It was crooked for sure, but Kate had assured all concerned that she'd seen worse at the hospital—and that even then the defect had been corrected well enough for the child to wear a proper shoe and walk with only a slight limp.

It should have been a joyous day, indeed, but words barely passed among the sullen trio until Hawke pulled the wagon up next to the New York House Hotel. Although its location on rough and tumble Front Street was not the best, the inn had been freshly renovated and it was one of the few establishments in Laramie in which Hawke figured a half-breed and his wife would be welcomed.

Dressed as John Winterhawke, Jr., businessman, in fresh jeans, subdued flannel shirt, and plain buckskin jacket, Hawke, who'd even taken the precaution of leaving his eagle feather hat at the ranch, climbed down from the wagon, gave Laccy a hand, then led her to the boardwalk in front of the hotel.

"Get two rooms," Hawke said, handing her a wad of bills. "One for us and one for Crowfoot."

The young man balked. "I will not—"

Hawke cut the kid off with both his tongue and sharp gaze. "You will do what we ask of you in town, son, remember?"

Crowfoot's bottom lip fell, but he nodded and said, "I remember. I will stay in the hotel."

"That's right." His attention back on Lacey, Hawke finished his instructions. "You and Crowfoot may as well go on over to see the doctor once you've taken care of the rooms." He paused, looking at her intently, but then went on with his instructions. "After you've finished there, meet me in front of Braddock Savings and Loan. That's at the other end of Second Street. By the time I've dropped the horses at the stables, ordered our supplies from Trabings Store, and taken care of business with Braddock, you two ought to be about done don't you think?"

She nodded, her gaze averted, and quietly said, "We'll be waiting for you out front of the savings and loan."

Then, Crowfoot in hand, Lacey stepped through the doors of the hotel and disappeared from view.

Although he tried not to think about her or the impossible situation she was in because of his carelessness, Hawke went about his business, distracted at best. All he could feel was numb inside; that and a terrible sense of loss. It was in that frame of mind that he finally approached his uncle's place of business. Though just one of several savings and loan companies Braddock had helped organize in Laramie, the impressive three-story building of brick and glass was the only to bear the man's name.

Striding across the lobby directly to the small desk placed squarely in front of Braddock's polished oak doors, Hawke announced himself to the secretary. "Excuse me, ma'am. I'm John Winterhawke, Jr., and I'd like a minute with William Braddock. Is he here?"

The young woman looked up at him, then gave a little start. "Oh, I, er, I'm not sure. Just a moment, please."

She backed her chair away from the desk, then scurried over to Braddock's doors, knocked, and opened one of them a crack. Moving as silently as he could, Hawke was right on her heels.

"There's a Mr. Winterhawke, Jr., out here to see you, Mr. Braddock. Are you in for him?" Better than a head taller than the attractive young woman, Hawke peered into the room.

"It looks to me like he is," he said, frightening the secretary so, she jumped and flattened herself against the jamb. Hawke pushed the door open all the way, then stepped around the woman.

Braddock, who hadn't said a thing yet, burst into boisterous laughter. "Even with all the schooling Ft. Laramie had to offer, it still didn't go far in civilizing a savage like you, did it, breed?"

Hawke shrugged, in no mood to put up with his uncle's insults a moment longer than he had to. "I've come on business, and I don't have a lot of time. Get out your ledger for Winterhawke Ranch. I want to pay off the deed."

The secretary started to back out of the doorway. "If you won't be needing me . . . "

"No, wait a minute, Pauline!" Braddock waved to the woman. "Get on in here and sit down. I might need you to, ah . . . jot down a note, or two."

Hawke smiled wryly, pleased to think that his uncle was too afraid of what his nephew-the-savage might do to allow himself to be trapped alone in a room with him. As Braddock dug through his files, Hawke couldn't help but notice that the secretary had taken a seat to the left of her employer—and that she was staring at him again, this time with a far more appreciative eye. Hawke winked at her just to see what she would do. Pauline winked right back, then gave him a crooked little smile. Braddock-trained all right, he thought with a twinge of pity. Then he turned back to his uncle.

Fiddling with his tawny mustache as he perused the papers before him, Braddock finally looked up from them and drew a beady-eyed gaze on his nephew. "Here are the new figures. How much of it do you think you can pay this year?"

Hawke stared at the number, hardly able to believe his eyes. "What the hell are you trying to do to me? This isn't even close to the amount we agreed on last spring!"

"Take a seat, breed, and I'll explain." But Hawke remained standing, glaring at the uncle he hated as the man went on with his lies. "You've got to admit yourself that the house and barn are worth ten times what they were four years ago—maybe more."

"Of course they are, you idiot, but I built them myself

with my own two hands. You can't raise the price on what I've done!"

He narrowed one amber eye. "I can do just about anything I want to as president of this company, and don't you forget it. Besides, there's been a lot of talk around town about the quartz gold mines popping up all over around Centennial way. Hell, the mineral rights alone on that property are probably worth more than the final figure I just gave you."

Hawke slapped his hands to the desk, leaning across the polished mahogany top to better look the man in his lying, cheating eyes. "You will not do this to me again," he said, his voice rough. "I have enough money on me to buy Winterhawke at a fair price, free and clear. I know it, and you know it. Now get me the deed, god damn it, or . . ."

"Or what?" Braddock had leaned so far back, his chair was pushed up against the wall. And his voice had lost its arrogant edge. "You gonna scalp me, or something?"

"Maybe," Hawke ground out. Then he made a mistake with the man that he couldn't have foreseen. "Just maybe I will lift your miserable scalp. You willing to take that chance, or are you going to do the right thing by your sister's son?"

Hostility replaced the fear in Braddock's expression the moment he heard the word sister. He spat into the spittoon at the foot of his desk, his amber eyes slits, and said, "Get out of my office, you no-good son of a bitch! You disgust me as much as your Indian-loving mother did!"

Hawke had never heard the man speak so of Mildred Braddock. And he didn't much care for it. "My Indian-*loving* mother? Don't you have that backwards, *Uncle?*" He pronounced the appellation as if it were the Arapaho word for shit.

"No, *nephew*, I do not." Braddock's naturally ruddy complexion took on a deeper hue. "My whore of a sister ran away with your father *after* she found out he'd knocked her up, not before!"

Cold fury swept through Hawke at those words and his hands tightened into white-knuckled fists. Could this possibly be true? For years on end, he'd been led to believe he was a product of rape, that his father had forcibly dragged his mother off during the night.

"You're lying," he said, almost certain for some reason that he was not.

"I wish that I was—almost as much as I wish that Mildred had died of consumption *before* she had a chance to give birth to the likes of you."

Sick inside as the vague image of his mother's sad eyes came to mind, Hawke had the fleeting thought that she'd probably died more of a broken heart than consumption. And he had a pretty good idea who was responsible for making her feel that way, too. As he thought of what he'd lost of his heritage, of how he himself had been taught to look on his paternal blood as somehow less than acceptable, he grew angry all over again.

Seething with rage, he growled, "How could you let me think what I did of my father all this time, you lousy bastard?"

"Your father, bah!" Again Braddock spit into the brass container. Beside him, Pauline flinched. "If there's a bastard in all this besides you, it's the big dumb savage that sired you. But don't worry about looking him up, if that's what you've got in mind—I fixed his ass good after he and Mildred disappeared, or didn't you know that either?"

Braddock's face was beet red now, his fat jowls jiggling continually. Although he was quite sure he didn't want to hear the rest of what the man had to say, Hawke morbidly asked, "No, sir, I didn't. Just what did you do to his ass?"

For a moment, it looked as if Braddock realized that he'd gone too far. But then his sheer joy in taunting Hawke overruled his better judgement. "Mildred's and my father was the post commander at the time that Arapaho scout went and 'kidnapped' his daughter. He had every right to send a detachment of soldiers after them, and he did." A grin that was more sneer spreading his mustache wide, Braddock went on to say, "I rode with the detail that day, and when we caught up to Mildred and her 'savage,' *I* had the honor of putting the bullet through that red bastard's heart myself."

This final bit of information proved too much for Hawke. Incapable of restraining himself any longer, he leapt on top of his uncle's desk and grabbed him by the throat, the sound of Pauline's screams ringing in his ears.

In the doctor's office, Lacey beamed after the man finished his evaluation. "And what you're saying then is that the boy has a good chance of walking with no limp a'tall after this operation?"

"I'd almost guarantee it."

"Did you hear that?" she asked Crowfoot, who was beaming as well. "Soon as we talk to Hawke and make all the arrangements, you'll be as good as new!"

"Yes, lady! Good as new!" Crowfoot hopped up from his chair. "Let's go tell Hawke now."

"In a minute, Lad." Lacey softened her voice. "There's something else I wish to discuss with the doctor that has nothing to do with you. Will you wait out front for a minute or two?"

Happy just thinking about his future, Crowfoot shrugged and limped out the door.

When she and the doctor were alone again, Lacey turned to him, anxiety adding a little quiver to her voice and a rush to her pulse. "There'd be one other wee problem I'd like to have your opinion about," she said. "Do you have the time?"

If not for the double-barreled Derringer Braddock pulled from his vest pocket at the same moment Hawke's fingers found the hollow of his throat, he might very well have breathed his last breath. But as the man swung the small pistol toward his head, Hawke knocked the gun from his hand, and then released him.

Picking up the weapon himself, Hawke slid off the desk and pointed the ivory handled pistol at the spot just above the bridge of Braddock's nose. He let the man sweat a moment before he finally slammed the gun down on the desktop and muttered, "You aren't worth going to prison over."

Then he turned his back and started for the door.

"You'll never get the deed to that ranch now, you bastard!" Braddock screamed after him. "You can get down on your knees and beg me, and it won't do you a damn bit of good!"

As his fingers touched down on the doorknob, Hawke looked over his shoulder at the quivering mass of flesh that made up his uncle. "I don't plan to set foot in this office again for any reason, much less beg you for a ranch I no longer want. Just know that if I can't have Winterhawke, no one can."

"What's that supposed to mean?"

"Just believe it. Believe, too, that you'll pay for this, Braddock. Somehow, someday, I'll see you pay, and pay dearly." His gaze and voice deadly, he added, "There's more than one way to skin a polecat—and without getting your stink all over my hands." That said, he let himself out of the office and slammed the door.

As Lacey and Crowfoot headed down the boardwalk toward Braddock Savings and Loan, she was practically bouncing down the street. What a fool she'd been to be so worried—her troubles were practically over! She automatically clicked her heels before remembering that she'd left her silver spurs behind at the ranch. She'd been sure they'd run out of luck, but oh, how she wished she could clink them together now! Between her own relief and Crowfoot's optimistic outlook, she could hardly wait to see Hawke to tell him the good news. Why, tonight they'd have to celebrate at the finest restaurant in town!

Just before they reached the correct building, the glass doors flew open, shattering one of them with a deafening crash as it slammed against the brick exterior of the business. Hawke strode through the doorway along with that explosion of glass, then turned on his heel and marched in Lacey's direction, the rumble of his angry boots against the boardwalk sounding like thunder.

She'd hardly had enough time to digest what she'd seen before he was upon her. "Oh, Christ, and by the nine orders of angels," she whispered under her breath. "Don't let these tidings be a match to my husband's anger."

"Our plans have changed," said Hawke, his murderous expression stripping away all hope that her prayers had been heard.

Gripping her painfully by the elbow before she could utter another word, Hawke turned Lacey around and started walking her back in the direction she'd come from. Then, gesturing for Crowfoot to follow them, her husband went on in the same wooden monotone as before. "I'm taking you two to the hotel now. I've got to ride out to the ranch for a couple of days, and when I get back to Laramie, we'll be moving on."

Lacey planted her feet. "Moving on? What does that mean?"

"Like I said, our plans have changed." His sage green eyes were devoid of their usual silvery sparkle, dull like moss as he briefly explained. "I've just found out that Winterhawke will never be ours to keep no matter how many horses I sell to the cavalry. I've decided to take Phantom and my best mares into the Snowy Range Mountains where I'll release them."

"B-but—"

"No buts about it. I'm not going to let anyone take over that ranch or the horses I've worked so hard to breed." He paused, grinding his teeth. "Once the livestock is taken care of, I'm going to burn Winterhawke Ranch to the ground. Then I'll come back for you two."

"Lord above," she cried, tears falling freely. "Please, Hawke, I beg of you, do not do this thing."

"Sorry, but I have to." On the move again, Hawke renewed his grip on Lacey, then turned to Crowfoot to issue a couple of orders. "I've got a mighty important job for you here in town. Think you can do it?"

His onyx eyes shining with worry, the mute boy simply nodded.

"You and Lacey are going to be alone in Laramie for two or three days. I want you to take good care of her for me. Don't let her out of your sight. Understand?"

Again Crowfoot nodded.

In front of the hotel now, Hawke took Lacey aside. "Go to your room and stay there except for meals. I'll be back as fast as I can." He took her by the shoulders, gave her a brief hug, and softened his voice just a little as he whispered, "It'll be all right. Someday, it'll be all right again." Then he released her and stormed across the dusty street.

"Hawke!" she called after him, her voice drowning in tears. But he didn't even look her away again. In the next second, the man she loved so dearly rounded the corner and disappeared from view. Lacey's knees buckled, and for a minute, she thought she might even collapse. Shadows drifted behind her eyes, warning her of an impending spell. *Not now,* Lord, she prayed. Not now with Hawke so distraught and everything he'd worked for in such jeopardy. If ever he needed her, it was now. Surely there was something she could do to help, but what?

As Lacey struggled to regain her composure, an idea occurred to her, a rather impetuous plan, she admitted to herself, but the only one she could think of. Why couldn't she simply march back to this dishonest banker's office and explain the situation? After all, what more could she and Hawke lose? And if she were successful, and actually talked this Braddock fellow into doing what was right, there might even be time to stop her husband from turning the horses he loved into the wild. Surely there would at least be enough time to keep him from burning the house down.

Growing more confident of the plan, she turned to Crowfoot and said, "I want to go back to this savings and loan company to try and find out what this is all about. Maybe I can get this Braddock fellow to show a bit of fairness to us. What do you think?"

Crowfoot frowned. "Hawke told me to keep you in my eyes, lady. I think this is not good."

"But I'm sure he did not mean it that literally." She took the boy's hand and started back down the boardwalk. "You can go with me and wait outside, knowing where I am the whole time. 'Twill be as good as in your eyes that way. I promise to hurry as fast as I can so you will not have to worry too long."

Although she could see the boy was not happy with the idea, he gave her a reluctant nod. When they reached their destination, Crowfoot sat down on the edge of the boardwalk, pointed a small brown finger at her and said, "I wait right here. You hurry."

Lacey gave that finger a little squeeze. "As fast as I can."

Then, wishing now more than ever that she'd had faith enough in her silver spurs to bring them along with her, she hurried down the street. Tiptoeing around the glass outside the doors to the building, she stepped through the one which no longer featured a barrier inside the frame, and skirted the bustling employees who were cleaning up the glass which had fallen inside the lobby. Pausing a moment, she scanned the desks lined up checkerboard-style throughout the room, then brightened as the name she sought came into view on an immense pair of doors toward the back of the building.

Approaching the small desk situated in front of those impressive doors, she said, "If you'll be excusing me, please, ma'am?"

The secretary glanced up at her. "Yes? Is there something I can do for you?"

Lacey straightened the jacket of her new brown dress, belatedly wondering how well her hair had held up during the long ride to town. Resisting the urge to touch her curls and find out, she said, "I would like to speak to your Mr. Braddock, please."

"And who shall I tell him is here?"

"'Tis . . . " She gulped. "'Tis Lacey Winterhawke come to call."

"Winter—oh." The young woman narrowed her gaze and looked Lacey up and down as she got out of her chair. "Ah, excuse me a minute? I'll just go see if he's in." Then she slipped through the doors and ducked inside the office.

Lacey had just enough time for a few second thoughts before the secretary reappeared, a nervous smile pulling her painted lips taut. "Please come this way, Ma'am. Mr. Braddock said he will see you now."

Following the secretary's lead, Lacey stepped inside the large, airy office and directed her gaze to the bulky man lounging in a chair behind the desk. As he looked her over with narrow amber eyes, he smoothed the tails of his mustache with one hand and lightly stroked his own belly with the other.

"Come on in," Braddock invited, a broad grin showing a remarkably perfect set of teeth. "I don't bite. At least, not as a rule." He laughed at his own joke, then pointed to the chair directly in front of his desk. "Have a seat."

As she crossed the room, Lacey picked up the aroma of polished wood, stagnant cigar smoke, and something musty, an odor not unlike mildew.

Speaking to his secretary, who'd followed along behind Lacey, Braddock said, "That's all, Pauline. I won't be needing you any longer."

"But—"

"I said, that's all."

Pauline, who wore a pained and rather irritated expression, gave Lacey a quick, meaningful glance, then turned and walked out of the room, careful to close the door behind her.

"My secretary informs me your name is Winterhawke," said Braddock, studying her features carefully. "I don't see how it's possible with a good-looking gal like you, but are you related to my nephew's father in some way?"

"Your nephew, sir? I can not imagine that I am since I do not think I know the man. Is he from Laramie?"

"No," Braddock said thoughtfully. "He runs, or I should say, ran a horse ranch up near Centennial for me. I didn't think a gal like—"

"Would you be speaking of Winterhawke Ranch?"

"I am, but the fellow I'm talking about is a half-breed, and probably doesn't—"

"Excuse me, sir," Lacey said, puzzled and shocked. "I believe we must be speaking of the same man, although I can not imagine why you refer to him as your nephew."

"Because he is my sister's bastard son. What's he to you?"

Lacey cringed over the way the banker had referred to him, but proudly said, "Hawke is my husband."

Braddock strangled on his own spittle. When he'd finished choking, he gazed at Lacey bug-eyed, and said, "You can't expect me to believe that a gal like you is tied up with that half-breed. What'd he pay you to waltz in here with that cock-and-bull story?"

"'Tis the truth!" Raising her chin a notch, she held her head high. "I married Hawke good and proper a year ago next month. But he did not e'er mention a word about you being his uncle."

Braddock laughed at the irony in that, for white men generally disavowed blood ties to Indians, not the other way around. "Assuming I'm idiot enough to believe that a fine piece of dry goods like you went and hitched yourself to my half-breed nephew, what possible good does he think it will do sending you to me? Did he figure I'd trade the deed to that ranch for a little fling with his woman? Is that it?"

Incensed, Lacey snapped, "My husband does not know that I've come to speak with you." And, if a little late occurring to her, she suddenly had a pretty good idea that he wouldn't have wanted her to talk with this man, either. But since she was already here, she went on with her mission. "I've come on my own to ask you to please find a way in your heart to make right by Hawke and the ranch. 'Tis the most important thing in his life."

"More important than you, you think?"

The man was leering at her, chuckling again and looking as if he enjoyed her discomfort tremendously. The effort beginning to weigh her down, Lacey kept her head high. "I would have to say, aye. 'Tis without question that Winterhawke Ranch is the thing my Hawke loves most. He loves the land and those horses as much as I love him: Utterly and completely."

"Is that a fact?"

Adjusting his trousers and the double V tails of his vest, Braddock pushed out of his chair and circled the desk. Stopping in front of Lacey's knees close enough to brush against them, he rested his backside against the edge of the mahogany top. "If you love that breed as much as all that, I expect you're willing to do just about anything you have to in order to get what he wants the most. Is that why you're here?"

Lacey recognized the trap in the man's question. "Aye," she admitted carefully. "So long as it was within reason, I would do almost anything for Hawke."

"Then why don't you stand up and let me have a better look at you. In fact, I'd like to see exactly what kind of a white woman would let herself be bedded by a no-good half-breed like that nephew of mine."

Lacey wasn't insulted for herself, but she could barely stand to hear such indignities spoken in her husband's name. Not bothering to conceal the loathing in her tone, she muttered, "If it be true that you are Hawke's blood uncle, I can not think why you would speak of him so dreadfully."

"I didn't ask you to think." With that, he reached down, grabbed Lacey's arm, and jerked her out of the chair. "And I didn't ask my sister to bring your miserable husband into this world, either." Painfully squeezing her arms, he demanded, "Tell me the truth—did he send you to me?"

Frightened by the man's tenacious grip and the evil she glimpsed in the pits of his eyes, Lacey's gaze darted from side to side as she sought an avenue of escape. "I—no, Hawke didn't send me here, but he probably knows that I came on my own by now, sir. He will not be very happy about it or what you are doing to me. Please let me go."

"Not yet, sugar." He released one of her arms long enough to drag a perfectly manicured finger across her lips. "That's an interesting little accent you've got there. Where are you from?"

She tried to twist out of his grasp then, but he quickly reclaimed her free arm. Still thinking of ways to escape, Lacey answered the question. "Ireland, sir."

"Is that so?" Braddock slid one of his hands down her arm to her waist, then dropped it even lower and cupped her bottom. He gave her a little squeeze as he asked, "Just what are you willing to do for that deed, you Irish beauty, you?"

Lacey brought her free fist to his chest, pounding against him as she said, "Nothing, sir! 'Twas a mistake me coming here, and I would like to go now."

"Not so fast, you little tease." With that, he spun around in a circle, taking Lacey with him, and then bent her over the top of his desk. "You're not near as friendly as you let on you'd be. How about a little kiss?"

He hovered over her, his thick lips open as they descended toward hers. At the last second before they could touch down, Lacey twisted her head to the side, avoiding him. There on the desk barely an inch from her nose, she saw a small gun. Was it loaded? she wondered.

Braddock slapped the side of her face, bringing her mouth back in line with his own, and then he tried to kiss her again. This time there was no escape as his lips clamped down on hers. Repulsed and terrified, Lacey bared her teeth against his probing tongue, then wriggled her hand free and groped for the gun.

Once the ivory handle was cradled in her palm, she swung the weapon up next to Braddock's temple, prayed that it contained a bullet, then twisted her mouth away from his, and demanded, "Get off of me now or I will shoot you!"

His expression riddled with surprise, Braddock released Lacey and abruptly stood up. "Whoa, now—be careful with that thing! It's loaded."

Her gaze and the barrels of the revolver aimed directly at the man's flushed face, Lacey struggled to her feet and brandished the weapon at him. "I-I wish to leave your office now," she said, her voice shaky. "If you will just be standing aside, please?"

Braddock took a sideways step as she'd requested, but when Lacey moved forward, he lunged at her, grasping the wrist of the hand which held the gun.

"Give me that, you stupid bitch!"

She screamed, fighting him for control of the gun, then spun in a circle as if dancing with the banker while they grappled for the revolver. Lacey could feel blunt fingernails digging into the back of her hand, tearing her fragile skin. She curled her fingers tighter around the grip, determined to keep the man from rendering her completely helpless, and then in the space of a heartbeat, a terrible explosion rent the air.

William Braddock stood there a moment, looking at her as if he were about to call her a stupid bitch again. Then he crumpled to the floor, his bloody fingers clutching the left side of his chest, and let out a gurgling gasp of surprise.

Stunned and horrified, Lacey stared down at the man through a little curlicue of smoke trailing off the end of the pistol. Had she *shot* him, or . . .

The door opened then, followed by the high-pitched scream of a woman.

"Oh, God! She's gone and shot Mr. Braddock!" Pauline turned toward her co-workers. "Somebody help him! Help!"

Shadows had filled the back of Lacey's mind by then, cold dark clouds of the same ilk as those which had kept her mute for so many years. If recognizing nothing else, she did know that she hadn't murdered just any man, but her husband's uncle. The enormity of the deed overwhelmed her so, Lacey didn't even bother to fight the tide of sensations rising up to sweep her away. Giving herself up to them instead, she lapsed into the friendly darkness of a deep, mind-numbing spell.

19

The Irish are a fair people;—they never
speak well of one another.

—Samuel Johnson

Crowfoot sat across the alley from Braddock
Savings and Loan, contentedly whittling a piece of mountain mahogany into another of his lupine creations. As he
worked, he allowed himself to believe, and for the first
time ever, that he might grow into a real person someday,
a man with normal working parts and the ability to communicate with the world at large. Hawke and Caleb had
been trying to convince him of that for years now, but
until the lady came along, he'd refused to even entertain
the notion. The lady got him thinking that way, and now
that the doctor insisted that his foot could be straightened out well enough to wear a regular shoe or boot,
Crowfoot not only entertained the notion, but relished
the idea of becoming more "civilized."

Maybe, he thought, taking his dreams one step further, he might even find himself a girl like Hawke's
someday, one that could understand the darkness inside
him and the pain it brought the way Lacey seemed to. He

wondered how the lady had come to understand his need for quiet moments and the periods of torment that came over him, forcing him to take himself off to the forest to release some of the rage inside. He wondered, too, if she'd experienced something like his own private misery. He'd felt that in her the day she'd set fire to the kitchen, then came to him to ease her suffering in silence.

But that was all Crowfoot had time to wonder about as a shot rang out in the building next door. Quickly sticking his knife into the smooth leather sheath Hawke had made for him, he hopped down from the edge of the boardwalk and scurried into the alley. Terrified of what might have happened, he sat there not knowing what else to do, and listened to the muffled screams and general confusion ringing off the walls inside the fancy building. Moments later, boots sounded on the boardwalk, and a blur of men ran past the alleyway where he was hiding.

Even though he was increasingly worried about Lacey's safety, Crowfoot remained huddled there in the alley until a couple of men, one wearing the badge of a lawman, shot past him on their way back to the savings and loan building. Too concerned about the lady by now to remain in hiding, he crept to the edge of the brick structure and peeked around the corner. A crowd had gathered outside the institution, all of them whispering amongst themselves in tones too low for him to overhear the words. Then at long last, the lawman stepped back outside again—and much to Crowfoot's horror, he had Lacey Winterhawke in tow, her hands manacled at her waist.

Impulsively jumping out from his hiding spot, Crowfoot called, "Lady, lady!"

But Lacey, her eyes downcast, didn't even glance up to acknowledge him. Like before, it was as if she couldn't see, hear, or speak. Crowfoot knew then that she was having one of her quiet times like the day in the barn, and that neither he nor the sheriff of Laramie would get her to talk until she was darn good and ready. As the trio passed by the spot where he stood watching, the sheriff reached out and cuffed Crowfoot alongside the head.

"Get on out of here, boy!" the sheriff snapped as he ushered Lacey down the boardwalk toward the court-house.

Afraid of most white men, but especially of those in authority, Crowfoot immediately ducked back into the alley. He stood there trembling near the corner of the building where the crowd was still milling around, and listened in on their conversations again. They were openly discussing a topic which sent a bolt of panic to his extremities—the murder of William Braddock, and the fact that Lacey Winterhawke had fired the bullet which killed him.

His lady, a *murderer?* Crowfoot couldn't imagine why she could have done such a thing, much less how, so he stayed there huddled in the alley a good long time as he tried to figure out what to do next. He hated the idea of leaving Lacey, not to mention the reprimand it would bring from Hawke, but there was nothing he could do for her now. The sheriff would never let a crippled Indian boy inside the jail to see her, and even if he did, Crowfoot was fairly certain nothing he could do or say would bring her around. Only one person he could think of had that ability. And he'd gone back to Winterhawke.

In spite of the fact that Hawke had instructed him not to let Lacey out of his sight, Crowfoot knew he had to go to the ranch to let Hawke know what had happened to his woman. The decision made, Crowfoot skulked through the streets of Laramie in the wolf-like manner he'd been taught, and made his way to the Front Street Stable and Carriage House where Hawke had left the wagon and one of the two horses who'd pulled the rig to town. He begged and pleaded with the liveryman to let him take the horse left behind, but the man turned a deaf ear to him. John Winterhawke had left the animal in his care, and John Winterhawke would have to come get the horse himself. Period. Crowfoot easily read the silent part of the statement in the stableman's eyes—he sure as hell wouldn't be giving up any animal to a filthy little Indian kid, no matter how much he begged.

After yet more indecision, Crowfoot waited until the night had reached its darkest peak and most of the town, save for the gambling establishments, had gone to bed. Then, knowing full well the authorities would hang him should he get caught in the act, he snuck back to the stables and stole the horse Hawke had given to him as his very own.

Undetected, Crowfoot rode out of town and straight through to Centennial, pausing here and there to rest his mount several times along the way. At dawn he reached Three Elk Ranch where he dashed into the house long enough to inform Caleb and Kate about Lacey's troubles with the law. After asking if they knew where Hawke had gone, then discovering that the Weatherspoons weren't even aware he'd returned from Laramie, Crowfoot resumed his journey. Just before noon, he finally arrived at the log home nestled in a forest of lodgepole pines, relieved to find it was still standing.

With the exception of the cowboy hired to watch over the place, Winterhawke Ranch was deserted.

Dressed in his full mountain man attire of buckskins including his eagle feather hat, Hawke stared out at the wide expanse of snow-splotched meadows near the glistening peak of Medicine Bow Mountain, and watched as his dreams raced out of his life. Phantom galloped through a thin patch of snow, kicking up flakes of ice with his heels, then wheeled around as if checking to make sure he'd truly escaped the man. He reared as if in victory, his nostrils blowing billows of fog, and pawed the air with his hooves. Then he took off again, a silvery shadow amongst the pines, until he could be seen no more.

Hawke was a mass of conflicting emotions late that afternoon as he watched his stallion disappear, for he above all understood and appreciated the exhilarating sense of freedom driving Phantom onward. But the terrible sense of loss, of finality, was too painful to contemplate, an indicator by his way of thinking, of his failure as a horse rancher. And that in turn, pointed out his failure as a husband.

He'd been so caught up in his own rage and pain, he hadn't even thought to ask Lacey what she wanted to do now that it looked like Winterhawke Ranch would stay in Braddock's hands. Worse, he hadn't even considered asking about her visit with the doctor. Were they going to have a baby? He didn't know because he'd gone off like a madman, not giving a moment's notice to anything or anyone but himself. Here he was with almost a full year of marriage under his belt, and he still behaved as if he were his own entity, a man who answered to no one.

He loved Lacey, there was no doubt in his mind about that, but he hadn't realized how selfish a thing love could be. He loved his wife on his terms and for the way she made him feel inside, but why hadn't he loved her enough to put his own needs aside and have a look at hers? Maybe it wasn't so much a question of love as anger, he thought, taking himself apart piece by piece. It didn't take an extraordinarily wise man to know that some of the anger he'd felt as he roared out of town had been directed at Lacey.

Right or wrong, it still rankled Hawke to think that

his own wife didn't want to bear his children—assuming of course that it was because she did not want to raise a passel of half-breeds. But what if her fears had nothing to do with the color of his skin at all? He'd never thought of looking for another answer, but now that he had, Hawke recalled the trouble he had bedding Lacey that first time, and how terribly afraid she'd been of the whole process. What if she were even more afraid of childbirth? It made a good measure of sense, now that he finally considered it.

Angry all over again, this time with himself, Hawke leaned back against his saddle, his pillow for the night, and went on with his self-examination. Funny, he thought, how insignificant a piece of land could be when placed in the proper perspective. He could easily replace Winterhawke Ranch and his yard full of fine horseflesh, but none of it meant a damn thing without Lacey—and he knew without a doubt that he could never replace the little Irish miss with the golden blue eyes. Not if he lived to be one hundred. Why hadn't he been smart enough to realize that before now? He hadn't even thought to tell her how much she meant to him.

The rest of the night, all Hawke could think about was getting back to town and letting Lacey know how much he loved and needed her. Then *together*, they would work out a plan. If she wanted to fight for Winterhawke—and he assumed she did since she'd even gone to the trouble of learning how to sew well enough to fashion curtains for their bedroom window—they would find a way to save the ranch together. As for Braddock—hell, maybe gaining revenge against him wasn't worth the trouble.

Hawke stayed the night on the spot where he'd turned the stud loose, then returned to Winterhawke the next morning armed with a new plan. If Lacey agreed, he would take the cash from this year's crop of three-year-olds, and if need be, use it all to have her hire a good attorney. Maybe in that way, they could force his uncle to set a firm price for Winterhawke, a fair-market figure which couldn't be changed according to the banker's whims or gut-deep hatred of his only living blood relation.

Finding some hope in this decision, after tending to his mount, a tired but less despondent Hawke started for the house to change back into his clothes for going to town. Then he heard someone scrambling down the ladder leading to the loft.

"Is that you, Hazelbaker?" he called. Turning around, he was shocked to see a small figure approaching him. "Crowfoot? What the hell are you doing here? Didn't I tell you to stay with Lacey? I told you not to let her—"

"Lady has troubles," he said, interrupting, but staying out of Hawke's reach. "I could not think of what to do but come after you."

"Troubles?" The hair along Hawke's spine stood up like a row of spikes. His first thoughts were of Lacey's pregnancy, and the possibility that something had gone wrong. Advancing on the boy, he caught him by the shoulders. "What's wrong with her? Is it something to do with the baby?"

Crowfoot paused, confused over the reference to a baby, but went on with his tale. "After you left town, lady tried to help you at the bank. She went to talk to Braddock, but—"

Struck by both horror and sudden rage, Hawke shook the boy. "She *what?*"

His survival instincts kicking in, Crowfoot snarled at Hawke, then wriggled free of his grasp and backed away. "I tell lady, don't go there, but she does not listen to me. I keep her in my eyes," he pointed at them, "but she will not stay there. She will not listen!"

The boy looked as if he were about to bolt and run,

and if he did that, Hawke was afraid he'd never know what had happened to his wife. Calming himself, he spoke tightly, but in a non-threatening tone as he asked, "So Lacey went to talk with Braddock. What did she say to him, and how . . . how did he treat her?"

Crowfoot shook his head. "I do not know any of these things. She kept me outside. I did not see what happened, but listened to people talking after the sheriff took her away."

"The *sheriff*? Christ almighty, what . . ." Hawke couldn't fathom a scenario which would bring the law down on his wife, so he wisely shut his mouth and urged the boy to go on. "What happened, Crowfoot? Just say it plain and simple."

"The people say that the banker, Braddock, is dead." He averted his gaze, unable to look Hawke in the eye as he told him the rest. "They say that lady shot him."

Once he got past the mind-freezing shock of those words, other than disbelief, Hawke's first thoughts were of his own culpability—and not just over the fact that he'd run out on Lacey threatening to burn down not just *his* ranch, but her home. Christ! What had he gotten her into in his quest to hide the shame of a family who treated him as an inferior, a shame he now knew that he didn't even deserve? Hawke couldn't bear to think about what Lacey might have suffered at Braddock's hands, of what the vile animal must have done to drive her to shoot him. If he did, he knew he'd go crazy, and then he wouldn't be of any help to her at all.

His throat so tight he could barely speak, he asked, "You're sure that Braddock is dead?"

Lowering his gaze and his head, the boy nodded.

"Christ." He drew in a painful breath, thinking not of his uncle, but of his wife. "How is Lacey doing? Did she ask for me?"

A tear rolled down Crowfoot's cheek, the first Hawke had ever seen on his sienna-colored skin. Then he raised his sad-eyed gaze and, voice cracking, said, "Lady not ask for Hawke. She not ask for anything." Then, as if he couldn't go on speaking, the boy placed his hands over his ears, then his mouth, and finally over his eyes.

His heart in the pit of his stomach, for he knew exactly the condition the boy was miming, Hawke found himself hoping that Crowfoot was right about the state of his uncle's health. If the son of a bitch wasn't already dead, he had an idea the man would be—and soon.

Caleb and Kate hadn't even bothered to change into fresh clothing the morning Crowfoot stopped by with his terrible news. They just bundled themselves and the baby into the wagon and took off for town, leaving the ranch foreman to oversee Three Elk and its cattle herd. When the boy informed Caleb that Hawke had vowed to turn his horses loose and then destroy the ranch, he knew that his friend would probably spend a day or two up in the Snowy Range before coming to his senses and returning to Laramie. No point in going after him either, for like himself, Hawke was a hard man to find when he wanted to be lost. The best plan, Caleb decided, would be to go to town and try to help Lacey in any way he could.

So after a long, uncomfortable journey, the Weatherspoons arrived in Laramie just as the sun was sliding over the very mountains where Lacey's husband was either losing or finding himself. They immediately went to the courthouse to make certain the tale Crowfoot had told them was true, and after finding that it was, Kate arranged for a private visit with Lacey in the room the sheriff had specified as a "female jail cell."

Caleb, who still felt awkward and uncomfortable

holding his fragile daughter, waited with her in his arms at the sheriff's office along with the deputy on duty. Looking down at her pretty little face, again he marveled at the miracle of birth. Kathleen was so tiny and delicate, he simply couldn't imagine her growing into a woman some day.

She stirred in her sleep then, stretching her little arms until her tiny fingers popped through the fold in the blanket. "Lord almighty," Caleb cooed to his daughter. "I don't see how in hell something so delicate-like and cute as you could share the blood of an old hog's butt like me. Remind me to skin your ma good when I see her—she musta had another rake besides me gathering up her hay crop."

"Your first?" asked the deputy from across the room.

His face red, Caleb glanced over to the man. "Uh, yep, she shore is. How can you tell?"

"I've had four myself." He laughed. "The first one always seems like it's gonna break or something if you even look at it cross-eyed."

"I know what you mean there, pardner. I feel like a regular board-hands with this little gal—scared half to death of her, in fact."

"You'll get over that with the next one. By the third, you'll be bouncing the kid off the floor."

Just thinking about that made Caleb hold the baby even closer to his chest, but before he could make a comment on the deputy's reckless suggestion, Kate burst into the room, her handkerchief to her nose.

"Oh, Caleb," she cried. "'Tis even worse than I thought with the lass." She hurried to his side, peeked at her sleeping daughter, then sat down. "They put her in a poorly made shack with cracks in the walls and a dirt floor! But even in such dreadful surroundings, I couldna get the lass to so much as blink at me. I'm thinking this could be the worst spell she's e'er had."

"Worst spell? What in tarnation does that mean?"

Taking her time to dab her tears and blow her nose, Kate finally said, "'Twere a term used for any kind of shock in the mad room at the hospital where I worked. With Lacey, 'tis, I suppose, like a nonphysical coma, you know? Where the mind is completely asleep but the body has suffered no trauma."

Trying to absorb all that, Caleb furrowed his brow. "How long will she be like that do you think?"

Fresh tears rolled down Kate's cheeks. "I dona know. I . . . I've seen spells that lasted for years on end."

Looking for a way to comfort his wife, Caleb carefully slipped his hand from beneath his daughter's body and patted Kate's back. "Don't you worry none, angel pie. That ain't gonna happen to Lacey, you'll see."

But she just cried harder.

Glancing at the deputy, who was taking in the whole scene, Caleb whispered, "Now don't carry on so, Katy. You'll upset little Kathleen, here."

She hiccuped. "I canna help it. If Lacey doesna speak soon, I am afraid that she, that . . . "

"The girl means an awful lot to you, doesn't she, darling?"

Her pale blue eyes awash in tears, Kate turned to him and murmured through a sob, "More than ye'll e'er know."

Slipping his arm around Kate's trembling shoulders, Caleb kept his silence as she cried herself dry. When he could be heard over her sobs, he turned toward the deputy and asked, "Isn't there some way for us to get that poor gal out of jail? I expect she could use a little of my wife's nursing about now."

"Sorry, pardner, but no chance in hell. She ain't got long to wait, anyways, what with her trial starting up tomorrow morning."

Kate abruptly stood up. "So soon?"

The deputy shrugged. "No point in waiting on this one. Got witnesses you know. She done it, and there ain't no way she can talk her way out of it."

"But the lass is sick! Can ye na see that?"

He jabbed a toothpick into his mouth and began cleaning his teeth. "Didn't look sick to me or the sheriff."

"She *canna* talk! 'Tis a sickness of it's own. Can ye na wait a wee bit for her to snap out of it?"

The deputy laughed. "There ain't nothing sick or strange about keeping the mouth shut when it comes to murder. Either they talk all the time insisting they're innocent, or they clam up like your friend in there. She'll snap out of it fast enough when Judge MacIver sentences her to hang tomorrow!"

The citizens of Laramie were proud of their new courthouse, a structure they also used as a general gathering place and party hall. Charity dances were a favorite there, and once on a very unusual Fourth of July, the hall was even used to shelter unprepared citizens who were caught by a surprise blizzard. No such luck today as a hot spell had descended on the valley, bringing uncomfortable temperatures outside and stifling conditions inside.

Today as the members of the jury filed back into the hall after breaking for a noonday meal, the building was serving its original purpose as a courtroom with Kate, Caleb, and their newborn daughter among the crowded gallery of spectators. The prosecution had presented their case in short order during the morning session, and now as Pauline Little was marched back up to the stand, Lacey's lawyer, Malcolm Webber, was about to begin the process of cross-examining the secretary.

Kate, who was still astounded to find women serving

on the jury—four women to eight men in this case—
turned to her husband and whispered, "Are ye thinking
maybe the women will be sympathetic to Lacey, or will
they toss in with this fast woman and all her lies?"

Caleb shook his head, not sure what to say to her.
Now that the case had been presented in no uncertain
terms, it didn't look good for Lacey. The secretary had
sworn that she'd dashed into her employer's office a second after the gunshot rang out to find the defendant
standing over the dead man, gun in hand. Worse yet, it
had come out that John Winterhawke, Jr. was William
Braddock's only living heir since the banker had no
will—and stood to inherit everything, including the ranch
he so coveted. Thus far, Lacey hadn't so much as reared
her head in her own defense, much less spoken out. And
that gave Caleb second thoughts about his decision not
to go after Hawke in the mountains. Maybe if he had
managed to find the man, things here would be different.

With a heavy sigh, he turned to his wife and admitted,
"I got to be honest with you, sugar. I'm plum worried
about the girl. It's gonna take a flat out miracle to get her
out of this one. A good bit more than a miracle, at that."

The doors to the courthouse slammed open then,
charging the air with a loud *bang* which was almost
enough to convince Caleb that a bolt of lightening had
come down from the sky, bringing with it the hoped for
miracle. He turned along with gallery to see what looked
like a wild man standing in the doorway.

The women gasped and the men seemed to shrink
against their chairs. Then Hawke strode into the suddenly
hushed room.

20

To lose one parent . . . may be regarded as a misfortune;
to lose both looks like carelessness.
—Oscar Wilde

He'd tied the leather thong around his forehead to keep the hair from his eyes, but dressed the way
he was in buckskins and leggings, Hawke's long flowing
locks did little to dispel the savage within the clothes or
to hide his raw outrage.

The gavel banged down as Judge MacIver said, "Come
in if you've a mind to, sir, and sit down. This court is in
order."

Spotting Caleb's white lipped expression among the
onlookers, Hawke moved over to where his friend was
seated on the aisle, and dropped down to his haunches.
Crowfoot, who was intimidated by the large crowd,
hovered just outside the courtroom, preferring to take
in the proceedings through an open window.

Ignoring the spectators who were still gawking at
him, Hawke turned to Caleb and quietly asked, "What's
happened so far?"

"Uh, not too much. The law took a turn asking questions of the folks who work at the bank, and now I guess Lacey's lawyer is gonna give it a go. That's him, Malcolm Webber, up there talking to the gal from Braddock's office."

With a quick glance toward the stand, Hawke turned back to his friend in surprise. "You hired a lawyer for Lacey?"

"Nope, the court did. I expect soon's the trial is over, though, they're gonna come after you to pay up."

He shrugged indifferently. "Has Lacey had a chance to explain what happened?"

Dragging his answer out, Caleb hemmed and hawed a minute, then said, "No, she, ah . . . ain't been called up to testify yet."

Nodding thoughtfully, Hawke turned his attention back to the stands to listen in on the cross-examination.

". . . and you were actually present in the room when Mr. Winterhawke assaulted Mr. Braddock?" asked Webber.

"Yes, sir, I was sitting right next to Mr. Braddock when the half-breed jumped over the desk and tried to strangle Mr. Braddock." She pointed at Hawke. "That's him right there, the fellow who just came into the courtroom."

The gallery gave a collective gasp, and Judge MacIver banged his gavel, demanding quiet. Then he turned to Webber and said, "Hurry this thing along a little, will you? Ask her something we don't already know."

Fresh out of law school, Webber's cheeks flushed brightly as he resumed his interrogation. "If memory serves from your earlier testimony, I believe you said that Mr. Braddock saved himself during the assault by pulling a gun on Mr. Winterhawke and ordering him from his office. Is that correct?"

Pauline delicately sniffed into her handkerchief. "Yes, sir, and if I may say so, I think if Mr. Braddock had put that gun away instead of leaving it lying on his desk, he'd . . . he'd be alive today." She collapsed into sobs after that, and the judge was forced to give her a moment to collect herself.

When he was able to resume questioning the witness, Webber quietly asked, "Now be very careful to remember the exact words if you can, and tell the court one more time what Mr. Winterhawke said to the deceased as he walked out of his office."

A heavily perspiring Judge MacIver intervened before she could. "Didn't I ask you to hurry this along?"

"Yes, your honor, but Miss Little's testimony is really all the court has by way of evidence. I want to make sure she's absolutely certain of the facts in this case."

With a weary sigh, the judge agreed. "You may proceed, but do remember to keep it moving along."

After a short nod of thanks, Webber went back to questioning the witness. "Please answer the question, Miss Little."

"Well, best as I can remember, he said something like; 'there's more than one way to get rid of a fellow like you, and I'll have someone else do it so I don't have to get blood on my hands.'"

Webber raised a cynical eyebrow. "Those were his *exact* words?"

From the gallery, Hawke leaned in close to Caleb and whispered, "I said there was more than one way to skin a polecat, and that I intended to do it without getting his stink all over me—where does she get blood in that?"

"I think those were his exact words," said Pauline. "He said something very much like that, anyway."

Hawke rolled his eyes. "She's not even close!"

Drumming his fingers against the witness box, Webber paused a long moment. "Fifteen or twenty minutes after Mr. Winterhawke left Braddock's office, the defendant requested an interview with him. Is that correct?"

She nodded, pointing at Lacey as she said, "That's her sitting right there."

Hawke strained to see his wife over the crowd, but all he could spot of her was a few wild coppery curlicues which had escaped from the bun at the back of her head.

"Please tell us one more time," Webber went on. "Exactly what happened after Mrs. Winterhawke entered the office of the deceased?"

"Well, I really can't say exactly since I wasn't in there, but she hadn't been in Mr. Braddock's office for more than, oh, I don't know, around ten minutes or so I guess, before I heard the gunshot."

"And did you hear loud arguing or anything of their conversation prior to that gunshot?"

She shook her head. "No, it was real quiet—even when I walked up near the door and listened long enough for her to say that she was Mrs. Winterhawke."

"And why did you do that?"

Pauline shrugged. "Curious I guess."

"Curious," Webber repeated. "After you heard the shot, what happened?"

"I raced through the door that same second, and saw that Mr. Braddock was lying on his back near his desk . . ." She choked back a sob. "He was dead, and that red-haired murderer was holding the gun that killed him!"

A buzz rippled through the crowd as if they hadn't heard this information before, even though they had during the opening statements and again during the prosecution's questioning of the witness. The judge banged his gavel to quiet the group, then asked Webber, "Are you quite finished with the witness?"

After a moment's reflection, he sighed and said, "Yes, I believe that I am."

"Good," said MacIver. "In that case, I suggest you call your client to the stand so we can wrap up the proceedings."

Casting a wary eye in Lacey's direction, again Webber sighed. "She, ah, hasn't been very cooperative so far, your honor. I don't—"

"She can cooperate or not, Mr. Webber, but she will come up to the stand and at least hear the charges against her before I send this trial to jury. Now go get her, young man."

His cheeks burning again, Webber hurried to the table where Lacey sat staring at the floor, helped her to her feet, and bodily led her to the witness stand. He then sat her down, lifted her right hand, exposing her scarred palm to the spectators, and held it upright throughout the swearing in. When asked to give her pledge at the end of the process, however, she remained silent.

"Mrs. Winterhawke," Judge MacIver warned in a deadly serious tone, "if you think you can avoid telling the truth in this court by refusing to swear yourself in, you are gravely mistaken. This trial, and the consequences of your actions, are indeed a matter of life or death where you are concerned, so I strongly suggest you take your pledge now."

Even from his spot on the courtroom floor, Hawke could see that Lacey's eyes and the depth of understanding there were as shallow as a teardrop. Turning to Caleb, he said in a strangled whisper, "Has she been like this since they arrested her?"

His eyes downcast, Caleb slowly nodded. "Kate says she's having some kind of spell."

Kate, listening to the conversation, leaned across her husband's lap. "'Tis a sickness Lacey thought cured long ago, Hawke. She canna understand what is going on around her, and she canna . . ."

But Hawke was no longer paying attention to Kate's description of his wife's condition. He knew exactly how debilitated Lacey was and had risen to his full height. Marching down the aisle toward her, his gaze pinned to her dazed features, his progress was suddenly stopped by the waist-high gate separating the gallery from the proceedings—not to mention the pair of strong hands tugging at his left arm. Trying to shrug the deputy off, he shouted at Lacey, praying to God that somewhere in her confusion she might hear his voice.

"Lacey! It's me, Hawke. For the love of God, snap out of it!"

Another pair of strong hands gripped his right arm, jerking him backwards, but Hawke wrapped his long muscular fingers around the gate in front of him and clung to it, still shouting at the woman he loved.

"Lacey! I'm begging you! Hear me, please hear me!"

"That's enough, sir!" The judge brought his gavel down three times, filling the air with a series of sharp *cracks* that sounded like rapid gunfire. "If you don't remove yourself from this court now, I'll find you in contempt and have you jailed."

Finally taking his troubled gaze off of his wife, Hawke turned to the judge, his voice hoarse with emotion, and begged, "Please, just give me five minutes alone with her! Just five minutes to get her talking again, then I've leave!"

"That would be highly irregular, and—"

"Something's wrong with her—can't you see that? Look into her eyes!"

Judge MacIver grudgingly glanced at Lacey and studied her a moment. "I can see that she's probably not quite herself, Mr. Winterhawke, but you should have had this little discussion with your wife long before this court convened." He raised the gavel again as if preparing to give his final order, but kept it hanging in mid-air as Hawke continued to plead his case.

"I've been up in the Snowy Range Mountains since I

left Braddock's office, and didn't even know until this morning what had happened to him or Lacey." His knuckles white where he gripped the rail, Hawke launched a final plea. "I just now got into town. Can't you show us—my wife—a little mercy and give us five measly minutes alone?"

Contemplating the request at last, the judge's gaze flickered between Hawke and Lacey. Finally, he raised his gavel and said, "Clear the court for a short recess!" After smashing the polished wood mallet to the bench one more time, he leaned over and quietly said to Hawke, "That's five minutes, Mr. Winterhawke, and not one second more. I'm going to clear this court of everyone except those two guards hanging onto your arms. They'll be posted at the back of the room with instructions to shoot you dead if you even look like you're thinking of sneaking your wife out of here. Is that understood?"

"Yes, sir, it is. And thank you."

As Judge MacIver climbed down from the bench, he signaled for the guards to release their prisoner and take up their positions. The moment he was free, Hawke vaulted over the gate and hurried to the witness box where Lacey still sat staring down at the floor.

Dropping to his knees, he took her hands in his. Then, keeping his voice low as the fascinated observers slowly left the courthouse, he begged, "Lacey, sweetheart, please listen to me. Hear me now—we don't have much time."

This got no response whatsoever, frustrating Hawke right down to his toenails. Remembering the items he'd brought with him just to cheer Lacey up, he reached into his back pocket and withdrew her lucky spurs.

Spinning the silver shamrocks at the heel of one spur as he spoke, he tried gentle coaxing one more time. "See what I brought for you? Want me to put them on your boots?"

Nothing, but he went ahead and attached one of the

spurs to her left boot, anyway. Still spinning the other spur under her nose, Hawke raised his voice. "Damn it, Lacey—pay attention to me. You're almost out of time! You've got to save yourself, you hear me? Save yourself, god damn it! I love you!"

Hawke had never seen a pair of eyes shudder before, but that's exactly what happened to Lacey. Her eyes shuddered as if caught by a sudden chill, then she trembled from head to toe. Was she coming out of it? he wondered, daring to hope it was true. She began to blink then, her eyes darting from side to side, so he continued to shout words of both encouragement and love.

Something disturbed Lacey's calm, her dark sense of peace.

She liked being unconscious inside herself, unaware of her surroundings, and fought against whatever or whoever dared to disturb her. The intrusion reminded her of bath night, one of the few memories she had left of her childhood. She loved to play "fish," floating face down in the big copper tub in the family castle whenever she got the chance. Then one night her mother came upon her that way, floating calmly and serenely like a giant stingray.

Of course her mother thought she'd drowned! The frantic woman dug her fingers into Lacey's tender shoulders and jerked her out of the water, violently disrupting the safety of her silent underwater world where nothing could hurt her—especially not the shouts and cries of her parents' endless arguments. Lacey felt as if she were abruptly being jerked out of the water again. Somewhere in the darkness of her mind, she heard Hawke's voice, verbal fingers this time, but still grappling with her, demanding that she come up for air. Or something. And then she caught his scent, the musky horse and pine aroma of the man she loved.

Lacey opened her eyes and cleared her vision until she

was able to focus on her husband. Realizing instantly that something was terribly wrong, but not what, she opened her mouth as if to speak. Hawke placed his finger across her lips, silencing her.

"I don't have much time to tell you what's going on here," he explained, his voice not only hoarse now, but raw with emotion. "You're in the Laramie courtroom, on trial for killing William Braddock—"

Lacey gasped. "Oh, my Lord!"

She tried to pull away from him, but Hawke held her hands fast. "I don't know what Braddock did to make you shoot him, but whatever it was, I know it must have been pretty awful." His jaw granite hard, he narrowed his gaze and instructed, "Tell the judge what he did, Lacey — spare no details, you hear me? Every last detail!"

Again her eyes shuddered. "B-but—"

"Do as I say, Lacey! Beg the court for mercy, get down on your knees if you have to and beg, but save yourself!"

She shuddered all over now, caught in her husband's intense gaze, and for a long moment, it was almost as if they were somewhere else, at some other time. She'd killed Hawke's uncle! Lacey remembered that now, the sight of the man falling to the floor at her feet, and yet Hawke didn't seem to be mad at her. Even stranger, she vaguely remembered words of love coming from him as she swam up through the surface of her spell. *I love you,* he'd said, not once, but several times over. Still locked in her husband's gaze, Lacey's eyes grew moist and her heart blossomed with love. Then a voice, not Hawke's, but that of a stranger broke into their private moment.

"Time's up, injun," said the bailiff.

Sliding his hands up her arms to take her by the shoulders, Hawke slowly rose to his feet. "Do whatever you have to, Lacey, but save yourself at any cost—understand?

Nothing else is important; not me, not Winterhawke
Ranch, nothing. Just save yourself, no matter what!"

His voice steeped in irritation, Judge MacIver said, "I
don't want to have to find you in contempt of court, Mr.
Winterhawke! If you do not take your seat now, I'll have
you removed from the courtroom. Bailiff, call the jury
and the spectators in at once!"

With one final long look into his wife's sparkling eyes,
Hawke folded the other spur into Lacey's hands, then
turned and strode down the center aisle, his spine and
stride as rigid as the trunk of a lodgepole pine.

It wasn't until he'd sat down beside Caleb that Lacey
finally glanced at her surroundings. People were everywhere, packed into the large courtroom and staring at her
as if she were some kind of freak. To her right, two men
were huddled against the bench, engaged in conversation
with the judge. She took a deep breath, longing to return
to the safety and comfort of the spell, but strengthened
herself instead by mentally repeating Hawke's words:
Save yourself. I love you.

The men to Lacey's right suddenly approached her. The
young one, a rather nervous looking fellow, said, "Hello,
Mrs. Winterhawke. My name is Malcolm Webber. I'm
your attorney. This," he swept his arm around toward the
older man, "is Anthony Silver, the prosecuting attorney."

The older man gave her a magnanimous smile, but
before she could decide how to respond to either of
them, her lawyer resumed speaking. "I realize this may
all seem a little strange to you after your, ah, recent ill-
ness, but we are in the middle of a trial and the judge has
directed us to proceed. After you're sworn in, Mr. Silver
will ask you some questions about the murder of William
Braddock. You, ah, do recall the incident, don't you?"

Nodding miserably, Lacey uttered a barely audible,
"Aye."

"Good. Just raise your right hand and repeat the pledge when you're asked. I'll be sitting right in front of you looking out for your interests as best as I can." He turned on his heel as if to leave, but then turned back to her, leaned in very close, and whispered, "Just one more thing—did you shoot Mr. Braddock? It's always a good idea for your lawyer to have some idea what we'll be getting into."

She swallowed hard, then said in that same wisp of a voice, "Aye, that I did, but 'twere an accident."

"I see." With that, he turned around and took a seat directly across from her.

Once Lacey was sworn in, the prosecutor wasted no time getting around to her. Still smiling that patronizing grin, he began to question her, his dramatic tone leaving no doubt in her mind that the man loved the sound of his own voice. "Try to relax, little lady. I'm going to ask you a few questions about yourself just to break the ice. I understand that you are married to one John Winterhawke, Jr., a half-breed Arapaho Indian who also happens to be the blood nephew of the deceased, William James Braddock. Is that correct?"

Her gaze rolling through the crowd until she found Hawke again, Lacey managed a wan smile as she said, "Aye, I married him one year ago on the eighteenth day of June."

"And when did Mr. Winterhawke inform you that he was related to Laramie's very successful William Braddock, a man who is listed in Triggs City Directory as a capitalist and one of our wealthier citizens?"

"Hawke ne'er mentioned the man was his uncle. I did not know."

Silver uttered a muffled chuckle, then turned to the jury with a cynical smile. "Now, Mrs. Winterhawke. Do you really expect any of us to believe that a, well, half-breed like your husband didn't go around bragging on the fact that he was related to such an esteemed man as William Braddock? It hardly seems likely."

"Hardly or no, Mr. Silver, 'tis the truth."

"I certainly hope so." He stopped directly in front of her and banged his fist against the witness box. "You did vow to tell the whole truth and nothing *but* the truth, did you not?"

The little bubble of confidence she'd managed to work up burst. "Aye, and I'm telling it, sir."

Looking slightly disappointed, the attorney paced in a small circle, his hands behind his back before he looked at Lacey and asked, "Not much of what I'm hearing about you is making sense, little lady. Perhaps we should start at the beginning so the court can get a better idea of what we're dealing with here."

"Mr. Silver," Judge MacIver said. "Were you paying attention when I asked Mr. Webber to keep things moving along? I had high hopes of getting this trial over with before the afternoon heat renders us all addle-brained."

"Begging the court's indulgence, your honor, I'm having just a little trouble understanding a few things. I will, of course, examine the witness with all due haste."

Permission granted with a wave of the judge's hand, Silver turned to Lacey again. "One of my biggest problems is how a lovely young girl like you came to marry this Winterhawke fellow. Did he compromise you in some way or—"

"I came from Ireland with Kate Quinlin to be a mail-order bride, sir." Her back up, Lacey forged ahead even though the attorney was preparing to ask another question. "My husband is a very honorable man, and I would appreciate it if you would apologize for the slander of his good name."

One of his finely arched eyebrows shot up at the request, but that was the only indication the lawyer gave that he'd been slightly taken aback by her demand. "Do forgive me, Mrs. Winterhawke. I meant no unkindness towards your husband, who I'm sure is a fine man, even if he didn't see fit to inform you he had family in Laramie. Now then." He strolled around in front of the jury, gauging their reactions to his last comment, then asked Lacey another question. "You say Mr. Winterhawke sent for you as a mail-order bride?"

"Well, not exactly. Kate was to be Caleb Weatherspoon's bride. She brought me along for a neighbor of his who turned out to be Hawke—ah, Mr. Winterhawke."

His eyes narrowed in contemplation at her words, then Silver walked right up to the witness box as if he suddenly smelled a little secret hidden in there. "You say that Kate "brought you with her" as if she'd done some wonderful favor for you." Again he looked her over. "I can't imagine why you would have any trouble finding yourself a husband in Ireland—just what did Kate take you away from, Mrs. Winterhawke?"

Frantic to find Hawke now, again Lacey's gaze swept the gallery. On her second pass through the throngs of spectators, she caught sight of Kate and Caleb. With a little gasp of surprise, she looked back at the attorney and said, "She—she took me away from St. Josephine's Hospital for Women in County Tipperary, sir."

He chuckled lightly. "You say that as if the hospital was your home. Where did you live, Mrs. Winterhawke?"

"I object!" declared Webber, jumping to his feet. "This has no relevance to the case whatsoever."

"Counselor?" the judge said to Silver. "Is there a really good reason for this line of questioning?"

"I believe there just might be if you'll bear with me a few moments more."

"Just a few, mind you," the judge cautioned. "Proceed."

"You haven't answered my question, Mrs. Winterhawke. Where did you live in Ireland?"

Lacey lowered her gaze and bowed her head. "At St. Josephine's Hospital for Women, sir."

"That seems rather odd. Why would a healthy-looking girl like you be living in a hospital? Were you injured in some way?"

She glanced at her palm. "Burned a little is all, sir."

"Burned," he repeated glancing down at her scar. "And how long did you live at the hospital for treatment of this little burn?"

Her head down, Lacey held out as long as she could.

"Answer the question, Mrs. Winterhawke," Judge MacIver insisted. "You are holding up these proceedings."

After a deep breath and a long sigh, Lacey admitted, "A wee bit more than . . . thirteen years, sir."

Both slender eyebrows shot up at this. Then Silver licked his thin lips like a predator. "Surely you're not trying to tell me you were being treated for such a small injury during that entire time."

"No sir, I am not." Giving it all up, Lacey raised her head and looked the attorney straight in the eye. "I was there most of that time because I was considered to be a mad girl."

"A mad girl? You mean—*insane?*"

After another long pause, she murmured, "Aye. They thought me insane."

The crowd came to life at that, the mass buzzing like a beehive, but above the sudden din, a female voice could be heard. "No, lass, 'tisn't true they thought that of ye!"

Judge MacIver banged his gavel. "Order! Madam, sit down and be quiet, or I will have you thrown from this courtroom!"

Kate dropped back down into her chair, and Silver turned on Lacey again. "There seems to be some conflicting statements regarding the state of your mental health.

What, may I ask, prompted the doctors in Ireland to pronounce you as insane, Mrs. Winterhawke?"

Unable to look anyone in the eye now, not even the pompous attorney, Lacey softly whispered her answer.

"What, Mrs. Winterhawke? I'm afraid the court did not hear you."

"Because," she stated a little louder. "I killed my mum and da."

The audience of bees became hornets as they swarmed about circulating their chatter and shocked outrage. Again Kate jumped to her feet, this time speaking even louder as she proclaimed, "No, lass! 'Twasn't ye caused yer parent's deaths!"

"Order!" shouted the judge, his gavel pitting the top of the bench. "I will have order in this courtroom, by God!"

By then, Kate had handed the baby to Caleb and made her way to the center aisle where she stood, tears streaming down her face. "'Twas me, lass. 'Twas me robbed ye of yer family."

21

The law is a sort of hocus-pocus science, that
smiles in yer face while it picks yer pocket.
                                    —Charles Macklin

In the chaos caused by Kate's statement, Judge
MacIver's gavel could not be heard. He ordered the
guards to clear the courtroom of everyone except for
Lacey, Hawke, and the Weatherspoons.

Now that his courtroom was quiet once again, the
judge turned to Kate Weatherspoon, who was standing
on the gallery side of the gate, and speared her with a
sharp-eyed gaze. "Now then, madam. Can you give me
one good reason why I should not have you jailed for
contempt of this court?"

"Begging yer pardon, yer honor, sir, but I couldna
allow the jury or the people of Laramie to think of the
poor lass as a murderer before her trial could e'en begin."
Kate clutched her breast, aware her husband had been
staring at her in abject shock since she'd made her confes-
sion. "The fire at O'Carroll castle is a burden of guilt I've
carried inside me lo these many years, one I thought to
take to the grave with me." She glanced at Lacey. "I canna

believe ye carried the same burden, lass! What e'er made ye think ye'd had a hand in the fire?"

Before she could answer, Judge MacIver stepped in. "Am I to assume, madam, you feel the need to clear this matter up before the trial can proceed?"

"Aye, and I think 'twould be best in all fairness."

He sighed heavily, then leaned back in his chair. "In that case, since it's becoming quite apparent to me that we are *not* going to have a speedy trial in this courtroom on such an ungodly hot afternoon, we might as well have a fair one. Do proceed, but please—don't drag this on any longer than necessary."

"I thank ye for yer consideration." Again she turned to the witness box. "Why, lass, are ye taking the blame for burning down yer family home?"

Lacey glanced at her palm, then out to the first row of spectator seating where Hawke sat beside Caleb. She saw no look of censure or disappointment in her husband's expression. Just a heavy sadness. Looking back at the woman who'd practically raised her and wondering why she was trying to take the blame for something Lacey herself had done, she answered the question.

"I can not remember anything of the night my parents died or of the fire that burned me. I only remember the nurses whispering amongst themselves. They thought I could not hear or understand what they said, but I could at first. They pointed at me, some saying I should be locked up but good for setting fire to the O'Carroll castle and killing off my parents. I thought it must be true."

"Lord forgive me, lass, but I swear by the cross o' Christ that I ne'er *dreamed* yer head was full up with such lies!" Kate buried her face in her hands and wept into them. After she'd collected herself, she wiped the moisture from her cheek with her daughter's burping cloth. "Do ye remember anything of me whilst ye were a wee thing growing up in the castle, lass?"

The question was so outlandish, Lacey thought for a moment that perhaps Kate was the one who'd gone mad. "No, why would I have known you then?"

She shrugged. "I seen ye once or twice. I was the low cook in the kitchen, working for yer dear mum and da, the one got ordered about by the higher-up cook to clean the messes and chop the onions."

Lacey was surprised—not by the fact she hadn't recognized Kate as an O'Carroll employee since she'd never been allowed to visit the kitchen—but to hear that the woman had once worked for the family! Wondering briefly if Kate had burned the castle down by setting fire to the kitchen the way she had at Winterhawke, Lacey asked, "Why have you ne'er told me this?"

"Because I hoped that ye truly had forgotten me, and didn't want to stir up yer memory." Ignoring another urge to glance at her husband and beg for his understanding, Kate went ahead with the story she'd hoped to take to the grave. "I don't know how to say this politely, lass, so I'll just be tellin' ye right straight—whilst a cook in your home, I caught yer father's fancy." She averted her gaze, unable to look Lacey in the eye as she went on. "I canna say I'm proud of myself, but I give him free rein with me, him countin' on my soft heart with stories of how yer mum turned him away night after night."

Lacey couldn't stifle a sudden gasp that was at least half whimper.

"I'm sorry to be tellin' ye this, lass, but if I don't, ye will not understand the rest. I turned up . . . " She canted her head, again drawn to beseech understanding from her husband, but quickly looked back at Lacey. "The night of the fire, I had just told yer father that I was to be havin' his child."

Lacey's mouth dropped open, but absolutely no sound came from her throat.

"'Tis the truth, lass." Kate went on easily now, free of her burden. "As ye might imagine, he didn't take it too well. Neither did . . ." She lowered her head and frowned at the memory. "Neither did yer mum."

"You told my mum all this?" Lacey didn't know at that moment whether she was more hurt or outraged.

"I was young at the time, lass, and foolish enough to believe yer father wanted to cart me off as his very own! I ne'er meant for any of this to happen, but it did." She closed her eyes to ward off yet another wave of tears "May God forgive me someday, it did."

Fanning herself with her free hand, Lacey thought that God might forgive the woman, but she wasn't sure she could. "Are you saying that when my da would not carry you away, you decided to burn him up?"

Kate stared across the suddenly vast distance between herself and Lacey, her shoulders slumped, and wearily said, "Ye'll probably have trouble believing me now, but the fire were an accident. Yer mum, da, and I had a terrible row in the upstairs study late that night after all the help had gone to the servants quarters. It ended with yer mum chasing after me threatenin' all kinds of bodily harm. I was afraid for my life, so I ran out of the room. At the very second I closed the door, something heavy made of glass shattered against it! I were sure then that she was trying to kill me! Panicked, I turned the key in the lock so she couldna follow me, and fled the house."

Kate paused, giving Lacey a moment of reflection. There were many terrible rows between her parents in that upstairs study, arguments little Lacey could hear well into the night as her bedroom was only three doors down the hall from what she'd begun to secretly call "the fighting room." She could not, however, remember the night in question.

"I ran outside to the garden," Kate continued, "threw myself to the ground, and cried till I could cry no more. When I finally looked up at the study window, is when I saw the flames and realized the room was ablaze. Near as I can figure, yer mum must have thrown one of her heavy crystal oil lamps at me. When I heard screams and realized yer parents were still in the room, I looked down and saw that I'd taken the key with me—I swear by the cross o' Christ I didn't knowingly take it from the lock."

"And so you left them there to die?" Lacey was gripping her lucky spur so hard, the shamrock had left a deep depression in her left palm.

"No, lass. I run back up the stairs to the study to save them, but it were too late. Ye were pounding on the door, yer poor little hand burned from trying to turn the blistering doorknob. I coulda get close enough to e'en try to fit the key back in the lock, so I grabbed ye up in my arms and saved ye best I could."

Memories of her mother's frantic screams assailed her, bringing with them a brief glimpse of the night in question. The key. Something about the key. Lacey dug at her fragile memory, gouging out clues, and she finally remembered fragments of the aftermath.

"I was found outside the castle by the firemen! They tended my burned hand, then opened the other to see if it were damaged, too. There was no burn there, but . . ." A wave of nausea rolled through Lacey. She swallowed, then swallowed again. "I was holding the key to the study. One of the men, Mr. O'Shaunnessey, I think, called me a very bad name, and then . . . then I think I must have passed out. I can not remember a thing after that."

"Ah, lass. 'Tis the reason, I think, they thought ye

killed yer mum and da." Kate's eyes closed again and her brow furrowed with pain. "I searched the garden for that key later, but when I couldna find it, I thought I just lost it somewheres else. I ne'er knew ye had it all along."

Tears welling up in her eyes, Lacey dropped her gaze to her lap and the silver spur.

Her voice even softer now, Kate said, "That key, by the way, wasna the only thing I lost that night. The babe I was carryin' couldna stand all the excitement, I guess. I spent the next three weeks in the hospital recovering from the miscarriage."

Lacey still didn't know how she felt about Kate at that moment, but at those words, she couldn't stop the burst of compassion in her heart. "I feel bad for you about the babe, Kate, but I feel worse for myself. I spent thirteen years in that hospital thinkin' I was a madwoman—with the nurses thinkin' that, too! Now it seems that I didn't belong there a'tall!"

Judge MacIver cleared his throat then, sounding as if he were about to bring the discussion to an end, but one sharp look from both Kate and Lacey changed his mind. Shrugging, he gestured for them to go on.

"No, lass," Kate said, picking up the conversation. "You didn't, but how was I to know what were in yer head? By the time I hired on there, ye'd been in a spell for two years. No one told me ye'd killed yer family. They just said you was a mute girl."

With a heavy sigh, Lacey leaned back in her chair and dropped her gaze to the floor.

"I come to work at St. Josephine's for only one reason, lass, and that was ye." Kate went on, her voice cracking now. "When I found out that ye was orphaned with no other family to take ye in, and locked up in the mad room of St. Josephine's, too, I felt my calling was with ye. I worked as a nursemaid for a confined lady a while, then used that reference to gain employment at the hospital. My only purpose was to be with ye and see that ye were well taken care of. I took ye on like the child I almost had, I guess, but I was glad to do it. I loved ye Lacey, and still do. I hope ye can find it in yer heart to forgive me someday."

With that, she spun in a slow circle and returned to her husband and child.

His own tone much less harsh than before, Judge MacIver turned to Lacey and said, "Let me see if I can get this straight myself. When you left Ireland, you were confined at the hospital and not free to go on your own?"

Her concentration shattered, Lacey did what she could to answer his questions honestly and clearly. "No, sir, I was not free to leave. Nurse Quinlin—Kate there—had to spirit me away in the night."

"In effect, you're saying that you ran away from the hospital?"

"Aye, sir, and come here with Kate because no man in Ireland would want an escaped mad girl as his wife."

"I see." He tapped a thoughtful finger against the bench. "So you came to Wyoming Territory and married the first man who'd have you without mentioning your previous mental history?"

"Aye," she admitted softly with a fair amount of shame. "That I did."

The judge glanced at Hawke, frowned and shook his head. Then he shouted to the guards at the back of the room. "I think we've done all we can in here. You may call in the jury and the gallery now. I'm ready to resume these proceedings."

Still fiddling with the little shamrock wheel on her spur, Lacey thought back to the questions the judge had asked of her, and in particular, to some of her answers. She glanced at Hawke, wondering what he thought of the exchange. His face was set and stony, unreadable, emotionless. As she stared at him, he stood up, gave her a long thoughtful look, then turned and walked out the door, fighting his way through the tide of incoming spectators.

Lacey's heart sank. Had he misunderstood what she meant when she said that she'd have married the first man who'd have her? She hadn't meant *exactly* that, but her poor mind was confused, lost in the puzzles of the past. Lacey thought of calling Hawke back inside, of begging him to listen so she could explain herself a little better, but then it was too late. Next thing she knew, the judge was giving the jury instructions to disregard her prior statement about killing her parents, and her interrogation was underway again.

After carefully explaining what Braddock had done to her in his office and how the gun had accidentally gone off, the case against Lacey Winterhawke finally went to jury. In less than thirty minutes, they returned with an innocent verdict, and Lacey was once again a free woman.

After the courtroom had cleared of spectators, and Lacey had attached the other spur to her boot, the Weatherspoons escorted her outside for a breath of fresh air. Shading herself against the bright afternoon sun, she glanced down the boardwalk to see Hawke standing alone at the end of the building. He looked as if he were staring a hole right through her, but she couldn't quite read his expression.

Desperate to get to him, Lacey turned to Kate. "There are many things we need to talk about, questions I have about my family, but I can not, well—"

"Go to yer husband, lass." Kate smiled indulgently. "Our wounds can wait a wee bit longer for the healing. I've a few things to explain to my own man, too." Then, cuddling her daughter in one arm, she hooked the other around Caleb's elbow, and the little family slowly walked down the street.

Anxiety building in her breast, Lacey started toward her husband. Not sure what he was thinking or feeling when she reached him, she awkwardly asked, "D-did you, ah, hear the verdict?"

"Every word." Hawke's eyes were guarded, suspicious. "I was listening through the window with Crowfoot."

Lacey glanced around, looking for him. "Where is the lad?"

"I asked him to wait up the street a ways so we could have some privacy."

Her uneasy gaze returning to Hawke's still-stony features, Lacey made an attempt to set things right. "I—I don't know where to begin, my husband. You must be very angry with me."

"I'm not angry, Irish." Hawke reached out and touched her cheek. "As for beginning, maybe you shouldn't even try. There's been enough said for one day."

"No, there hasn't. I have to explain what I meant when the judge asked me if I married the first willing man."

"No, you don't." An ironic grin brightened his expression a little. "I had a feeling from the first time we met that there was something wrong with you—why else would a pretty little thing like you want to hitch up with a man like me?"

"Because I was afraid when I first come here, Hawke. I suppose 'twas true the day I first met you that I'd have agreed to marry any man, but only so I wouldn't be a burden to Kate any longer. I didn't have the means to live on my own, or knowledge of any skills, so I thought if I married Caleb's neighbor, Kate's and my troubles would be over. I ne'er thought of the trouble I would be causing you."

Again he touched her cheek, this time with a gentle sadness. "You haven't been much by way of trouble, Lacey. You don't need to say any of this."

"Aye, but I do." She moved close to him, sliding her hand along the chiseled contours of his jaw. "I want you to know that by the time of our wedding, I already felt differently about the whole thing. I felt stronger as a lass on my own, but still hoped mightily that you'd marry with me. I was honored even then, Hawke, to think that someone like you would accept me as your wife. I still am." The stone beneath her fingers softened a little. "If you tell me that you don't want me by your side any longer, I will go away and ne'er trouble you again—but know, too, that if you ask this of me, you'll know my pain as your own, for my soul's within you."

One of Hawke's eyes twitched a little and his Adam's apple bobbed as if he were having difficulty swallowing. But he didn't speak. He couldn't.

Encouraged, Lacey went on. "All I want is to live with you at Winterhawke. If that be what you—" Then at once, she remembered. "Oh, Lord! The ranch!"

Hawke shook his dark head. "I couldn't destroy it." His voice was husky, strained. "How could I? Winterhawke is your home as much as mine."

"And the horses?"

He smiled at last. "I couldn't turn the mares loose with such young foals, but I did release Phantom up in the Snowy Range."

"Oh, but Hawke—now he's lost to you!"

Adding a chuckle to the smile, Hawke said, "Not really In fact, I'm kind of looking forward to tracking him down again."

Daring to think that now maybe everything would be all right, Lacey let her head fall against her husband's chest. Instead of allowing her this moment of comfort, he gently took her by the shoulders and held her at arm's length.

"What happened at the doctor's office, Lacey?"

She suspected what he was asking about, but saved it

for last. "Oh, 'tis wonderful news! Crowfoot can be helped."

"I already know that. What did the doctor say about you? Are you with child?"

"Aye, my husband." Lacey grinned broadly, aglow from within. "That I am."

"You don't look terribly upset. I thought you didn't want to have children."

"Aye, but that was because I thought any babe I bore would be born mad like me. The doctor told me that probably would not happen, but now even that does not matter—I was ne'er truly mad, so the babe is sure to be all right!"

"That's what you've been so upset about?" Still confused, Hawke hadn't truly grasped the idea that he was to become a father. "What about the difficulties you'll have raising the children of a half-breed?"

"A half-breed? Oh, Hawke." Lacey knew exactly what he was referring to and why he couldn't get it out of his mind—he'd carried a burden not so unlike her own all his life, too. Tears welling in her eyes, she softly said, "My only concern was that I might be forced to give the man I love a mad child. I have told you many times before that your Indian blood makes no difference a'tall—in fact, I've grown rather fond of that side of you. Will you ne'er believe that of me, my husband?"

Hawke closed his eyes, and Lacey thought she heard him utter a low groan or growl.

"We are going to have a baby," she went on to say, tears spilling down her cheeks. "Please try to find a way to be happy about this, husband."

Hawke abruptly released her, turned his back, and for a moment, Lacey wasn't exactly sure how he was taking the news. He took three deep breaths, his back heaving mightily, then he swung back around to face her again. He opened his mouth as if to speak, but something caught Hawke's gaze over the top of her head. Lacey glanced over her shoulder to see that several curious onlookers still stood on the boardwalk watching their exchange.

Without a word, Hawke turned Lacey toward him, lifted her off her feet, and carried her around the corner, down the alley, and to the back of the building where they finally found complete privacy. Again he opened his mouth as if to say something, but instead, reached into his shirt pocket and withdrew his ledger. After flipping the pages to a blank sheet, Hawke moistened the tip of his pencil and began to write.

Amused, Lacey watched him awhile, but finally grew impatient and snatched the ledger out of her husband's hand in mid-scrawl. He didn't object, but smiled that dazzling smile of his as she scanned the heading: *Loving Lacey*.

The first entry in the *Reasons For* column read:

She's the only female in all of Wyoming Territory willing to marry a hard-headed man like me.

Lacey glanced up at Hawke in surprise, met his gaze, and gave him a shy smile. Then she read entry number two; *Because I can't help myself.*

Smiling to herself now, Lacey scanned number three, then reread it to make sure of what she'd seen; *She's having my baby and wants it as much as I do.*

"Oh, Hawke," she murmured as again her gaze shot up to his. This time when their eyes met, it left them both a little misty.

Catching her breath, Lacey read number four, and burst into giggles; *Because I really, really can't help myself.*

And number five filled her heart to bursting; *Because she is the sun, the moon, earth, wind, and fire to me.*

The last entry in that column was scrawled across the page, since Hawke had been writing it when she snatched the book away. *Because I—*

Giving a grin as big as all of Wyoming, Lacey glanced to the top of the ledger where the *Against Loving Lacey* column started. It had but one entry; *It's too damn embarrassing to tell her how much I love her in public.*

With tears rolling down her cheeks, Lacey let the slender book fall from her fingers as she threw her arms around Hawke's neck and whispered, "And I love you, too, my husband."

Then, kissing him with all the love and passion she felt inside, she reminded him of yet another entry which belonged in the *Reasons For Loving Lacey* column.

Epilogue

> Out of the kitchen comes the tune.
> —An old Irish saying

Hawke didn't get the opportunity to enjoy rounding Phantom up again. When they returned to Winterhawke Ranch the following day, the stallion was standing in the lush meadow which bordered the mare's enclosure, calling to his "girls." A bucket of grain was the final persuasion that coaxed the silvery stud back into his own corral, and there he was happy to keep watch over his lovely ladies.

Lacey and Kate had worked out their troubles by then, too, and came up with an agreement; since neither of them wanted to live in the past, they decided never to look on it again.

Thanksgiving supper was held at Winterhawke Ranch that year—not because Lacey suddenly became adept at cooking, or because Hawke's culinary talents moved beyond simple stews and roasts, but because the log house was bigger than the Weatherspoons'. With three babies and an eleven-year old boy among them, the weary adults needed all the room they could get.

Shortly after the twins were born in October, Crowfoot had finally agreed to move into the house. His surge of protectiveness made it impossible for him to let them out of his sight for more than an hour at a time. He bedded down in the babies' bedroom, still content to lie upon the little straw mattress he'd fashioned in the barn. This arrangement was fine with Lacey, who wasn't getting much sleep, and Hawke was darn near agreeable to anything, so awed was he over the perfect little boy and girl he and Lacey had created.

As William Braddock's only living relative, Hawke did indeed inherit everything the man owned, including Winterhawke Ranch. Other than their home, which Hawke had considered as his own property anyway, the inheritance didn't really mean so much to him. He and his wife were content just to live in peace to raise their family and the horses. Of course, the extra money Braddock's holdings afforded them did come in handy here and there. Especially for frivolous, nonessential items. Like sterling silver spurs.

Eyeing the pair of miniature spurs hanging from a wire above each of his red-haired babies, Hawke impulsively reached out and flicked the tiny shamrock wheels at the backs, setting all four of them to spinning. For luck, he told himself. Not that the Winterhawke family felt they needed any more than they already had. But just for luck.

GLORY IN THE SPLENDOR OF SUMMER WITH

HarperMonogram's

101 Days of Romance

BUY 3 BOOKS, GET 1 FREE!

Take a book to the beach, relax by the pool, or read in the most quiet and romantic spot in your home. You can live through love all summer long when you redeem this exciting offer from HarperMonogram. Buy any three HarperMonogram romances in June, July, or August, and get a fourth book sent to you for FREE. See next page for the list of top-selling novels and romances by your favorite authors that you can choose from for your premium!

101 Days of Romance
BUY 3 BOOKS, GET 1 FREE!

CHOOSE A FREE BOOK FROM THIS OUTSTANDING
LIST OF AUTHORS AND TITLES:

HarperMonogram

___LORD OF THE NIGHT Susan Wiggs 0-06-108052-7
___ORCHIDS IN MOONLIGHT Patricia Hagan 0-06-108038-1
___TEARS OF JADE Leigh Riker 0-06-108047-0
___DIAMOND IN THE ROUGH Millie Criswell 0-06-108093-4
___HIGHLAND LOVE SONG Constance O'Banyon 0-06-108121-3
___CHEYENNE AMBER Catherine Anderson 0-06-108061-6
___OUTRAGEOUS Christina Dodd 0-06-108151-5
___THE COURT OF THREE SISTERS Marianne Willman 0-06-108053-5
___DIAMOND Sharon Sala 0-06-108196-5
___MOMENTS Georgia Bockoven 0-06-108164-7

HarperPaperbacks

___THE SECRET SISTERS Ann Maxwell 0-06-104236-6
___EVERYWHERE THAT MARY WENT Lisa Scottoline 0-06-104293-5
___NOTHING PERSONAL Eileen Dreyer 0-06-104275-7
___OTHER LOVERS Erin Pizzey 0-06-109032-8
___MAGIC HOUR Susan Isaacs 0-06-109948-1
___A WOMAN BETRAYED Barbara Delinsky 0-06-104034-7
___OUTER BANKS Anne Rivers Siddons 0-06-109973-2
___KEEPER OF THE LIGHT Diane Chamberlain 0-06-109040-9
___ALMONDS AND RAISINS Maisie Mosco 0-06-100142-2
___HERE I STAY Barbara Michaels 0-06-100726-9

To receive your free book, simply send in this coupon **and** your store receipt with the purchase prices circled. You may take part in this exclusive offer as many times as you wish, but all qualifying purchases must be made by September 4, 1995, and all requests must be postmarked by October 4, 1995. Please allow 6-8 weeks for delivery.

MAIL TO: HarperCollins Publishers
P.O. Box 588 Dunmore, PA 18512-0588

Name_____

Address_____

City_____State_____Zip_____

Offer is subject to availability. HarperPaperbacks may make substitutions for requested titles.

H09511